Judgment Day

PATRICK REINKEN

SIMON & SCHUSTER

SIMON & SCHUSTER
Rockefeller Center
1230 Avenue of the Americas
New York, NY 10020

Designed by Edith Fowler
Manufactured in the United States of America

10 9 8 7 6 5 4 3 2 1

Library of Congress Cataloging-in-Publication Data

Reinken, Patrick.
  Judgment day / Patrick Reinken.
    p.   cm.
  I. Title.
PS3568.E494J83   1996
813'.54 — dc20   96-17051   CIP
ISBN 0-684-80762-9

Acknowledgments

Many people have helped at many different stages of this book. Thanks go to the late Jay Garon and to Jean Free, Nancy Coffey, and everyone else at Garon-Brooke for their initial belief and support and for all the effort that followed. Thanks also go to Michael Korda, Chuck Adams, Cheryl Weinstein and everyone at Simon & Schuster for everything they did to polish the manuscript and make it shine as much as it possibly could. Finally, thanks go to everyone who read and commented on the manuscript in its various incarnations, including my wife Cindy, who read it first; my sister Deb and her husband Kevin McElroy; Laura Anderson; Kirsten and Greg Sonbuchner; Joe O'Brien; and Elizabeth Johnson Heying. I couldn't have done this without these people—any shortcomings that are left here are purely mine.

For my son Brian.

INTRODUCTION

The Day Before

A TINY RIVULET of water rinsed slowly through the gutter, winding down between occasional pieces of ice and over a leaf, the plastic lid to a fast-food drink cup, a torn parking ticket from the previous November. The narrow thaw washed along as a small, thin cascade into the sewer, where it fell into a pool with a distant smattering reminiscent of long-forgotten rain.

It had not rained since late fall, when an Alberta clipper sprang up and turned suddenly southward in a twisting wind, pushing the Canadian chill deep into the Midwest. The drizzle that was falling then turned into a glassy ice storm, sheeting the city in a thin crystal layer before covering it with almost three feet of powdery snow in a blanket a hundred miles wide. The pack remained throughout the winter, receding only in the last week to let the first hints of the still-frozen earth and the buried garden hoses and other implements of spring and summer emerge into rare sunlight.

A footfall dropped into the steady little stream, diverting it momentarily around the black, thick-soled boot before it could once again flow unimpeded, carrying with it a brownish, melting, and formless blob of slush from the shoe.

The man dipped under the yellow barrier tape and walked over close to the building, avoiding larger chunks of tinted glass while a galaxy of buckshot-sized shards crunched underfoot. He shot one picture. The quick bolt of a flashbulb flared back at him from the ground-level windows. People behind the pane pulled suddenly back, but then they were up against the glass again like insects attracted to bright lights.

Eleven floors above their heads, the wind rushed into the building through a gaping hole. Papers scattered around the office in a miniature whirlwind.

Another picture and a small flash of lightning. Then another. No real words were exchanged between the sparse and uniformed crowd of people outside. Just "here" and a picture.

"Here" and another picture.

"Now here."

Someone stretched a Stanley Leverlock tape out seven or eight feet, until its tip reached a few inches beyond the body's feet and the canary-yellow-labeled silver tape casing rested a few more inches beyond the head. The photographer backed up to get the entire measuring tape inside the box that was etched into the view-finder. Another picture whirred out, and he pulled it from the camera without looking, putting it with all the others into a gallon-sized Ziploc bag.

"Here." A different angle.

"Okay" was his simple and repeated response. The bulb brightly outlined a shoe, ten feet or so away but matching the one that the man still wore. The photographer's nose was numb. It was a warm March day, but the breeze coming down the side of the building whipped across and chilled uncovered faces.

"Get one here." A finger point.

He stepped up and shot down. The camera whirred again and the photo slid out to show head and shoulders, three hairline cracks improbably radiating out through the sidewalk from underneath the face. A single paint-ball spot of red blood spiked out from beneath the broken nose in a spiny moon that was only half visible. Into the Ziploc.

"Chalk him," someone said, and he was surprised, as always, that this was not simply melodrama but was actually done.

Someone bent with a spray can of "chalk." Not really chalk,

because it could sometimes rinse away too quickly. Cool blue paint, lining out the shape of a dead man.

"Let's bag him," someone said. "What's the time?"

"Six fifty," the photographer answered.

A coroner stepped back. Three men stepped forward.

The man had hit left shoulder down, that arm telescoping cruelly under the weight and velocity until his left elbow stuck up behind his right ear. The left side of the head was intact apparently, if encased only by the soft shell of scalp and an undoubtedly jig-sawed skull. Intact except for a running gash at the back and for the left eye, which exploded on impact, leaving a pool of sticky clear fluid and the spiked blood ball. He hadn't thought it possible to burst an eye that way, actually, but the Polaroids wouldn't lie. The pictures never did.

The men positioned themselves as a gurney covered in white sheets was pulled up.

A bag of opaque plastic also sat atop the gurney, its zippered seam spread open. The photographer thought oddly about high school biology, where he once dissected a formaldehyde-pickled frog. The frog's skin was peeled back the same way, and his reaction was still the same — he got queasy seeing things spread open like that.

The men tugged slightly, four pair of yellow-gloved hands, then six. A pant leg stuck, frosted to still-ice-cold pavement at the crotch. One of the men slipped a wide and flat metal plate steadily under the body to free it anywhere it resisted. They called it the "spatula" anywhere other than in public. But not here, of course. Too unseemly. This was its sole use — scraping frozen or partly frozen bodies from cold streets and sidewalks, however they got there. It was used a lot in some winters, rarely in others.

Another flash of light. The motor whirred and the Ziploc collection grew.

The body was stiff because of the cold. Rigor mortis had come and gone, according to the coroner, but the 30–35 degree tempera-tures achieved largely the same result. A twisted leg would remain twisted for hours and would stay blue forever.

Gentle hands worked at the head. The spatula was set aside. It would only have scalped him, given the conditions. The white lab coat that he wore made a soft ripping sound as they lifted, like the sound heard when the laundry left overnight on the first fall day of frost is dragged from the line the following morning. A light crackling crunch and rasp, then it's off.

The photographer noticed a deep, clotted cut running three inches across one of the man's palms, and he stopped the men to take a picture. He waved them on as he slipped that picture, too, into his Ziploc.

They moved the body to the stretcher, and there was another flash and whir. They loaded the body as more pictures were taken. The full scene with the blue outline of paint. A minimal but still perceptible valley in the walk, dotted by the spiny red ball and the three cracks running out like tiny roads seen from miles up.

The ambulance sped off as the sun was just edging up on the horizon, the first rays piercing out like the diamond on a ring—a small but fierce beacon above the distant line of still-black land.

He looked down at the Minnesota River, which ran beside the building, and he watched the last chunks of the ice floe edge slowly along it. The river lay just beyond a nature preserve, where nude trees reached up without a hint of life. Patches of last November's uncollected leaves were visible, surrounding scattered, lingering islands of snow.

The river looked inviting, just a touch of darkish blue-gray reflecting now from its surface as the sun edged higher and caught the water between the moving ice.

Inviting, he thought, *but still deadly cold.*

He dropped the camera into a cavernous coat pocket and turned quickly away.

Part One

TUESDAY
WEDNESDAY

The First Day

1

THE BARBER WASHED HIS HANDS.

When he woke up each morning, it was what he always did. No matter how tired or groggy, he washed his hands. The sound of the water sometimes made him want to pee but he always held it in until he used the antibacterial soap on both sides of both hands, in between his fingers and up his wrists, almost to the elbows.

He laid out his tools on the nightstand next to his bed, then went into the kitchen to get a blueberry muffin. He poured a small glass of grapefruit juice. It was really too bitter, but that was good for him, so he always drank it in the mornings, even if he would drink something else — something stronger maybe — later. He brought the food back to his nightstand and set the muffin and juice at one corner, away from his work area so he wouldn't knock anything over and make a mess.

He opened the drawer and pulled out a white handkerchief, its corners pulled together in a tight little knot. He drank a small gulp of juice, then set his narrow fingers on the knot, quickly working it out and spreading the corners wide. The splayed-open handkerchief sat square on the nightstand.

A loop of hair lay in the middle. It was long, easily more than a foot and a half. As it had to be. And it shone brightly, the result of three careful washings last night. An application of conditioner, too. A tint of coppery gold reflected off it under the yellowish light on the nightstand. The shine caught in his eyes and glassed them over as he set to work.

He straightened the looped hair out to full length, stretching and spreading it into a narrow hill that was almost as thick as his pinky. With a comb, he carefully separated the hairs farther, taking care to be gentle. He misted them once with a spray bottle he had picked up at K mart, sending down a fine, sparkling dampness that beaded just momentarily on the blond strands before soaking in.

He worked them into three groups, then knotted the three at one end before carefully laying them out again. Starting at the knot, he twisted his way down, crossing one over the other, always laying the third between the other two. He pushed down on the braid with a forefinger every inch or so, pulling down to tighten the twists. Seeing a hair sticking up, he undid an inch and a half to retie it. Seeing another and assessing its length, he stopped momentarily and extracted it painstakingly from the bunch.

No goddamned messes. Just like he'd always been warned. *Nothing out of place.*

He braided again and hummed a tune that lingered in his head from maybe as far back as childhood. Distantly, he wondered at its title, which escaped him as he concentrated on the job at hand. A favorite of his mother's, he knew. He always hummed his mother's favorites. He paused for a moment and took a bite of the muffin. Then the Barber braided again and continued to hum.

When he finished his work, he emptied the juice glass, his lips tightening and his teeth clenching as he felt saliva glands purse in his mouth, then he laid the braid out to its full length. He measured it. Sixteen and a half inches. A little short, he thought, but it would just have to do.

He sprayed it once more, stretched it tight, and rolled it back into the handkerchief. He put that back into the drawer and collected the tools, setting them in the drawer next to the rolled-up cloth.

He glanced at the clock. It was almost seven. He would have to hurry through his shower.

2

MARGARET WASHBURN simultaneously rubbed her left shoulder, kneading a sharp shoulder blade that was numb with the stiff pain of bad sleep in a bad bed, and slapped at the ringing alarm with her free hand. The clock was an old Baby Ben, a black windup model with a broken plastic face, chartreuse glow-in-dark hands and numbers, and a bell for a ringer. She had never owned a clock radio; had never been and never would be awakened to the sound of music. Always the staccato and poor rattle of the Baby Ben, one of the bells inside muted by a crack. It had cost her a dollar uncountable years ago, and, like everything else in Maggie's life, it showed.

She rolled and shoved without success at the man beside her. A mop of blackish hair tangled out from beneath a collapsed and stained feather pillow. He didn't really move, barely even stirred, and she stopped trying to wake him, concentrating instead on what else ailed her this morning.

Her throat ached, she realized, the dry raspy scratch and raw redness that she associated with her move to Phoenix making her cough lightly. She rattled the phlegm in it to clear it. She awoke with that every morning now, and with its not-too-distant cousin, the dull ache in the chest.

A perpetual patient of every free medical program that came along, Maggie had seen a medical clinic doctor — or maybe it was a physician's assistant — about the cough. He put a cold stethoscope head on her back and then on her right breast and pronounced that she had bronchitis in both lungs while he copped a feel. She'd told him that squeezes cost five bucks, and he pulled his hand quickly from her shirt, a blotchy red flush climbing his face and running across his pimpled, freckled forehead.

That was almost seven months ago. He had given her a pre-scription for erythromycin and told her that he would give her one for sulfa if that didn't work. She didn't know the difference and didn't particularly care. She did know, however, that the erythro turned out to be a horse pill that she couldn't swallow. She'd taken only one before hocking them as prescription barbiturates.

She never went back for a follow-up or for different medication. She never did with any of the other free programs, and she wasn't planning on starting with some horny kid playing doctor.

Maggie swung her legs over the edge of the bed and reached to pull the thin curtain away from the window. She looked out at the cars on Van Buren as she licked at the corners of her mouth, feeling a crack of dryness running across her lip on the left side. There was a metallic taste, not of blood but of the near-blood rawness of damaged skin. She tried to clear her throat again and had only partial success while setting off a dull throbbing headache that raced across her temples before settling deeply behind her eyes.

It was still dark out, but somewhere the sun was already swinging into position to bake the valley up to 85 or 90 degrees. Not hot for Phoenix, unless it was March, which of course it was. Another blazing day. As close to literal hell as you could come.

She rubbed at her shoulder again and contemplated the heat, the beer plus whatever else she drank last night, the overall strange combination of pain and numbness racking her body, and the as-yet-unrecognized man lying next to her. Maggie thought of getting a small glass of water, craved getting a small glass of water, but she decided that she really didn't feel quite up to the ten-foot walk across the apartment.

She lay back instead, her head cleaving her own nearly empty feather pillow in half. Blindly, she reached over to the tabletop and felt for the money. It was still there, and she picked it up, rubbing apart the two bills and squinting her eyes back open. One hundred dollars, a payment for an entire night, and she didn't remember having to do anything that she really hated or that would make her feel like trash. That was rare on Van Buren.

Maggie started to tuck the cash into one cup of the thin bra that she still wore but thought better of it and reached down to slip the money under the mattress. She felt carefully with one finger and hooked the bills between a bare spring and the worn tick. That accomplished, she brought her hand back up and rested it across her head.

Her forehead was warm. Probably a little too warm. It was maybe 75 degrees in the room already, but Maggie made no effort to open the window. It would have been senseless. If the smog from the street didn't get to her tender lungs, the heat from the rapidly rising temperatures would. It'd be cooler shut up inside she thought. She let her eyes remain closed.

She was rattled by one spat of coughing just after falling back asleep, but she reflexively swallowed whatever it was that came up, drifting automatically into a deeper sleep. She was dimly aware of the man's hand rubbing across her thin shoulder and down her front.

3

THE SKY ROLLED BY, and Jonathan Patchett's stomach rolled a little with it as the elevator slipped steadily up the building's side. The elevator's curved glass wall stared out over the receding ground that spread out from around the Minneapolis Exchange Tower. The ground below was cut and etched by streets, traffic moving slowly along in the last dark vestiges of standard time.

Beyond the neighboring buildings, the wintry ground, patched here and there by snow now dirty after a full season of cold, reached across the slightly graded hills and valleys of the upper Mississippi. The river itself flowed only a few hundred yards to the east, dropping in a creamy froth over St. Anthony Falls before moving on to St. Paul. It was still locked with ice and impassable there, but the river would soon open to the traffic that originally put these cities on the map, carrying grain to points farther south.

Patchett turned away from the elevator's glass wall and faced the door. The slight crease above each eye wrinkled as he watched an electronic display tick the floors soundlessly away. He marveled in slight dread at the speed, leaning against the wall. He ran a hand through his unkempt, roughly cut blond hair.

Every day, every single business morning and frequently more often, he rode up through this building with a haunting thought hanging in his mind like a slim ghost. Every day he wondered why he did it, and every day it always came to him easily, although with more than a whisper of guilt.

He rode the building for money. Not for love of the work. Not for some idealistic notion of service or anything similarly noble. Not anymore, and not for a long time, really. Now, it was for the money, and for the money alone.

He bent and lifted his briefcase with a slight sigh as the elevator gave a *ding* at the arrival of his floor. Patchett stepped off into the maroon and blue austerity of Allen, Sander & Flare, forty-four floors up in the MET Building.

"Morning," he said automatically, emotionlessly to the receptionist. She nodded a quick hello before becoming reengrossed in the novel that was spread open in front of her. An average man with a tall frame and fair looks marked mainly by a barely crooked nose, Patchett was the type who received little attention from her. The fact that he was an associate only clinched that.

She was one of the ones who were doing their time at Allen, Sander solely to meet and eventually marry the "right" attorney. She was always dressed flawlessly in her effort, invariably in conservative-toned skirts cut short enough or slit high enough to show admirably proportioned legs. She wore shimmering blouses in a rainbow of shades, cinching them tightly at her narrow waist to draw attention to other proportions. The blouses were of the type that always threatened to tent open, leaving any man near her wondering if perhaps he could play the angles right and worrying if she would notice. Auburn hair and green eyes surrounding a *Vogue* face completed the just about perfect picture.

Patchett did his best to ignore it all. He'd had his share of misfortune with women and had no intention of opening up the potential for more. His first wife came from the Southern California school of tanned skin, freckled cleavage, and long, sun-washed flowing hair that used to wrap her shoulders seductively when she emerged from an ocean swim before it dried to a fluttering, feathered softness. But at the end, barely eighteen months later, those looks and a Barbie-doll figure hadn't mattered at all, weighed against her impossible intolerance and dim intellect.

The second wife was different. Different enough to have made a lasting impact that would have been more pronounced — and more positive, he thought now — if she were still around.

But she's not, came the ever-present reminder in the back of his thoughts. Those words were seemingly eternal there, etched as razor-sharp, self-preservational alarms that blared whenever his mind turned to Liz.

She's not around. Not anymore.

With that thought ringing in his head, Patchett pushed aside any attention he might have shown the receptionist. He picked up a small stack of pink message slips, flicking through them idly with his free hand. His expression freely registered his varying state of mind as he read the name on each one. It looked to be a bad day — a tally of seven messages, at least five of them from people to whom he would just as soon not speak. He crammed them into his trench coat pocket and moved toward his office.

The floor was covered by a somber crimson carpet that the building management railed against with each day's call for special vacuuming; the wallpaper was cloth, narrowly piped blue and maroon. All in all, thought Patchett, it was an overly depressing scene, one made even worse by the art that so obnoxiously dominated the hallways.

Patchett maneuvered around a glass sculpture of an unidentified creature never seen except possibly in the depths of hell. It erupted from the corner by his office, and he was forever smacking a knee on it and announcing that he would personally melt it into tumblers if it wasn't moved. It never was, and he never did, of course. The ten-thousand-dollar price tag and a nagging thought that he might actually have to be a partner in the firm in a couple years prevented that from ever happening.

Once inside his office, Patchett dropped his briefcase on a

chair and shrugged the trench coat off, hanging it on the hook behind the door before moving to his desk. Four distinct piles of paper cluttered one side of the desk, with offspring sheets of paper scattered across the blotter. Patchett picked up a sheet off the floor, glanced at it for a moment, and slapped it onto the nearest pile.

He plucked a stapled collection of papers from his chair and scanned them briefly before sitting with a slight groan. It was a draft memo, and the siege of red marks instantly told him that he'd spend hours justifying the work to a belligerent partner who because of self-imposed distance wouldn't have the slightest notion about the case. Already aggravated by the thought, he rubbed a hand through his hair and flipped the draft onto the appropriate pile.

Taking a blank time sheet from a drawer, he scrawled the date across the top and pulled a small work diary from his breast pocket. Reading the calendar for March 11, the previous day, Patchett absently scratched in the hours for the different files he'd worked on, largely guessing at the specific amounts of time. He wrote down a couple hours for consulting with a patent attorney for Thomas Yeutter, who for the third time was trying to get approval on a sewing bobbin, then recorded another three-plus hours for drafting an answer to a complaint against Axton Associates, accused — probably correctly — of churning the accounts of their securities customers. The last entry of any real size was an hour for Ingersoll Electronics, whose subsidiary had manufactured the light socket incorporated into an egg incubator that burned down most of De-Smet Elementary, a grade school on the south edge of the city. Patchett totaled up the time, calculated it against how much he needed to bill for the month, then added an extra hour to Ingersoll for good measure.

The exciting life of a senior associate, he thought, examining the time sheet — a client that burns down schools, a man consumed by a goal of achieving the better sewing bobbin, and a group of ten overpaid and undereducated men who probably felt that it was their right to trade client portfolios on a whispery whim. It wasn't a pretty picture.

He quickly jotted down the rest of the entries, every one of which was three-tenths of an hour for a telephone call for some faceless name on a numbered file. None of the calls had lasted anywhere near that long, but each entry reported that time anyway. That was the result of the firm's longstanding policy of never charging for less than eighteen minutes on any given action for a client. If you sneezed on a file, you billed eighteen minutes, even if the only thing you did was wipe off the spit.

It was a forty-two-dollar charge for what was actually no more than a three-minute call for any of the files. Make enough calls like that, Patchett thought, and pretty soon you don't have to do any real work at all.

He set the time sheet aside and pulled the messages back out, quickly skimming them again. He crumpled two immediately and tossed them toward the trash can. He spiked the next four on a needle spindle. Only the last one actually held his attention.

That message was from Ben Flare, the partner in charge of the Weber BioTech file. The company that once had been Weber Pharmaceuticals was the foundling of Rowe Weber, a passable "industrialist" who managed, admittedly with great difficulty and far from great grades, to obtain a doctorate in biochemistry. He clearly wasn't talented enough to make anything of that degree himself, but it made him conversant with those brilliant enough to make good use of Weber family money.

That money was in fact Rowe Weber's only real asset, and it was one that he originally obtained only by default. His father had carefully nickel-and-dimed it away while building Weber Industrial Equipment, a farm and shipping implement manufacturer that once was the pharmaceutical company's parent. Emphasis on the *once*, Patchett reminded himself.

The pharmaceuticals company was Rowe Weber's baby from the instant his father funded it as an unadmitted but painfully obvious employment haven for his overly ambitious and vastly underqualified only child. Since the first day that he'd set foot in his own office, with its river view and mountainous desk hand-crafted from some no-doubt scarce Brazilian hardwood, Rowe Weber had nurtured the company along, supported by his father's routine infusions of capital and by moderate sales of the firm's only truly successful product—an antihypertensive that doctors in the know turned to after the three or four best-selling products failed or were contraindicated for a patient.

Rowe had so cared for the company, in fact, that he fought bitterly to maintain control of it following his father's stroke. When the 1980s vultures swooped in on Weber Industrial, the prodigal son had his father declared incompetent and moved himself into the front office. From that position, over the next few years, he steadily dismantled his father's company by selling first one part, then another. The farm equipment manufacturer. A shipping arm. A controlling interest in Pennsylvania Steel with a matching participation in Minnesota Range Coal, Incorporated. That steel package, fourth largest in the country at the time, went for a premium in a U.S. market with dust on its blue ribbon awards from postwar America.

Feeding the predators, Rowe himself achieved what they would have accomplished in the end—he sucked the value out of Weber Industrial by selling its constituent parts at prices that collectively totaled more than the intact company's worth. Weber Industrial ceased to exist on January 1, 1993, and the only part that remained was Rowe Weber's small pharmaceutical company.

Not quite three months later, Henry Weber was dead. The elder Weber went without knowing what his son had done. Without, in fact, having uttered or apparently having had a coherent thought in more than four years.

Rowe Weber hadn't cried. He hadn't attended the service. Patchett himself was there, and the one thing that he remembered clearly was that Henry's boy was nowhere to be seen. Rowe was content merely to collect his father's life insurance—reported in the Minneapolis *Star Tribune* as another $1.78 million for Rowe's coffers—and march back into Weber Pharmaceuticals to sit at his private chunk of rain forest and do nothing more than watch the Minnesota River ooze by. Around him in the Weber Building sat the pharmaceutical company, the sole surviving entity from an enterprise that for years was the industrial backbone of upper-Midwest agriculture and shipping. But no more.

All told, Rowe came back to Weber with, if reports were to be believed, a company a few hundred million dollars wealthier and with his own ambition still intact. Without his father's constant oversight, however, he had breathed a little easier but was self-driven a little more. His father had built the company, Rowe knew, but any real mark to be made needed to be made without the shadow of Henry Weber over the doorstep.

As always, the answer for Rowe lay in money—the one asset he possessed. And so the younger Weber, at forty-seven sowing the oats of blind ambition, began to buy himself some talent.

When Marcus Clifton, B.S., M.S., M.D., and Ph.D., bolted from Cal Tech to join Weber Pharmaceuticals, industry observers sat up and took a little notice. Weber at that point was still only one product, and it carried the marks of a company with a checkered past and a future in which it was seemingly going nowhere fast. Clifton, among the top five viral researchers in the nation, was an unlikely Weber employee.

Jonathan Patchett knew now what those industry observers didn't know then. He knew why Clifton made that move. The answer was hidden in the Weber Pharmaceuticals stock offering prospectus, buried in company documents encased in sealable folders marked with bright orange WEBER—EYES ONLY stickers and kept in a central repository in the firm. When the company went public, those offering documents disclosed a new name—Weber BioTech. And they also disclosed Marc Clifton's motivation in green spades—he received more than $800,000 in compensation that year, with stock options pushing that amount into a researcher's stratosphere above that. As a researcher he was, in short, paid as much as several chief executives in major companies across the country.

And Patchett knew the similar motivations for the other nomads to Weber, all of whom had impressive if somewhat lesser income lines in the Weber prospectuses. Thomas Rifkind, Alexander Tomlin, and Kenneth Miller all came to Weber over the next year and a half, all with outsized talents and all with compensation packages just as large.

Rifkind's move immediately prompted a suit, Patchett also

knew. That, too, was mentioned somewhere among the punched, clipped, and stapled towers of documents that were pigeonholed away in the stickered folders of Allen, Sander's file room. There had been shaded allegations of piracy, but those disappeared, along with the claim, in less than a month. Again, the magic of Weber's pocketbook, Patchett expected, although that was most assuredly *not* shown in those documents. Nor was the fact that Rifkind himself was gone within three months after that. Weber was a bad place to make waves, and Rifkind came in splashing.

Patchett looked at the final message form again. Look into Tomlin, was all it said, but Patchett didn't need any more than that. He read the newspapers, and he knew without even really thinking — had known early this morning, in fact — that he'd need the Weber file now. All of it. And he'd have to get in touch with Anne.

Anne Matheson was one of five legal assistants originally assigned to the team that handled the Weber work. She was, if Patchett remembered right, the one who did the background work on the Weber researchers, and that made her the one he needed to see.

The company's signing of the researchers had prompted intense speculation, Patchett recalled. Research publications, typically aloof from such matters, even responded in their own way, with no less than four major publications crying that the researchers had sold out and denied the world all the benefits of their considerable talents, which were now exiled to a doom of producing more and better blood pressure drugs. Researchers in a backwater could not, after all, compete with researchers in the respected halls of learning.

Rowe Weber had eaten that attention up, just as he had all the even more massive avalanche of publicity that followed. Patchett could remember a meeting in Weber's office, with Rowe standing and striding around his desk to pluck one journal from a shelf, laughing uncharacteristically as he held it out to Jonathan and to Ben Flare, with whom Patchett made that trip to the Weber Building. It was still the only time that Patchett ever heard Weber laugh, and, almost two and a half years of unceasing attention later, the attorney could still hear that unusual sound, even though the particular article was long forgotten. Patchett remembered Rowe laughing perfectly well. He remembered him laughing very hard.

"Idn't that just a kick in the ass?" Weber said that day, and he pronounced it just that way — *idn't* — despite that science degree.

"Idn't it just?" Patchett said now to no one in particular. He stepped out the door and headed toward the file room.

4

THE BROKER SAT bored at his desk in the offices of Carlysle and Thomas. His name was Ian Anderson, and his office sat precariously at one edge of the Multifoods Tower, where it should have looked out toward the Minneapolis suburbs. From his floor squarely in the middle of the three Carlysle and Thomas levels in the building, Anderson instead looked across the small ream of paper cornered on his desk and out the window sliver that was his apportionment of the view. A pillar blocked what should have been a continuation of the window. All told, he had a view maybe two feet wide, all of which faced south. Directly into the Marriott Hotel, which sat only twenty or so feet away.

The hotel was oddly triangular in shape, with one point confronting the Multifoods building like a spear. When Ian Anderson looked out his window, he saw only hotel.

If he went up to the window and craned when the lighting was right, he could actually see *into* the hotel. And very occasionally, he watched to glimpse the businesswomen staying at the hotel as they dressed in early morning preparation for their work. It was only the thought of those possibilities that brought him into the office early in the morning.

He was contemplating rising and going to the window to see if anyone was in view, but a buy order for Weber BioTech crawled across the computer screen ticker on his desk at that moment, reminding him of a call he was planning to make to one of his clients. This particular client — actually the blind trust for the client — purchased a small holding in Weber about a month after the company's public offering. Anderson at one point had thought that it would cost him his job.

Weber originally issued publicly at $6.00 a share. It was an embarrassingly low opening for a biotechnology firm, but it was also Weber, and the Street acted on that knowledge and an over-sized issue with a vengeance, obligingly correcting the price down even further, dropping it to 3⅞ within the day. When it hit 3½, Anderson had made some calls.

He hadn't known much about Weber. Only that it was a local, in St. Paul. Bloomington maybe. And it was, of course, some type of medical company. But he didn't think it was necessary to investi-gate it further. That wasn't really his speciality. In fact, it was rarely the speciality of a company where the brokers usually knew less about stocks than the average dog.

Anderson instead called precisely three clients, each of them among a select group with six-to seven-figure portfolios, each with substantial cash accounts from dividend and sale pour-ins. He told each one of them the same thing: Weber, a new offer, was un-derpriced at 3¾ and carried a short-term sell target of 5¼. There was money to be made. Were they interested?

Two had bitten. One of those put down around $100,000 to buy nearly 29,000 shares. When Weber dropped to 2⅛ within two weeks, that client contacted a supervisor and asked for Anderson's head on a plate. The supervisor sold the shares, and the client walked with a loss of not quite $40,000, most of it covered by Carlysle and Thomas to avoid the otherwise inevitable lawsuit. It wasn't a stunning loss by any means, given the amounts of money shifting around. But then again, it wasn't Anderson's biggest sale of Weber.

That particular sale was to the Caldwell X. Young Living Trust, operated on behalf of the Honorable Caldwell X. Young, Chief Judge for the United States Court of Appeals for the Eighth Circuit. Because of the judge's profession, the trust was supposed to be blind — the judge was to have no say.

Real life knows no rules, Anderson reminded himself now, thinking back to the purchase. That buy order, almost $300,000, was stamped with the official but unspoken judicial seal of approval from Chief Judge Young himself.

"Sounds good," Young had said, a man of few words.

Anderson remembered the conversation well. Short and extremely to the point. The judge was a pointed man who was accustomed to pointed discussions.

"There's around $697,000 in the account," Anderson told the judge that day. "I recommend a position of 100,000 to 150,000. That's around 28,500 to, say, 43,500 shares." There was a short silence, no more than three or four seconds.

"Three hundred," Young said then.

Anderson hadn't skipped a beat. "We'll call it eighty-five thousand shares."

"Sounds good," the judge replied. "Sounds good," and he had hung up. The deal was done and the papers out in less than ten minutes.

A $300,000 purchase of a 3½ point stock can create a minirise in itself, and Anderson would have done okay to run at the price bump that followed. He didn't do that, and the trust took a beating for weeks, right up until Ian Anderson nearly lost his job at the other client's request. But there were times in his life that he thought maybe he operated under the special watch of some higher force, and that time two-plus years ago was the biggest.

The buzz that morning cut through the electronic lifelines that tie brokerage houses together, phone and computer veins and arteries that were almost bursting with information. Anderson caught the first word at a late rumor stage, but even at that point, it was still only a vague hint that Weber was preparing an announcement. A dread feeling had crossed Anderson's heart and pulsed his temples for exactly twenty-four minutes, a stretch that he remembered intimately, with a nervousness that racked him each time he recollected it. His ears still grew warm and his stomach tightened in a slow, rolling turn.

His phone had rung twice after those twenty-four minutes, an outside call. Ian picked the receiver up to the office's D.C. branch.

"Ian," said the voice at the other end, "word is that Weber's set for a move out there. Any ideas?"

At first, Anderson thought it was some forgotten press connection, the papers maybe picking up a rumble on a slow news day. But then he recognized the voice and connected it dimly with Clayton or Clifford or Something Tarker. He remembered the last name. An unusual one. But the first name escaped him. Tarker had addressed Anderson with the pseudofamiliarity that was common but still uncomfortable between affiliated offices with employees who didn't know each other.

"No," Anderson said then. Simple and truthful.

"Bets are on product line." It was a leading statement, with a barely hidden request for a responsive confirmation. Anderson recalled now that Clifford — it was Clifford — Tarker was a blustery, overbearing type, prone to thinking that he was in control of everything he touched and everyone he met. And he was attempting control in that conversation, too, oblivious to the fact that Anderson would have told one of his own colleagues if he had known anything.

"Someone's on it," Anderson lied. "Working through Weber. You'll be first to hear after us."

He'd made a quick call after hanging up on Tarker. Carlysle and Thomas of course had no one "on it," and Anderson's tottering career, not insignificantly linked to Weber, was nominating him as the candidate of choice that day.

Anderson couldn't tap any source at Weber or at anything close to Weber, so he tried the other end. He'd worked his thumb across weathered Rolodex cards that sat at his elbow, flipping to a card marked FDA. It bore Nicholas Callestanza's name and number.

Callestanza was a college friend, a good one, who gravitated toward medical school as Ian earned an MBA. They spoke occasionally and occupied permanent slots on each other's Christmas card lists.

Very occasionally, Anderson completed a trade for Callestanza. No questions, no concerns, just a hand between friends.

Anderson reached for the same hand that morning, and Callestanza answered on one ring. It had been 8:00 A.M. D.C. time.

"Nick Callestanza."

"Nick, Ian Anderson. How're you?"

"Great!" Callestanza's voice seemed genuinely pleased. His voice rattled slightly on Anderson's speakerphone. "Keeping busy. No complaints," he said. Anderson had stood and moved to the window, bent and craned to look at the hotel.

". . . thinking about calling you," Callestanza continued. "I need to be up in Madison next month. I was thinking maybe . . ."

Anderson stopped paying attention as Callestanza made social niceties. He was looking out the window, where he had caught a glimpse of what appeared to be a young brunette.

He remembered her well now, too, even over the intervening years. She had been standing at her hotel window, oblivious to the fact that workers in the next building could see her in her well-lighted room in the darkness of a Minnesota winter morning. She had been drinking coffee. Maybe tea. And she had been naked.

Anderson remembered that very well indeed. A vivid image of her body remained with him. As she had lifted a white china cup to her lips, he could see her nipples, cocoa-brown and hard against the whiteness of her skin. He could see them still.

"That sounds good," he'd said when Callestanza stopped abruptly, the broker having no idea what the other man was saying. Then Anderson had taken another glimpse over at the woman before reluctantly pulling his attention back in the general direction of the phone.

"Listen, Nick, I need a quick favor from you, if you could." He glanced out again, but the woman was gone, and he turned his still somewhat distracted mind to the conversation.

A cautious silence stilled the line. Callestanza's noticeably less certain voice cut through. In truth, Anderson knew, Nick probably expected this for years, but that wouldn't have made it any easier to hear that morning.

"Sure," Callestanza had said, slight hesitation stalling the response. "Name it."

Anderson moved back to the desk, where he lifted the receiver to his ear. He collected the cord with his free hand and sat down.

"I need for you to check out a company called Weber BioTech for me. Word is that they're developing something that may have landed out your way. Something that might make the market a little jumpy."

Another pause, this time briefer. "Hang on."

Anderson could recall that wait as well. He could recall each and every aspect of it. Wondering if the brunette was back in the window. Wondering what Chief Judge Young was planning for Anderson's soon-to-be-on-the-street ass. Ian had wiped a finger across the framed diploma on the wall. It came away furred by a fine layer of dust, and he wondered idly where else he might hang it to collect some more. Nick was gone five minutes, no more.

"Ian?"

Anderson started a little and then sat forward. "Yup." Nonchalant. He could have been knitting for all the excitement in his voice.

"Packets arrived this morning. A new drug application by the looks of it. Lots of boxes. Lots of paper. Probably just the tip of it all." Callestanza sounded nonchalant for a moment also, but the change in his voice was perceptible as he continued.

"Now, I asked around a little, and no one can confirm it for me." Another pause, with Anderson resisting the temptation to prompt.

"Some people—*some* people, Ian—say it's an AIDS drug." The silence at that point was stretched and pure, almost crystalline in its permanence and frightening in its sheer clarity. Anderson had thought when he concentrated for one second that he could hear Callestanza's heart beating rhythmically through the knotted phone cord.

"What kind of drug?" Anderson said finally, hoping against all hopes for what Callestanza said next.

"A preventive vaccine," Nick replied, "called Prohiva. Spelled like it sounds." Anderson heard him rustling through papers across the miles. "That's all I know, Ian. And you didn't hear it from me." The last part was emphasized.

"Thanks."

Ian had rocked the phone into the base and plucked a cigarette from the pack of Merits in his breast pocket, lighting it between his lips without thinking. The tip glowed orange and then grayed as he drew heavily on the cigarette. The world turned very suddenly in Ian Anderson's favor that day. He had pulled very deeply on that smoke.

The word that Weber was submitting an investigational new drug application — an indy — to start the FDA approval process was late in the game. The Street typically heard about it long before the papers actually hit Washington. But Anderson thought maybe he was still early enough, so he'd made two quick phone calls. First to his manager. Then, approval obtained against the manager's better judgment, a second to Caldwell Young. It was time to increase the position. After four minutes' discussion, extensive for the judge, Young agreed to $100,000 more. Another 47,000 shares at the price then. More than two years later, Anderson watched the Weber quote tick glowingly across his screen: 43⅝.

It was enormously overpriced until you factored in the income potential, but biotech stocks didn't trade on past earnings anyway. It was always seat-of-the-pants stuff, guesses at what might happen or what traders knew would happen. Guesses cast as "projections" about what a company would do, could do, might do. Maybe.

In this case, Ian Anderson had done better than a lot, because he *knew* what would happen. The product was indeed an AIDS drug. A preventive AIDS *vaccine*, thank you very much, and Weber stock had erupted on announcement of the submission for FDA approval.

Up over $8.00 per share the first half hour, formal — sometimes informal — exchange mechanisms stepped in to control trading. They hadn't mattered in the end, and the stock price peaked at 53⅞ in six months.

A year and a half later, it held steady at a few dollars less. The trust held a paper profit of more than five million dollars. The judge was ecstatic but noncomplimentary due to "blindness." Ian Anderson continued to smoke his Merits in this office.

$43^5/8$ and going on the third year.

Anderson itched now, and he reached to the phone, lips pulling a last drag from a cigarette before he crushed a smoldering filter out into his empty coffee cup. He called Nick Callestanza almost monthly for updates, not wanting to blow a profit like that because of some fuck-up, but suddenly it seemed that he hadn't talked to his old friend in a long, long time. Much too long for such close friends. He dialed quickly and stood, listening to the distant D.C. phone ringing on the speaker as he moved to the window. He craned his neck toward the hotel.

Seven fifteen, the best time for viewing.

5

PATCHETT WHEELED a dolly like a pro, a habit long ago picked up as a senior high schooler employed at a Safeway, and he maneuvered the stacked boxes around the explosive glass sculpture outside the door, rolling them into his office and sliding them onto the floor. Setting the dolly aside, he grabbed each box in turn and set them around the office, stacking them against other boxes left from other files and older, completed projects that were now largely forgotten, their boxes remaining behind. That cardboard wall was the only decoration in the white-walled office, and it was growing yet again.

The three boxes Patchett was adding represented that small portion of the Weber BioTech file that was most likely to include anything relevant about Alexander Tomlin. Patchett had frankly hoped he would be able to simply pull a folder marked TOMLIN. No such luck. He ended up with the boxes instead, each of which contained at least ten individual folders. Each folder in turn held any number of separate reports, papers, filings, or other mind-boggling pieces of information, all of it needing to be examined.

He looked again at the labels pasted to the box ends. GENETICS INFORMATION was the most promising, but its contents were the least likely to be understood, particularly the thickest folder in the box. That one read only ANTISENSE. Even the term made Patchett wince, but the five inches of material in the folder positively made him shake. He dimly remembered looking through it once before and being able to comprehend about ten pages of it. All of those were diagrams.

The box labeled PERSONNEL was just the opposite. It was probably insignificant information, but it would be fully understandable. Patchett recalled that box as well but didn't recollect ever reading anything on Tomlin, which was no surprise. The personnel angle and its role in the FDA approval had been the easiest, so it was given to the legal assistants. Patchett thought that Anne would have some knowledge of any personnel information on Tomlin, and he set the box aside.

Then there naturally was the middle ground. The third box held the bulk of the investigational new drug application to the FDA. Without its attachments, it crammed the box. With them, it would have filled — and overflowed — the room.

In that box was an overview report that detailed, in lay terms, the vaccine and the company and science behind it. It was essentially a press release, of course, a condensation and explanation of all the rest of the mumbo-jumbo that most reporters wouldn't have the time, energy, or intellect to digest for their television sound bites and news column blurbs. That report had been the bulk of the firm's work, along with making sure that Weber dotted its *i*'s and crossed its *t*'s in organizing the submissions to follow the arcane requirements of the Food, Drug and Cosmetic Act of 1938.

The box also contained the briefest reports on the scientific analysis of the same information. Those were wholly prepared by Weber researchers, Tomlin probably chief among them, and Patchett never even tried to comprehend them. He also largely shied away from the truckload of appendices to the reports, in deference to their multiple references to both genetics and complex chemicals. He had taken a look at one of the appendices once, with its multihyphenated and italicized terms, and slapped the document closed. For a moment, he'd seen a glimpse of Greek characters interspersed in the reports, and that was all it took.

He reached now for the overview, settling into his chair as he thumbed that report open to refresh his memory, somewhat faded in the seven — no, eight — months since he last touched the project. He saw the diagram first. The studded golf ball that was the human immunodeficiency virus, the AIDS virus, was marked blackly on the page, a corner cloven out of the diagram to reveal a schematic of the protein coat that was the ball's surface and the strands of genetic materials that were its core.

The words in the opening introduction were comfortably familiar even if distant. He'd written them more than two years ago:

PROHIVA: PREVENTING THE 20TH-CENTURY PLAGUE

The human immunodeficiency virus (HIV) has been the primary focus of immunology and disease response research since the infection caused by HIV — acquired immune deficiency syndrome (AIDS) — was first identified in 1981. Since that first published report of five deaths, the steady progression of HIV and AIDS has resulted first in an epidemic and more recently in a worldwide pandemic — 50,000 U.S. AIDS cases and 150,000 worldwide cases in 1987 has grown to 100,000 U.S. AIDS cases and perhaps 400,000 worldwide cases, with millions more infected by and carrying HIV. By the early 1990s, 1 in 100 American men and 1 in 250 Americans overall carried HIV. Now, that overall number exceeds 1 in 225. By the end of this century, the total number of persons infected by HIV worldwide will be in the tens of millions, possibly even exceeding 125 million. Almost 10 percent of those infected will be children.

Most ominously, this 20th-century plague was ultimately determined to have a mortality of 100% for those who developed "full-blown" AIDS, and infection by HIV is invariably linked to eventual development of that status. No treatment is available for the disease other than immunological boosters such as azidothymidine (AZT) and companion drugs such as DDC (dideoxycytidine), which together showed some limited—though controverted—ability to delay onset of the disease, if not to avoid AIDS altogether.

Patchett smiled at the ease and smoothness of the language and at the utter catastrophe that it suggested, precisely the picture that they wanted to give to the news organizations. A masterfully simplistic and clear work, the press had eaten it up for a solid month, largely without ever confirming the sometimes generous estimates. Even now, Patchett weekly saw language culled from the overview in newspapers and magazines reporting on the status of the approval process.

The fundamental problem lay in the virus itself. As a retrovirus, HIV infects cells by copying itself directly into a cell's DNA. Additionally, HIV proved to have great mutability and is, in fact, the most variable virus known. It also can lie deceptively dormant for a latency period of years before erupting into disease. Finally, the hallmark of HIV—it attacks cells of the immune system itself, and the body's counterattack on HIV-infected cells is, therefore, a destruction of the very immune system "killer T cells" that are responsible for fighting infection. This bodily defense mechanism destroys its own cells and provides opportunity for further spread as healthy T cells attack infected ones and themselves become infected. An answer to HIV necessarily had to confront these problems.

That is the achievement of Prohiva.

Traditional vaccinology focuses on injection of "dead" viruses or of noninfectious portions or attenuations of the virus. Either method is designed to stimulate antibody production. The first, however, raised issues of the efficacy of "killing" viruses, particularly a virus known for its dormancy. The second presented expense concerns and questions regarding how much of the virus or its component parts could be shed without destroying the ability to stimulate the optimal antibody production.

Prohiva walks both lines with proven results. Prohiva is based on a simple premise: the surest stimulator of antibodies —and thereby immune response—is the entire virus itself. Prohiva therefore maintains the integrity of the virus but negates its effects and characteristics by "blanking" portions of the viral genes through the application of cutting-edge antisense technology.

HIV is an RNA virus — it contains only half of the nucleic acid ladder found in a typical DNA gene. "Antisense" is a series of nucleic acids that can lock with the nucleic chain of the RNA in the HIV genes. Even in a "locked-up" state with antisense, the HIV genes have been found to maintain their ability to infiltrate cells, triggering the antibody reaction. Nevertheless, they lose their ability to replicate and mutate because of the blocking effect of antisense on key portions of HIV genes. In essence, therefore, the application of the antisense nucleic acids creates HIV genetic "blanks."

These blanks stimulate antibodies, but because they cannot replicate, they do not spread infection. In addition, the antibodies produced by the genetic blanks are generic — they have been found to respond to *all identified* HIV forms. Through this production of generic antibodies, which will be stored in the body's immunologic memory, any HIV infection will be attacked from the outset.

As for the genetic blanks themselves, they, too, will be attacked. The integration of the genetic blanks will leave antigen "flags" on infected cells, just as any HIV infection does. These flags will attract the antibodies, which will, in turn, attract killer T cells to destroy the infection. No infection will spread from the genetic blanks to the attacking T cells — the blanks cannot replicate.

The end result — generic antibodies to HIV infection that are stored in immunologic memory, to be supplemented by boosters as needed, without infection from the vaccine itself. Any subsequent HIV infection can be addressed.

Prohiva can prevent further spread of this 20th-century plague.

A soft rap at the door interrupted Patchett.

"Yes?" he said, and was pleased to see Anne Matheson's face when the door opened. As was typical, her soft blond hair tumbled uncontrolled across her forehead in a pageboy cut. The sun streaking brightly in from behind him caught in her almost-navy eyes. He waved her in.

"Got your message," she said. "What's up?"

"Heard the news?"

"Tomlin, right?"

"Cops peeled him from the sidewalk in front of the Weber Building early yesterday morning. Rowe Weber was on the phone to Ben Flare by noon. Flare left a message for me within an hour. And now I'm calling you. Wasn't Tomlin part of your stuff?"

Anne nodded. "He *was* my stuff. Head genetics researcher. Chief brain at Weber on the genetic mapping and interaction of the antisense chemicals."

Anne instantly lost him, even with the refresher read-through. There was a reason that Patchett was a lawyer. A penchant for words had never been denied him, and he always managed well enough with that, but he'd never really gotten far past the cover of any science book.

He looked now from Anne to the GENETICS INFORMATION box sitting at her feet on the floor, and he rubbed briefly at his eyes, then pushed a hand back through his hair. Flare wanted information by the end of the week, a seemingly impossible time line, and Patchett had a passing moment where he considered just going to Ben and telling him that there was nothing special about Tomlin. Nothing that should be addressed or brought to the FDA's attention, despite the untimely passing of Weber's chief geneticist.

"Sit down," he said instead, sounding aggravated. He gestured to a chair. Anne sat opposite him at the small table in his office and looked briefly at the materials scattered haphazardly in front of him.

"Let me guess," she said. "FDA updates because of Tomlin's death?"

Patchett nodded, eyes closed tight with already-present frustration. "I'm doing my homework," he said. "It's due Friday, and I think I'm going fail the final."

"Looks like you've barely started studying."

"Thanks for the support," he said sarcastically. He leaned back in the chair and looked out the window. He vacantly tapped at the open report with his pen. "To tell you the truth, I'm a little uncomfortable, a little uncertain, about exactly what it is that I'm supposed to be looking for. *Anything that looks like it might matter to the FDA*, says Ben. Well, that's real nice, but I'm not even sure that I understand most of the information in these files, some of which went out with my name at the bottom of it." He shook his head, then looked over at her and smiled a bitterly wise, knowing grin. "That's why I called you."

She expected that this was coming, and she was glad it was Patchett. He was always relatively undemanding and was usually friendly, even if typically a little sharp. More important, he appreciated the fact that her brain worked, too, and he was free with delegation of responsibility.

Anne Matheson's brain, in fact, worked exceptionally well. As a legal assistant, she was the best. As a biology student at the university, she was also among the best.

Patchett knew that Anne had come to college and work the hard way—by scraping things together in a family life that was, by all appearances, a taboo subject. He also knew that she performed exceptionally well in both—a consistent honors student in a difficult major who held down a challenging job while doing virtually flawless work. That was why he turned to her when the Weber team was formed in the first place, and it was why he had consistently relied on her whenever a Weber issue came up since then.

This particular issue, of course, was a perfect fit, given her earlier work, and Patchett was pleased it would involve her. It naturally didn't hurt that Anne was also attractive, unmarried, and only twenty-five, but Patchett admonished himself once again at that thought. An attractive woman could be a problem, he knew. Still, he told himself, it was always better to be working with her, and he could always look.

Truth be known, Patchett probably could have managed the work alone. Tomlin's death wasn't likely to raise any new considerations for the FDA submission. The last nonhuman studies were almost complete, after all, at least judging by the loose talk around the office and out of Washington, and the relevant files wouldn't be insurmountable. The medicine was still the same, so those files would not need review. But the extra hand would be useful. And then there were those eyes, black in some light, blue in others . . .

"What's the latest on where we are with FDA?" Anne suddenly asked him.

"Poised on the brink of Phase Three," the attorney said, shaking his gaze off. He sat forward and shuffled aimlessly through the papers on the desk, as though searching for more information on that point.

"Remind me what that is compared to everything that's come along so far," Anne said then. "First the indy . . ." She trailed off, and Patchett picked up her lead with the part of the story that *was* familiar to him. The part of the story that he actually understood.

"First the indy," he said, nodding. "The investigational new drug application. That usually gets filed a month before human testing, then there's a thirty-day pretesting period for FDA to analyze the application and determine the testing process. But there's also usually a hold during that period, and that delays testing."

"And that happened here?"

Patchett nodded again.

"And that's when FDA decided to use animal testing for the first two phases?" Anne asked.

Patchett nodded a third time. "The first phase is typically around fifty people, and they're tested with the drug to determine or confirm pharmacologic effects — to find out what the drug actually does *as a drug*."

"And the second phase?"

"That one's larger. Maybe several hundred patients, tested to get a preliminary understanding of the drug's effectiveness, which is the big issue in ultimately getting approval."

"But no human testing in those two phases, right?" Anne emphasized.

"None," Patchett answered. "Prohiva early on met with highly particularized FDA examination, for obvious reasons."

"HIV is no ordinary virus."

"Not by any stretch of the imagination. HIV is no ordinary virus, AIDS is no ordinary disease, and Prohiva's no ordinary shot in the arm."

"So Weber ended up with animals for the first phases."

"That's right," Patchett said. "The company had completed five animal studies and had another one going even before the indy was submitted. Those all used chimps because nothing similar to HIV was carried in rats or mice. All that early testing was incredibly expensive, but they did it diligently and methodically, all in hopes of easing through FDA approval."

"Didn't matter," Anne said.

"Nope," Patchett replied, a thin smile on his face. He seemed pleased by the memory of Weber BioTech's problem, despite the fact the company was a client.

"The presubmission animal test results were successful," he went on, "but it didn't matter at all. FDA put a seven-month hold on the indy application while it considered whether human testing would be allowed in the two early phases. Rowe Weber met almost daily with FDA administrators for one of those months, alternately cajoling and threatening everyone he came across. And they still came down on the side of animal testing in the first two phases."

Patchett smiled again at the recollection. "*God,* Rowe screamed about that," he said softly, shaking his head slowly.

"You don't like this company, do you?" Anne asked, catching that look. Patchett hesitated a moment before speaking, but the tight, edgy smile never disappeared.

"It's a client, Anne," he said, as though she hadn't known that. "I don't think there's any room here for ideas of *like* or *dislike.* We just do the work, and we do it as best we can."

Anne smiled then, too, knowing that Patchett believed what he said, but also knowing he didn't really care much for Weber BioTech just the same. "So it did more animal testing," she said.

"Two phases of it," Patchett replied. "And as of now, more than two years of additional time."

"I remember the complaints about how slow the phase studies were going."

"Rowe screamed about that, too," Patchett said. "He knew that everyone was being slow and cautious because of the latency factor built into HIV's genes. You couldn't go too fast when you had a disease that might take years to manifest itself. But Rowe constantly argued that latency was eradicated along with the 'active' sections of the eight HIV genes, and he was always pointing out FDA's own public promise of expediting AIDS drug approvals."

"Has he finally had some effect?" Anne asked.

"Maybe," Patchett answered. "The word is that FDA's planning to approve human testing in Phase Three sometime soon. That might be a result of Rowe's getting to them finally. More likely it's public pressure and Eugene Wall. You remember him?"

"Counsel to the FDA secretary," Anne answered instantly. "And former senior senator from Minnesota."

"And good friend to Rowe Weber," Patchett added. "I've heard that FDA was inundated with letters and calls about Prohiva, and Wall might have used that public response and a little internal pressure to speed things up for his friend."

"So we're looking at Phase Three."

"Phase Three and a dead researcher."

"And what are your thoughts on how to go about looking into that?"

Patchett tipped back in the chair again, leaning it onto its hind legs as he reached over to a desk drawer, pulled it out, and grabbed a yellow legal pad from inside. Plucking a pen from his breast pocket, he took brisk notes as he spoke.

"As you can see, I pulled the genetics file and the main papers from the indy." He pointed vaguely toward the boxes. "I've also got the personnel materials you guys pulled together. I don't know if Tomlin's file is in there. I didn't see it . . ."

"My office," Anne said. "Been there for months."

"Good. I was afraid we'd lost it." With all the security codes, the numbers of which he was always forgetting, Patchett doubted that was possible, but lost files were hardly a rarity in a law firm.

"My plan right now is to review what's here," he said. "I'll go through all the personnel files except Tomlin's to see if there's anything worthwhile in them. Shouldn't take too long. You take a look at Tomlin's. You know him and that file better anyway. Look for interesting things, personal things." He scribbled on the pad.

"We should also eventually take a look at the indy file," he added, "but I'd need your help with the genetics stuff." Anne nodded and scratched a note of her own on the ubiquitous pad that legal assistants carried.

"And we'll want to look at a few more things beyond that, too," Patchett continued. "Tomlin might have had some personal papers at the office. Those might help. We should also probably talk to the people at Weber, see if anything was up with him."

"He should have had a ton of notes," Anne said.

"I'll call over to Weber to find out where they keep them." Patchett wrote something else.

"Was he married?" he asked then. There was no mention of a wife or family in the newspaper report.

Anne shook her head. "Never, according to the records. No wife, no kids. No real family. A brother, I think." She thought about it, couldn't remember for sure. "Iowa maybe."

"Girlfriend?"

"Not the kind of thing that's in a lot of company records, Jon."

"Gay?"

"*Also* not the kind of thing that's in a lot of company records." Anne shook her head at the question.

Patchett made a final note. "So we have an apparently unattached, brilliant man with a personality only in his work?"

"Pretty much."

The attorney scratched at his head and stared out the window, frowning slightly. The Capitol was just visible at the horizon. A steady drip of water from melting ice lined down the window glass, severing the view of the distant building precisely in two.

"So we start with these, I guess," he said, sounding uncertain. "Then we move on to company records. We see what we have, maybe get a few ideas and follow up, then let Ben know that there's nothing to add. Just a dead, lonely guy. We're in and out quick. Sound good?"

It sounded relatively easy, if nothing else, and Anne appreciated that. There were exams coming up in a couple weeks, and she didn't need any extra work getting in the way. This, at least, could be taken care of fairly simply.

"I'll let you know what I find out, if anything," she said, standing and moving out the door.

"Fine," he said. When she left, he turned to the box before him and, with another slight groan, pulled out the first folder.

Ian Anderson was doing some expectant imagining and fast calculations as he hung up the phone on Nick Callestanza. *Four days to the FDA's approval of Phase III studies.*

Anderson pulled the judge's file and opened it to the Weber listing. A figure of 132,000 shares stared back — 132,000 shares currently listed at 43⅝.

An FDA announcement, he figured, would eventually rocket the share price to around 75. Maybe 80 to 85. The value of the judge's stock would soar above $10 million dollars. *Amazing.*

Anderson thought again of the past two-plus years. He had indeed come close to losing his job but instead made millions for his client.

"This is one fucking strange world," he said. He lit a Merit, smiling, and leaned back in his chair. Maybe he'd take the day off.

6

HIS NAME was the only thing he remembered, really.

Gordon Grant. Last name like the president. It wasn't on the chart.

He was stretched on his back, though he didn't think he'd ever slept that way until he came here, where other people took care of him and fed him and turned him and cleaned up after him. Even had to wipe him off, and it was embarrassing to think about that when the dementia floated far enough away for him to understand.

He was stretched out flat, his head resting on his right cheek on a pillow that was starkly yellow from age and, had Gordon been able to tell, pungently fresh from overbleaching.

He could dimly feel a small cake of residue that crackled around a narrow tube winding its way from a machine at the side of the bed into his right nostril. It fed into his trachea and from there reached almost to his bronchi, which rattled with each movement of air fed into him. The tube was crystal clear, a cylinder of curved ice.

Gordon opened one eye with an effort, saw nothing but the curtain drawn around his bed, struggled to keep the eye open, and succeeded. He spoke without sound, mouth moving in utterance of a voiceless whisper that no one could have heard even if an actual noise had been made. He tried to say only one word: "thirsty."

He distantly registered the sounds from the other patients scattered beyond the wall of white pulled around him, listening vacantly to the occasional cough or rustle of sheets.

Gordon carefully raised one arm to rub at his mouth. He noticed the brownish lumps on that arm and ignored them, the sight of them conveying nothing to his mind, which right now was again understanding very little. More of the small lumps, almost purplish in color, patched across both of his legs.

The chart hooked to the foot of his bed listed this as Kaposi's sarcoma. *KS*, it said. It was extraordinarily rare except in AIDS victims, and Gordon's chart listed that as well: ACQUIRED IMMUNE DEFICIENCY SYNDROME stretched in an almost-unintelligible scrawl across the top sheet.

And others: advanced *Pneumocystis carinii* pneumonia, intestinal cryptosporidiosis, AIDS-related dementia, and partial paralysis of lower limbs, a host of infections and maladies crept down the page and through Gordon's thin frame. A list of tests sought confirmation of others.

He coughed dryly and could feel the tube in his chest.

Somewhere in the recesses of a mind that was rapidly losing its battle to infection, Gordon wondered how he had wound up here. Wondered, in fact, just exactly where this was.

He was still a virgin at twenty-two. Never had sex with a woman. Nor with a man, for that matter. No shared needles or drug use of any kind. No transfusions.

Even if he was able to think clearly, he would not have associated his current state with the man who had handed him the small flyer on a narrow street extending off the Strip, almost two years ago. That scrap of paper had only a line for his name and address, with an offer of a hundred dollars for participating. The money was a lot to Gordon Grant then, even though it meant nothing to him now, and he took the offer.

He didn't recall that anymore, as his eyes closed. He could feel only the tube in his nose and the pain in his chest.

7

By LATE AFTERNOON, Patchett was buried in personnel files, which spread around his desk in a rough fan centered on what was becoming an increasingly — almost infuriatingly — uncomfortable chair. So far, he'd found very little in the indy box, just as expected. The folders were filled only with technical information. Some of it mentioned Tomlin. Some, in fact, was prepared by him. But there was almost nothing that seemed particularly tied to Tomlin's untimely demise. Nothing specific to be brought to the attention of the FDA.

The box also contained the summary reports for the preapplication studies of Prohiva. Amazingly enough, each monkey in the studies was named and numbered and reported with a listing of inoculations, exposures, time frames, and a boggling array of minutia. Patchett knew how to find out how much and what kind of food any damn one of them ate on any damn given day, but he knew precious little more about Alexander Tomlin.

More than the expected lack of information from the indy file, though, Patchett was afraid of not finding anything at all in the personnel files. True, he didn't anticipate volumes of facts, or even a few facts, culled from these snapshot pictures of the Weber employees, particularly since he didn't even have Tomlin's file to examine.

He kept thinking that perhaps Anne would make something of that file, would pull together some bare shred of news that would prove that the diligent search was thoroughly performed. Perhaps. But Patchett doubted that as well. He'd told Anne the simple truth, one that anyone in their place probably already would have accepted — they weren't going to find anything.

Close the books and let's fucking move on, Patchett thought abruptly, but the disturbingly eager rush and threat of carelessness in that sat the attorney up straight in his chair, alarmed. There was a time, he knew — a time in the not too distant past — when more thorough objectivity and an unassailable patience in his work and his life would have made his still-echoing thought unthinkable.

Patchett settled himself, elbows on the desk, and he searched as best he could back through the frayed fabric of his past few years, digging for some window of calm reflection through which he could view this. He searched for whatever remnants he had of a rationality that would best serve him now, that would best serve his client. And he knew as he did so that he owed the company — the *client* — that much, however ambivalent his feelings might otherwise be.

His fingers dug at his temples as he forced himself to think through what he knew of Tomlin again, and they pushed harder at the attorney's realization that the things he did know *were* in fact as sparse and straightforward as they seemed. Tomlin's life apparently really was a simple story, and that was the lingering problem that naggingly, *annoyingly,* caught in the attorney's mind. Patchett found himself wondering what that early morning thought of Tomlin's could have been, what fleeting reflection had passed through the mind of this simple and straightforward man, ultimately pushing him out that window.

Patchett closed the file of one of the research chemists, shutting it against an employee handbook black-and-white photo of an unknown face at Weber, and he rolled his chair back to stand and move to the window. He looked out across the city. The lakes — Harriet and Calhoun — were just visible at the far edge of his southeastern view, their still-iced surfaces glinting white in the full and high afternoon sun.

He glanced down, looking toward but not seeing the street running below. From the forty-fourth floor, the building was too high to actually see the sidewalk, the passing cars. The angle of the building prevented that. But he could imagine it, he thought confidently, and he knew that Tomlin — only eleven stories up — would have been able to see his own street lighted below him as he leaned out of the Weber Building into the brisk and dark air. Patchett again wondered what tipped Tomlin out and down, what pushed him past that initial explosive and hesitating fear that anyone would have felt. He reached back to the desk and slipped the legal pad from it, plucked a pen out, and scratched a note.

Working on what? was all it said.

If he could find out what Tomlin was working on, he thought, what specific aspect of this project that consumed his life for years, then that might be something legitimate to raise with Flare.

In the end, Patchett wanted to be able to respond at some level, just as any attorney with a project wants. He wanted to think this through as best he could, as best as he at least *once* was able to, and he wanted to come up with the result that served the task and the client's needs. That, he felt, wasn't too much to ask in the end.

He moved to the stacked folders and flipped through the personnel files to find the reports on the people who worked with Tomlin most closely. Marc Clifton, the $800,000 virologist. Patchett set it aside. Kenneth Miller, another virologist. On top of Clifton's. Michael Kasselton, a lab tech whose report listed work with Tomlin on the antisense. Rebecca Cartaway, Tomlin's secretary. The stack grew. Patchett continued to sift through the files.

Anne tore the top sheet from the pad, filing the page and its jottings from her conversation with Patchett in a NOTES folder from her own file on Alexander Tomlin. She kept a file for each project, with subfiles for various papers. All were slipped into the narrow bookshelf at the narrow end of her narrow office.

She didn't have a window. No legal assistant did. So she didn't have plants. There was only an array of photographic prints — waterfalls and mountains in Montana. Anne had never visited there, had never had the money to get even that far, but she hoped to.

Besides the prints, what everyone noticed first was the stark neatness. The folders in the bookshelf. Under those, a small library of biology books, pirated from throw-away bins at the university. Above the folders, a framed photograph. Her mother. There was no photo of her father, nor of her stepfather, both of whom were long gone from her life. She never wanted a picture of either man. Would never have one or willingly look at one again.

The notes put away, Anne sat and reached for the telephone. She didn't intend to examine Tomlin's file for relevant information to be passed on to Patchett or Flare or Rowe Weber. She knew the file intimately, could recite it virtually word for word, as she could everything else she worked on for months at a time.

Like Patchett, Anne had known reading the morning paper that Tomlin's work and life would be scrutinized by the firm, Weber, and probably the FDA. Major researchers didn't just leap off buildings after a monumental medical breakthrough without raising eyebrows in the scientific community. Everyone would be looking hard at Alexander Tomlin and what might have gone wrong, and Anne had guessed correctly that she would be one of those doing a lot of the looking.

She was exceptionally qualified for it because of her knowledge of the man's life. She did know that file — Alexander Tomlin had been forty-eight years old. Undergraduate degree at Stanford in microbiology and genetics. Medical school at Johns Hopkins. Back to Stanford for a Ph.D. Genetics again.

He worked for two years as a researcher at a large pharmaceuticals firm in San Francisco. Nine years at a different drug firm, this time in Portland. Then to Weber. He was there only around four years before his death. He'd fit in perfectly, spearheading key elements of the Prohiva project.

Tomlin was never married and, to the best of anyone's knowledge, had no girlfriends, boyfriends, any kind of friends, really. And that was pretty much all that the various paper tracings in the files revealed about Alexander Tomlin.

So Anne turned to the phone. It was, in a sense, her best weapon, putting her in touch with a few key contacts whom she kept and maintained from friendships or working relationships. Each of the contacts could supply different information, with each different fact telling a separate part of what might be Tomlin's story. After they were all put together—if she could find them—who knew what those pieces would show.

She called the credit bureau first and asked for Brad Martin. He was a high school friend, a good one.

"It's me," she said when he answered. She'd slept with four guys in high school, and he was one of the them. They went their separate ways after graduation but remained good friends ever since. The effort at anything more failed miserably, but they had unfailingly assisted each other since that time.

"Hey, how're you doin'?" he said, but then instantly added, "business or pleasure?"

"Business. Sorry."

"No problem. What do you need?" His intimate niceness came through to Anne, and she again regretted for a moment that something with Brad never worked out. But he was a man whom mothers, not their daughters, loved.

"I have a guy named Alexander Tomlin," she said, reading off a Social Security number. "He lived at 432 Eagle Mountain Avenue. That's in Burnsville. Worked in Bloomington at Weber BioTech as a geneticist. Died yesterday after a hundred-foot plunge."

"Tough hop. And what's this Tomlin to you?"

She could hear him punching at the computer keys and knew that the information on Tomlin was already coming up on Brad's screen across town. It was really too easy, she thought. A connection helped, of course, but the truth was that anyone who knew a person's Social Security number could get reams of information on that person with the simple push of a few buttons.

"He worked on Prohiva," Anne replied, pushing aside any fleeting concerns for the privacy of persons either dead or alive. "Heard of it?"

"AIDS drug?"

"HIV preventive vaccine, actually," she said. "We did the FDA approval papers for it. Tomlin worked a lot on the stuff, and now we have to know if there's anything we should be telling the FDA about him because of his death."

"He didn't take the secret with him, did he?"

"Funny. Do I get anything or not?"

"Depends," he said. "We having dinner sometime? Friday, maybe?"

"Busy. I've got finals coming up. Make it three weeks, your treat."

That was good enough, and Martin read off what appeared on his computer screen. "There were two credit cards, a Visa from CentralBanc and an American Express gold." He gave her the numbers for both, and she jotted them down.

"No delinquent charges on those. No delinquencies on the house, either. In fact, it looks like he owned it outright. It's been paid off for" — he paused, flipping through screens — "for a year."

"Two cars," he went on, "both also paid off. There were credit checks by two apartment complexes within the last year. Both in Bloomington, fairly close to his job by the looks of it." He read off the addresses while she wrote them down.

"Neither is listed as a residence address?" she asked.

"No. But there's another apartment listed as a rental in his name."

"Where at?"

"Old Shakopee Road, 1740, number 411." That, too, would be near the Weber Building. Anne added the address to her notes.

"Crash pad maybe?" Martin asked.

Anne considered that, thought it probable. Tomlin worked long hours, and even Burnsville could seem far away, especially in winter. So he'd have a place to sleep when the working hours got long. Lord knows he could certainly afford it with the pay scale at Weber.

"Probably." She chewed on her pen. "What else you got?"

"Not much. No judgments, no real debts. A bank account, of course. Norwest savings. Checking account, too, judging by the number. No bouncing going on, though. All in all, a pretty boring guy."

Anne raised her eyes and nodded silently at that, pulling at the scrap of hair that dropped now across her face. The information wasn't much, but it gave her two or three lines that might have good hooks on the ends.

"Is Linda still at Norwest?" she asked. Another contact and a mutual friend.

"Long gone."

Anne checked off the bank numbers. Bank accounts were tight information, and she didn't want to run any risk with those without help from the inside. She scribbled a circle around the credit card numbers instead and began to run through a list of names, trying to think if she knew anyone at CentralBanc or American Express.

"You want a written report with this?" he asked.

"How much?"

"Twenty-five bucks, but I'll let it slide for that date."

Anne smiled. "Deal. Can you get it in the mail today?" She heard him pecking at the keyboard and already knew the answer.

"It'll be there," he said.

"Thanks," she replied. He reminded her of the date in three weeks. She would forget. He would forgive.

Patchett drank noisily from a glass of sour orange juice, which was too warm and far too straight, and watched as Ben Flare continued to flip through a *Penthouse*. Flare had kept a monthly copy of the magazine in his desk for as long as Patchett could remember, and he thumbed it routinely during the day. Never when there was a woman around, mind you, but almost incessantly when he was, as was typical, shooting the shit with one of the guys.

"You gonna make it tonight?" he said to Patchett, turning the magazine on its side. Flare's face twisted in a grimace.

"And miss the opportunity to have Melissa force another one of her girlfriends on me?" Patchett replied. The tone was a little sharp, but he doubted Ben noticed. "You know I never pass on that," he added for good measure. He drank again and wished for something to liven up the drink. It was already late in the day, and he always finished — and occasionally began — his days with a screwdriver or two. Or three.

"I'll try to control her," Flare said weakly.

Melissa Flare was unfortunately a stereotypical partner's wife. Too much time on her hands and too much money in her pocketbook, she busied herself with shopping and society, usually intermingling them in a frenzied afternoon of gossip and store hopping. When she got near Patchett, though, she focused on only one thing — matchmaking him disastrously with a spectacularly poor selection of women.

It'd been natural, probably. Maybe unavoidable. Flare was Patchett's mentor of sorts, had recruited him in law school and teased him away from a brief stint in the prosecutor's office, then shepherded him through the early years in the firm. Melissa, who was really too young to be called *Mrs.* Flare, apparently took it upon herself to watch over the rest of his life, whatever small amount that was. Patchett resented it but typically avoided putting up too big a fuss. Partnership was, after all, the goal, and that road ran directly through Ben Flare and his irritating wife.

"Not that big a deal, Ben," Patchett lied. It carried an almost sweet sound that he'd perfected whenever the subject of Melissa Flare came up.

Ben wasn't paying attention, his gaze instead fixed again on the magazine. He turned it to show Patchett.

Two women were contorted on the page, so wound together that Patchett couldn't tell which legs belonged to whom. He didn't know whether to feel excited or repulsed, and he was surprised when he felt both. He nodded to Flare, mouth tightening in a forced grin.

"Nice," he said. It sounded insincere, and he knew it.

Flare looked again at the picture. "Nice? Christ, Jon, sometimes I wonder if you're gay." He flipped a couple more pages before closing the magazine and tossing it into an open drawer. He pushed the drawer closed with a wing-tipped foot.

"Would it get your wife off my back?" Patchett asked almost hopefully.

Flare laughed. "No way. She knows some guys she'd like to set up, too." The magazine put away and the small talk handled, Flare turned to a little business. That was probably to justify billing an hour before leaving for the evening, Patchett figured. Ben Flare never missed a chance like that.

"What have you got on Tomlin?" he asked.

Patchett was afraid this would be the particular business that Flare would discuss. He was one of those partners who didn't seem to comprehend that projects didn't just magically get done during any short time period between the assignment and the next time the partner happened to see you.

"He only died yesterday, Ben," Patchett said as patiently as he could. "All I've got is a lot of paper and one moderate-sized dent in the sidewalk outside Weber's building. That's assuming, of course, that Rowe hasn't had the chance to have someone fill that in."

Flare smiled and leaned back in the chair, rocking it gently and twirling slightly side to side. His belly hung out over a cinched belt, wrinkles stretching up from the pant line across the bloused, starchy white fabric of his shirt. There were slight yellow stains under each arm, Patchett noticed as Flare locked his hands behind his head and spoke.

"He's a little apeshit about this, you know, just between you and me."

"I'd be a little apeshit, too," Patchett said. "Suicide's pretty unsettling as it is, but having one of your top guys jump out of your building is probably enough to ruin even one of Rowe's days."

"His week, I think. Maybe month. He's convinced now that the FDA will halt the investigation. I'm pretty sure that'd put him off his lunch for an entire year." Flare laughed.

Patchett stood. "Well, you can tell him he doesn't have to worry," he said. He pulled at the door and stepped out. "We'll find whatever there is to find. If anything."

"Tonight," Flare reminded as Patchett started down the hall.

Patchett waved back in resignation.

•

The phone was answered on the second ring.

"Can I help you?"

It was Anne's third call to American Express. The first one was short. Anne hadn't gotten past telling the service representative Tomlin's name before she was shot down. It wasn't American Express's policy to give out information to anyone but the cardholder, she was told. And since she was a woman, she obviously wasn't Alexander Tomlin. End of conversation. No information.

She got only a little further the next time. Although the company operator was a man this time, making the odds of a female caller's learning something slightly better, she wasn't able to get past the screening question about Tomlin's mother's maiden name.

She called the third time only because she was shut down so convincingly when calling CentralBanc that she gave up instantly on them and because screening questions were inconsistently asked. When the next representative answered, a man, she was again partway home.

"My name is Sharon Keyes," she began, the name coming from nowhere. "I'm at the finance office of Weber BioTech?" She said it as a question, as though expecting a response, and the operator obliged.

"Yes?" The door to Tomlin's credit records cracked open.

"Alexander Tomlin from our company had an American Express account? We prepared an end-of-year reimbursement for him, and he thinks that he's missed — well, actually, he thinks that *we've* missed — some of his charges? They were reimbursable?"

"Yes?"

"I was calling to check on some charges he thinks were on his AmEx card. Could I do that?"

"Corporate or personal card?"

"Personal." It was a guess that she hoped was correct. If she was wrong, this would be a short call, too.

"Number?"

She gave him Tomlin's account number, reading it from the notes from her conversation with Brad.

"Just a moment while I pull up the file."

She barely breathed for a few silent seconds, waiting for the inevitable question, any question. The one she got was unexpected, and she breathed easier.

"What do you need to know?" The door flew open now, and she ran through.

It was improper, of course. Almost certainly illegal. The conversation with Brad had been as well, as was the credit report that would arrive tomorrow. All in all, it was quite a day for breaking the law. If Patchett or any of the other attorneys did it, they'd be sanctioned by the state bar and probably suspended, possibly stripped of a license.

But she wasn't Patchett, and neither he nor anyone else would know of it. Under the unspoken lawyers' code, that was enough, because the information didn't seem improper if you didn't know how it was obtained. Attorneys wanted results, and if you gave them those results, they didn't ask a lot of questions about how you arrived at them, at least as long as they weren't implicated and the information could be used for the particular purpose at hand. Very Machiavellian. Very illegal. Very real.

"I just have a list of a couple things he says he charged for business? I was thinking maybe that you could confirm them for me?"

"Sure."

Just before calling, Anne jotted down a number of likely credit card charges, and she skimmed down that list now, picking one out and hoping to hit something blindly.

"He said there were a bunch of gas charges?" That was an easy one only vaguely stated and likely to be found.

"I see one in . . . July," the representative confirmed.

"No," she said. "He specifically said March."

"None then. Two in December, though. One in Kanab, Utah. The other in Vegas."

"Those are here," Anne said, writing the information down. He was telling her the amounts, but she was already trying to think of where to go next. As expected, she was suddenly flying without any beacons.

"And a rental car, too?" she asked, figuring it'd make sense. Few people would drive to Las Vegas from Minnesota in December, but Tomlin bought gas.

"I show an Avis rental on December third, returned on the fourteenth. Las Vegas."

"That's the one."

"$142.53," he said. She ignored that as well.

"And the plane tickets, too?"

"Uh, yes. United Airlines. Charged in November."

"That's right," she said. The operator's helpfulness told Anne that he thought they were working together to clear up this poor guy's receipts and get him his reimbursements. The company's rules apparently knew no bounds where money was the issue. Anne wrote the information down, ignoring the amount that followed.

"He also said something about an airline charge earlier in the year," she said, fishing a little deeper. "But I don't see that record. Does that show up?"

There was only a moment's delay. "No, I don't see that. Maybe another card?"

"Well, that's what I said, but he's a doctor, so . . ." The unspoken explanation worked.

"I still show an airline trip about a year and a half ago, mid-1994. That wouldn't be it, would it?"

"I don't think so. Was it in June?"

"May one is the charge date."

"Vegas again?" She was far out on the limb now, and the bough was bending precipitously.

"Well, there's another car rental there at that time. May four to twenty-one."

"No," she said. "I remember that. It was something else." She hesitated deliberately, recording this, too, as she shuffled her papers in a feigned search for Tomlin's misplaced receipts.

"Anything else?" he asked.

"I don't think so. We got the Vegas trip." She paused again, then pushed a little further. "Any meals there?"

"Nope," he said. "I really only see a few other charges, all local to the Minneapolis area. A couple of things last Christmas, some flowers around Valentine's Day, that kind of thing."

"No, that's definitely not ours," she said. She desperately wanted to ask about the flowers. They intrigued her. But she wasn't likely to learn anything more, and she couldn't push a clearly nonbusiness expense. She decided to go with her luck.

"I guess I have all we need. I told him I was sure he got all his reimbursements. Thanks for convincing me I'm not crazy."

"Certainly. And thank you for calling American Express."

You're more than welcome, Anne thought as she hung up. She read through her notes and filled in some gaps. A productive call.

Patchett glanced at the clock—6:00—and then at the stack of personnel files still tottering unread on the desk. The sun was nearly set, the sky and the sheet of clouds hanging in it slowly rotating through ever-changing shades of pink and crimson and purple. Dinner was at 7:30. Flare's home was only twenty minutes away. That left more than an hour to share with documents—an hour he couldn't possibly imagine filling, particularly after a drink or two.

He sat down and reluctantly pulled a file from the stack. He opened it, setting his glass down beside it and lifting his briefcase up onto his lap. He popped the snaps and drew a flask from inside.

Guessing at two fingers, Patchett poured the clear liquor into the glass, then added an extra splash. It filled it to the rim, watering the leftover juice to a runny orange, and he recapped the bottle and slipped it back into the briefcase.

The juice had the quick and slight bitterness of alcohol, but he barely noticed it after the first taste, and he knew that he wouldn't notice it at all after the entire glass.

He sat back and began to read the file, a yawn of frustrated boredom already stretching his mouth wide. He doubted he would make it.

8

HE WAS ODD. That much was certain. Melissa Flare could think of no other way to characterize him as she moved the cart briskly between the loaded shelves of food. Jon Patchett simply was odd.

It wasn't that she thought he didn't like women, as her husband so quickly and easily had suggested to Patchett himself just minutes before Melissa began making her way through the store. In fact, she was certain Patchett was straight. He was just too . . . well . . . *normal* not to be, she thought.

She'd considered testing him herself to make sure. She had a pretty good body, despite her self-perceived old age of thirty-three, but she'd never gotten around to trying it. Had never found just the right opportunity. And then, of course, there was Ben to consider. She supposed he would have found out eventually, and that simply wouldn't do. He was no prize catch to be sure, but his name was still on the paychecks that mattered.

So she contented herself with trying to set Patchett up with various eligible friends. After all, he might have been odd, but he was still a well-paid man himself, with prospects for even more.

Melissa figured that the biggest barrier to finding someone who fit with him was his damn edge. Patchett's outlook was gritty on almost everything. It was a demeanor, Melissa thought, that strangely suited his attractive but slightly off-kilter features, his consistently borderline-rumpled look, and his ragtag haircut.

That outlook did stand in the way, just like everything else that was detached and unknown and personal in him. Patchett never discussed anything of his life before he came to Allen, Sander, other than a very occasional, passing reference to two former wives. He'd apparently loved them — one of them, at least, to judge by the way he spoke of her — but there was no evidence of either woman's ever really having existed other than the fleeting mentions. There was only the brief comment here and there, or scattered statements coming out of the blue and serving in no way to fill in the gaps in everything that Patchett presumably knew before coming to the firm.

Melissa was content to leave that past in the dark. Her interest instead was in the future Mrs. Patchett. It was, in a sense, a kind of diverting hobby, one she fully intended to see through. She smiled at the thought. It might take some doing, she knew, but it would get done.

Melissa plucked a jar of olives from the shelf, the last of a few forgotten items for the dinner, and she made her way toward the front of the store.

9

THE BARBER watched the sun go down, sitting on a park bench that was emblazoned with words now mostly worn smooth by weather and usage and a strictly enforced city law against vandals. Only three things — JESUS, L.B., and FUCK — still read clearly.

He watched the sun intently. From the moment he had arrived in the park, just as the sun first dropped below the ceiling of March clouds, he'd stared at it until it swung down across the short distance to the horizon and slipped below it. Just before it disappeared, its brightness sat fat and red-orange against the dark earth. Branches in a nearby copse cut across it in the angles of a crazed latticework. His face grew cool when the sun disappeared. The 45 degree temperature of early evening hinted at a spring that was only temporarily waylaid by the latest snowstorm.

Even the sheet of clouds threatened spring, looking and smelling of rain rather than the coldness of snow, and that upset him in a way. Rain tended to keep people out of the park. At least with snow, they still came out consistently. And skiers could always be found.

Of course, every bad thing came with something good in it. His mother once told him that, and she'd been right. As usual.

So, even though spring brought rain, more people eventually would come as temperatures rose. On clear days, there'd be dozens of them each night in each park. And even more women would pass by, some of them jogging maybe, long hair drifting out behind them. Long tanned legs.

The prospect excited him. But it distantly alarmed him, too, as he considered it. More people meant being even more careful. Choosing the parks more selectively. Waiting till later at night. Or maybe the very early morning. Maybe an afternoon, when most people were at work. He might have to take a summer afternoon off some day.

He worked slowly through the good and bad points of spring and summer and then moved on to fall, alternately becoming aroused and dejected at the opportunities and implications of the various times of the year. He considered these things until he became enraptured again by the song blaring into his head from the speakers of the Walkman headphones that were pushed into his ears.

It was an old Dean Martin track. Old by the Barber's standards anyway. Dino was pretty much done with recording by the time the Barber was a kid. No one he knew ever listened to that stuff, certainly.

But he listened now. In fact, he'd listened to this song exactly six times since first sitting on the bench earlier in the evening. This was the seventh.

His mother had loved Dean, too. She even loved Martin and Lewis, though she had never watched the telethon in her life. She'd never been able to tolerate Jerry alone and always blamed him for breaking up the team, no matter what others said. Actions like that weren't to be rewarded, she'd always told her son. She was right. Of course.

He was reminding himself of that lesson and of his mother's infallibility when he saw the woman striding along the bicycle path on the opposite curve of the lake. She was making good time, so she'd be near him soon, and that was good. He glanced at his watch and scanned the park.

He kept listening to the music, turned it up a little, and watched as she moved toward him. She was alone, with the light only now really beginning to leak from the sky. And she had long hair, flowing a fiery orange-red in a bobbing mane behind her. *Just like the sun*, he thought, and fabulously long, he could tell even from here. Just like Kimberly's — silken in a glistening flow without any whorish crimping or perming to mar its smoothness. He would've settled for wavy hair, had done so once before. But he didn't have to worry about that with this one.

He stood just as she walked past a boat launch that was pulled up onto a frozen beach. She was still coming toward him, arms swinging with the artificial speed of walkers. He turned and began to walk away from her, slowly.

He was genuinely surprised at his luck and took it as a good sign. He'd gone to a park three days in a row last month before finding someone just right. And even then he wound up going for fairly short hair. It was good quality, of course, and he felt again its glassy softness as he ran his thumb along the braided cord deep in one coat pocket. But so short, not much over his minimum fifteen inches. Too short to really be the best, the *ideal* length.

But it had been almost past time then, and he'd felt the uneasiness that once before racked him when he actually failed to find the right one. It happened just that one time. Of the two times per month over the last three months, he'd failed to find her just one time. He would never, *could* never, go back to that park again. That wasn't right.

It was a different park each time. Always. The Twin Cities overflowed wonderfully, tantalizingly, with parks, and he would visit each one of them.

But never *that* one again. And never Loring, he supposed. Loring was where the queers were. His mother had always told him that, too, and he knew that this was true as well. Queers and diseases and who knew what else. Probably some things that he wasn't able to see the one time that he went there. He might find the right woman there, he knew, but he also knew that she just might turn out to be a man.

He shuddered and muttered quietly to himself, "*Queers.*" The woman would have heard him, would also probably have noticed him slipping on thin leather gloves, black against his pale skin, but her own headphones blared her own music into her own head. The distractions of exercise numbed by cold and transfixed by noise.

She didn't notice him. Not even as she passed and he stared at her shimmery red hair. It waved out as she walked past, and he moved to touch it but checked himself.

He glanced once over his shoulder and saw no one. The sky was getting to be too dark, the wind suddenly starting to bite too coldly for people to be in the park. It was cold enough that it was probably to be — certainly would be, he knew — her last trip around the small lake this evening.

He pulled the cord from his pocket and felt the frenzy build instantly inside him as he caught sight of its pieces twisted together. One end was wrapped around two fingers on his right hand; his left caught the other end swiftly and rotated the thin rope into a quick tourniquet on that hand's fingers. His fingertips turned purple and hot beneath the gloves as the blood flow restricted.

He was behind the woman in two steps as she moved in front of him, and his arms were up and around her in the third. The cord caught her just above her larynx, crushing out a startled sound as he jerked back. Her head snapped toward him, and he pulled tighter as her arms first flailed out and then reached to her neck. There was fearful astonishment in her eyes as her head came back almost to his shoulder. She stood off balance as she struggled to slip a finger under the cord buried in her neck.

The braided hair *was* short, and he swore with a passing fear that it wasn't usable after all. But he was able to just cross the ends behind her head anyway. His wrists formed a cruel X against the back of her neck as he yanked tighter.

It took almost forty seconds before she collapsed against him. She'd clawed at her own neck once, failing to tear away the cord that etched its furrow into her soft skin. She'd clawed at his gloved hand once as well, snapping a nail back on the thin leather.

He tugged harder for ten more seconds, then dragged her into the trees as he searched for people. Once there, he untwisted the cord from his fingers, then recrossed it behind her head and tied it fiercely into a tight knot. The narrow hair rope again bit deep into her neck.

That done, he took a pair of embroidery scissors from a pocket. Turning her head, he gathered a small section of hair where it lay longest, directly down her back. He ran it through gloved fingers, admiring it against the blackness of the leather. He cut it at the scalp and returned the scissors to his pocket.

Always the hair, he reminded himself. Always take the hair first, or the dirt and snow might ruin it. He knew that now. Learned it by experience.

No goddamned messes. Mother again. Right as always. And so he'd learned how to do it.

Looping the ends together, he fashioned a loose knot and set it, too, into his pocket. Carefully.

He turned again to the woman. Her face was almost black against the gray snow and dark earth in the first tints of night. He reached down and tugged at the top of her sweatpants.

Dino blared in his head.

10

PATCHETT WAS LATE, of course, the result of a side trip for fortification. That was a necessity when dealing with Melissa Flare. When dealing with everyone and everything in his life, for that matter. But the night had gone relatively smoothly anyway, and they were past the appetizer and main dish — both exquisitely prepared and both, no doubt, catered — and were well on their way through an after-dinner salad. It was an abominable practice, Patchett thought. He liked salads little enough as it was without having them as dessert. He made no comment, though, not wanting to fuss too much given the unexpectedly acceptable conversation.

But even as he thought of that, the subject turned to Patchett's love life. He should have seen it coming, too, as he looked across a salad decorated with sunflower seeds and unidentifiable sprigs. He was searching for salad dressing that wasn't there, but his face fell on Melissa's eyes, which were searching for openings in the conversation.

They'd already covered the other usual subjects. "They" mainly meaning Patchett and Ben Flare, and "usual subjects" meaning anything related to the law. It was surprising, really. Men who bitched constantly about the law and how much they disliked their jobs while they practiced it all day seemed fixated on talking about practicing it at all other times.

Ben had told his latest war stories, and Patchett had laughed at all the appropriate parts. The lubrication of the drinks at work and another before dinner, with a liberal splash of wine now sitting at his right elbow, made that easier.

Patchett told his own stories then, too, but he ran out of the updates of his legal career. So the door was wide open when he gazed across the salad and saw Melissa. He thought he could actually see her winding up and taking a deep breath before plunging into her favorite topic. He visibly braced and froze in midreach for the pepper.

"So," she said slowly, with deliberate and almost cautious emphasis, "Jon, have you been seeing anyone lately?" Her face brightened noticeably as she said it, and Patchett bit back the first response that came to him on the soft edge of the booze.

"Nope," he said simply. He gave up the brief search for the salad dressing and the reach for the pepper and decided to just forage on the lettuce leaves instead. "Not even really looking, Missy," he added. "You know how that goes."

She did know. He was always telling her that he wasn't looking for anyone anymore. He had tried marriage before. Twice. Had tried an occasional date, too. But ever coming close to the talismanic labels, "seeing someone" or "looking for someone?" That was long done, and Patchett made no secret of that fact with Melissa or with anyone else.

"Well," Melissa said, "I know what you say, but I don't think you're giving yourself the benefit of the doubt."

That was an odd statement even for Melissa, with a suggestion that Patchett maybe thought he wasn't good enough to attract a woman. He let that slide, too. Crunched on the seeds. At the head of the table, Ben sat apparently engrossed in his own salad, attention fixed on it as though the only leafy green vegetables on earth had magically materialized on his plate. Melissa went on to the inevitable.

"You know, I have a good friend from the health club. She's very sweet. Pretty. Keeps herself fit. She's divorced."

Patchett contemplated the relevance of this as he chewed. He tapped at the plate with his fork.

"I'm not interested, Melissa," he finally managed, speaking past a lettuce leaf dangling in the corner of his mouth.

"But you haven't even met her."

"I'm *really* not interested," he emphasized as patiently as he could. He could feel the blood swim warmly through his head, pushed by alcohol. He looked at Ben, who was finished with his salad but was now mesmerized in varying fits by the bare plate and his glass of beer.

"Well, I think you should keep trying," Melissa said. "There's someone for everyone, they say. Susan's very nice, and she's very pretty, with a nice little figure. You never know. Someone to keep you company—"

She didn't finish the thought.

"Melissa, listen." Patchett set his fork down. It clinked loudly on the plate. Ben snapped out of his seeming trance at the sharp sound and looked up. Patchett spoke calmly and clearly, but with the artificial courage and near-bluster of more than one drink.

"I have been married. More than once. You know that. I married one of them because she was sweet and pretty and because she had a *nice little figure*. In fact, I married her because she had a *great* little figure. And, sure, she kept me company. But I ruined her life after about eighteen months of my company."

Melissa Flare's gaze was fixed like that of a child being calmly but sharply scolded.

"And *then*"—he went on, his voice rising, but he cut the statement off even before the next words were fully formed.

"Then . . . ," he said again before faltering once more. He scratched his fingers slowly and deliberately through his hair, leaving it jutting, then he mopped at the suddenly tired, suddenly *weary* look on his face.

"It doesn't matter," he said through a web of fingers still stretched across his mouth. "I just don't think I'm cut out for it," he added quietly. "You and Ben are. A lot of people out there are, and that's great. But I know that I'm not, and it's gonna take one whole hell of a lot more than a pretty woman with a nice body to convince me otherwise. I'm sorry."

His words hung heavy in the room. Patchett picked the fork up and speared at the last piece of lettuce, lifting it to his mouth. Melissa slowly reached for her own fork and began to eat. Ben simply sat.

There was no more conversation about dating.

11

"WHAT'S THE MATTER WITH YOU? You don't know what the *fuck* you talkin' about," Jesse Cole said. He walked down the street with his friends, keeping one eye on any passing traffic as they moved. Thomas was dribbling a basketball, a dull orange-brown one with the worn surface of schoolyard games, and Michael—MK, he always said he wanted to be called—was emptying the last drink from a hip flask into his mouth, tilting his head back so far that he threatened to tip over. He swayed a little.

They always kept an eye on the street. All three of them wore colors, Starter jackets in the bright fire engine red of Kansas City's football team, with the single word "Chiefs" emblazoned across their backs and the "KC" arrowhead targeted over their hearts. Red tennis shoes, high-top Converse Chucks, unlaced. And you didn't wear colors without watching the street anytime you walked it. Especially at night.

They were dead center in the middle of South Central L.A., an area marked on a map by thick freeway lines—I-40, 405, the 110. In everyone's memories, the area was defined largely by references to years and the riots associated with them. The 1965 Watts riot. The 1992 Rodney King riot and its hotheaded little sequels. And always the Riot Yet to Come. It wasn't an area where you walked at night without all senses up and active.

They all knew guys, some girls, too, who had gotten caught in a drive-by. Jesse's older brother was hit in one a year back. A .22-caliber slug caught him in the jaw, lacing its way in a fine hole through his right cheek and exiting just below the ear. The doctor pronounced him lucky. Jesse himself, now twenty-three, was expected to be less stupid.

So they watched the street.

They'd been talking about Tina. They'd seen her minutes before, riding with someone none of them knew, and that sparked the questions about what she was doing. It was especially a question in Jesse's mind, since he and Tina had gone separate ways less than a week before. Now she was with some guy no one had ever seen. Which was *bullshit*.

"Man, we know *exactly* what we're talkin' about." Thomas didn't take his eyes off the ball as he continued to put Jesse on the spot in an attempt to finally get him past the girl.

"You don't know who the hell he is," Jesse said. "I don't know who the hell he is. An' I don't care. She can do whatever the fuck she wants. I am free of that fuckin' chain." He smiled at this, if only for the benefit of the guys with him. It actually pissed him off that she was with someone else, but he couldn't let it show.

His friends stopped at the intersection and looked over at him. Jesse could see even in the low light of the sole burning streetlamp that Michael's eyelids were leaden across bloodshot eyes.

"Fuckin' chain is right," Michael managed in a staggering street drawl. He weakly jabbed a finger in Jesse's direction. "That's all she ever was for you, man. A *fuck*. And you *know* it, man. That's prolly all she is for that guy, too." He gestured wildly in the general direction of the Pacific Ocean. The empty bottle dropped from his hand and spit a glass shard off from one thick corner as it tumbled into the street.

"Fuck you, man," Jesse replied, quietly now. He gave his friend a soft shove, a *you're drunk and full of bullshit* push that nearly knocked Michael off the curb.

"Get him outta here," Jesse said to Thomas, who caught the ball in one hand and reached out with the other to take hold of Michael's jacket. "Get him home and outta my sight. Fuckin' stinkin' drunk is all you are. Don't know what the hell you talkin' about." Jesse turned and headed up the street for the final two-block walk to his house. "Fuckin' drunk," he muttered into the night.

Thomas pushed at MK to move him down the street the other way. "Move, shithead," he said softly, and Michael mumbled something in reply that Thomas missed. They crossed the street and moved into the darkness, Thomas with the basketball propping up one arm while his other one handled his friend, guiding him up onto the curb on the opposite side and steering him in a relatively straight line down the sidewalk.

They had watched the black men since the three left the McDonald's, following them in the car at a distance until they recognized where the men were heading. Then they drove ahead and parked on the side street, waiting for the three to reappear.

When they saw them, they slid down out of sight until the three men moved past. Two white men sitting in a parked car in South Central was not a picture to present to anyone, and it was probably a good way to get killed. That wasn't the idea.

They watched until the three disappeared, then slipped out of the car and followed, dipping into and out of the numerous shadows on the poorly lighted street. Considering where they were, they were both somewhat surprised at the lack of activity. But it was a late Tuesday night — no, it was Wednesday morning, 3:00 A.M. They hugged the shadows. Even South Central slept sometimes.

The two men stopped when Jesse and his friends came to the intersection and had their parting. They could hear the conversation well enough. One of the three was a loud drunk. They watched them separate and allowed time for Jesse to move down the street by himself.

Stupid, one of them thought. This was originally planned as a drive-by, but the idea was killed because of the potential troubles from witnesses who might identify two white guys. White men weren't involved in too many drive-by shootings in this neighborhood.

But Jesse Cole and his friends were neatly resolving the witness problem, and the two men stepped from the shadows to jog silently up behind Jesse as he made his way alone along the street.

Their tennis shoes made only the softest sounds as the men moved, narrowing the distance. As they drew nearer, each pulled a small handgun from a jacket pocket and held it tightly against his leg. Barrels were elongated oddly by silencers screwed into the tips.

Jesse didn't hear them until they were almost on him.

He heard their footsteps first. No pair of tennis shoes could make grown men running up the street into stealth artists. The soft *fwap-fwap, fwap-fwap* — rhythmic pairs of footsteps in syncopation — gave them away.

Jesse ran without looking back. Like keeping an eye on traffic, it was another habit learned the hard way in L.A. You ran when someone you didn't know was chasing you. You ran as fast and as far as you could, and you didn't look back.

It crossed his mind that it might be Thomas and MK, but he remembered Michael's condition and instantly realized that he would have been able to hear him blocks away. Jesse ran harder.

The red jacket, unbuttoned to the bottom snap, parachuted out behind him, and he jerked it down around and across his back as he ran, feeling for the snaps to secure it. He couldn't tell if the footsteps were closer or not, but he knew that starting from a walk hurt his chances.

He'd barely covered a half block when the first hitch in his chest came, making him wince as he ran, his breath suddenly jumping and panting between his lips. There was a sharp point, just off his sternum on the left side. Then again.

Jesse was getting over a bad cold and was still a little short of breath. It wasn't the best time for a predawn run. He reached for his side and pushed his hand against the quick pain, trying to deaden it.

From the corner of one eye, Jesse could see the houses flying by, their daytime-bright but flaking colors flashing past as the grays and blacks of the dead of night. No light shone in any of them.

He heard his own feet slapping at the ground, mixing with the sounds of the men behind him as he passed his house. It occurred to him to head for the door, but he knew that he couldn't get it unlocked and open, get in, and relock it before the men would be on him. And then they'd be in the house, with his mother and brother, one younger sister. When you were being chased, you didn't go home if you gave a shit about your family. That was a final unspoken lesson of South Central for this night.

Jesse veered right and cut across the street instead, feet smacking on the asphalt hardness as he passed the old Dodge Dart that was the family's car, sitting at the curb.

The men were still behind him, and he saw that they were closer — no more than ten yards or so back — when he risked a glance over his shoulder. He realized with a start that they were white, and the abrupt thought that he was running from cops flashed across his mind.

He tried to push harder. The pointed pain in his chest became a bolt, and he coughed sharply. It felt like a stab, and Jesse pressed his hand more firmly against it.

He jumped to the opposite curb and continued across the sidewalk and into the Smalls' yard, heading for the rear of the house. Just beyond the chain-link fence that circled the backyard was an alley. If the fence slowed them down, then he figured he'd have a chance at either hiding in one of the dingy garages lining the alley or reaching the street another block down. The traffic would be a little heavier there, his chances a little better.

He hit the fence at a jump, impaling his left hand neatly on one of the crossed wires that lined the top bar. The pain was quick, blinding, searing, but Jesse barely noticed as he vaulted over. The wires caught and held for a second, tearing a half-inch chunk from his palm and dislocating the middle bone in that hand. He hit the ground at a stagger, thrown off balance by the snagged hand until it tore free. Then he was off across the spotted and worn backyard, making his way to the next fence and the alleyway beyond.

His chest hitched again with another flash of pain as he jumped at the back fence. Distantly, Jesse heard what sounded like an extra footfall from the far edge of the yard behind him. The quiet, muffled sound of a slap on a pillow.

The shot caught him in the upper right shoulder, piercing the Chiefs' *F* and pivoting him as it knocked him over the fence and into the alley with the blunt force of a hammer. Jesse landed face-down, the dirt puffing up around his head and the gravel in the alley drive cutting into his cheek.

Jesse Cole screamed for help, already knowing that none would come.

They immediately hurdled the fence after him, nearly landing on Jesse Cole's prone body.

"Do it," one said fiercely to the other, and Jesse struggled to stand. A thin, bubbled spittle of blood came from his mouth while a steady line ran from his nose. One of the guns crashed against the back of his head, and he collapsed forward again into the dusty, oiled surface of the alley.

The men bent over him, and one of them reached into a pocket, fumbling there as he grabbed a capped, hypodermic-tipped syringe with a latex-gloved hand. He pulled the syringe out and passed his gun to his companion.

Slipping the protective cap off the needle, the man studied Jesse for only a moment before lifting the maimed hand and plunging the hypodermic into the open wound. The fingers convulsed like a dying spider before spreading open again. Even in the darkness, they could see the chamber fill with blood, velvety-black in the light of the not-quite-full moon.

He drew three cc's, then, using great care, held the needle up in the best light available and carefully slipped the cap back on it.

He drew a plastic case from the pocket and set the full syringe inside it, put the case back into a pocket.

He nodded at the man with the guns, who leaned toward Jesse as the other man backed away. The gunman kept some distance as he stretched a silenced pistol toward Jesse's head. A gloved finger mashed rapidly on the trigger three times. The gun puffed the pillow-slapping sound each time a slug fired into Jesse's head. The gunman formed a precise triangle running from behind Jesse's left ear and across and up the back of his skull.

They turned and made their way quickly down the alley, moving in the center packed surface, leaving no footprints as they swiftly jogged back toward the car. A dog barked down the street.

The Second Day

12

ANNE DROPPED a clutch of biology books and work assignments onto her desk and hung the empty bookbag on the hook behind the door. It was 7:30 on the nose. She always tried to get in early. The office was quieter, the competing demands therefore fewer. She could get more done.

She stacked the books neatly on one corner. The top one, microbiology, was her first final, just two weeks away. She'd brought the books to study during what was supposed to be a lunch hour, but she'd never really gotten a lunch hour since shortly after she started at the firm, and she didn't really expect one today. Those were the perils, she supposed, of success in your job, combined with considerable efforts to get out of that very same job.

Anne sat and pressed thoughts of everything else — finals, grades, eventual graduation, a new job — out of her mind. The legal pad still in front of her contained her notes from the conversations with the credit bureau and American Express. She read through them and made more notes in a "to do" list for the day.

She knew from the credit card company that Tomlin was in Vegas in early December. Once before that as well, almost two years ago in May. She wanted to pin down those dates, and she scratched a call to United Airlines as the first thing on her list.

She didn't expect much from the rental car company since it couldn't tell her what she really needed to know. That, of course, was what Tomlin was doing in Las Vegas. One trip and she might not give it a second thought. But two trips, one not long after the initial FDA application, was worth a few more calls.

She weighed calling Weber BioTech to ask about the trip to Nevada. She knew that there might be a simple business explanation, one that the company could readily provide. But she wasn't examining Weber specifically. She was just trying to learn more about Alexander Tomlin and any matters, business or personal, that might have affected his work before his death. The more she could learn from independent sources, she figured, the better off she'd be. Any call to Weber could wait.

Looking again at her notes, Anne saw that the bank account numbers were still unchecked. She considered following up, thought of phone calls there, and ruled them out once more, at least for the time being. A checking account record might track Tomlin more effectively than anything else for as far back as the record reached. But calls that dug into bank files were quite a bit different from getting a friend to spill some information or conning a clerk into confirming something you supposedly already knew. Without a contact, they were risky business. She boxed the account numbers off and wrote *Later?* beside them.

That left only Tomlin's apartment address, besides the unhelpful but curious fact of the flower and gift purchases. All in all, it was turning out to be a sorry list of leads.

She studied the address for a moment, trying to picture where it was. Old Shakopee Road was a long, meandering stretch that ran east to west along the southern edge of Bloomington. Along with the Minnesota River and some marshy lakes, the road cut Bloomington, Minneapolis, and the northern suburbs off from the rolling hills and homes of the south.

She didn't imagine that she could get into the apartment, although that, too, could reveal a lot about Tomlin. She considered trying to get someone from the rental office to let her in, but she immediately dismissed the thought as too precarious, too open a position.

She could, however, make a visit out there, talk to some people who knew Tomlin. Apartment dwellers were notoriously poor neighbors and would almost certainly be closemouthed, particularly where the neighbor in question probably only slept there once a month. Particularly when that neighbor was now dead. But she might come across someone.

Anne checked off the address and wrote it down on a second list. She had errands up in Bloomington. She would stop by the apartment, see what happened. You never knew.

She set the list aside and pulled out the Yellow Pages, flipping through to "airlines." She found the number for United Airlines customer service, then picked up the phone and began to dial, already preparing her story.

At 9:47, Patchett sat at his own desk, rubbing at the throbbing dullness that lined his head with leaden weight. It was later than his usual arrival time, but his head was pounding a little more than was typical, even for him. After dinner, he'd celebrated his confrontation with Melissa in true style by going home and polishing off two or three beers. Or maybe it was four or five. Whatever the number, they had, as always, glossed over the upset or issue of the evening. But the booze had also unsettled him this time, despite all his experience with alcohol. He crashed on the couch and remained there until around 3:00 A.M., then stumbled into bed.

There hadn't been a hangover then, at least not that he could recall. But one was visiting him with a vengeance now, and it felt like it was fixing to stay there for a few years.

He rubbed with both hands at his face, running them across his eyes and back through his mop of hair. He propped his head on his hands and scanned the accumulated mess on his desk. With one hand, he reached down and pushed idly through the morning mail and through the usual array of law firm junk.

The newspaper sat at the bottom, its front page screaming about another murder by a serial killer the press insanely dubbed the "Barber." Minneapolis, it seemed, was joining the ranks of all great murder cities. Patchett rubbed again at his eyes, puffy red and swollen.

He scanned the article with one eye, closing the other one against a quick upsurge of pain that came from studying the small print. Word had leaked from the police long ago that the victims, all women, had had their long hair cut off. And they were all strangled and, judging by poorly veiled references from the authorities, raped.

Patchett winced at seeing it. The written words and their unwritten intimations made the pain in his head throb against the pulse from his heart, and he closed the other eye to momentarily blacken the world. He counted slowly to himself, pacing the calmness as it crept slowly back over the sudden, brilliant pain shaking his body, then he read on.

Beyond the usual paltry information, repeated again in this latest article, there was precious little word about the investigation or motives or "methods of operation" or any of the usual murder story adornments. And, Patchett noted, there was a conspicuous lack of a police rendering or even a description of a suspect. Apparently there were no real witnesses, then.

The sixth murder in only four months. An unusually fast-paced killer, Patchett thought, and the police from all appearances had no clue.

Two murders within a single week, for two out of the past three months. The third month, the month before last, there was only one murder, for reasons unknown. With this morning's news, it would take one more woman to complete this month's macabre set —people wouldn't take odds that this would be another single for the Barber. Women across the Twin Cities would be shearing their hair off, and the parks, always the site of the murders, would be deserted.

Patchett's head throbbed uncontrollably just thinking about yet another angry issue in an angry world. Particularly *that* issue.

He tossed the paper into the garbage can, and it flapped and rattled to a muffled *thunk* in the bottom. He pulled an aspirin bottle from his drawer and retrieved the vodka from the briefcase, splashing some into a glass of juice. He washed two tablets down, hoping that they might achieve what the earlier four hadn't. The booze was just insurance. Patchett capped the flask but kept it close, sliding it into a file and pushing the file back onto a nearby bookshelf.

The Weber personnel files glared back at him from the shelf, their untouched pages accusing him silently, and Patchett pulled out two of them. Marc Clifton and Kenneth Miller. The two men worked closer to Tomlin than anyone except his secretary and possibly his assistant, and the assistant was now in grad school in Michigan. Patchett resigned himself to starting with Clifton and Miller, then talking to the secretary and tracking down the lab assistant, if necessary.

He also needed to see Tomlin's files, although the thought of examining the presumably incomprehensible scribblings of a geneticist set his head ringing a little louder. His eyes were watering at the prospect.

He wanted to put it all off till tomorrow, but Flare's likely anger at that discouraged him. It would be best to finish as soon as possible.

He would schedule interviews with Clifton and Miller for the early afternoon, giving his head time to recuperate somewhat, then hit Tomlin's files later in the day. The files would probably take another visit as well. The sheer volume of the Prohiva papers necessitated keeping only the most recent work in researchers' offices and labs. Older materials, boxed by the thousands, would be warehoused in the basement. Getting the authorization to examine those files would alone take twenty-four hours. Security was understandably tight.

Patchett reluctantly dialed the Weber number. He began his day.

13

THE SMELL OF COFFEE was thick and expensive. Rowe Weber drank a French gourmet roast, and it brewed constantly in his dark office, permanently steaming its scent into the air and carpet and furnishings. Over that smell floated the smoky sweetness of Borkum Riff tobacco. An inconsistent odor from Weber's inconsistent pipe use, it drifted only occasionally through the room as people walked through the office, stirring the scents as they passed. The pipe, a meerschaum from Weber's collection, sat on the edge of the massive desk.

Weber tapped at it absently with a pencil, drinking from a cup emblazoned with the company's WB logo. The coffee was black and strongly bittersweet, and the steam from its rainbow-oiled surface wafted past his nondescript brown eyes, past the somewhat bulbous, once-broken nose, past the still-thick but gray-fringed brown of his hair. He studied a handwritten note on the desk: "C. Wall, L.A. — Phoenix if time. No word on Steffens. Grant hopefully Seattle."

Lew Franck, special assistant to the CEO, had talked to Clark Wall that morning. Franck sat on the opposite side of the desk. He had no coffee; Weber never offered it to visitors or employees in his office, and they never asked.

Franck watched Weber and sat patiently, waiting for him to speak. You didn't ask for coffee, and you didn't prompt Rowe Weber. Rowe alternated between sipping at the coffee and chewing on the pencil.

"You talked to Clark?" he asked finally.

Franck stirred and shifted in the uncomfortable chair. It was stiffly Victorian. He knew very well that Weber picked the furniture precisely because it *was* uncomfortable. People who were too comfortable didn't pay attention. Franck himself actually would have preferred to stand, but Weber also frowned on that. Standing people presented too much physical presence over sitting people, so everyone also sat in Weber's office, where the CEO's chair — lifted two inches off the floor by a riser behind the desk — looked slightly down across the room.

"This morning," Franck said, "five thirty." That was for Rowe's benefit more than anything else. Franck took every opportunity to point out that he, too, worked hard for this company. Most of the time, he doubted that Rowe ever picked up on it.

Weber sucked at the coffee, a soft slurping sound, and Franck watched as the steam wafted past the man's weathered face and the varied color of the prematurely graying hair. Rowe appeared deep in thought, as always, gazing at some distant spot seen only by him. The crow's-feet at the corners of his eyes, the edge of the color fading from his hair, and the rough, almost clumsy features all aged him past his years, lulling some people into believing that he was older, in decline, moving inexorably downhill. Smarter people never assumed that.

"What'd he have to say?" Weber asked into the coffee cup.

"Cole's dead."

Weber digested this news briefly, his face showing possibly only resigned discouragement, but not surprise. Franck waited. When Weber was ready to talk, Franck knew, he'd talk. When he was ready to listen, he'd let people know. This Rowe Weber, the *real* Rowe Weber, was quite different from the corporate persona projected to the public. He was garrulous and confidently in command in that forum, but in the private world that still clicked behind the doors of Weber BioTech, he was bizarrely intense and almost . . . eccentric, Franck decided.

"How?" Weber finally prompted.

"The, uh, usual," Franck replied softly and somewhat nervously, shifting in his chair and already readying himself for any variety of possible reactions to his news. No matter how often Franck delivered information like this to Weber — and it'd been too often over the past year — it still made him uneasy. You just didn't get accustomed to announcing people's deaths, and it wasn't made easier by the circumstances.

"Three gunshots to the head," Franck went on, quietly and almost apologetically, as if he were sorry for having to bring this news. "Close range. The police have no witnesses."

"Did Clark get a chance to see Cole himself?" Weber asked. Franck glanced up and caught a surprisingly tired look in Rowe's eyes before Weber could look away, toward and out the narrow window at the side of the room.

"Yes."

"And how'd he look?" Weber asked. The question sounded reluctant, as if Rowe didn't really want to know the answer. He stared past the coffee, still held before him, and across the glistening, deeply reflective surface of the desk. He seemed to study Franck, who looked briefly into his own lap, where his hands sat knotted.

"He appeared healthy," Franck answered. Then he added, "Except for the holes in his head, of course."

Weber closed his eyes at that. He set the coffee cup down carefully. There was only the slightest *tick* in the otherwise still room as the cup touched the desk. Weber lifted a hand and ran it across closed eyes, then reached for the pipe and pulled a bag from the drawer. He took a small wad of tobacco from the bag and tamped it into the meerschaum's bowl. Franck only watched, still trying to gauge Weber's mood by his ever-changing reaction to the news.

Rowe set the tobacco pouch aside and plucked a match from a small gold-plated smoking box on the desk. He struck the match and rested it against the pipe bowl, pulling the flame down into the tobacco with a long draw on the stem. The bowl smoldered, and smoke poured gently from Weber's mouth, escaping around the pipe stem. The tobacco caught and glowed orange against the whiteness of the meerschaum clay.

"I suppose in any event," he said softly, shaking the match out, "that Jesse Cole's lucky in a way." Weber's voice was perfectly flat and empty. "In a way," he said again, quietly thoughtful. "Given the possibilities." The words drifted off as he watched the thin line of smoke float off the match's burned head.

"Any luck finding the others?" Rowe said after a few moments. He drew on the pipe again, then puffed the smoke out, and the room began to fill with a fresher scent of the Borkum Riff. "My notes tell me that we didn't have anything on Steffens last time. Any change?"

Franck shook his head. He would have preferred to start with one of the others besides Steffens, but that choice wasn't his to make. "We lost his trail originally in Philadelphia. We thought maybe we had found him again last week in Harrisburg, but that didn't check out. Someone's on it at all times, of course."

"Of course." There was a tone of uneasy impatience in Rowe's voice. "Do we have any idea how a drifter from Nevada wound up in Pennsylvania in the first place?"

Franck shook his head again.

"*Christ*, what a mess," Weber muttered softly, leaning forward, elbows on the desk as he slowly scratched his forehead with the pipe stem. "What about Washburn?"

"We know she's in Phoenix," Franck answered. "We think she's turning tricks out of some local hotel down there. Clark is leaving L.A. this afternoon, and he'll be there by early evening. He'll pin down her location once he's there. Finding her won't be a problem."

"Lew," Weber said slowly, "I have heard that too many times before to believe it now. Tell Clark to make *sure* that it's not a problem this time."

"Fine."

"How about Grant?"

Like Steffens, Gordon Grant was a bad choice for Franck, but Grant was the last one on the list. There was no one else to talk about. Not anymore.

"We're still looking for him in Seattle," Franck said. "We know he was sick, and we've checked the hospitals, but we can't find any listing for him. He might be listed as a John Doe, but there are really too many to check out quickly. We can't just go in and ask for these people, after all, but we're going to do what we can to find him as soon as possible."

Weber sucked on the pipe, drawing hard, and the tobacco glowed fiercely. A faint orange-red cast shone on Weber's face in the slightly darkened room. Weber held the smoke for a few seconds before blowing it slowly from pursed lips.

"You do that, Lew," he said when the smoke was thick above his head. "And remember just how important it is. If it takes an extra man, then send Burke. But you find Grant and the others, and you find them fast. Before someone else does." Franck thought there was the barest edge of dread in that statement as he stood to leave.

"One more thing," Weber said, stopping his assistant just as Franck grabbed the doorknob.

Franck turned. "Yes?"

"You're aware that I've asked Ben Flare to look into Alex's death?" Weber said, and Franck nodded. "I think it's appropriate," Weber went on, "and I'm sure they'll be looking through files and what-not. In fact, Ben tells me that we can expect to have Patchett out here today. So while they're looking around, while Patchett's here, I truly think it's in everyone's best interests to demonstrate that we're fully in control of what's going on. I want it perfectly clear — there are to be no mistakes at all. Understood?"

Franck nodded a final time, then turned and stepped out the door. He left Weber behind, frowning in the cloud of smoke.

14

IAN ANDERSON also sat in smoke, the butt of the ever-present Merit between his fingers just winking out as he stared at the computer ticker. He was watching for Weber quotes, mesmerized by the rapidly crawling scrawl of codes and numbers flitting across the bottom of the screen. When Weber flashed by, as it did once every couple of minutes or so, Anderson could feel his heart skip a beat.

From around $44.00 per share the previous afternoon, Weber stock had risen steadily if slowly to $49.50. It had settled in there for the last hour, slipping below and jumping above that figure every few minutes.

The price climb both encouraged and scared Anderson. He was elated to see it rise as a confirmation of Callestanza's news that the FDA would allow Phase III tests. Whispers about the FDA's upcoming action were clearly heard by more people than just Anderson, and the early trades were already advancing the stock price.

He considered for a moment that he might have underestimated the initial rise that would result from the FDA's announcement of Phase III testing. If the FDA truly was planning on approving human testing of Prohiva in a new phase, then perhaps the stock *would* pass $70.00 or $75.00 per share, given the indications that he was now seeing still three days away from the announcement. He was almost giddy at the thought.

Somewhat more sobering considerations rapidly followed, however, and Anderson worried at their implications. Any company expecting a major positive announcement would experience stock inflation immediately before publication of the news. That was to be expected in a world where leaks were common and communications were instantaneous. Even the SEC overlooked some of that activity.

But if the action in a stock is excessive, then the SEC's dogs start to come out, so Anderson was keeping one eye focused on the shifts in price. A five-dollar increase in a historically poor performer was enough to raise eyebrows. Increases above that might motivate the powers that be to make some examinations into trading in that company's shares.

That was something Anderson most assuredly did not want. Although there were no trades in Weber stock after the judge last upped his holdings, Anderson didn't feel up to government scrutiny that might cut broadly across traders. And he doubted very seriously that the judge would be up to it, either.

For the next five minutes, a variety of thoughts crossed Ian Anderson's mind. The most important and the most disturbing was the passing notion that he should cash out the judge's shares and take the formidable profit that was already ripe to be plucked. Weber's increases would be startling in a few days, and few people after the fact would examine someone who sold all shares prior to an increase like that.

He didn't even think that selling at this point would be trading on insider information. The information right now suggested enormous growth. A sale that avoided that growth surely wouldn't violate the law. At least he didn't think so.

Anderson quickly dismissed that thought with a recognition that the judge would never go for it but then immediately contemplated an even more disturbing possibility. *What if,* he wondered, *the FDA* wasn't *going to approve human testing for Phase III? What if it was going to announce continued testing on monkeys?*

Virtually anything short of actual full approval for human testing could be a disaster for Weber stock. When the FDA sneezed on a product approval, the stock market for that company caught cold, and it was a cold that was known to cause deaths. The biotechnology market was full of horror stories about stock plunges following less than wholly favorable FDA announcements. It wouldn't even take an outright disapproval. Something that serious could destroy Weber BioTech almost instantly, but just about anything less than complete approval for Phase III would still be a severe blow that would set Weber's stock price back perhaps as much as 50 percent.

Anderson considered that, too, and actually lifted the phone to call the judge before setting it back in its cradle. He could imagine how that conversation would go. Even if he convinced the judge to sell, which he doubted, he'd be out the door the second the FDA issued a fully favorable announcement and the stock skyrocketed.

No, Anderson knew his best bet lay squarely on the accuracy of the information. He trusted Nick Callestanza, at least to some degree, if for no other reason than because he knew that Callestanza had a few illegal trades of his own under his belt. A few trades that might encourage him to be straight about what he knew. And the market indicators suggested positive results on top of it.

Anderson knew he was in the ring for this one, and he knew it was going to be a whirlwind ride. He already felt it in his stomach as he watched Weber tick by.

51.

15

ANNE PARKED HER CAR in front of one of the five buildings that sat just off Old Shakopee Road. Tomlin's apartment was in number 1740, and the sign on the building nearest her declared that this was the one.

She got out, went in, and trotted up four flights of stairs. The complex carried the distinct marks of the end of winter — grass brown from the cold and soiled from street-plowed snow, painted trim cracked with peeling lines that showed wood underneath, trees bare, street gutters lined with gravel and a crusted build up of dirt, plastic carpet runners down the stairs. But a renovated freshness concealed what otherwise would have been passed off as early 1980s apartment complex style — brick, squared, and institutional. There was no security system, though, and Anne was thankful to escape the patchwork of lies over intercoms that it would have taken to get in.

She found apartment 411 and knocked softly on the door. Nothing. She knocked again, louder, and the hollow wood sound filled the empty hallway. No response again.

"Dead men tell no tales," she muttered to herself. She moved to the next door down.

When there was no response there, either, she quickly became convinced that it wouldn't pan out, that this would be just one more dead end for a dead man, but she moved to the door on the other side of Tomlin's apartment. The knock there also echoed, calling no one.

Her watch said 11:05, and Anne swore at her timing. She was too early for people to come home to lunch and too late to catch them before work. She stepped down to the next apartment.

She'd knocked on that door and on two more doors across the hall before she saw anyone — a young woman answered the next knock. A baby sat hitched on one of her hips.

"Yes?" the woman asked. There was a soft drawl in her voice.

"Hi. My name's Patty Sumner," Anne lied. "I was wondering if I could take just a minute of your time to ask you about your neighbor down the hall? Alexander Tomlin?" She pointed to Tomlin's door, the number just visible in the gleaming slant of low hallway lights.

The woman followed the gesture, then turned back to Anne. "I don't know any Alexander Tomlin," she said. "What's wrong?"

"I'm an investigator," Anne said, concealing her job in the overbroad term. "Mr. Tomlin killed himself very early Monday morning." She had just the right tone of remorse in her voice, and she glanced at the floor in a seeming moment of respect for the dead. "Maybe you heard?"

"No," the woman said. "I didn't hear anything like that." She hesitated while she bumped the baby higher against her waist. "Did this guy go out with her or something?"

Anne looked up from smiling at the baby, thinking for a second that she misheard the woman. Or that this woman herself had misunderstood. "Go out with who?" Anne asked.

"With the lady who lives there," the woman replied. She was stroking the baby's head, slicking thick, black hair back like a miniature Jack Nicholson. "That's not a man's apartment." She pointed toward 411. "It's a woman lives there. I see her every day, but I never saw no guy."

Anne looked down the hall toward the apartment, understanding dawning on her. "Do you know her name?" she said softly, still staring toward the door.

"Nah. She's real quiet. Keeps to herself."

"What's she look like?"

The woman looked at Anne carefully. "Is she in any trouble?"

Anne shook her head. "No. We just might have to talk to her, that's all."

The woman accepted that. "Your height maybe. Black hair, past the shoulders. Pale skin. Looks like she's never been out in the sun in her life." The woman smiled. "Medium build. Not real skinny or fat, just kinda average. Kinda pretty, but not too, you know?" Anne pulled a small notepad from her purse and started writing. The woman narrowed her eyes.

"She's not a murderer or anything, right?"

Anne closed the pad at that, regretting taking it out in the first place. "No, not at all," she said in her most comforting voice. "Probably just a mistake."

"You want me to tell her you were looking for her?"

"No. No need," Anne said. "Thanks for your time. Sorry if it was a bother." The woman nodded once and swung the door closed.

Anne considered the description as she walked down the stairs and out to her car. With that description, and with the apartment's registration to Tomlin, she found she wasn't surprised that she knew exactly who lived in apartment 411.

Anne had gone to the Weber Building once during the indy work to collect some files. Even over the intervening months, she remembered the startling black hair of the woman who helped her that day. That woman was her size, average build. Plain and pretty and pale. You could almost see the veins in her face, her skin was so light.

The woman who had helped her had been Alexander Tomlin's secretary.

Rebecca Cartaway.

Patchett thanked Rebecca and reentered the small conference room. It was his office for the day, a stark and tight unadorned cubicle in which he so far had sat for two hours while Kenneth Miller chain-smoked his way, and Patchett's way, through a wholly useless interview. Patchett could still smell the smoke. It permeated his clothes, bringing him back to college days when he would awaken every weekend morning, and some weekday mornings, smelling like the dance-floor pits of meat market bars. It was a smell that would hang with him all day, one that would probably revisit him in the shower as he washed himself clean tomorrow morning.

He pushed that thought away as he sat down before Marcus Clifton, who was impatiently twitching one foot while studying

Patchett with the supposedly detached but silently critical eye of a researcher. His legs were crossed, and the neat patent leather shoe bobbed in the air with the jaunty jerk of a marionette dance.

"Sorry if I've kept you, Dr. Clifton," Patchett said, sitting down. "And I apologize in advance for taking your time." Patchett set his briefcase back on the conference table and popped it open.

"As I'm sure you're aware," he continued, "we're trying to make sure that Dr. Tomlin's death won't create any problems or questions in the approval for Prohiva. I hope I'll be able to get you out of here shortly."

Patchett pulled a tablet from the briefcase and turned a page of his notes to scan a jotted overview of the morning's conversation with Miller. "Dr. Miller and I have gone over most of the basic facts again, the roles of everyone in the research, Dr. Tomlin's role in particular, things like that. So what I'd like to ask you about is your work with Dr. Tomlin and your impressions of him, specifically in the past few months."

Patchett was ticking off notes, writing in a few extra words. He glanced up at Clifton when he reached the end of the sheets on Miller. "But I wonder if we could just start with a refresher, for me, on your own background." Patchett slashed a line across the page and scratched the doctor's name under it.

Clifton frowned briefly at the request, an inclination picked up after his lucrative dash to Weber, but it disappeared quickly, and he spun through a well-worn speech about his education and job experiences. He spoke rapidly and in virtual stream of consciousness, a seamless weaving of every fact that came to his mind at any given point. When Clifton got to the move to Weber fifteen minutes later, Patchett looked up once at a pause, but the doctor proceeded, oblivious to the fact that the attorney before him was already fairly well informed of Clifton's background.

It was an old approach, maybe, but a common one. You always learned whatever you could about people before talking with them. It gave you the edge and removed theirs, making them more at ease with the naturally confrontational style of investigational interviews. The more someone talked about his personal background, the more likely that person was to either spill something up front or to give something up later by assuming false confidence in the face of the initial, more friendly questions.

So Patchett let Clifton talk, and he stopped him only after the doctor began speaking about the development of Prohiva.

"Who originated the project?" he asked on Clifton's casual mention of the initiation of the Prohiva research.

"Couldn't really say for sure," Clifton said. He shrugged his shoulders as if to emphasize the point. "AIDS drugs are a hot research area. Have been for years. I'd expect any pharmaceutical or biotechnology company to be doing some form of research related to AIDS and HIV."

Clifton laced his fingers together and leaned forward on the table, propped on elbows, arms up like a praying mantis. "Were I to guess at an individual, Mr. Patchett, I suppose that it might very well be Rowe Weber. As I'm sure you're aware, Rowe is very much a hands-on CEO, and research projects sometimes funnel directly through him at early stages, though he doesn't actually begin them himself."

"Is he actively involved in research?"

Clifton shook his head. "No, not really. He'll keep tabs on progress, cut research that's going nowhere. Things like that. But he doesn't slip on a lab coat very often."

Patchett knew that, as well, from his earlier refresher course on Rowe Weber. "How about on Prohiva?" he asked. "Same thing there?"

Clifton nodded. "Especially there, I'd say. Dr. Weber," he said, slightly emphasizing the title, "is neither a geneticist nor a virologist, and a meaningful role on Prohiva virtually demanded training in one or the other of those two fields."

"That was where you came in?" Patchett asked.

"Yes, I was the lead virologist. I headed the research on the HIV side. Understanding viral actions, antibody reactions and immune system response in general, and so on. If you're knowledgeable in virology, I'd be happy to discuss it in depth." At that, Clifton leaned back, hands still knitted together but resting now on his stomach. He looked utterly at ease. Totally confident.

Patchett heard the condescending twinge in Clifton's statement and saw the presumptive smile, and he ignored them both. "And Dr. Tomlin worked on the genetics side, of course," he said.

"That's right," Clifton answered, nodding slowly. The sound of a teacher rewarding a dim student resonated in the air. "Genetic makeup of both the virus and the antisense acids."

"And you and he then worked jointly to bring those two research areas together and formulate what ultimately became Prohiva?" Patchett was taking notes, but both he and Clifton knew that this was essentially old information covered almost two years before in the initial indy application and still set out weekly in some news source or another. They both knew it despite Patchett's innocent and curious questioning and Clifton's high-handed attitude.

"Also correct," Clifton said, nodding as an additional confirmation. He glanced at his watch, more as an intentional sign of a man impatiently waiting for something to end than in curiosity about the time. Patchett noticed but ignored it.

"Any special problems that might have developed in the course of Dr. Tomlin's research?" he asked. "Any specific issues? Trouble areas?"

"No," Clifton said immediately, somewhat too quickly. "Not that I recall." He gazed steadily at Patchett, then away, then back to the attorney. In that moment, with that answer, Clifton seemed suddenly and horribly put out by the questions.

"What about more recently?" Patchett said patiently. He wasn't prepared to let Clifton go just because the doctor didn't want to take the time to talk. "Any particular problems that Dr. Tomlin was coming across in his later work?"

Clifton shifted in his seat, then leaned forward once more, chin almost touching the table. "Frankly, Mr. Patchett, Alex Tomlin and I were not the closest of friends, and he did not come to me with his work problems.

"But I will say this. He was an incredibly intelligent — in fact, he was a brilliant — researcher and that drug exists because of that brilliance. I would hardly say that he had any difficulty or problems in his work, given the success of the vaccine." Clifton leaned back again at that, recrossing long legs.

"Dr. Clifton, I assure you that I didn't intend to denigrate Dr. Tomlin's work. Or your work or this vaccine, for that matter." Patchett spoke with a quiet determination emphasized only by a cool stare and a calm flip to a new page of paper. It shone cleanly up between them, waiting to be filled. Patchett poised the pen above it. "But something motivated that man. Something put him out that window. And I think it's important, and Dr. Weber apparently thinks it's important, that we find out what that was before the FDA asks." Patchett felt a gentle swell of anger rising in him, and he bit it back to continue.

"What was Dr. Tomlin doing in terms of Prohiva research most recently?" he asked then.

Clifton hesitated. His voice was smooth and calm when he spoke, a practiced tone of authority that filled the small room.

"Dr. Tomlin's last work was performed just prior to the first submission to the FDA, which would have been, what, two, two and a half years ago? He and I performed final examinations of our chimps and macaques to verify their health and blood work. I don't believe he touched anything on the project after that."

Patchett was surprised, but he concealed it by concentrating his attention on the paper in front of him, where he began to write. No blinking, no reaction, despite the incongruous suggestions that Tomlin wholly ignored Prohiva for the past two years.

"He must have been working on something, though, I assume?" Patchett was speaking into the table, still intent on his notes, as he tried to fit this report of Tomlin's lack of involvement with everything that he'd heard over the months since the application, everything that he would have assumed about completion of Prohiva.

"Certainly," Clifton answered.

"Do you know what that might have been?"

"He was a geneticist, and I know there are a variety of genetics-based products being researched, all of which are, naturally, very confidential."

"And he would have been working on one of those?"

"That I don't know for sure," Clifton said. "Genetics is a broad field, Mr. Patchett, and it's getting broader as each new biotech product suggests new applications of gene manipulation technology. As I've said, Dr. Tomlin was a brilliant man, and, for all I know, he was off on another project."

Clifton's face was suddenly etched with a passing smile of what could only be characterized as poorly feigned admiration for another man. A *good doctor?* Patchett wondered, seeing that smile. Absolutely. *An actor?* Patchett didn't think so.

"He was an intense fellow," Clifton said almost wistfully. The smile lingered and even broadened. "Alex focused on one thing for days, sometimes weeks at a time. Prohiva was his life for years. But once that was done, I imagine that all the other ideas that were bottled up inside him for so long started to come spilling out." Clifton's eyes looked keenly, narrowly at the attorney sitting across the table from him.

"I don't believe you can imagine what it's like, Mr. Patchett," he said. The condescending tone was rising again. "You have to understand medical researchers and their peculiarities to appreciate how Alex probably felt when Prohiva was done."

"Why don't you try to help me understand, then, doctor?" Patchett replied. He capped the pen and dropped it to the pad, where it rolled and then sat mute, a marker made silent by Patchett's own rising frustration with Clifton.

Clifton's gaze leveled once more, and a sardonic grin replaced the smugly content and controlled one that faced Patchett before. The change was so abrupt that it looked as though Clifton changed it with the click of a button. The doctor's mouth tightened in a slitting arc as he spoke.

"All right, Mr. Patchett," he said clearly and a little too loudly, leaning again up to the table. "It's like a good fuck."

The last word almost echoed in the room, the sound of it lingering uncomfortably between the two men. "It's intense until the end," Clifton went on, "then there's the drop-off, and then you're kind of disappointed even though a minute before you thought it was the greatest experience of your life. But you forget about it in a minute, and your attention goes to other things. You understand that, counselor?"

Now Patchett leaned forward, one elbow on the table, and he spoke softly but firmly past a finger pressed tight against his lips. "You mean to tell me, doctor, that Alexander Tomlin finished what may be the most important medical breakthrough in decades and then he just rolled over to something else, leaving it alone during an intense examination of the very product he worked so hard on?"

The chair creaked slightly as Clifton shifted in it again. "You don't understand this profession," he said, "and you can't understand him. This is *stress*, Mr. Patchett." Clifton's arms were out, gesturing as though he were referring to the very walls. "Pure and simple, it's as clean a dose of stress as you can get."

He pointed a finger at the attorney. "You consider the facts. This is a business, and it has all the pressures of a business. But it's also medicine, right? And it has all the pressures of medicine. Now Dr. Tomlin—he might have leaned toward the medical aspects, particularly focusing on those considerations. Other people may focus on the business aspects. But everyone feels the pressures of both, and the stress is virtually unbelievable at times.

"In this business, you could be sitting behind something that will get you worldwide fame and maybe a Nobel Prize. People are examining it, studying what you've done for years, to see if they're going to let you go ahead. To see if they *approve*. Would you want to throw yourself into that examination? When you know you've already busted your ass to make sure it's right? Could you handle that?" Clifton shook his head to answer his own questions.

"That's stress, Mr. Patchett," he said. "That's this job."

"You think he couldn't handle the pressure?" Patchett said.

Clifton looked away and bit gently at his lower lip. "Maybe," he said finally. "I couldn't really say for sure. But what I do know is that Alex Tomlin was a little flighty, a little . . . I guess maybe *crazy* might even be a good word. In light of that and knowing this job and what it's like, I'm just saying that maybe I'm not too surprised that Alex did what he did."

Patchett pulled the cap from the pen, wrote something down, looked back at Clifton. "He ever give you any reason to think he was going to do something like this?"

"No, but as I said, we weren't real close." Clifton smiled. "We were competitors, in a sense, you know. Competing for Rowe to fund different projects. Competing on the best way to perfect Prohiva. Competitors aren't real close."

"Who won that competition, Dr. Clifton?"

Clifton didn't answer, instead abruptly standing to leave. "I think I've told you pretty much all I know, Mr. Patchett. Is there anything else?"

Patchett studied his face for any sign that would show him what he needed to know, what he thought Clifton could tell him to resolve the fresh, nagging, and uncertain confusions in his own mind. The attorney glanced at his notes.

"Just one more thing," he said. "I recognize, as you've indicated, that you weren't overly friendly with Dr. Tomlin. But do you know if he had any real personal life? Did he do anything outside work?"

For a moment, Patchett thought the doctor would actually give him some substantive answer. But Clifton just shook his head. "No, sir," he said finally. "We just weren't real close." He opened the door and left the room, pulling the door closed behind him and shutting Patchett inside.

The attorney set the pen down once more and braced his head in his hands. His hangover had been dulling up to the afternoon, but it threatened a revolt now.

"So tell me this, Dr. Clifton," he said to the empty room, "which side do you focus on? Business? Medicine? Something else entirely?" Patchett wondered about that. He wondered if Dr. Clifton had maybe known Tomlin a little better than he let on. Because then Patchett began to feel that maybe — just maybe — he actually had.

Anne called Jon but got his secretary.

"Is he in?" Anne asked.

"Out for the rest of the day. He's at Weber."

Anne expected as much. She was at a pay phone at the college. After leaving the apartment, she'd gone back to the office to look for Patchett but hadn't found him. She assumed then that he was out at Weber trying to learn something from the people there.

She hadn't left a message, instead deciding that the most important thing for her was to get the hell out of the office after all. She had a class that evening and another tomorrow, and she still hadn't done the reading, with finals always looming. So she blew off work for the rest of the day, with an idea toward doing the same tomorrow, and she'd left.

But Rebecca Cartaway's presence in the apartment chewed on her all afternoon, right up until Anne decided to try to talk it over with Jon. Now, of course, she couldn't find him.

"Do you want to try to reach him over there?" the secretary was asking.

Anne thought it over before deciding against it. She doubted she would be able to get in touch with him there, and she didn't particularly like the idea of leaving a message that involved Rebecca in a place where Rebecca would almost certainly hear of it.

"No," she said. "Could you just give him a message? Could you tell him that I think that Rebecca Cartaway and Tomlin might have been sleeping together?"

"Sure," the other woman said, a slight laugh in her voice. "I'll see that he gets it first thing in the morning."

"Thanks. And you can tell him that I'll be around Friday morning if he wants to see me." That would give her until the day after tomorrow. Time enough to actually get something done with her own overstressed life.

Anne hung up the phone, her thoughts on Rebecca Cartaway. That Rebecca and Tomlin were involved with each other seemed pretty clear. Tomlin's credit record referenced an address where Rebecca lived. Anne assumed that Tomlin had been paying for the apartment, which would put it in his name, and he was probably supporting Rebecca there. Somewhat romantic in a kind of sleazy way, she thought.

She headed up the stairs toward the library.

Rebecca brought only one box of materials into the small conference room, setting it on the table in front of Patchett.

"That's it?" he said.

She nodded, and Patchett lifted the lid to look into the box. Rebecca moved out the door, shutting it behind her.

There were only two folders in the box, neither of them thick, and Patchett was already thinking back to his conversation with Clifton. The virologist's suggestion was basically that Tomlin was a brilliant kook who finished work on Prohiva, then just turned to any number of other projects.

It was possible, he supposed, that Tomlin actually was taking it easier following the FDA submission, but that didn't explain a virtual absence of signs of other work. After all, two years had passed since Tomlin supposedly washed his hands of Prohiva and set his talents to other things. But this? Patchett looked into the box again.

Two years and two files. Patchett wished that his work was as paper free, and he knew immediately that Tomlin's wasn't. Medical research produced reams — *volumes* — of paper. In two years, one researcher's notes would fill dozens of these boxes.

The explanation, Patchett assumed, was buried in the warehouse downstairs. There was enough room there to hold decades of research records, and it was entirely possible that Tomlin, a superachiever by all accounts, produced so much that his records were routinely cleared out and moved down.

That consideration, though, would need to wait a day. Patchett had the authorization to examine warehouse documents and could begin that work tomorrow. Until then, he would have to content himself with the two files in front of him.

He picked one up, read with a groan the label identifying a disease he had never heard of, and he began to page through it.

16

MAGGIE WALKED the Phoenix night on Van Buren. Each night, starting at 7:00, she would step out and walk the street. Sometimes alone, sometimes with another girl, always making her way slowly downtown. Some nights, she'd go quite a distance before she was stopped by a man driving by. Other nights, she barely got a block. Later, after a midevening lull in business and then past 2:00 in the morning when the people kicked out onto the street by the closing bars had all dissipated under the still-glowing lights of the city, the numbers would begin to pick up. A different group of people, to be sure, looking for different things. But business was business.

But that'd be later. At 7:00, just out into the dry warmth of the evening, Maggie would see only the boldest of men — those who were willing to cruise down Van Buren and pick up the prostitutes even in the last waning hours of sunlight. She pushed her hair back and stepped out, turning toward the skyscrapers, hotels, and businesses sitting distant but large before her.

All in all, she felt okay. When you considered the day, in fact, she was doing pretty damn well. By the afternoon, the rattle in her chest had erupted in a sharp staccato burst of pain and coughing that once put her on the floor. That bout continued for a full ten minutes, until people in the next room banged on the wall and she was able to pull herself up and into the kitchenette for a glass of water.

The coughing had abated a little as she rinsed her mouth and spit the water out. She'd been mildly alarmed to see a thick gob of something, with a clear streak of blood floating through it like the color in a cat's-eye marble, all rinsing down the drain. It took three full glasses of water to get that taste out of her mouth.

Maggie continued down the street, tugging at the belt of a short skirt to hike it up. The skirt seemed shorter and tighter on her a couple months back, but it hung on her now, dropping away from slender hips. As she pulled at it, she made a mental note to check back at the clinic after all. Whatever she had, she clearly wasn't getting any better. Losing a little weight, by the looks of it. She cinched the narrow belt one notch tighter, looking down to see knobby knees. It'd have to do, she thought, and walked on.

Maggie crossed a street and continued toward the buildings of downtown Phoenix, lighted against the orange backdrop of the edge of the Arizona sunset. The buildings looked terrifically huge in the magnifying heat of the desert air.

She cracked her gum and walked slowly and with a slight

swaying jaunt. She coughed occasionally or wiped at a runny nose. Maybe she'd go to the clinic tomorrow, she thought, rubbing a hand across the back of her neck and finding it hot. The hand came back with a light tinge of perfumed sweat and an already-present residue of grime. Even in March, walking a street meant working up a sticky sweat and coming away dusty.

She looked again at the buildings, a block closer, and wondered if she'd be there before anyone stopped her. She'd made the entire distance a couple of times before, finding herself walking in the reversed shadows of night. All the light came from the ground up, casting a sinister illumination into the air. Buildings reached up into blackness beyond the line of sight. Downtown was like a purgatory, though—all the truly washed-out showed up on the shores of Central Avenue there—and she didn't want this night or any other to be a night in purgatory.

She was considering moving to a different street when a maroon Mercury Sable pulled to the curb. The night caught a touch of promise. She walked over to the opening passenger door.

"Hi there," said a young man inside. A big man, maybe twenty-four or twenty-five, and he was leaning into the middle of the seat. There was a thin black briefcase resting in the backseat.

"Hey," she said. She hesitated for a moment, giving him an opportunity to avoid any unnecessary embarrassment. "You aren't just looking for directions, are you?" she said then.

He smiled and patted the seat beside him. "Not if you've got something better." She got in, and the Sable pulled back onto Van Buren.

There was an awkward pause as they drove a few blocks. "Where you wanna go?" she said.

"Not my neighborhood," he replied. "I'm an out-of-towner."

"Then turn here." He turned and followed her directions for five minutes, moving through the steadily more deserted, squared-off streets of Phoenix.

"How's here?" she asked, and she pointed to an alley. He pulled in and turned off the car and headlights.

"How much?" he asked.

"What for?"

"Straight."

"Sixty bucks. One hundred for a night. One-forty for no con-dom. One-eighty for a night and no condom." She cracked her gum.

"A true professional," he said. He pulled out a wallet and opened it to find two fifties and two twenties. He passed them to her and she tucked them into her small purse with carefully hidden satisfaction. Definitely not purgatory. After this, she could skip the rest of the night and just sleep.

She arched her back and began to pull her shirt up.

"Skip it," he said. "Just the skirt."

She looked at him, shrugged, and pulled the top back down. "You're paying," she said. She unfastened the belt and slipped her skirt onto the floor. Pink striped panties landed on top of the crumpled pile.

He reached over her and pulled the seat release lever, and she leaned backward as the seat back folded open behind her.

"Turn over," he said.

"You said straight. That'd be two hundred."

"I *meant* straight. Turn over."

She did, and it brought a mercifully short spasm of coughing. She was afraid it would cause questions, as it did one time before, and she held her breath against the possibility while he fumbled himself over behind her. She needed the money that was latched into her purse; she didn't need this guy to start asking about a cold.

When it was clear that he hadn't even noticed, she relaxed, listening to what sounded like him unfastening his pants. She felt the car rock gently as he struggled to pull them down, kneeling behind her on the floor of the car's passenger side.

She felt him pushing against her as he reached up and clutched at the briefcase, which lay now on the seat next to her head. He grabbed the handle and lifted it, then tipped it over onto the floor behind the driver's seat.

He rested his hand where the case had been. Then he was inside her. She propped her chin on her hands and waited for him to finish.

●

He left her where he'd picked her up, pulling over to the curb. She went without a word, and he offered none as well.

Then Cal Cross pulled away from the curb and headed toward the airport. There was a 10:30 flight home, the common end to his common business trips.

The trips occurred every couple of months, and they always ended the same way—with some girl from some corner in some motel or car. He wouldn't have done it except that he missed the variety of women from his premarriage days. So he indulged every so often.

He rubbed absently at his crotch, trying to relieve the dull burn that was only now fading. He'd hoped that it would be gone by now. His doctor had diagnosed some kind of infection and given him some antibiotics. Those were gone, but the infection was apparently still there. He squirmed as he stopped at a light, thinking with a touch of irony that he probably gave something to the prostitute.

But Cross had another infection, too, though he didn't know about that one as he sat waiting before accelerating on the green. He had just paid $140.00 for one brief moment between Maggie Washburn's legs, and he got something in return for his effort.

A particularly virulent form of HIV was coursing into his bloodstream. He could have counted the actual organisms on the fingers of both hands. There were fewer than ten of the viruses, the smallest living things, and they were moving across thin membranes and through the convenient infection site into his bloodstream.

Cal Cross would be on a plane within an hour and would be home in about three. He would be dead in a little less than two years, a tragically short period of time following HIV exposure. His wife would follow four months later. Maggie Washburn would be long gone by then.

17

PATCHETT WATCHED silently from a seat on his balcony as the stars winked on. There was a vodka in one hand. Another screwdriver, actually, but it was mixed so strong that it looked like strangely cloudy water. He sipped at it. The drink made him feel warm against the chill of the early spring breeze that was cutting across Minneapolis. He could just see the bare branches of the trees swaying against the final violet tint at the horizon.

He was studying the lights of the sky and the lights of the city, the former only barely visible in the proximity of the latter. Patchett was a downtown dweller, loving the look of the buildings towering around and above him. It was a small consolation to his life that his drudging job gave him the income to afford this apartment.

Harrison arrived on the balcony through the open door and leaped onto Patchett's lap, his strong purr already pleasantly breaking the still evening. Patchett owned two cats before he found Harrison on a walk home from work. The first was McCartney, the second Lennon. Both were now dead, but Harrison lived on, and Patchett avoided thinking about any time when another cat would replace him. He couldn't imagine naming a cat "Starr," and he would never call it "Ringo." It sounded too much like a feline disease.

He scratched at the cat's striped ears and it mewed back an acknowledgment.

"So," Patchett said, "you gonna figure this one out for me?" The cat purred and looked up at him through slitted yellow eyes.

Tomlin's office files hadn't helped. The two folders contained sketchy information on two projects that Tomlin thought of starting at some point. Nothing on Prohiva. Nothing on any work in progress. They were a puzzling set of papers, mainly because of what wasn't in them.

Anne's message puzzled him, too. He wasn't sure how she knew that Rebecca and Tomlin were involved with each other, but he hadn't known Anne to be wrong before, and he didn't expect that she was now. But he was at a loss to figure out how Rebecca might fit into this picture.

Her very presence sent ripples, almost tides, through the one theory that previously was their best guess about Tomlin's suicide. He no longer appeared to be the despondent and lonely researcher they had originally believed. A girlfriend, maybe a lover as Anne apparently assumed, supported by Tomlin in an apartment? It hardly seemed plausible, but Patchett would clearly have to speak with Rebecca Cartaway. In truth, he could barely even begin to fathom how he would handle that issue, another bothersome complication on the lengthening list.

And there was Clifton to consider. That discussion seemed a pointedly delivered quilt of half-truths cut back for Patchett's benefit, but Patchett was at a loss to figure out why that would've been done. Clifton's unrestrained dislike of Tomlin didn't explain it, particularly given his similarly unabashed admiration of his deceased "competitor."

Patchett felt something that he rarely experienced as a lawyer —the case was slipping away from him. Just yesterday, it was relatively straightforward. Ask a few questions, confirm that Tomlin was just a victim of his own depression, and close the issue. Nothing to report to the FDA.

He considered the situation now. A researcher who inconceivably did nothing for two years. Probably disliked by co-workers but probably involved in a serious relationship that carried all the markings of a quiet love affair. And with those considerations, Patchett felt something else as well, approaching inescapably on the tail of the thoughts about Tomlin.

Every so often, ever since his marriages . . . well, since Liz, anyway . . . there'd been a growing swell of loss and loneliness that threatened to overwhelm him. Something that would strip him of control of his life. A sense, perhaps, that was somewhat similar to something Tomlin might have felt. Perhaps.

Patchett always dealt with it as best he knew how, but he also saw distantly that he'd been running for years and would someday have nowhere left to run. It would, quite simply, all catch up. He wondered what would happen then. Where he would be, what his life — or what remained of it — would be.

But someday wasn't here yet, and he pushed his frustration with life, with the losses, with all the accumulated debris seemingly rising around him — he pushed that back. True, he missed Liz. True, he missed *someone*. A companion, not of the type that Melissa Flare pushed on him but one who would care enough to understand and to help him understand.

Patchett sipped again at the drink. His only companion.

Harrison stood and stretched abruptly, giving up on the cold and moving indoors. And Patchett stood also, stretching his own tall frame.

He gazed over the ledge, looking over the railing and down from his apartment on the fifteenth floor. He scooped some melting snow from a corner, the last vestige of winter still on the balcony, and balled it into a soft mass. He dropped the snowball over the edge, and it spun slowly and dramatically as it tumbled through the air. He lost sight of it briefly as it fell into the darkness, but it came into view again under the streetlights far below.

It hit with a distant and ever-so-soft sigh, spreading wet snow in a five-foot spray across the sidewalk. Patchett looked at the dark circle far below him. Wondering. And imagining.

He went inside and drew the door closed.

Part Two

THURSDAY
FRIDAY

The Third Day

18

As REQUIRED, Patchett checked in at the Weber document ware-house in the basement at precisely 7:30 the next morning. He'd wanted to speak to Rebecca before then but hadn't found her in, so he headed down to the lower level, a path well known from his frequent visits during the indy application and his less frequent forays since that time.

Weber guarded its documents and the information they con-tained with security befitting the National Archives. Beyond the cinder-block walls ahead would be an inner steel wall. Beyond that, a layer of concrete sandwiched a yard of dirt against the inner cinder blocks. Then another steel wall. Together, the basement walls were a barrier almost five feet thick.

Of the papers in this area, which filled two underground levels of the Weber Building, virtually all related in one way or another to the development of Prohiva. From the first memo, which sketched out a broad plan to raise capital to fund research, the entire story of Prohiva was held here, in these boxes and folders.

All research notes. Investigational forms for the "lesser pri-mate" studies. Formulas and charts and diagrams. Final reports later found not to be final and therefore marked by SEE LATER REPORT stamps. A complete copy of the indy file.

The new drug application was here, too, completed and waiting for submission after the end of Phase III. Results from those tests were to be filled in. The application submitted. The adulation received. The money raked in.

Patchett surveyed only the initial racks of files, standing from his position outside the check-in point. He never actually wandered back into the stacks and just rummaged through them. The company wouldn't allow it, citing legitimate concerns for "organizational integrity." In short, he interpreted, the company didn't want him fucking up the filing.

Instead, it always pulled the requested information and set it up for him in a basement office. That, he assumed, would also be his destination this morning.

He pushed a small button on the counter and heard a distant buzzing from some place lost in the back of the room. He waited until the attendant appeared, an older, brawny man with a throaty and booming voice.

"Mr. Patchett?" the man asked.

"The same."

"I'll need an ID before setting you up. I hear you know the procedures pretty well."

"Oh yes," Patchett said. He was already reaching for his wallet, and he drew out his driver's license, which the man studied and compared to his face before filing the license in a small box.

"Mr. Franck had all the documents you asked for collected in the office. I'll ask you to sign this first, though." He passed Patchett a clipboard under the glass-encased mesh fence that separated them. A chart filled the page on the clipboard, listing dates, names, signatures, and check-in/check-out times. Lew Franck's name was scrawled on the line immediately above Patchett's blank. Franck had spent about six hours down here the previous afternoon. *Serves the little worm right*, Patchett thought, but he was also already dreading the amount of time that this threatened. If Franck had pulled the documents in six hours, it'd probably take twenty to comb through them.

Patchett signed the sheet with an inaudible sigh and passed

the clipboard back to the attendant, who took it under the glass wall and studied the signature. As always when Patchett came into this basement, he wondered briefly if they were going to fingerprint him next.

"Fine," the man said. "I'll buzz you through the door on your right." Patchett glanced at the door. "Follow that hallway to the second door on the left. All the documents are set up in there."

The man reached under the counter and pushed an unseen door release. Patchett heard another buzz, and the door clicked. He picked up his briefcase and pushed through.

The second door on the left opened to a familiar office that was decorated with spartan furniture with a distinct Salvation Army appearance. Much of the indy work that Patchett had done started in this room. But the room looked dramatically different now as he walked in.

Ringing the walls of the small office were cartons and cartons of papers, stacked in sometimes tottering columns around the space. By quick count, Patchett saw thirty-five to forty bankers' boxes, with three or four bigger ones thrown in for good measure. They all gave off the musty, attic-dust smell of stored paper, and it filled the air.

Alexander Tomlin's role in Prohiva sat filed and boxed neatly before him, and Patchett immediately upped the estimate for a thorough review. This was a week of work that needed to be encapsulated in a day. Patchett set the briefcase on a chair and shrugged his coat into a corner.

He scratched his head and considered trying to track Anne down, knowing immediately that he wouldn't. Her message said that she would be available Friday, and that meant she'd be in classes today. He didn't blame her. Standing in front of the boxes, he wished that he'd pressed a greater sense of urgency on her before, but he realized that he hadn't been operating under that urgency himself.

Patchett moved to the nearest cartons and began to examine them. Each was labeled, a date and a short reference marking the box ends. He skimmed them and swore.

All dealt with Prohiva; there were no documents from anything else that Tomlin might have done, although Patchett had expressly requested those things as well. That suggested that even more papers and more time spent were lying in wait for him.

He skipped the first boxes, passing over what appeared to be Tomlin's oldest papers from the earliest work, moving instead to documents that were prepared only after Prohiva took its relatively final form. If there was something to be found that would be of importance to the FDA, it wouldn't be in material that involved some earlier approach to the problem.

Patchett pulled a box labeled INITIAL PROHIVA RESEARCH NOTES — 35 PADS, and he sat down. He lifted the lid and counted out exactly thirty-five legal pads. Single pages leaked out of some of them, presumably memos or documents that Tomlin slipped inside the back covers. Patchett pulled the first pad out and once again immersed himself in the paper.

19

THERE WAS VIGOROUS DEBATE in the news about NCAP requirements. The National Care Plan had been in effect for just months, and its budget and its bureaucracy were already straining, a major portion of that strain coming from AIDS.

The language of NCAP was clear — its stated goal was to extend basic medical care to every American — but there was a lawsuit in Texas that was trying to figure out exactly what that meant. The plaintiffs wanted to interpret the plan and its effectuating statute broadly. There must be, the thinking went, some effective limit, some reasonability standard on the extent to which care would be provided. After all, the statute said "basic" medical care. Without that limit, NCAP would continue to hemorrhage taxpayer money until its empty shell had to be abandoned, its noble goal going with it.

At Kingland Memorial Hospital, which sat overlooking a distant view of a blue-tinted Puget Sound and the harborside clutter of Seattle–Tacoma, the goal actually wasn't so noble, and the effort and funds purportedly spent in NCAP's name were even more misguided. NCAP coverage for AIDS was a bonanza for the small medical center. The government continued to make NCAP payments despite money problems, just as it was obligated to do, and Kingland was reaping the benefits.

AIDS victims were stacked almost bed to bed in the hospital, fully filling two wings of the main building. Most of the patients were either homeless, taken from the streets in a four-or five-state area, or they were abandoned by their former friends and family. They were collected by Kingland Memorial, and Kingland collected from the government while providing a clean, if desolate, place for its patients to die. Outside the hospital, and even inside it in some circles away from the AIDS wings, there were common references to the "death wards."

Gordon Grant was there, rasping soundlessly for yet another drink of water to soothe his cracked and dry lips. He'd come into Kingland as a John Doe, and he would leave it the same way. Grant went into cardiac arrest at 12:14 in the afternoon on Thursday. The shrill *scree* from the monitor startled the charge nurse at her station, and she knocked a Diet Coke over when she jumped. The brown syrupy liquid fizzed as it stained across a chart and dropped to a foaming puddle on the floor.

"Shit," she said softly, and one of the other nurses turned to help her.

"Which one?" she said.

"One fourteen." The charge nurse punched a button to silence the sharp noise.

"No code?"

"No code."

As a "no code," no effort would be made to preserve this John Doe's life. Truth be known, he wouldn't even have been monitored a few months previously, but this was, after all, on NCAP money. The patients on the death wards had the works. Both nurses continued to watch the monitors for a moment, then turned to other things.

Gordon Grant died at 12:21.

20

PATCHETT SEARCHED the documents all morning and well into the afternoon and found nothing. He went through the volumes of papers for more than eight hours, taking breaks only to stand and work the unsettlingly numerous kinks out of his body or to use the restroom. Each time he spent more than five minutes without Tomlin's notes in front of him, though, he had only to look around the room to be prompted to press on.

Tomlin was retentive enough to write in precise, almost type-like lettering and surprisingly complete and succinct sentences, filling one yellow legal pad before moving on to another. That made the task a little easier for Patchett, who skimmed the notes quickly, searching mainly for names or records of conversations or meetings. But it made it difficult as well, increasing vastly the number of pages prepared for any one conversation, any meeting or conference, any particular day.

Patchett was paging through the next to last pad of the final box of Tomlin's notes, yawning and cursing his luck and the time now lost. The boxes contained virtually nothing that caught his eye. The few boxes from the last year and a half were in fact almost empty by comparison to the earlier filings.

He was bracing for searches through different documents when he found himself flipping back and forth in the notes, eyes suddenly struggling to blink tiredness away. He read one page carefully, puzzling over it, then skipped to the next before turning back again.

Tomlin's notes, the very model of research efficiency, suddenly didn't make sense. The sentence that ran across the page break, even to Patchett's untrained eye, was gibberish. At the bottom of one page, it said, "Research into Lot 179 is," and on the next, it continued, "last June. Clifton anticipates approval anyway." Then the notes ended.

Patchett reached over to the box and grabbed the last yellow pad propped at the far end. That pad was completely blank, a small tail of paper dangling from a top corner.

Peeling back the cardboard binder on the top of the second pad, Patchett carefully fingered through the remaining pieces. He counted seven pages that were torn out.

Patchett set the pad aside but continued to stare at it. He wondered briefly why a blank pad would be filed, but he knew at the same moment that the pad contained writing when originally placed in the box.

Why, then, wasn't it taken out when the notes were torn out, rather than leaving a blank pad in the file? But the attorney immediately understood this as well, and he spun the box around to read the label on the end again. 42 PADS, this one said.

In the world of the law, Patchett long ago learned that it was better to use a half-truth than any visible lie, and that lesson came back to him now as he looked from the blank legal pad to the box, with its clear record of forty-two pads.

Half-truths, he thought. *Half-truths but no lies.*

The pad couldn't be taken, so the notes were. So long as there were forty-two pads, Patchett realized, it wouldn't matter what they contained. You checked out a box with forty-two pads, you returned a box with forty-two pads. No one would look farther than that. No one would check more closely, he was certain.

No one would check *at all.* There'd be no harm. No foul.

Patchett thought suddenly of the other pad with Tomlin's notes, and he picked it up and turned to the back. Finding the last page break, he bent back the binding of that pad as well.

Two sheets were missing.

"Research into Lot 179 is," and then two missing pages. He dropped the pad on the table. It landed on its painfully silent successor.

Patchett hurried to the boxes against one wall. Suddenly, it was startlingly important, *crucially* important to find a document that he knew existed. That he actually prepared himself.

The box he searched for and found was labeled TOMLIN — IND APPLICATION — SUMMARY REPORTS. Patchett hoisted the carton to the table and threw off its top. He found the overview report and then its six-month update, and he slid this thin brief out to page briskly through it to the appendices.

The update contained ten of them, little snippets of largely irrelevant information designed to flavor the original application and, more important, to keep the application and Weber in the news. There was nothing substantive in them — lists of researchers, of study dates and subjects. But in the ninth appendix, there was a list of lot numbers for Prohiva, with the ultimate disposition of each production of the vaccine.

Patchett turned to that list and ran his finger down the page. Lot 179, he found, was among the last produced and was made as the indy was being submitted. He traced a line across the page, noting the production date and the amount produced — 300 doses, enough to inoculate as many chimps. The appendix also identified the production facility — as with all the lots, 179 was made in the Bloomington building itself. Then, under "disposition," there were two words: "none" and "destroyed."

Patchett closed the appendix and tossed it, too, onto the table. It landed on the two legal pads. The words in Tomlin's notes ran through the attorney's head.

Research into Lot 179 is . . . And Patchett wondered what Tomlin had written on the next page in that neat and precise handwriting now gone. Research, he presumed, was not done on destroyed lots of vaccine. And even if it was researched and then destroyed, the disposition wouldn't also be listed as "none."

There was no date on the appendix nine reference to the destruction of Lot 179, and Patchett closed his eyes and tried to remember where he originally got the information in that appendix. He didn't have the slightest idea. He supposed that Weber itself likely fed him the appendix almost as produced.

He sat again, the two notepads and one document stacked in front of him, the box beside them, and he worked his fingers into the knot in the back of his neck. Yesterday's hangover had passed in the night, but a bottle of aspirin couldn't pull the new pain out of there. He kneaded at it anyway, eyes focused on the label on the box.

He wanted desperately to comb these notes further, but the box said forty-two notepads, and he couldn't very well take one or two away with him, especially if they were altered. He reached into the box to open a slot at the back for the two legal pads.

His hand grazed a paper as he moved the other pads forward, slicing an unseen cut across the back of his index finger, and Patchett jerked his hand back. He immediately sucked at the cut, which began to sting, and he reached back into the box to pull a paper out from under the notes.

He knew what it was the instant he touched the smooth silkiness. A fax. Curled and unfilable as they spin off facsimile machines, faxes were invariably lost. His own files, he knew, were dotted with misplaced and crushed pieces of the fragile paper. He pulled this one out and spread it on the table.

The fax was handwritten, its words scratched and crawling in crooked lines over the page:

179 is almost done. Finally. I hope last trip to southwest. Tomlin's wrapped up in the study. Hasn't said much since we got back. May be good sign for approval. Bancroft's going along, though. Rayes wishy-washy. Usual for both of course. Need to talk.

The initials at the bottom were M. M. C., and Patchett didn't have to search far back in his memory for that person.

Marc Clifton.

He spread the paper out farther, rolling its crumpled top edge flat. A phone number was there, and Patchett scribbled it down on his pad, along with the name "Bateman 24-Hour Copy Center," which ran alongside it. A 520 area code. He didn't know it.

He examined the paper another time, checking the date. The missing notes were from around January 1995. The fax said December 12 of the same year, just four months back now. The research that Tomlin mentioned in the notes was apparently almost done by the time of the fax, and Patchett knew only one thing clearly. Whatever that research was, it hadn't involved destruction of Lot 179.

Patchett almost pocketed the fax but stopped short. What he didn't know about Lot 179, about Tomlin, about Marc Clifton or anything else that loomed large here was extensive. But there was a lingering feeling in the air suddenly, a chill feeling, and that feeling carried the very distant but still-threatening taint of fraud. Patchett knew that the slip in his hand could be one piece of evidence of that potential fraud.

More ominous than that was his own role, which began to etch its way in understanding across the attorney's wrinkling brow. He hadn't actively participated in any fraud, nor had the firm, at least not to the best of his knowledge. He didn't even know it *was* fraud, for that matter. But if it was, it could pull his firm down along with everything else, and that was a whirlpool Patchett most assuredly did not want to be in.

He set the fax on the table gently, as though it were infected with poison, and it rolled slightly into a curl to stare menacingly at him. Patchett's mind was reeling as he leaned back slowly in the chair. He tried to calm his accelerating thoughts to think things through.

He wasn't in a position to suggest fraud on anyone's part, and he knew it was foolish to even consider it. All he had was an undefinable mistrust of Marc Clifton, some missing notes from a suicidal researcher, and a lot of vaccine that was reportedly destroyed but that instead ended up in some project in the southwest. It might be suspicious, he supposed, but it wasn't really fraud.

Which left him with another consideration — the fact that Weber BioTech, soaring above him even now, was a client. In truth, Patchett never operated under a feeling that he was uncontrollably guided by the noble edicts of the Rules of Professional Conduct, the attorneys' self-imposed scheme to avoid other regulation. Those rules established that the client was his utmost responsibility, short of truth before the court, but neither he nor most other lawyers he knew felt consumed by the particularly loyalistic fire that drove some of his colleagues to throw all sensibilities to the wind.

But Weber wasn't just a client, he reminded himself then. It was an *important* client, doing important things.

Patchett stared at the fax again. Its words were almost burned into his memory already, but he took no chances, pulling over his legal pad and copying the message verbatim. He also wrote down the excerpt from Tomlin's notes, running from the reference to Lot 179, across the page break, and then through the out-of-place language on the next page.

After he finished, Patchett dropped the fax back into the bottom of the box and slipped the two legal pads in on top of it. He also replaced the update report in its own box, recovered both boxes, and stacked them in their places.

He contemplated leaving but had a sudden question about whether he would be back to have this opportunity another time. He lifted a box of formal reports to the table and opened it.

Research into Lot 179 is . . . he was thinking as he did that. Over and over, the words ran through his mind.

Research into Lot 179 is . . .

And then, unavoidably, the other thought came to him.

Half-truths. But no lies.

And all he could think of then was Marc Clifton. "We were competitors," Clifton had said. "He was brilliant," he had said. "He was crazy."

Patchett wondered which were Clifton's half-truths, what lies they concealed. He flipped open a folder.

21

THE TRUCK was a metallic copper color that might once have been brown, a 1989 Chevy three-quarter-ton pickup that rattled as it moved toward the heights of the Kaibab Plateau, twenty-five twisting miles of rutted Arizona blacktop road away. It was early in the month for Alfre Rayes to be heading to the small trailer that sat in House Rock Flat in the high desert on the opposite side of the Kaibab, but it was, in a sense, a special occasion. Not special because he had an early opportunity to tend to the Navajo in the insignificant clinic across Marble Canyon, east of the flat. He wouldn't make this trip just for that "opportunity." The clinic work was only something he tolerated for the small amount of extra income it provided.

No, this was a unique trip because Dr. Rayes was never going back to Kanab, at least not as someone tied inexorably to the dismal future of that dismal town. He'd sold his small house there, a herculean task in Kanab, which was little more than a desert gas stop perched against the red clay bluffs of extreme southern Utah. And he did it in anticipation of getting out altogether, of packing his meager bags and removing himself from Kanab, from Utah, Arizona, Nevada, from the entire history that chased him all his life until he landed desperate and broke in this high Sonoran desert of the southwest canyonlands.

There would be one more trip to Kanab for Rayes, of course, and to the Canyonlands Hospital. That would be to deliver his resignation, just days or perhaps even hours away. At that moment, he would finally be making a move that suggested he was in control of his own life. At that point, he hoped that maybe *he* would be dictating his own future. Maybe.

It had never been that way before. Rayes originally went to medical school so he could someday support an extended family of twelve that still lived, to the best of his knowledge, in the Mexican ghettos of San Diego. He'd despised it, hating everything about the grinding, burn-out existence that was modern med school. But the press of family and an understanding that he alone of all of them had some chance to pull them up kept him there.

His grades were excellent, a steady stream of high marks that would outshine the second-rate medical school he attended. His way after school would have been set, if not at the highest level of achievement, then at some respectable level under that.

And then his family learned he was a homosexual. After that, things had begun to go steadily, uncontrollably wrong. Communication with them all but disappeared, along with the family ties and support he had always enjoyed and had, in fact, taken for granted. And Rayes, for the first but not for the last time, began the slow drift.

Rayes thought now that the drift was the one unerring trait of his life — the slow-motion walk through his existence. He was pushed, pulled, or buoyed by tides beyond his control.

He'd been done with classes when all the bad things truly began back then, a young resident gearing toward a modest but healthy profession in general practice. The drift had carried him away from that life, but Rayes had still moved in the direction of his momentum, landing without fanfare in an unknown medical partnership in El Cajon, up the Alvarado Freeway and over the dry shoreline mountains from San Diego.

Looking back, as he now watched the desert roll steadily toward the wooded and still snow-fringed top of the Kaibab, Rayes wondered if the time in El Cajon was the low point or if perhaps the past two years were worse, with the up and down of brushes with fame and of running on what must clearly be the edge of the law. It was a close call, but Rayes thought El Cajon. For now anyway.

He was barely in that first medical partnership for a year when new trouble started. It wasn't trouble *then*, of course — it was love. One of the other doctors, an experienced thirty-nine to Rayes's then twenty-eight years. He'd been married, with two kids. He'd been gay. They learned of each other through the course of that year, and the growing friendship between colleagues turned into a three-month affair.

All of which had been broken up by Marguerite Ruval. The day that Marguerite came into the office was diamond pure in Rayes's memory, a picture still seen painfully distinct through years that were only like a magnifying sheet of glass.

The clear southern California sun had not quite cut through the smog that crawled over the mountains from San Diego and, to the north, from Los Angeles. There was the unbearable heat common to August in the California desert highlands.

Marguerite Ruval was seven years old back then, and she was infected with a well-developed case of meningitis. Anyone who saw her, anyone who touched her and felt the heat pouring from her small body should instantly have understood that she needed to be in the hospital and not in her father's arms in a medical office. Marguerite was well on her way to dying.

Rayes never learned the entire story of Marguerite's entrance into his life. He was away from the office when she arrived, and she was hidden away in an examining room when he did get there. But he eventually knew that she had been in the waiting room for almost two hours while her Spanish-speaking father struggled to understand and be understood.

The first thing Rayes himself discovered on arriving that day was that Marguerite would never get to be eight, or, if she did, she would never comprehend it. When Rayes was called into that room, what he noticed immediately was the doctor, leaning over the child with a stethoscope pressed to the little girl's chest. He felt and recalled, as always, the quick surge of mixed love and excitement. The next thing he noticed, though, was that Marguerite was almost burning alive with fever and that she very clearly was dying.

The next events in Rayes's life were frenzied, automatic reactions he barely remembered now. The utter confusion and frustration and fear on the face of this man he loved, a man who had left an intensely sick girl lingering in a waiting room. The instant understanding that his friend had no idea what was wrong. The scream that Marguerite issued, the only sound Rayes ever heard her make, when he lifted her head so her chin touched her chest. The recognition of meningitis and the knowledge that Marguerite would not survive.

There were calls for an ambulance and a failed attempt to locate a medevac helicopter. The ambulance took twenty minutes, and it faced another twenty to the nearest capable hospital.

Marguerite died two days later.

Rayes never blamed him for the death. There are those times in everyone's life when you are suddenly overwhelmed by everything around you, when you freeze transfixed in helpless and incapacitating fear, like a deer caught in the headlights of an oncoming car. But he could never forgive what happened afterward.

The lawsuit was inevitable. The news of the relationship between the doctors, on the other hand, was a surprising issue. It arose subtly at first — innocuous questions in the depositions. After a year, though, it was clear that this single issue, which bore no relationship to little Marguerite Ruval or to her fate, was obsessing the prestigious doctor and husband. They parted, bitterly.

Rayes walked with a one-hundred-thousand-dollar lump sum severance payment from the partnership. It agreed to pick up any liability assessed to him. He returned once, for an additional deposition, and he eventually learned of the settlement. Blame, he heard suggested, was laid on him.

Rayes went away on steadily more-embittered waters.

The drift this time carried him to virtually every major metropolitan area west of the Rockies, with intermittent stops farther east and one foray into Canada. Always the search was the same. Always the result was preordained. The medical community, Rayes came to realize, was nothing more than a series of closely connected small towns with long memories. Alfre Rayes's reputation, justified or not, had spread fast.

The hundred-thousand-dollars got him through three years on the drift before depositing him unceremoniously in Las Vegas, the perennial refuge of cast-outs. There he encountered his first work in the clinics that catered to the unspoken underclass. He did a stint in Vegas for a couple of years before finally fleeing to one of the tiny towns dotting the other unseen world of America, one full of casual people oddly separated from the rush of life in the 1990s.

His position in Kanab at Canyonlands was also essentially at a clinic, treating the colds and fevers and snake and spider bites common in the area. Falls from rocks. Heat stress. Alfre Rayes hadn't come far. He hadn't thought that he would escape.

In time, the thoughts of never escaping led him inexorably to extend his medical services in a largely failing effort to get whatever income he could from the desert communities spreading out across the lands north of the Grand Canyon. The medical work for the

Navajo, marked by monthly visits to the bare edge of their vast Arizona reservation, were just such an effort.

It lingered that way for another year, twelve more months ticked off what Rayes had concluded was his inescapable destiny of uncontrolled movement toward nowhere. Only after that year did he finally reopen connections to Vegas. Only after that time did he come into his most recent work, which found him, incredibly enough, in the alcohol-scented, dingy-tiled rooms of community clinics.

Where he met Eric Bancroft.

The thought that kept Rayes going since that time was that he would never see Vegas again when this was all done. Never, in fact, see Kanab or Bancroft or clinics or deserts or any of the rest of it again.

That thought brought the well of moralistic guilt swelling up through him, perhaps the last vestige of the man he'd been before being battered by the lifelong backlash against his homosexuality and the effort to stay in his profession. The guilt came back to him, as always.

He tried to push it from his mind, concentrating instead on the road as it cut through the emptiness now interspersed with the first trees of the Kaibab. As he watched, he was struck by the simple beauty of the plateau, the stillness of the desert, marked by the flecks of blooming cacti and the scrubs of the trees of the lower elevations. Perhaps he would want to see this again after all, he thought, seeing those things. Sometime long after this time, sometime when enough years were behind him to dull the world that he'd built around himself, that still was being built. Perhaps he'd want to see it again then.

Perhaps.

The truck roared up the mountainside.

22

THE ELEVENTH FLOOR was deserted by the time Patchett got there. Office lights were off. Secretaries' lights, too, the ranks of blocked-off stations dim, chairs pushed in, and papers filed. That was a Weber BioTech requirement, Patchett knew. All desks were to be neatly organized each night. A place for everything. Everything in its place.

Everything except Patchett himself. He moved through the hall, not with stealth but with the quiet, soft movements of someone alone in the office at night. Someone who wasn't expected to be, wasn't *supposed* to be there.

Patchett wasn't really alone, of course. There was a security guard when he signed out of the document warehouse. Another one outside the elevator up here. And the attorney did have authorization to go to this floor. At least in some sense.

He'd hoped without justification that Rebecca would still be there, not getting to talk with her during the day. The documents were too numerous; he'd skimmed the last boxes as it was.

The guards were able to tell him that Rebecca was long gone. Patchett asked to leave her a note and, sensing that wasn't enough to get him through, to check a file left at her desk. There was no file, but the guards recognized him and allowed him a couple of minutes.

Rebecca's desk, like the others, was neat almost to a fault. Patchett rolled her chair out, the sound of its wheels grinding on a carpet protector and grating out into the hall. He sat and pulled a pen from a cup on her desk. No memo or message pad or other paper was visible, so he took a business card from his breast pocket and wrote a note on the back: "Would like to talk with you, if possible. Will call you tomorrow." He stood and dropped the card on her chair, pushing the chair back into its precise Weber place.

As he stood, his eyes fell on her Rolodex, and curiosity more than anything made him reach over and start to flick through the cards. He turned through the tabs to find *T*. There was a card for Tomlin, headed only "Alex" in what was obviously Rebecca's own flowing handwriting. A home phone number was written beneath the name.

Patchett supposed that having a Rolodex card for your boss wasn't unusual, even when that card carried the perhaps too familiar first name. He thought that maybe even his own secretary would have one tucked away at her desk, with his name on it. But it struck Patchett oddly as a confirmation of the relationship that he knew still only through Anne's somewhat cryptic message.

He thumbed to *C*. There was no listing for Clifton in Rebecca's cards, but Patchett checked under *M* to be sure, looking for Marc. Nothing there, either, but Patchett could see Clifton's office even as he stood at Rebecca's desk, and he also vaguely thought he had once heard that Rebecca was Clifton's secretary at one time. If that was right, then the listing should be there, lost in the never-thinned ranks of a Rolodex. Still, no card.

He was flipping the cards back and pushing the Rolodex to the corner when he stopped and pulled it out again. He glanced up to check the darkened hallway, the sign of a man suddenly aware he was doing something he ought not do. And he turned to *B*, looking for the first of the unknown names from the fax.

Bancroft's name and address were there. Dr. Eric Bancroft, at Mercy General Hospital in Las Vegas. Patchett took another business card from his pocket and wrote down Bancroft's name and address, adding all three of the phone numbers that followed on the card.

He turned to *R* and found Dr. Alfre Rayes. Kanab, Utah. Patchett then retrieved a third business card to record Rayes's name and the one phone number that was listed. "Canyonlands Hospital," it said. Patchett closed the Rolodex and pushed it back against the phone. The business cards with addresses and numbers went into his pocket.

He noticed the whistling then, and his first, somewhat irrational, fear was that it was the distant sound of an alarm, triggered in some way by his presence. But stepping away from the desk, he saw the source.

At the end of the hall, a few yards from Rebecca's desk, Tomlin's office door stood closed, the yellow police barrier tapes declaring the office off limits. Patchett could hear the wind more clearly now as he stood in the hall. It sucked under the door. Beyond that door, the breeze would be pulling out through the unrepaired window, past the temporary cover — wood, plastic, whatever it was — and into the dark night.

Patchett went to the door.

He looked back one more time, scanning the hall again for witnesses to what was more clearly beginning to tread on ground that he wouldn't want to label, before reaching through the tape and twisting the knob. The door opened easily as the wind caught it, and it swung into the room. A few papers on the desks behind him rattled briefly and were answered by the flutterings of some papers scattered across the floor inside the office. Patchett ducked under the tape and into the room and shut the door behind him.

Tomlin's office was a coal mine, dark and with the kind of chill that didn't bother at first but that eventually would cut its way through all clothing, moving deeply into a body to make bones ache. The building's heating system couldn't keep up with the steady sucking force through the shattered window.

In the dark, seeing nothing, the first thing Patchett noticed was the smell. A cloying sweetness hung in the brisk air despite the wind, a scent that existed in defiance of the ventilation. He smelled more deeply and caught it once more. Its identification floated at the edge of his mind until he reached for the desk lamp and turned it on, chasing the odor away with a sudden island of light that fell on the blotter.

The hole was covered. A large section of plywood was pressed against the window frame, small glints of reflected light showing the heads of nails that were buried in the ceiling and walls to hold the wood in place. Strips of duct tape also ran across the top, strapping the wood to the remaining section of glass on one side.

The room was a disaster. A few sheets of paper occasionally floated on wafts across the floor, pushed by the steady whistling breeze into darting movements around the furniture. Some golf-ball-sized chunks of glass were spread under the window. A small radio sat strangely alone behind the door.

Patchett moved to the file cabinet and opened the top drawer, cringing at the cold bar in his hand and the shriek of metal on metal. It was empty, and he checked the others, finding them mostly cleared out as well. He found assorted sheets and memos, fractions of the papers that would have passed through this man's hands.

He moved over to the desk and sat in the chair. Before Patchett pulled open the deep drawers on either side of the drab piece of furniture, the question of illegality again rose in his mind, but he patted it comfortably down before it grew too large. The unanswered questions he had asked himself over the last few hours had planted a seed of doubting interest in him, and he wanted to know the answers more and more with each passing moment, regardless of the consequences.

He pulled open one of the drawers and ran a hand through assorted odds and ends inside, quickly looking through them and finding only the typical appliances of businesspeople. A pair of scissors, a stapler, tape dispenser, and a virtual cemetery of various writing tools. Orphaned paper clips littered the bottom. Enough, probably, for an entire box. He shut the drawer and turned to the other one.

This one was empty, without even a stray memo to indicate what was once inside. Patchett noted the file runners, though. Long metal supports lined the sides of the drawer. They would have held hanging folders, but the folders were gone, leaving only the grayed rub marks to hint at what might have been there. He closed the drawer.

The top drawer was, like the file cabinet, a repository of straggling pieces of papers. Patchett lifted out a dozen or so sheets of various sizes and colors and shapes, different dates marking them, handwriting on some and not on others. The attorney set them on the desk and flipped through them one by one, skimming for things he didn't know, things he knew he wouldn't find.

Patchett was almost to the bottom of the stack when he came to the pictures. There were four of them there, and he glanced through those as well.

The first two were of some undefinable office party. Secretaries and two or three of the researchers were collected around a small cake sitting on one of the desks, undoubtedly outside the door closed darkly in front of him. Patchett smiled despite himself, seeing Tomlin and Rebecca in the second picture, standing next to each other, turned face-to-face in conversation.

He recognized the people in the third picture also. Tomlin was there again, Marc Clifton beside him. And there, next to Clifton, was Rowe Weber, the look on his face one of impatient indulgence at having the photo taken. Patchett smiled once more at that, then turned to the last picture.

He could instantly tell that this one was different. Its corners were bent roughly, as though it had been carried in a pocket at some point, and the picture's black back showed clearly that the camera had been a Polaroid. Squarely in the middle of the photo stood four men leaning against the dust-dulled fender of what looked to be a late model blue Buick. The car was a dark and vibrant contrast to the deep reds of the earth surrounding them.

The desert of the southwest, Patchett realized with an almost nervous start. Probably somewhere near Las Vegas. Maybe Kanab, Utah. The sparse grass was almost invisible in the picture — soft, greenish-tan wisps against the burned umber of the dirt. Patchett could just make out a rock outcropping that jutted up sharply in the background.

Alexander Tomlin was one of the men. He was at the left, head turned and eyes fixed on something off to that side. He was smiling under the desert sun, one arm thrown around the shoulders of a man Patchett didn't know. That second man appeared to be Hispanic, a sharply but casually dressed professional whose darker skin made him noticeable beside the pale complexions of the other three. Were Patchett to guess, he expected that it was Alfre Rayes. That man's arm, in turn, was around another man Patchett didn't know, but he hazarded it would be Eric Bancroft.

Bancroft looked uncomfortable in an overstarched cotton shirt and pressed blue jeans. Both were too small against an overweight frame. The doctor was a big man. A huge man, Patchett amended. His bulk pressed against and spread across the car fender. Alone of the four, Bancroft stood unsmiling, black Ray-Ban aviators hiding his eyes and tossing teardrop-shaped shadows down a sweaty, full-mooned face.

Clifton completed the set as the fourth figure, standing off to the right, hands in pockets in front of the Buick's nose. A superfluous jacket was draped over one arm. *All form*, Patchett thought suddenly. *All form with nothing underneath. Just like our discussion*, the attorney couldn't help thinking.

Friends, Patchett thought at seeing this last picture. The men here look like four friends on a pleasure trip, stopping at a roadside rest area. Getting a drink before moving on.

He sat back, tucking the picture into the inside pocket of his jacket without a second thought. He figured the picture wasn't evidence anyway, the police and whoever else cared apparently not wanting to claim it. But that thought made Patchett question whether a search was completed yet. The picture slipped snugly into his pocket, Patchett figured they should have finished any search and would have taken anything that mattered to them. *Certainly* they would have. That thought and the string of unanswered questions kept the photo deep in his pocket.

He swiveled the chair and studied what might have been one of Alex Tomlin's last views, finding himself unexpectedly wondering if some people had in fact been in that view. The windows, boarded halfway over, loomed above him, a fiberboard slash against the white wall and the black, pinlighted night seen through the remaining glass. Patchett could see a jagged edge of the broken pane, reaching just out from beneath the cover of the board at the side nearest him, and he stood to examine it.

Even in the dim light from the desk lamp, he could see the

greenish tint of the glass and the thickness that should have walled the night out of the room. The window was an inch through, maybe more, the product of an energy consciousness that would have been common at the time of the building's construction. He rapped at the intact window, listening to the low-pitched *dunk-dunk* sound of knuckles tapping against thick glass.

Standing back, he gauged the size of the missing sheet, which ran perhaps five feet across and six to seven feet high. He wondered how much force it must have taken for Tomlin to punch that window out, and he looked through the barren and chill room for anything the researcher might have used to accomplish that task. Only the chair stood out as a possibility, and Patchett dismissed that on trying to lift it. Nothing else came to mind.

He studied the glass again, examining the broken corner that hung out from under the wood barrier, his eyes tight with the look of questions and confusion. Stepping out of the light, he caught the faint shine from a clump of hair still sticking to the sharp fringe of the hole. Patchett bent closer, and he could see the smear of blood that stained the window at this edge, painting the glass at the break. Intent on the stain, he didn't notice when the door swung silently open.

"Find something, Mr. Patchett?" a voice behind him asked softly. Clifton stood in the door, and Patchett jerked around to see the silhouette blocked out against the light from the hallway, the dark X of the barrier tape crossing Clifton's shadow chest. The doctor's features filled in as he ducked under the tape and stepped into the room where the desk lamp's weak glow could shine across his face. The papers on the floor danced vigorously with the door open once more. They swept alternately from Clifton and the doorway to Patchett and the window. Patchett's heart pounded in his ears.

"Thought I would see where this latest task of mine began, Dr. Clifton." The attorney's voice seemed a booming echo in the small and cold room. His words were artificially calm with the trained smoothness that he somehow found when standing to make his first comments to a court or jury.

"I see," Clifton said as he moved farther into the room. He sat on the edge of the desk. "This is where it started, all right. But I thought that even you — *especially you* — would respect a police barrier." Clifton gestured his head idly at the doorway.

Patchett attempted an easy smile and glanced down in an almost shameful look of embarrassment that was entirely for Clifton's benefit. "Actually," he said, "I can." And then he added, for spite alone, "At least as well as you can."

He moved slowly, casually from the window, crossing directly in front of Clifton and just inches away. Clifton leaned back as Patchett moved to place himself against the backlighting from the hall. *A much more favorable position*, Patchett thought. His heart slowed slightly to a steady thud that pushed repeatedly in his chest.

"Why are you up here anyway?" Clifton demanded.

"Well, for better or worse, it is my job. At least for right now. But maybe I should ask you why you're here as well, doctor. I assume your own research went late tonight?"

Clifton's answer was clinically cool. "Curiosity," he said flatly. "The trademark and probably the curse of my own job."

Patchett ducked under the police tape and immediately enjoyed the comparative warmth of the hallway. "As with mine," he said. "The problem with both our professions, I suppose. Always looking for answers. Aren't we?" Patchett smiled a grin that was bitterly tight, like a razor-sharp slice across his face. He didn't expect an answer and didn't intend to wait for one. "Never content till we find them," he added then. He turned and moved down the hall, hearing the door close behind him, but he didn't look back until he was at the elevator.

The guard stood there still, oblivious to the fact that a couple of minutes turned out to be fifteen. He was overweight, his belly stretching the cheap blue shirt open to reveal snatches of the off-white T-shirt underneath. A tinny-looking badge was pinned to his breast, identifying him meaninglessly as a security officer. He carried no weapon of any kind.

"Find what you need, Mr. Patchett?" the man asked.

"Don't really know that," Patchett replied, forcing a smile.

"Not yet, anyway, but it's a start, I guess." His heart was slowing to normal.

"Well, you let us know if you need anything else."

"You can be assured I'll do that." The elevator arrived, and Patchett stepped on and descended down and out of the Weber Building.

The Fourth Day

23

PATCHETT SQUINTED against the dull light of the overcast morning, then took a drink from another day's juice-laced vodka as he stared at the photograph in his hand. The two business cards with Bancroft's and Rayes's names and numbers sat next to the phone, a sheet of paper beside them. The fax message was written on the paper, the phone number of the Bateman 24-Hour Copy Center stringing across the bottom.

The area code in the fax was for Arizona, but Patchett couldn't track the number down any more closely. He didn't have access to an exchange directory. So that number, along with those of the two doctors, was on a short list of phone calls. It was to be a day packed with phone calls, Patchett realized, swearing lightly to himself.

He sipped at the drink, feeling its strange mix of warming coolness and the slight but mercifully numbing effect seep into his body. Yet another hangover ached against his temples, milder this time but still bracing, the by-product of another night's poring over another seemingly bottomless bottle.

The overnight return of winter was making it worse. Outside the window, Patchett could see the light skiff of snow that was temporarily hiding the brown drudgery of prespring. The coating would last no more than a day before the steadily shifting fronts of March brought temperatures back up. In the meantime, the mercury was down five degrees both inside and outside, crossing the thin boundary between just bearable and uncomfortably cold. Patchett pulled again at his suit coat, drawing it tighter against his shoulders.

He'd set the picture down and was concentrating only on the chill in the room and the empty whiteness of his walls when Anne tapped at the open door and stuck her head in.

"Got your message," she said. He'd left it last night as soon as he got home, wanting to speak with her first thing this morning.

"And I got yours," he said in reply.

"Rebecca and Tomlin?"

"I'm a little curious to find out how you've deduced this," he said, sitting back. He squinted up at her, head throbbing once lightly at his movement. Anne sat down, setting a steaming mug of coffee on the front edge of Patchett's desk. She briefly ran through her trip to the apartment complex and her conversation with the woman there.

"Do I want to know how you found out it was his apartment?" Patchett asked when she finished.

Anne shrugged. "Showed up on his credit report," she said, hesitating only a second before going on. "Did you get the chance to talk to Rebecca about it?"

"No. I was tied up with the damn documents all day. I left her a message," Patchett said with exasperation, then he added, thinking of Clifton in Tomlin's office. "I hope she got it. Told her I would call her today."

"Ask her about Las Vegas."

Patchett sat forward as he picked up a pen and found his notes. "And what do you know about Las Vegas?" he asked. He was thinking about Eric Bancroft, the picture of four men in the desert, the fax machine probably out there somewhere as well. He was thinking about Alfre Rayes and Kanab, Utah.

He'd looked Kanab up on the map. It was a dot perched precariously over Arizona, and it looked to be about 150 to 200 miles from Vegas, roughly dead center in the middle of nowhere, judging by the barren area surrounding it.

"Tomlin was there at least twice," Anne said. "Once in mid-May of '94. The latest time in December last year."

"Around the twelfth?"

Now she looked mildly surprised. "How'd you know?"

"I have ways, too, you know," Patchett said levelly. He thought again of the fax. "What else?"

"Not too much. I don't think it was a vacation, though. The charges for the trip showed up on American Express, but there's no record of hotels. He could've paid cash, but that doesn't seem to fit. Most people on vacation don't pay cash for hotel bills, particularly for long stays."

"How long?"

"A little under three weeks the first time and about a week and a half the second."

Patchett nodded at her to go on.

"Most people on business don't pay cash, either, of course. So I'm assuming he met someone there. Or maybe the company owns a home there or something."

"Met someone," Patchett said. By his tone, it was a statement, not a suggestion.

"Who?"

"Dr. Eric Bancroft most likely. Maybe a man named Alfre Rayes. Also a doctor. Bancroft's in Vegas. Rayes is in a town not too far away called Kanab. That's in—"

"Utah," Anne interrupted. "It fits. Tomlin had a gas charge in Kanab on the December trip. How did these two come up?"

Patchett told her about his search through the documents and the discovery of the fax. He handed his notes over, and she read the transcription. When she handed them back, he gave her the photo.

"Tomlin on the left," she said, "and that's Clifton, right?" She was pointing to the man standing apart on the right. Patchett nodded. "I guess these two are Rayes and Bancroft?"

"Presumably. I didn't have the opportunity to ask anyone, and I'm not sure I will."

"Why?"

"I took this out of Tomlin's desk," he said simply. He watched for her reaction, saw none, and understood that someone who dug into credit card files probably wouldn't look too hard at stealing a snapshot out of a dead man's desk.

"Right after I found it, Marc Clifton showed up, so I could have asked him."

"But?" Anne prompted.

Patchett's response faltered with the cautious slowness of a man speaking carefully. "I'm, uh" — he tried before pressing a finger tight against his lips — "I'm not sure I know what to think about Clifton," he finally said. "Not really sure at all."

"I take it the discussion with Dr. Clifton didn't go too well?"

"The discussion with Dr. Clifton went just fine, if you don't mind the shoveling."

"What'd he say?"

Patchett laughed lightly and bitterly in response. "More like what he *didn't* say. What he couldn't tell me." Patchett shook his head at the thought of the prior day's conversations.

"I asked Clifton about problems in researching Prohiva," he explained, "but the doctor said there weren't any. I asked him about Tomlin's latest work on Prohiva, and he said Tomlin hadn't done any since the indy two years ago. I asked him what Tomlin was working on during that time. Clifton said he didn't know."

"Not impossible," Anne said.

"No," Patchett agreed, "it's not. But you didn't hear him. The answers were too easy, the responses too . . . pat, I guess. After all, this is a man who worked with Tomlin for months or years. Spent almost every waking moment with him more than likely. But he couldn't — or he *wouldn't* — tell me anything about him."

He pointed at the picture still in her hand. "More important, he was clearly still working with Tomlin within the last couple of years."

"This could have been taken before," Anne said, playing the devil's advocate.

"I don't think so," Patchett replied, shaking his head. "You and

I both know now that Tomlin was down there those two times, and that picture is from one of them."

"How do you know that?"

"Read the license plate."

Anne looked at the picture more closely. The front bumper of the car was just visible behind Clifton, the license plate right at the edge of the photo and behind his knee. It was a Nevada tag, and, although it was difficult to read, she saw that it carried a sticker marked 95.

"It was the first trip, then," Anne said. "The one in May." She held the picture up for Patchett to see. "This picture was taken in the higher level deserts north of the Grand Canyon. It'd be cold up there in December, maybe even some snow. But these men are in shirtsleeves and sunglasses."

Patchett looked at the jacket slung over Clifton's arm.

"All right," he said, impressed. "We know they were both there in May 1994. And we know they were probably with Bancroft and Rayes and that these two" — he pointed at the two figures in the middle of the photo — "are probably those two gentlemen."

"But we still don't know *why* they were there," Anne interjected, and Patchett lifted a finger to keep her from going on. He passed the sheet with the fax message back to her. She read it another time.

"Lot 179?" she said, and Patchett nodded. "What is it?"

"You know that production of medications is divided into lots?" the attorney asked.

"Sure."

"Well, Weber produced maybe two hundred fifty lots of the submitted Prohiva formula. The last fifty were for Phases One and Two. The FDA used them and is still using them." Patchett wrote the first number on the pad, then added the other numbers with each reference, counting down against the original 250.

"The first one hundred to one hundred fifty were used by Weber itself in the preliminary primate studies. But the remaining fifty-odd lots were destroyed. That accounts for all lots, give or take select ones scattered throughout and found to be unusable for some reason."

"And Lot 179?" she asked.

"Listed in our papers as destroyed. No usage ever made."

She considered this, reread the fax. "*Lot 179 is almost done.* That could refer to destruction of the lot."

Patchett shook his head. "Makes no sense," he said. "The information that the lot was destroyed dates from before this fax. Also, you don't go to Arizona, which is where the fax is from, to destroy something made and stored here, something that would have been tested here."

Anne started to say something, but Patchett cut her off.

"Plus," he said quietly, a note of puzzlement in his tone, "there's another reference to Lot 179 in Tomlin's notes, all of which I supposedly got. Very late in those notes, around January 1995, Tomlin writes, '*Research into Lot 179 is . . .*' But the next pages are gone." Patchett told her about the missing pages, the forty-two pads.

"So they were there in May 1994," he said, counting a chronology of points on his fingers. "Tomlin noted research in January 1995, Clifton faxed that 179 was almost done in December of the same year, and Tomlin was dead four months later. That's a long time on a Prohiva research project that, according to Clifton, Tomlin wasn't even on. And it's a *very* unsatisfactory result."

"So Tomlin worked on Prohiva to the end," Anne said thoughtfully.

"That's right. But we have only the slightest hints at what he did." Patchett gestured at the photo, at his own sparse notes.

They both were silent. Thirty seconds, forty-five, almost a minute.

"Which leaves us with what?" Anne said finally.

"A lot of questions."

"Like why Clifton said Tomlin wasn't working on Prohiva the last two years?"

"That first. And what Tomlin did in that time. What was Lot 179? Who are Bancroft and Rayes? What happened in Arizona or Nevada or Utah or wherever the hell they were?"

"And Rebecca?" Anne said.

"And Rebecca," Patchett agreed. "Maybe she can help us figure out why a man who supposedly had no real problems in his life is dead."

"So what do we need to do?"

"Well, we start with what we *do* know. I'm going to make some calls today. Rebecca first, I think. Then Bancroft and Rayes, to see if I can find out who they are, what their roles were. And we need to track down this fax number to see where it leads."

"What can I do?"

"I want to speak with Rebecca myself," Patchett said, "and I want to hear what Bancroft and Rayes have to say, too. You try the fax and get back to me this afternoon."

Anne copied the number down.

"You around tomorrow?" he asked while she wrote. "I'd like to talk this out with you after hearing what these people have to say, but I can't say for sure how long it'll take to get hold of them."

"Tomorrow night," she said. She capped the pen and stuck it and the note into a pocket. "It's Saturday, so we have makeup classes during the day."

"I'll be at home," Patchett said. "Give me a call there or stop by. Does that work out all right?"

"No problem." Anne grabbed her coffee and stood to leave but paused, then turned to him. She pulled back the lock of hair that flipped across her face as she moved, and she tucked it behind an ear. She bit her lower lip before speaking, a questioning look briefly crossing her face.

"What are we talking about here, Jon?" she said. There was a note of doubt in her voice. A note of concern. "I mean, in the end?"

Patchett picked up the photograph from where Anne left it on the desk. He looked across the four men and settled on Tomlin, who still looked cheerfully away from the camera, eyes narrowed against the sun and toward something unknown.

And it was things unknown that lingered and flew in Patchett's mind. Layers upon layers of questions towering above something hidden, something buried that he wasn't sure he wanted to consider. He wondered what the path through those layers looked like.

"I guess that maybe we might be talking about murder," he

said reluctantly, looking up. He heard the overwhelming doubt in his own voice and felt a near tremor of trepidation that it triggered in him.

Anne blinked quickly. "You think Tomlin was murdered?" she said incredulously.

Patchett considered it again, staring at the picture, still thinking about everything they didn't know. "I think," he said slowly, "that Dr. Tomlin was working on this project despite what Clifton says. I think Tomlin was working on something that supposedly didn't exist." The image of Tomlin's dark and cold office came to him, the papers gone, the shattered window with the blood and hair at its sharp edge.

"And I think that Alexander Tomlin, or anybody else, wouldn't have the strength to break out that window in his office. It was an inch thick, Anne," he said, and he looked up at her again, studying her dark blue eyes for a reaction, a confirmation of his own tentative questions. "No more than five by six or seven feet. It would've taken something, some kind of tool or weapon, to break that out, and there wasn't one around."

He thought now of all this information. "I really don't know what to think beyond that" was all he said in answering her question.

"Why would anyone kill him?" Anne asked.

"That's an even harder one," Patchett replied quietly, "and the truth is that I simply don't know that, either. But we're not done. Not yet. We still have a few other people to talk to." He was speaking cautiously, listening to his own words, not sure if he liked what he heard. Not sure if it was *right*.

"And then?" Anne asked, and Patchett looked up at her a final time.

"Then we'll figure out what we have to do," he said.

24

MAGGIE WHEEZED despite the steady spring downpour, and a cough shook her. In Arizona, the rains usually began in January rushes and stretched into March scatterings. Early in the year, two, maybe three nights of rain would fall per week.

The rains would return in August, the dark clouds once again rising above Superstition Mountain to the east, pushing the dry desert air into the city on brand-hot stinging winds. The Apache who once lived in the Valley of the Sun believed the mountain was the home of the thunder gods, and the superstition came to life during the rainy season.

And it was raining now, the pounding and smattering sound of the sudden Arizona storm rattling the tin roofs of nearby sheds with the staccato barks of pellets against tin cans. The gutters were overflowing, pouring rivers into the streets in a desert city with no storm sewers.

The moisture didn't help her. Maggie's body was racked by the coughing, one hand cupped and pressed forcefully against her mouth to muffle it, to push it back inside. The other hand was fisted into her sternum, her body arched over it. She was on the floor, braced on her knees. The sound was dry and almost absent, made vacant by the repeated emptying of air from her lungs.

She knew this would pass, the fits always did, but the fear that it was a heart attack or a rupture or *something* that pounded into her chest flew through her mind. The flare of pain shooting through her and the stunning numbness that ran across her shoulders always brought that thought. But it was no heart attack. It was the bronchitis, severe and sharp and alarming, and it would pass.

Maggie had been coughing for almost an hour and was on the floor for half of that. Ever since she got out of bed — actually since she was *driven* out by the pain that worked her every morning — she'd been coughing.

The usual glass of water didn't help. She threw that up five minutes after getting it down. The slick puddle still on the floor showed the streak of red that was more and more common in the various fluids she coughed up. There was a matching stain on the floor of the bathroom, an attack from the previous night that had kept her off the street for the first time in a month. She didn't have the energy to clean it up, and it sat there as a cruel reminder of the debilitating force of a recurrence.

It came in waves that way. For the last two months, Maggie's energy came in frustrating ebbs and flows, in direct relation to the spasms of coughing. More ebbs recently, she thought, but the cough itself was now slowly dying. She tipped forward to rest on her hands, then leaned over to sit on one thin hip before lying down. She wiped the back of a hand across an ashen and sweat-beaded forehead. Her breath was grating but calm, and Maggie almost fell asleep, eyes dropping closed in the long-awaited respite.

The thunder boomed distantly over the mountain as she rested, the sound for a moment muffling the first soft knock on the door. When the knock came once more, sounding out after the thunder died and competing only with the steady wash of the rain, it startled her. She rolled to look up at the door.

She was expecting no one and in fact knew only two people well enough for them to know where she lived. She tried to remember if she'd scheduled a trick. She sometimes did that, but she knew that this wasn't one of those times. Any john she got these days was found on the street; no regulars had come back for months.

The knock came again, and Maggie lay down on the floor, her head resting on one arm. She would not answer it. She didn't know who it was, and she didn't have the energy to find out. The coughing over, Maggie wanted only to rest. For a minute maybe, or maybe all day.

The thought of work tonight came to her, and she ignored it along with the knocking. Maggie slept the uneasy sleep of the sick. Her breath wheezed.

The big man knocked again, the third time. When there was still no answer, he glanced at the scrap of paper in his hand, checking the address. It was the right place, and he tucked the slip into the inside pocket on his sport coat. His hand graced the hard steel butt of a semiautomatic tucked under one arm.

He moved away with no glance back. If she wasn't there, then she wasn't there. There was no use parading his face around for no reason, given the circumstances.

In the parking lot, he slipped behind the wheel of his rental, running a hand through wet close-cropped hair, and he slumped his large and broad frame down slightly in the seat. He watched the door of the building closely, eyes never turning away.

The address in his pocket came from a contact who hadn't been wrong before. Maggie Washburn lived in that apartment, he felt certain, and she would show up sooner or later.

When she did, he would kill her. He didn't know exactly how that would play out right now, but he was confident that it would happen.

The man was as confident of that as he was of his ability to do it. He was asked personally to do this, and he was asked because of his "unique abilities." He'd heard that with his own ears.

Your unique abilities. The words still rang.

Those unique abilities consisted of precisely one skill that had proven valuable within the past few months — the man was an excellent hunter. For virtually all his twenty-four years, the big man was a hunter. Rifle, bow, pistol, even a crossbow a couple of times. And that experience had made him valuable recently.

Because of your unique abilities.

The list he had originally been given was eighteen names long, but some select pruning had shrunk it to just three. The man thought that Grant was probably off it already, too, although he'd heard secondhand that Rowe Weber was still scurrying to find Mr. Grant. If Grant was gone, as the big man expected, that'd leave only two, and Maggie Washburn was first up on deck.

He stared out from the car like a hunter in a blind, shadows dropping across his face. He looked first to see if anyone else might be watching Maggie's building. Watching as he himself was. Waiting for her maybe, as he himself was. He thought he'd seen that after Jesse Cole. Moving down that alleyway after killing the boy, the man thought he'd caught sight of someone watching in the distance. And so he checked for someone now. He was, after all, an excellent hunter, and he needed to keep attentive to everything around him. Given the circumstances.

He looked at the building only after scanning the parking lot. He tried to pick out Maggie's window, watching for any movement —any twitching or passing of shadows. She'd be there soon, he knew.

Until then, he could wait.

25

"Rebecca Cartaway, please."

"One moment."

Patchett heard the click of hold and then only silence after that while he waited. The photograph of the four men still sat before him, and he tapped at it with a finger. He was studying the background, trying to make out the mountains or bluffs or what-ever they were that edged into the hazed sky. They stood a distant purple-red above the men's heads. Miles off in a place that looked as though it would make even the slightest distance impassable.

"This is Rebecca."

"Ms. Cartaway. Jon Patchett," he said, snapping his mind back out of the desert. "I left a note for you last night? Asking to talk to you?"

"Yes, Mr. Patchett, I got it."

Patchett felt himself ease just knowing that Clifton hadn't found the note. "I was hoping we could speak about Alex Tomlin," he said.

There was a slight pause on the line. "I'm really not sure what I could tell you about him."

"Well, it's my understanding, Ms. Cartaway, that you and Mr. Tomlin had something of a relationship. I'd like to talk with you about that."

Patchett waited eagerly for a response, hoping that Anne was right and that he wasn't making a fool of himself. Hoping that Rebecca in any event wouldn't just deny it before saying good-bye with a slam of the phone. "Are you available this afternoon?" he asked.

There was a longer hesitation on Rebecca's end, and Patchett heard the kind of muffled conversation that can only come through a covered phone. Rebecca was talking to someone else.

"I'm afraid that won't be possible, Mr. Patchett," she said when she came back on the line. Patchett felt his blood rush, and he pictured Clifton standing over her shoulder. Standing there and giving instructions mingled with poorly veiled threats.

"I see," he said slowly. "Then maybe you'd be available tomorrow sometime?"

"No, sir. Actually, I won't be able to take any time here at all. We're incredibly busy this morning, what with the FDA's call. We'll all be in tomorrow, too."

Patchett shot forward in the chair as she said it. He caught the ever-present cup with an elbow and it rocketed off the desk, delivering a spray of orange against the wall.

"The FDA?"

"Yes," she said, a cautious and uncertain sound in her voice. "I assumed that everyone there already heard."

"Heard *what?*" Patchett asked, almost snapping at her. "What did it say?"

"The FDA told Dr. Weber that it was preparing to announce approval for Phase Three, at our earliest convenience, or something like that. That means tomorrow for Dr. Weber, of course. The place is going a little crazy trying to organize the conference, responses, and all that and still trying to begin scheduling the new testing procedures."

"Well, what about a —" Patchett stopped himself as he heard Rebecca cover the phone to speak again to someone else.

"Is there any way to get together away from the office?" he said when she returned, as calmly as he could manage. "It's really very important."

There was a final moment of nervous silence as Rebecca considered this. "I should be home around eight tonight," she said.

Patchett dug frantically through the various scraps of paper in front of him, searching for and finding the address that Anne had given him. "Old Shakopee Road?"

"I'm at my parents' now," she said instantly. "I moved out of Alex's apartment. I assume you knew it was Alex's."

Patchett felt the embarrassment common to his intrusive profession. "Yes."

She gave him the address.

"Thank you, Ms. Cartaway," he said, but she had already hung up.

26

WEBER STOOD watching out the window in his office, puffing at his pipe, adding to the low-level cloud of blue smoke that hung and twisted above his head, the sunlight streaming through the window and catching in it.

He was smoking more frequently now and had been for the past few months. Both the delicately pungent scent of the tobacco and the deadening effect of the smoke eased the slight case of nerves that Weber was uncharacteristically experiencing recently.

But no more. He hoped, anyway, with the sense of relief washing coolly over him even as he ran the FDA's message through his mind again. He drew at the pipe and glanced away from the scene outside, looking down at the carpet. He saw a small frayed area, and he made a mental note to have it fixed before realizing that he soon wouldn't care about frayed carpets or anxious nerves or projects, reports, analyses, or any of the other fucking little nuisances that seeped from the very pores of the building that towered around him.

The world has shifted once more, he thought. It shifted almost while no one was watching.

Rowe smiled at that idea even as he lifted the sheet of paper to read the actual words. It was a fax, one of dozens he received daily in an annoying age of instantaneous telecommunication. But this one, Rowe thought, this one was changing his life — his life *and* the world — like no other.

At its top was the number of the Food and Drug Administration, and the copy was on FDA stationery. "We are pleased," it began, and he smiled instantly even at that, "we are pleased to confirm that the Administration has granted approval for Phase III testing to begin on the above-referenced application. This phase will consist of double-blind control group studies with human participants, to begin at your earliest convenience. A formal announcement will be made at your instruction within the week, schedules permitting. Additional information will follow."

It was signed by the assistant deputy secretary. She'd called Weber that morning, and the fax had followed. Rowe had been smiling pretty much ever since, the satisfaction at finally reading those words thrilling him.

He turned back into the room, still grinning, still enjoying the unavoidable feel of success — of *life* — coursing through him. Despite the coldness outside, despite the darkness that seemed to wrap around the world for the past months, winter was ending, the sunlight streaming in behind him through the smoke and casting his cut-out shadow along the floor in a stretched and flat effigy.

Winter was ending. Gradually, the world was slipping out of that bond.

It was time to move.

27

ERIC BANCROFT'S private line was ringing, and that surprised him. He tried to imagine who it would be but couldn't. The number had been changed after his wife kicked him out of their house almost eight months ago. Once gone, he didn't want to consider looking back, so he'd severed that cord as cleanly as possible.

It wouldn't be his father, either. He was in the Virgin Islands on some old-timers' cruise, probably screwing as many old ladies as he could lay his hands on and maybe a few young ones, too. Bancroft had heard from him just a couple of days ago.

But the only others who knew this number were a few people at Weber, and he didn't expect them to be calling. The phone rang a third time, and Bancroft thought maybe they were calling to discuss the FDA letter.

He held a copy of the fax in front of him. It had arrived about an hour ago, with a note scrawled across the bottom: "Came this A.M. Things looking good all around. I'll call soon." Bancroft hadn't thought that "soon" would be within an hour.

He pulled himself with a grunt off the low couch and moved to the phone sitting on his desk. He tugged at his pants as he walked, hitching them up higher under the massive stomach. Eric Bancroft's pants were perpetually dropping or being pushed down by the various bulges on his body so that they habitually sagged across his butt like windless sails or sheets on a clothesline. He scratched a finger through a jowly set of chins as he picked up the phone.

" 'Lo?" he said. He propped a heavy thigh on one edge of the desk, ignoring the sound as the desk creaked a slight protest at one front corner.

"Dr. Bancroft?"

Bancroft felt an immediate twinge of nervous suspicion. No

one calling on this line would call him "Dr. Bancroft," and he didn't recognize this man's voice.

"Yes?" he said. The tenor of doubt was audible across the line with the unintended apprehension in his voice.

"My name is Jon Patchett, sir, and I'm calling from Minneapolis. I'm an attorney here, doing some investigatory work for Weber BioTech. I'm calling because your name came up in conjunction with some work you might have done on a Weber vaccine called Prohiva. I'm sure you've heard of it."

Bancroft quickly found his voice and responded. "I never worked on Prohiva," he said. Probably too abrupt and too loud, he realized, but he'd spoken it almost without thinking. "How'd you get this number, Mr. —"

"Patchett. Jon Patchett. I found this number in the working papers of a Dr. Alexander Tomlin, who was a Weber researcher."

"I know who he is, Mr. Patchett."

"You've worked with him, then?"

Bancroft mentally ran through the possible explanations for Tomlin's having his number and instantly discarded them one by one. "I said I know him," he said instead. "Not that I worked with him. What's this about?"

"Well, doctor," Patchett replied, "I'll be frank with you — I'm not really sure what this is about." There was a pause, and Bancroft could hear a door closing on Patchett's end. "Dr. Tomlin is dead, sir. Were you aware of that?"

"No, I wasn't," Bancroft said, trying to hit the appropriate note of mixed surprise and remorse. "How?"

"He took his own life. And to make the story short, the company has asked me to chase through Dr. Tomlin's papers to make sure there's nothing that needs to be addressed in the FDA application process because of his death. You said you have heard of Prohiva, correct?" Patchett was swinging to a tone of cross-examination by force of habit.

"Of course, Mr. Patchett. I do read."

"Certainly. I'm sorry. But I believe you said you didn't work on that vaccine with Dr. Tomlin?"

"That's right."

Bancroft wiped at his brow as he listened to the still line. The air was heavy with the humidity of a spring rain, and it sat on his skin in a clammy, slick coat.

"Then I'm afraid I'm somewhat confused, sir," the attorney said, the sound of his voice confirming his words.

"How's that, Mr. Patchett?"

"Well, doctor, your name shows up on a document that refers to a Lot 179. Now, I assumed that this lot number referred to Prohiva, but you've said you didn't work on Prohiva."

"That's correct. Twice now, I think."

"Yes, sir. Twice." More empty air. "Do you recall any Lot 179 on other projects on which you worked with Dr. Tomlin?"

Bancroft hesitated, learning a quick lesson from the attorney's deliberate pace. He considered the easy lie but knew with brutal clarity that tying Lot 179 to something else would be far worse than a simple disclaimer.

"No," he said, "I don't recall any Lot 179 at all."

"But you did work on other projects with Dr. Tomlin, isn't that right?"

Bancroft hadn't seen that in the question, and he jumped immediately to deny it before catching himself first. He honestly couldn't even remember if he'd already admitted having worked with Tomlin or not.

"Yes," he said, opting for the truth with eyes closed. He'd almost created a longer loose thread. He couldn't really deny working with Tomlin. The phone number was in the guy's damn notes.

"What would that work have been on?"

Bancroft's imagination rattled through a dozen possibilities and selected the one that seemed most plausible, given his location. "Tuberculosis," he said, and the sound was of incongruous relief at finding anything at all to say. "Dr. Tomlin was considering work on a genetic treatment for tuberculosis."

"Tuberculosis," Patchett repeated in the voice of someone writing something down. "That would fit," he added for good measure. "Was that work down there?"

The doctor struggled to think of the myriad implications from this question and decided to avoid it instead.

"Mr. Patchett, what's the relevance of all this to your concerns or to approval for this, this Prohiva?"

"Actually, doctor," the attorney said slowly, thoughtfully, "I was wondering the same thing. You see, I'm just trying to find out what Dr. Tomlin was working on the last few months. If it wasn't Prohiva, then there's nothing to tell the FDA."

"It wasn't Prohiva," Bancroft said. "Not when he was here with me."

"And that would have been . . . when, sir?"

Bancroft shifted the phone to his other hand and rubbed at his face. The hand came away soaked, a line of water running down it, onto his wrist, and dropping to make a wet dot on his pant leg.

"December," he said. The truth. Or at least half of it. It was the only answer he could give, and he knew it. He wondered if Patchett knew it, too.

"Do you do any other work for Weber BioTech, Dr. Bancroft?"

"I should explain," Bancroft said, and he backtracked by the seat of his pants to fill in details. "I didn't actually do any research work with Dr. Tomlin. We briefly discussed doing something in terms of the tuberculosis thing, but it never came together."

"Could you tell me how you got together in the first place?"

The doctor recognized the long hallway of lies that this question pointed him down, and he stepped outside of it. "Mr. Patchett," he said, his voice as heavy as his body, "I'm afraid I'm going to have to cut this short. I've got a very pressing meeting in a few minutes."

The silence from the other end of the line was somewhat longer this time. "I understand perfectly, Dr. Bancroft." Bancroft thought maybe the attorney's voice was slightly changed in that statement, but Patchett was going on. "Just one more question, though, if I could."

"Certainly." Bancroft desperately wanted to hang up and end this conversation.

"Do you know a Dr. Marcus Clifton?"

Bancroft hesitated again. He already admitted knowing, meeting with, Tomlin. He didn't see how he could really deny knowing Clifton. But he tried. As he spoke, he wondered if his phone number was also in Clifton's files, and he hoped that it wasn't.

"I know of Dr. Clifton, Mr. Patchett. As I said, I *do* read. But I've never had the pleasure of meeting him. Is he still at Weber?"

"He is," Patchett said. "Perhaps you'll have the opportunity to meet him sometime in the future."

"Perhaps," Bancroft said.

"For now, sir, I'd like to thank you for your time." The conversation was mercifully coming to a close.

"Of course."

Bancroft hung up the phone, then dragged it over to the couch. He lay down heavily, his form creating a canyon in the oversoft padding of the couch as he dialed a number from memory. He had some concerns about why an attorney was calling him with questions to which he didn't know the correct answers. Very troublesome, very knowing questions.

He was on a burn as the call began ringing through.

Patchett stared at the phone with a swirling look of stunned disbelief and bitter disappointment. Bancroft had thrown up a nest of lies, and Patchett knew that the slightest breath of truth could push it aside. *Leaving what?* he wondered, and he found that he didn't know.

"You lying shit," he whispered tightly.

He took no notes during the conversation. He hadn't needed to. Everything Bancroft said, every word of which Patchett was convinced was made up on the spot, was firm in Patchett's memory.

Patchett shook his head disgustedly as he read the other card and punched in the phone number. The sound chirped across a speaker and filled his office, and he set the card aside and fixed his gaze out the window at the cloudy sky. The smooth belly of the clouds from last night had rippled and broken up, and the sun cut across the city, steadily eating the thin layer of snow.

"Canyonlands Hospital."

"Dr. Rayes, please."

"I'm sorry. Dr. Rayes isn't in yet. May I take a message and have him call you?"

Patchett looked at the clock; 10:30, it would be 9:30 in Utah. The days apparently began late in the desert. But Rayes was a doctor, after all.

"When do you expect him in?"

"I'm not really sure. Would you like to try to reach him on his cellular phone?"

"Please." Patchett wanted to talk to Rayes as soon as possible, and Bancroft, he already feared, might have had the same idea. The receptionist gave him the number, and Patchett wrote it down and thanked her, still watching as the clouds dissolved a little more before his eyes, the blue sky fighting back and the sunlight slipping through.

He began to dial.

"I . . ." Bancroft sputtered before there was yet another interruption from the other end of the line. "I . . ." he began again. Then, "He . . ." A final pause. "He knew enough," Bancroft finally managed, trying to sound firm but knowing he was failing.

Eric Bancroft was a malleable man. A follower, not a leader. Everyone who dealt with him knew it, just as he knew it himself in the rare introspective moments he experienced. He was malleable, and he was therefore subject to being cowed. Even given the geographic distance between the participants in the conversation, even given the fact that Bancroft himself started this call full of hot self-righteousness and anger, he was being cowed now.

"He fully explained who he was and what he was doing," he was saying, his words already less sharp, more reticent and cautious. "I just . . ." He waited for silence from the other end, then started again. "I just want to know how he got my name," he said. It sounded almost calm. "That's all," he added quietly.

He listened to an explanation that didn't really explain, knowing that it didn't matter anyway.

"Yes," he said then. And again, "Yes." And finally, "Yes, I . . . I understand.

"I understand," he said. The line died.

•

The connection was amazingly poor. Despite all the progress on communications, Patchett thought, the trumpeting of capabilities was muted by the realities of the packed airwaves of 1996. Rayes's voice alternated from perfect clarity to a switch-hitting session between a Salt Lake City radio station and what seemed to be a third party's call from New York.

"Who did you say you were?" Rayes was asking. Patchett thought he heard the rumble of an engine, one that needed tuning, and he realized that Rayes was speaking to him from a car. No great wonder that reception was bad.

"Jon Patchett, an attorney in Minneapolis." He was almost shouting to be heard, his voice trying and obviously failing to cut through the static that floated intermittently across the line. "I'm calling about Dr. Alexander Tomlin."

There was a sudden burst of noise and Patchett swore as he reached to break the connection and try again, but Rayes's voice cut back through the sound. It was unexpectedly crisp, and Patchett looked up, half expecting to find the doctor in the room with him.

"What about him?" Rayes asked. Patchett could hear the soft Hispanic accent that lilted his voice.

"He's dead," Patchett replied. Simple. Straightforward. To the point. He'd walked carefully around Bancroft; he'd go directly at Rayes.

"I know," Rayes said, and the line erupted again with a combination of static and the distantly rumbling echo of the car engine.

"How well did you know him?" Patchett spoke slowly and as clearly as possible.

"What is that to you, Mr. Patchett?"

It was the one question that Patchett was certainly expecting, and he launched again into his recitation of Weber's original request for someone to look into Tomlin's death. He breezed through it as a now well-known tale, wondering how much of it actually filtered through to Rayes's car, traveling somewhere across the desert almost two thousand miles away.

"I did not work on it," Rayes said when Patchett finished.

Rayes's language carried the precise enunciation, the smooth rhythm of years of practice and training, but Patchett still hesitated at the doctor's response, surprised at the anticipation in it. Patchett was no further than reporting Weber's assignment and had asked no questions, but Rayes was already giving him answers.

"Excuse me?" the attorney said, thinking he hadn't heard right.

"I did not work on it," Rayes repeated. His voice was suddenly even clearer as the connection lightened. It burst over the phone in the steady and structured pace of one accustomed to dealing with poor phone connections.

"Prohiva," he said. "I had nothing to do with it." The answer carried the hallmarks of what Patchett recognized might be coached responses — too quick and too thoughtless. Too easy.

"That's fine, doctor," Patchett said, jotting a note, "but I'm actually more interested in anything else you might have worked on with Dr. Tomlin."

He knew there was no point in overemphasizing Prohiva in speaking with Rayes. Flags would probably be flying soon if they weren't already, and Patchett in any case knew perfectly well that Rayes had worked on Prohiva, despite what the doctor told him. The picture, the fax, the conversations with Clifton and Bancroft all told enough of the story that Rayes himself lied to avoid. The four men were in the desert to work on something related to the vaccine. Patchett didn't need to know that now. He only needed to know what that work was.

"I ran into him down here late last year sometime," Rayes was saying. "We talked about a couple of projects."

Patchett tried to imagine how that discussion would have gone. One of the top geneticists in the country was just chatting about projects with a clinic doctor from Kanab, Utah? The attorney chalked the unlikely picture up as a tale that no one had thought through, that no one probably ever thought would be uttered.

"A tuberculosis project?"

Rayes's end of the conversation grew almost ominously still. "No," he said finally. Even against the slowly returning static, Patchett could hear the unsure tone. He found himself trying to guess just how Dr. Rayes felt right now as he rolled across the desert, confronting questions that he obviously hadn't thought would be asked.

"Can you remember any of those projects then, sir?"

The answer was lost in the flurry, but Patchett didn't really need to hear it to ask his next question.

"Have you ever heard of a Lot 179, Dr. Rayes?" He smiled as the rasping of the open line surged and abated without other sound. Rayes was clearly trying to think it through, but the pause was too long.

"I do not recall any specific discussions of lots or anything. We talked only generally about the types of research in which he was involved."

Any quick and firm ease that Rayes earlier displayed was gone. In the space of less than a minute, the doctor had gone from answering unasked questions to guessing at answers to others, his tone haunted with the constant edge of hesitation. The characteristic signs, Patchett knew, of unexpected discovery.

He questioned how old Rayes would be and, remembering the picture, guessed he was maybe thirty-three or thirty-four. He would be fairly early in his medical career and was, Patchett hoped, even earlier in a potentially criminal one. The attorney felt almost sorry, and it came to him with uneasy certainty that Alfre Rayes's life might well be headed in quite another direction already. It swung that clearly in the last minute. Just as clearly, Patchett knew that he would have to talk with this man directly, face-to-face, to learn what he really needed to know. Perhaps to give him the chance to swing it back, if that was still possible.

"I can't thank you enough for your time," Patchett said quietly, setting his pen aside and turning again to gaze out the window. He watched a plane rise from the ground and move steadily toward an unreached point of disappearance in the sky.

He supposed that Rayes hadn't heard him, but the doctor spoke nonetheless. "I am sorry if I could not be of more help." His voice, too, sounded quiet. The static died out as Rayes hung up, and Patchett studied the sky until the plane slipped entirely from his sight above the clouds.

I will see you soon, he thought to himself. He wondered what the desert was like in March.

28

THE BARBER took a break. As always, he set aside his work at precisely 3:30, stacking it carefully in a short column to one side, and he walked slowly to the bathroom. He would sit there for ten minutes.

His life had been structured in this same way for as long as he could recall. His mother long ago taught him about regularity in your life and how important it was, and it was a lesson he learned very well. Amazingly well. He learned all his lessons well.

No goddamned messes, he reminded himself even at thinking that.

His mother was a brilliant and loving woman, he thought, full of information and wisdom to pass on to her only child. And she was a tough bitch, too, he added as an afterthought. She'd died only after a sixth blow from the tire iron that he wielded with a vengeance that day. She was a wonderful woman. He still missed her sometimes.

The one other woman who was ever as important to him was Kimberly. She'd moved in next door to him a few years ago, and he loved her instantly, in the intense and distant way that only truly terrifying love can be. At one point, he looked for her every day for three weeks straight. Whenever he was at his apartment back then, he listened for her and watched to get even a glimpse of her long, smooth hair. Her beautiful hair.

And when he actually met her? Actually spoke with her? Even now, it seemed that he was only watching, not really talking with her and hearing the lyrical sound of her laugh.

A laugh? With him?

And it wasn't so bad for a time after that. Just being with her, seeing the hair grace and frame her features in a smooth and shimmering flow, hearing her voice and touching her lightly.

Then there was the relationship that followed. An amazing mixed bag of her loveliness intertwined inextricably with his own insecurities, with his ultimate fear of losing her to one of the myriad men she must come across and win over with her beauty each day.

A year and a half. A short time to him, but one marked with all the highest and lowest points of his life. To her, he imagined, it must have eventually seemed interminable. Her beauty, her life — everything she offered — had been trapped with him.

And in the end, she was even tougher than his mother. *In more ways than one*, he thought now. He'd beaten Kimberly to death. It took nearly an hour.

He still remembered that afternoon in her apartment — *or was it his?* — a measuring cup clenched in one of his hands to hold something he'd been borrowing. The coolness of the room's air conditioning chilled him occasionally even now. There was the light smell of flowers from the daffodils in a vase on the butcher-block dinette table. The place mat beneath the flowers was a shocking turquoise, in contrast to the luminous yellow color of the blossoms.

Not her flowers, though, he remembered then. His. She gave them to him that day, and so it would have been his home. Or maybe *their* home.

Maybe.

The picture of Kimberly in his mind was etched clearly as well, her body prone on the kitchen floor, feet near the stove, head next to the refrigerator. One moment she was laughing, head tipped back. The next, there was an enormous amount of blood, an unthinkable pool of it. Each blow from the rolling pin that he had used sprayed the blood across the white enamel surfaces of the appliances, painting them with red leopard spots.

But her hair. What he remembered most was her hair, and he shook at the image now. When he'd touched it, the blood drained down it and dripped onto the floor, staining a red track across his wrist. He had ruined her beautiful, *fucking* hair.

No goddamned messes! He forgot that lesson that one time, but he wouldn't forget it again — he was more careful after that. Ever so much more careful. With each of the others, he took his time. There were no more goddamned messes, certainly.

He thought of the last one and felt the excitement begin to build within him. When he thought of the red strands of hair still hidden in the night stand at home, waiting to be worked, twisted, tied, he began to harden. He reached down and took hold of himself, wishing he could see that hair once more right now. Wanting to feel it tickle across his body.

His mother once warned him against this, too, and she whipped his hand the one time she caught him. She used a razor strop, and he didn't know what that was then, but the memory of his swollen and painfully immobile fingers still hung with him. "This'll teach you," she'd said. "Never," she added after that.

His mother had loved him enough to tell him those things, and he remembered them still. But she was dead within a week of that day.

He supposed it was odd that he wasn't seriously suspected in the investigation that followed. Nor in the one that trailed on Kimberly's death a few years later. But it was a violent world. He told one of the officers just exactly that, when asked about break-ins during the questions about his mother's death.

The image of the officer's sharply pressed, incredibly and precisely crisp blue uniform was intact in his memory along with the other pictures. The gun and club strapped to hips, the bland and vaguely bored questions of a young man who carried himself with the shield-shaped badge of artificially imposed importance.

"Any break-ins lately?" the officer had asked. He was writing in a small blue pad with a small blue pen that the Barber remembered very well. The policeman asked the question because the locks on the house were splintered away from the door frame. But the Barber did that himself. After Mom but before the police.

"All the time," he told the officer. His voice had quavered

slightly. "It's a violent area. It's a violent world." He'd shaken his head and, for his mother, worked up a few tears. The young policeman understood. He went on his precise, unwrinkled way, and the Barber never saw him again.

But he learned another lesson from that. His mother taught him never to lie, but the officer taught him that you didn't have to lie if they didn't ask the right questions. The officer didn't ask the right questions. It was a very valuable lesson.

The Barber's head began to swim a little as his pulse accelerated, and he began, as usual, to think about the women whose hair had run through his fingers. It would happen again soon, he knew.

This weekend maybe. There might be more people around, but he could find someone alone. He was pretty sure he could find someone. He would say good-bye to winter the right way.

The excitement built as he thought about that, and his feet trembled against the small tiles of the bathroom floor.

He thought of beautiful hair.

29

As HE STUDIED the city, watching the steady outbound stream of end-of-day traffic building throughout the late afternoon, Patchett was contemplating whether Rayes or Bancroft was the weak link in the chain. There always was one, he knew, and he figured here it was Rayes. Both men were poor liars, so it came down to determining which would be the most persistent liar. The other one by process of elimination was to be the door through which Patchett would have to find any answers to his questions.

He was thinking through the documents one more time, puzzling over Lew Franck's possible role. Franck had spent six hours with the materials before Patchett was able to touch them. Not enough time to fully review them and far too much if you were only collating them. But Patchett thought that six hours might be just enough to study a few key areas that you already knew. A few hours to do that and another couple to pull out certain assorted items, maybe. Maybe throw in a little time to discuss it before pulling papers.

Discuss it with whom? Rayes and Bancroft would be involved, he imagined. Maybe or maybe not Clifton, too, although Patchett knew that his opinion on that was clouded more by personal dislike than by anything resembling evidence. Kenneth Miller stood an outside chance also. Maybe even Rowe Weber himself, for that matter. The truth was that anyone at Weber BioTech could have gotten in the files. Anyone there could be involved.

It was at that point, his mind tracing every suspicion, that Patchett looked up and noticed Ben Flare standing over him.

"Tomlin?" Flare asked.

Patchett nodded and set his notes from the conversation with Clifton on the stack of materials nearest him. The pad covered the picture of the four men.

"Find anything?"

Patchett almost told the whole story in a cathartic rush, but caution overcame him. *Know what you're saying,* he warned himself. *Know it well.* He fully understood all the implications inherent in an attack on a partner's biggest client. He didn't like those implications.

"Maybe," he said, squinting up at Flare and nonchalantly rolling down first one sleeve, then the other. He calmly and methodically buttoned the cuff of each as he spoke. "Nothing too definite, though. I'll know better by Monday."

"You won't be on this by Monday," Flare said, and Patchett froze. Flare's face was set sternly, gray hair flanking granite features.

"What's wrong?" Patchett asked. Flare's look drove away thoughts of Rayes, Clifton, Bancroft—all of them—as Patchett abruptly considered the stability of his job. Flare's tone didn't sound like removal from a case or assignment. It sounded like removal from the firm. Patchett questioned at the same time if he should be more concerned, but that consideration was driven away by the sudden crack in Flare's stony face. The partner smiled.

"Lew Franck just called," he said, pausing for effect. *Lew*

Franck probably destroys evidence, Patchett thought instantly and unavoidably during the brief silence that followed that statement. *Lew Franck may be a liar*, he added after that. All the questions blazed back into life at the mention of Franck's name.

"The FDA has approved Prohiva for Phase Three," Flare went on. An enormous grin now spread across his face, one that Patchett had otherwise seen only when Flare was bullshitting over the girlie magazines.

Patchett forced a smile and avoided telling Flare that he already knew this news. He should have passed it on, and Flare would be pissed that he hadn't.

"Great," Patchett said, but he doubted that he sounded as though he meant it. Flare didn't appear to notice. He leaned against the far wall, arms crossed over his chest in a well-satisfied look.

"The formal announcement will come tomorrow. Rowe wanted it as soon as possible, and the FDA's open to doing it that way." Patchett nodded, not knowing how else to respond. He rocked uneasily in his chair, tipping it on its back legs.

The smile on Flare's face deadened a bit, and his brow dropped as he studied Patchett. "You should be happier, Jon. You put a lot of work into this. Besides, it gets you off the hook on Tomlin."

The chair stopped rocking. "How's that?" Patchett said, confused.

"It's done," Flare replied. "It's all done. The FDA obviously doesn't care about him."

"Did it even know?" Patchett asked immediately.

Flare shrugged. "I don't know if that should concern us," he said, taken aback by Patchett's reaction. Flare's smile was totally gone, replaced by the startled look of pinched eyebrows. His voice was stern and level. "It doesn't matter now anyway," he continued slowly. "This thing is home free." He turned and stepped to the door. Patchett stood and moved around the desk.

"I'd like to follow up on this still, Ben," he said, and Flare froze in the doorway. He turned to Patchett, standing now beside the desk.

"What do you know, Jon?" he asked softly.

"Nothing." The lie was surprisingly automatic and easy and, Patchett thought nervously, not remarkably far from the truth. "I just don't believe in leaving things half done."

Flare studied him with a careful eye, hesitating at the request, an unusual one for Patchett. The partner seemed to consider it for a moment, his mouth hanging open as if ready to speak, then he bit softly at his lip in a look of difficult decision. "Leave this half done," he said. "We'll have enough to do on this without chasing down dead men."

Patchett considered objecting but hesitated himself, then retreated, bringing a bare smile back to Flare's face with a just-right "okay" and a nod of the head. "It's done."

"Great," Flare said, and he was gone down the hall.

Patchett sat with a sigh, head in hands, fingers knotting in frustration through his hair as he silently assessed his options. He supposed he was as relieved as he was upset in the end. After all, given the potential complications, he knew that he should be thankful this was over.

But even as he was thinking that, something unseen and unknown tugged at whatever semblance of a conscience he kept despite his job. It was the questions, he knew. All the questions and mysteries suddenly surrounding him. Suddenly surrounding Alexander Tomlin and Marc Clifton and, above all, Weber BioTech and its precious vaccine. The client and its work. The *firm's* work.

He'd started with a small mystery and pieced together what he could, and it pointed only to all the new mysteries, all the new questions. A rank of them, seemingly stretching without end.

But now done, he warned himself. *Any questions no longer matter.* But those reminders were already growing weaker in his mind with each passing second.

It wasn't done, he knew, because he couldn't *let* it be done. He felt the compulsion of wanting to know more and knowing at the same time that it might just be important for him to do exactly that.

As Patchett looked up and out the window once more, feeling the rush of excitement that descends at recognition that he was doing what he thought was best, what he thought was right, he already knew that he would meet with Rebecca tonight. Would do it *despite* Flare. And he would learn what he could from her, would discuss it with Anne tomorrow night, and then they could be in Las Vegas on Sunday or Monday.

Before he could simply walk away from this, he needed to talk with Rayes and Bancroft face-to-face. He wanted to see these men and judge them better. Patchett himself was surprised at the drive behind that thought, at the unusual push in him to do something, anything, beyond the usual routine responses he'd grown accustomed to.

And whatever it was he would do, it needed to be soon. An FDA announcement tomorrow, and who knew what would come next. He wondered how long it would take to initiate the Phase III studies. A week at least, he assumed, to prepare the vaccine and distribute it. He had that week, at the outside.

"One week," he said to himself, rising and stepping to the window. The actual sound of that deadline echoing in his ears and against the office's walls unnerved him, and he instantly doubted again whether he should — maybe whether he *could* — do what he was contemplating. Whether he would find anything in the end or merely play out some foolishness he'd conceived. Whether any of that would matter.

Patchett tugged at the drawstring on the blinds, and they dropped closed with a clatter, hiding his own reflected image away.

One week.

"Is this the Bateman 24-Hour Copy Center?"

It took twenty minutes just to track down this latest phone number. The exchange on the fax led only to northern Arizona, and Anne couldn't narrow it down any more for directory assistance. So she asked them to check virtually every town or roadside stop in the area for the copy center. A rash of red X's dotted the map spread in front of her, ruling out points of population based on a toneless operator's rejections. Anne said a quiet prayer that this was the right place.

"Yes, it is."

She asked for the fax number, her heart pounding with each digit read back to her. When the last one matched the number in her notes, it was like hitting the lottery.

"Could you tell me where you're located?" Anne asked to confirm the name circled by her red marker. There was a surprising twinge of nervousness in her voice.

"Intersection of Fifteenth and North Navajo," the man at the other end said. "Next to the Burger King."

"No," Anne said, shaking her head although no one could see her. "What city?"

The clerk chuckled at the question. "Page," he answered.

"Arizona, right?"

"Just like always."

Anne hung up. Smartass.

30

THE JANITOR had worked in the Weber Building ever since it existed. An insignificant small job, of course, not like the white-coated men and women he saw each night. Some were awake, some asleep as he moved silently through the building, collecting the scraps of paper that daily littered the floor in the careless shuffle of everyday business.

Garbage, too — he emptied the garbage cans every night, replacing the liners with new ones, the opaque plastic bags even now rustling from a tab on his cart as he pushed it into the elevator. The liners wouldn't stay up right if you didn't tie them just so, he knew. Then if you put garbage in the can, the liner would collapse to the bottom, and that would make it pretty much useless. That was one of the little secrets that he learned to keep his job. Know how to tie the liner right so that it didn't fall down. You had to watch the details.

He'd learned other things, too, working at Weber. He knew that Dr. Weber up on twelve was almost always there, and he could hear him talking to all sorts of people late at night, sometimes into the morning. It was difficult to get his garbage because of that. Weber talked to scientists, doctors, lawyers, stock people, lots of others the janitor couldn't even begin to identify. You could learn only so much from one-sided snips of conversations, after all.

He also knew that Dr. Tomlin — who was dead now — was fooling around with his secretary. That one wasn't too hard to figure out at all. You could hear them every now and then, doing it in his office late at night. The first time the janitor heard that kind of muffled fightinglike sound, he didn't know what it was, and he walked right in.

"Garbage," he'd said. They always told you to identify yourself if you were walking into an office where someone was working, or if maybe you went into the ladies' room to change the toilet paper or fill the tampon machine if you worked the day shift. "Janitor," he always said then, although he didn't really know what the ladies were supposed to do if they were in there.

And he didn't really know what Dr. Tomlin and his lady friend would have done, either, because they looked pretty much immobile that night, connected as they were and all. So he moved on and came back later to get that garbage. All the times after that, whenever he heard noises coming from Dr. Tomlin's office, he picked the garbage up later.

He didn't go into Dr. Tomlin's office last Sunday night because of that. There was the fightinglike noise again, although it sounded a little different that time, as the janitor recollected. But it went on for a long time, more than an hour maybe.

He didn't collect Dr. Tomlin's garbage at all that night, but it was no big deal because Dr. Tomlin was dead the next day. Kind of strange how things work out that way sometimes. Like how he hadn't seen any garbage anyway when he peeked in later. A mess, sure, but no garbage.

He pushed the cart off the elevator and onto the cement floor of the storage room. There was only one garbage can in the room, and he moved toward it, the wheels grating against the concrete. The can was one of the big ones. He slipped its lid off and lifted it to empty the contents into the carrier on the cart. The usual array of papers tumbled out, some crumpled, some whole, some shredded. He recapped the can and set it back, rolling on.

When he first saw the vials, he thought maybe they were something new, and he moved toward the shelf, sneaking a quick glance around. He knew there'd be no one down here — there was only one person here even in the day — but he checked anyway. You had to mind the details.

He pulled the plastic-wrapped box from the shelf and stared into the stacked layers. Each box held maybe twenty-five small glass bottles, each of them capped with a shiny metal band that was centered with a red-orange rubber stopper. He read the box label carefully to see if he'd noticed the vials before.

PROHIVA, the box said, 2.5 CC. A tiny number ran underneath — LOT 512. He realized on working his way through the label that he had seen this before, but it was in the other storage room, not here, where they only kept stuff that was ready to go out. He was curious about when they moved the vials here, thinking he really should have seen them earlier.

He set the box back on the shelf, replacing it exactly as he found it. *Pay attention to details*, he reminded himself. You kept your job by minding the details. The janitor rolled the cart down the hallway.

31

REBECCA'S PARENTS, and Rebecca now, too, for that matter, lived in a middle-class haven in Golden Valley, a distinctly middle-class, close-to-the-city suburb. The houses all sat on narrow footprints in oversized lots, the winter-brown lawns stretching impossibly large around each one. It was a neighborhood of yard lights, the homes built long before more practical street lamps dotted the corners in the newer areas. Each light cast a haunting circle of yellow in front of its house, the trees occasionally breaking the glow with shadows like thin partial eclipses. The patches of light looked like ragged, cogged wheels on the yards.

Patchett was scanning the numbers, searching each house for its address and cursing the ones that were hidden in the night shadows that hung under the eaves. When he finally spotted the house he was looking for, he swung the car up the slight hill into the driveway. His headlights shone briefly across the door of a one-car garage, revealing chartreuse-shaded paint that badly needed another coat. The white trim looked better.

Patchett parked and turned the car off, stepped out, and walked to the door. Only one light was on inside, a living-room lamp visible through sheer white curtains. He could hear the television, and he caught the faint blue cast through the window.

Rebecca's father answered Patchett's knock. He was a tall man who gave his plain, angled features and the jet black color of his hair to his daughter. Patchett stuck out his hand.

"Jon Patchett. I need to speak to — "

"I know," the man said. He didn't take the hand, and Patchett lowered it, an almost apologetic look crossing his face.

"Is she here?"

"She is," Rebecca's father answered, and Patchett saw her then, over her father's shoulder at the top of the varnished wooden stairway that reached up behind the man. Out of the Weber office, away from the desks and the suits and bustle and buried here in her parents' house, Rebecca Cartaway looked like a college student home for the weekend. She wasn't Tomlin's lover here, Patchett knew. She was this man's daughter. Gone was the image of the secretary having an affair with her boss, replaced by this picture of naïve youth, still untainted by everything certain to hit her in the future. Patchett unexpectedly felt the outsider, standing on the family's porch and intruding on their seemingly simple lives in the dark and brisk night.

"May I speak with her?" He looked from daughter to father and back.

Mr. Cartaway leaned against the door edge and lowered his

voice to shut it off to everyone but Patchett. "I don't like this," he said in a harsh whisper. "I don't like it at all. I've always thought that her sleeping around with that guy was trouble — for God's sake, he was damn near my age — and now you're here to show me I'm right. But I'll tell you right now — "

"Dad?" Rebecca said from the stairs. Patchett heard the child in that word and in her tone, and he looked up at her to also see it in her sweatpants and a ratty T-shirt, her own black hair pulled back in a dangling ponytail, her eyes tired. She looked dressed for a sleepover.

"I'll tell you right now," Rebecca's father said again, his voice lower still, "she doesn't need any shit from you or anyone else. She's had enough problems with this, with all these people always pushing at her."

"Mr. Cartaway," Patchett said softly in reply, "I'm only here to ask a couple of questions. That's all. I'm not here to make trouble for Rebecca or anyone else."

Cartaway studied him and reluctantly stepped aside. He didn't even watch as Patchett walked in. He just shut the door and moved slowly back toward the glowing television in the nearby living room. Patchett saw Rebecca's mother peering at him over the back of a worn plaid-upholstered chair. Patchett smiled as warmly as he could manage, but she turned away.

"I'm just unpacking a few things upstairs," Rebecca said. "We can talk up there." She walked up, and Patchett followed.

Rebecca's room was the room of every child who returned home — a strange and slightly discomfiting mixture of the past and the present, blended together with the just-cleaned smell of sickly sweet lemon-scented furniture polish. Stuffed animals lined one wall, a Care Bear by a drape-covered window, Mickey Mouse and Pluto in another corner.

But Patchett saw a bra hanging carelessly from one bedpost before Rebecca caught it with a finger and flung it discreetly into the closet. A slightly wrinkled work skirt and jacket hung akimbo on the doorknob.

"What is it you wanted to talk about, Mr. Patchett?" Rebecca asked, but Patchett knew that they both were well aware of the answer to that question. She knelt on the floor and began to lift odds and ends from a hand-me-down cardboard box that was emblazoned with the single scratched-out word CHRISTMAS. He saw a clock, an iron, a hair dryer, an assortment of books. More boxes sat next to the stuffed animals.

"I wanted to talk about Alex Tomlin," he began, and he noticed that she didn't react at all. She would've had a chance to prepare herself this time, of course.

"What about him?"

"You two were in a relationship?"

"We were lovers, Mr. Patchett." Rebecca was stacking the books on a small dresser. Patchett saw pulp romances mixed with a peppering of mysteries. "I loved him, and I think he loved me." Her voice wavered only once, right at the end of the statement, but the attorney suddenly doubted whether she was going to make it through all of his questions.

"There was a time," she was saying, "when I thought we'd get married. Talked about it a few times, in fact."

Patchett saw the dampness well up uncontrollably in her eyes then, and he immediately hated himself for being there, for so needing the information that was locked away behind her fragile façade that he had to stand here in her room, cutting open her life. He had been talking with her less than a minute, and she was already near tears. He waited, shifting from foot to foot, uncomfortable with her too-apparent and too-raw pain.

Rebecca started to say something else but stopped. "Sorry," she said instead, and she wiped her eyes with a stretched-up sleeve of her T-shirt. He could see the wet spots darkening the cloth when she let it go.

"I told myself I wouldn't do this," she said. "I've been trying to gear up for it all day." She laughed lightly, the warbling sound of someone laughing through tears. "Didn't work." Patchett smiled a weak look of sympathy.

"Truth is," she continued, moving to a second box, "that we hadn't talked about that for quite a while."

"Why?"

"Too many problems. On both sides." She glanced up at him with a knowing look, and Patchett felt exposed, feeling as though this woman could instantly tell that he, too, had some fragilities of his own that lingered in him from better, less bitter days.

Rebecca's still-moist eyes glistened fantastically against her pale skin. She wore no makeup and needed none. *Classic good looks*, they might have called them. The simple face of a young woman made almost tragically remarkable by the events that were swirling around her.

"What kind of problems?" he asked, leaning against the wall, hands in his overcoat pockets.

Rebecca's gaze fixed on an unknown point before turning to him. The look was already duller. Drier.

"I heard my father, Mr. Patchett. He always thinks I can't hear him when he whispers to anyone, but I can. He used to whisper about the guys I dated in high school. He whispered about Alex. A *lot*. And now he's whispering to you *about* Alex. He never approved."

"Of the fact that you two were involved?"

She nodded. Patchett tried to imagine if he would approve of having a twenty-year-old daughter sleeping with her almost fifty-year-old lover. He couldn't imagine he would.

"Age problem?" he said, speaking his thought.

"Among others. He thought Alex paid attention to me because he only wanted a . . . What were his words?" She gazed at Patchett, gauging him. "I think he said that Alex was only around because he wanted a *young fuck*." She smiled now, a bittersweet one, and Patchett knew that it had taken a long time for her to reach a point where she was able to do even that.

"That's why I moved out originally," Rebecca continued. "*He wants a young fuck*, and I was gone."

"But you're back now."

"But I'm back now," she agreed, nodding. "I didn't set foot in this house for probably two years until three nights ago. Didn't speak to my father for a year and a half.

"But I frankly don't have too many other options right now," she said. "Alex paid for my apartment, and the pay at Weber stinks. At least for secretaries. So I couldn't afford to stay there, and I don't think I have the energy to find another place or the roommate that I'd probably need to pay for it." She was unpacking without watching, moving the various small pieces of her life from their small boxes back into this small room.

"I'm only twenty," she said. "I don't really have the resources I should have to be out there alone. On the other hand, I'm *already* twenty, and I'm moving back into my parents' house. Pretty pathetic, huh?"

It was a question he didn't want to answer. "Mind if I sit?" he asked instead.

"Sure, sorry, go ahead." She gestured at the bed, which was the only place to sit down, and Patchett pulled off his coat and sat. The bed was the overly soft kind common to kids' rooms, and it would've killed anyone over twenty-five who slept on it. He sank deep into the mattress.

"What about on his side?" he asked.

"What do you mean?" She was on her third box, and she turned light blue eyes back to him as she stacked objects around her, recluttering the room.

"You said there were too many problems on both sides."

"Oh," she said, focusing again on the box. "His job. He was always working on that vaccine. Every time I wanted to do something, to see him, he was working on his precious project. It was supposed to get better recently. He told me he'd try. And it did for a while. But only for a while. Then his work took him again. It was different, I suppose, but still the same."

"Travel, too?"

"A couple of times," she said. "And he was gone for two or three weeks each time. There were a few problems with that, too."

"Because he was away?"

"Yeah. It's not that he didn't write or anything. I got cards every couple of days, and a letter once or twice each time. It's not the same, though." She stopped lifting sweaters from the box in front of her, and she looked at him.

"I suppose that latest trip was when I first started to get pretty concerned," she said.

Patchett's warning lights glared red.

"Why?"

"That was when he said he'd change. Something spooked him, I think, but I don't remember what anymore. So he came home and played the perfect boyfriend for a couple of months. Then it was like he fell off the earth after that. I hadn't talked to him for maybe a week before he died.

"I was starting to imagine what it'd be like to be married to him. He'd be working all the time or traveling or something. There one minute, gone the next. Talking with you one second, rushing off after that. Never around for the things that everyone says should matter. That'd be rough, I think."

"Where'd he go when he traveled?" Patchett thought he knew the answer to this, too, and Rebecca didn't disappoint him.

"Las Vegas that time. Time before, too."

"Any idea what he was working on down there?"

"Prohiva," she said without hesitation. "It was always Prohiva with Alex."

"Anything more specific?"

"No. Truth is, Mr. Patchett, I wasn't really interested in his work. I was pretty much up to my neck in that stuff as it was, and I didn't have the time to figure out specifics. I was just seeing him because, you know, because I liked him. I *loved* him. He was a nice guy. Just a really nice guy." She was getting a glassy look again. Patchett spoke to head it off.

"Did he ever mention a Lot 179?"

"No," she said, thinking about it, "not that I recall."

"How about men named Alfre Rayes or Eric Bancroft?"

"I've spoken to them both, but I don't really know who they are. I'm sure I have phone numbers for them at the office."

I'm sure you do, too, Patchett thought without saying it.

"Like I said," Rebecca continued, "I really wasn't interested in his work. His letters are in here somewhere, though, and you're welcome to see them if I find them." She was looking at the small mountain of boxes on the floor. "He might have mentioned those things in one of them. God knows he was always talking about his work."

Patchett heard the shake in her voice returning.

"I'm sure I'll come across them somewhere in here." She was on the verge of new tears.

"I'd like to take a look when you find them," Patchett said warily. "If it's no trouble."

"No," she said. She wiped again at her eyes as her voice steadied. "They'll turn up tonight or tomorrow. I'll get them to you."

With that, Patchett found that the conversation was suddenly at an end, and he stood, collecting his coat. He felt a dull ache in his back from sitting on the bed. His spine cracked as he stood. There was little youth in him anymore.

"Anything else you need to know?" Rebecca asked as she stood up beside him, still wiping at her face, and Patchett knew that he had to ask. He searched for the right words but couldn't find them.

"Why do you think he did it?" he finally asked, fearing the pain it would trigger in her but craving the answer she might have. Rebecca's eyes, wetness lingering in them, leveled at him, and her voice was cool and calm in a stream of words that flowed out after a brief pause.

"I don't know," she said. "Sometimes I think I'll wake up and find out that it was just a dream because I just really didn't think he'd ever do something like this." She sniffed back a slight gasp.

"I said before that I thought he loved me. And I *do* think that. But he loved his research even more. And he loved that vaccine more than anything else. I just can't believe he would have given up on that, even if he gave up on everything else. Even if he gave up on me."

He waited for her to compose herself, thinking he should reach out to comfort her but certain it was the wrong thing to do. So he only waited again, awkwardly.

"I'm sorry," she finally said, and she wiped one more time at damp eyes.

"*I* am sorry," Patchett said, "for bringing all of this back up."

She nodded. "It's okay," she said. "I'm sure it'll get better. I'm sure it'll be fine. They say it will be, anyway." And she gave him a look of impossibly warm certainty to back up her words.

At that moment, Patchett knew that Rebecca was struggling in that worst-of-all-possible worlds — caught between the idealistic and innocent visions of the young and the much colder and harder lessons-learned mentality of imposed maturity. Looking again at the room, the attorney wondered how long it had been since his own idealisms were washed away in the steady, erosive run of years and experiences, leaving whatever was left in him now.

But at the same time, looking at Rebecca and seeing the glimmer of idealism still displayed in her life even here, even despite the circumstances, Patchett wondered why that loss of idealism happened. Why it *had* to happen. And whether it did.

Rebecca walked him to the door downstairs without another word, then opened it. "I'll get you the letters when I find them," she said, and Patchett stepped out. He could see her parents watching closely from the living room.

"I appreciate it. Sorry for the inconvenience."

She closed the door, and Patchett walked to the car, got in, and drove into the night.

The man watched them at the door, long enough to recognize the woman in the picture. When Patchett came here, the man following the attorney was confused and a little curious. The address didn't match any of the ones given to him, and he didn't know who answered the door. But it was apparent that someone else was there, too, and he knew that it was that person whom Patchett had come to see.

He waited almost half an hour, the slow drudge of house and clock watching numbing his mind into a lull of thoughtlessness. He hated that the most — the steady droop of eyelids that was almost unavoidable in surveillance. That and the bobbing head that always followed.

He was at that stage, his head snapping back from the steering wheel, then drifting toward it once more. But Patchett came out, and the man woke suddenly.

He saw her then, standing briefly in the light from the porch lamp, and he knew immediately that she was the one in the picture. The same precise features, the thick hair. She looked childlike in stocking feet. An unremarkable and average woman, he thought, but definitely the one in the photo. He sat up slightly.

His attention peaked higher as Patchett started the car and began driving away. He took a last glimpse at her picture, using the light from a yard lamp, then dropped the photo to the passenger seat.

The man shook off the last edge of his exhaustion, started his own car, and headed after the shrinking taillights.

32

IN BED LATER that night, the unknown and unseen man long gone, Patchett jerked awake with a start, shooting upright and almost shaking as he struggled with the seeming reality of a terrifying dream already fleeing from his mind. From that dream, he still clearly held an image of Liz — the final image, the most shattering image — and he rubbed at his forehead to push it even further away, finding a thin layer of sweat. The sheets were damp with the perspiration from his back.

The picture that awakened him frayed more at the edge of his mind, and it floated disturbingly there for a precarious moment before vanishing into grayness. After that, there was only one thing that remained from the dream's intertwining mélange of images, and he jumped out of bed with the thought still hammering in his mind. He jogged into the next room and over to the dinette table. Papers spread across it in a disorganized array, and he fumbled through them in a flurry. He picked out one sheet, blank except for a few stray jottings that now meant nothing to him, found a pencil that was dulled by the scribblings that he made late into last night, and searched for the Weber BioTech prospectus.

He didn't find it until he went to his briefcase and emptied the contents onto the floor. The prospectus tumbled out on top of the assorted paraphernalia that always accumulated in the small case, and he plucked it out.

He was looking for something specific, and he found it almost instantly, flipping through the nearly memorized pages. Moving back to the dinette, he wrote the numbers down on the sheet of paper and set the prospectus aside.

He repeated the searching process at a kitchen drawer, opening it to the dismay and ever-present shock at the junk that was collected in there. He found the ancient calculator at the bottom, and he flicked it on expecting it to be dead. When the small red figures lit up, he smiled and went back to the table.

Patchett grabbed the sheet and set it beside him. He began to punch in numbers nervously, forgetting altogether the other images that slipped away into the fog of awakened sleep.

They were gone.

Part Three

SATURDAY

SUNDAY

MONDAY

The Fifth Day

33

THE ASSISTANT deputy secretary stood before a rank of microphones under glaring snow-white lights that chased any hint of darkness from the conference room on the third floor of the FDA building. The assembled horde was scattered before her on folding chairs that creaked and whined as reporters shifted forward and back. The steady burr of unintelligible conversation droned in the air, punctuated by an occasional laugh, the call of a name, or a shout for a sound or camera check.

The mixture was typical of what she saw at other press conferences—mainly science and medical reporters, with a few "life" editors and a miscellaneous potpourri of Capitol Hill and White House castoffs dotted here and there among the faces that were slowly quieting and turning to her. She heard one or two live feeds introducing her and falling silent.

She was nervous. She recognized the faces and knew the routine, but the stakes here were uncharacteristically high, the crowd unusually full. Word about the announcement clearly was already out. The questions would be pointed, and the answers probably overly short or, God forbid, nonexistent.

She glanced at the monitor screen next to her and silently

cursed herself and Rowe Weber. She shouldn't have left the date to him, or she should at least have insisted that a Weber representative appear live. The screen, hooked to a feed from Minneapolis, was blanked with a Weber BioTech logo. It looked like a damn advertisement, just as her own assistant earlier had warned it would.

"Ladies and gentlemen, please, let's get started," she said. "The Food and Drug Administration is very pleased this morning to announce that we have approved for Phase Three testing a promising preventive HIV vaccine. Yesterday, we informed officials at Weber BioTech in Bloomington, Minnesota, that human studies on Prohiva could begin at their earliest convenience."

Almost a third of the people in the room immediately jumped up from their seats and rushed toward the back wall and the doors there.

The race was on.

In New York, the weekend/overnights erupted and spun Weber stock up $11.00 in a little under two minutes. In ten more minutes, after Weber jumped 35 percent of its value, the trading automatically shut down under sales imbalance regulations specifically governing the overnights, the concession that had made real off-hours trading possible at all.

The same thing wasn't true at unofficial trading counters across the country and in London and Tokyo, of course. Operated by the brokerage houses themselves, the traders took buy and sell orders for another two hours before approaching what they perceived would be the ceiling for Weber BioTech. When the market reopened Monday, they would complete those trades as soon as the stock climbed above the particular purchase prices, and they would sell when it hit other, preordained numbers, up or down.

Across the country, the brokerage trading, which skirted the edge of federal securities laws, peaked at around $95.00 a share. That was the price the brokers were comfortable with. That was the price, they determined, that was sufficiently under the ultimate projected ceiling for Weber BioTech stock. Any shares still held by the brokerages at that price could be unloaded later to realize any remaining profit whenever the stock finally hit its high. But until Monday, they would have to hold their collective breath waiting on the outcome.

Rowe Weber's smiling and unblinking face stared out across the crowd from the blue-hued picture on the monitor. The conference was nearing its end, and it was going extremely well, relaxing the secretary as she stood watching the crowd. The questions were almost fawning, in the nature of "How big an impact does this have on your company?" and "What do you plan to do next?" It was the product of press deference cultivated by Weber over the time since the original submission, she supposed.

Weber was his usual public self—cheerful and glib in an open, nonoffensive way, and the press was eating from his hand all morning. "Tremendously excited," he was saying. "We all knew that this was an excellent product, and we are confident of its full approval after Phase Three. We view this as just one more movement toward that, toward what we see as the eventual eradication of HIV and AIDS from this country and the world." It was a scripted TelePrompTer response that sat in front of Weber in Minneapolis, out of view of the people in D.C.

The room clamored as reporters stood with questions. Weber could not see them; no cross-feed was established, so the secretary pointed to the gray-haired woman in front. She continued standing while the others sat.

"Dr. Weber," the woman said precisely. Her words, delivered in a crisp, educated English tone, were soft but were clearly chosen after extended deliberation. "How has the death of Dr. Alexander Tomlin affected your company?" She continued to stand, staring at the flat, discolored image on the monitor.

Were the color better, they might have noticed a change. But it was not, and they did not. Weber spoke with a suddenly more solemn voice, in a smooth, heartfelt tone.

"We all miss Alex very much," he said. He spoke slowly. "And I'm sure we will continue to miss his incredibly valuable contributions to this company in the coming months and years. But we recognize that there is no finer testament to the value and capabilities of Dr. Tomlin than the FDA's announcement this morning. Dr. Tomlin committed great efforts to fighting HIV, and we are now seeing the fruits of that labor. And what we have seen is that those efforts, and that life, have achieved something valuable to us all." This, too, was scripted, although Weber frankly hadn't expected the question to be asked.

"With that," he said over the again-standing crowd, "I would thank all of you and, of course, the FDA. We are working to go ahead on this project at full speed, and we must get back to that. Thank you." The picture froze on his last gesture, hand raised in a wave to a crowd that he had never seen.

"Thank you," the secretary said, bending to the microphones from her position beside the podium. They squealed once more, but overall, everything had gone fine. Thank God. She decided to reward herself with a nice, cold stiff drink.

The crowd began to disperse, and the lights clicked off.

34

ERIC BANCROFT was appreciably calmer than he had been during the previous day's phone conversations. That was due in no small part to the soothing effect of the assurances he'd received and to the equally pleasing announcement of approval and its concurrent ring of money. But credit also needed to be given to the exceptionally large doses of Xanax that he had choked down yesterday and on awaking groggily this morning.

Bancroft was numb to the world, and, at least for now, that was precisely how he wanted it. He poked at a mountain of pasta, a rapidly cooling lunch that sat before him, and shoveled a mouthful in. One noodle caught across his chin and dragged a stripe of red into his mouth. He wiped at it idly with the napkin wrapped around one hand but missed.

Everything was going to be okay, he convinced himself for probably the sixth time that day. Everything would be fine. They had guaranteed that, and they were never wrong. That was a comforting thought that guided him as he continued to eat.

There was a quiet, unmoving smoothness to his world. For the first time in a long time, Bancroft was calm.

House Rock Valley was as empty as always as Rayes cruised along Route 89A. It ran roughly east-west in a straight-line arrow that gradually bent to arc in a tracing along the southern edge of the Vermilion Cliffs — an artificial and narrow asphalt shadow under the red earth of that jagged wall. The road ran through a world of ecosystems in a couple hours' drive. From the pine forests on the Kaibab Plateau, it twisted and swept in switchbacks and runs down more than three thousand feet to the valley floor. It ran across the open spaces there in a bound that lulled drivers into speeds they would never attempt under normal circumstances. But the open spaces of the flat, particularly when broiled by a summer sun that shimmered the horizon, were no normal circumstances. They were like the surface of Mars, red and desolate and virtually deserted.

Speeding was not a problem. There was exactly one Arizona highway patrol car that covered 89A, and its route was usually limited to the run from Jacob Lake above the Grand Canyon, northwest past Fredonia to the Utah border. The eastern stretch of 89A was too sparse, leading only to the sharp lip of Marble Canyon, which dropped in a dizzying plunge to the Colorado River.

East of the river was the vast reach of the reservation of the Navajo Nation, and the highway was patrolled there by the Navajo Tribal Police. State patrol had jurisdiction, too, but it wasn't asserted on the seventy-five-mile length that skirted along the canyon and the reservation's edge from Navajo Bridge on the Colorado down to the small town of Cameron. There, the tourists heading for the Grand Canyon's south rim attracted more attention, and the regular patrols from Flagstaff would swarm over the area.

But here on the flats of House Rock, there was no one to see as Rayes turned south on an unpaved, unmarked, virtually indistinguishable trail of a ranch road. Dust kicked up in a red plume as he drove the fifteen-mile distance before stopping to unlatch the fence.

It looked as though it were dropped out of the sky—a new barbed-wire barrier that stretched out into the desert and across the road. Some of the others had wanted razor wire, and Rayes spent an entire day talking people out of it. The valley was sparsely populated, was in fact decorated by only a handful of ranches like this one, but somebody would come across it soon enough and would raise an eyebrow to razor wire in the desert.

He pulled through, jumped back out, and shut the gate, then continued down the road another five miles. When he shut off the truck and got out, he noticed that the desert air, marked by a breeze, the early scent of cactus blossoms, and an utter lack of sound, was growing cool in an afternoon sky misleadingly clear of clouds. He pulled a jacket from the cab and walked down a slight slope, then up another slope, moving slowly and feeling the breeze against his skin.

Winter in northern Arizona was a lingering season that probed deeply into spring and even summer. Nights there could kill a person well into May, and a combination of evening chills and daytime heat could get it done surprisingly easily. Rayes pulled the jacket collar tight against his neck as he moved up the rise to a short overlooking edge before picking out and sitting on one of the scattered round stones whose presence told the tale of this region's prehistoric submersion by water.

He looked down at the site from the small bluff, shading his eyes against the sun. When he squinted, the naturally tan face crinkled at the eyes, lines spreading out from the corners like the sunrays that beat those wrinkles into his face in the first place.

It looked the same. It always looked the same to him now. A barely discernible patch squared into the desert floor. It was melting more convincingly into the scenery with each passing day, with each dust storm or rain. It would soon be indistinguishable, a thing forgotten, hidden, and Rayes felt the delicate tug of guilt pull at him once more.

There is, he consoled himself, *a higher good being achieved here. There is a purpose and a goal that will be furthered.*

And that goal, his voice came back to him, *is lining your pockets. You're a moneyed man, Alfre Rayes,* the voice was saying to him. *The higher good is making you wealthy and making others fabulously rich. And is the price paid any balance for that? And don't you of all people know that it isn't?*

Rayes didn't know the answer to those questions, and he hoped he never would. Instead, he confronted his doubts with the shaky counter that more was to be achieved from everything that was already done than could be perceived from merely looking at the pocketbooks of a few men.

The vaccine was itself a huge technological advancement. The technology and its possibilities, he told himself again, must be fully understood to be grasped and made a proper tool. And the way to do that somehow lay in that square patch of earth.

He stood and turned, taking a last long look over one shoulder before retreating the way he'd come, moving through the slight dip toward the truck, which stood insignificantly on the rise in the short distance. The sun warmed his back, moving him along as it tried and failed to push away the growing chill. Rayes made his steady way back.

35

"YOU'RE BEING A PUSSY." The man's voice crackled over the phone line. It was assuredly the most unjudicial comment that Chief Judge Young had ever made to Ian Anderson in all the time that Anderson had handled the judge's Weber stock. The broker doubted it would be the last, though — after hours of deliberating, after a couple of days of it in fact, Anderson was telling the judge that it was time for the Caldwell X. Young Living Trust to bid its adieu to the biotechnology company.

Anderson had thought this out thoroughly, considering it from more angles than he ever looked at anything. With the stock at around 60 and certain to climb, they could sell on Monday, not raise a single eyebrow, and realize a profit of $7.5 million. That would be an appreciation of almost 2000 percent over the few years that the shares were held. Pretty damn good for what was essentially a lark in the first place.

The judge wasn't so content. With his characteristic abruptness, Young called Anderson a name that the broker last heard in grade school. Anderson wouldn't even have expected that the judge knew that word, but it still reverberated over the silent line.

"Your Honor," Anderson finally managed in his best kiss-ass tone, "I hardly think that it's being a pussy, to use your word, if you make a profit of more than seven million dollars."

"There's more to be made. That stock'll climb for weeks, maybe months."

"Maybe so," Anderson conceded, "but the FDA could find something wrong in the same amount of time, and I don't think I need to tell you that, if it does, it's the end of this stock. Of this *company*. Weber is very much a one-trick pony, and without approval for Prohiva, there is quite simply nothing there."

Young didn't even take the time to consider it. "Don't sell," he said bluntly. The line hummed its disconnection.

Anderson hung up and mesmerized himself with the figure on the Quotron: $59.50. "Trading suspended" flashed below it.

The broker reached for a cigarette that wasn't there before remembering he had burned through the entire pack during the FDA announcement and the on-the-heels meteoric rise of the stock. He fumbled through the desk and found none there as well.

"Fuck," he said softly, eyes closed tightly as he tried to calm himself enough to think.

The one thought that kept running through his progressively more agitated mind was to sell. With one call he could unload those shares even in suspended trading, at a price significantly higher than the final close. The profit could easily go as high as $10 million, and there would legally be nothing that Caldwell Young could do about it.

Except ruin your pitiful life, of course was his next thought.

Young couldn't bitch too loudly about trading in his blind trust, and the trustee, who long ago deferred to the supposed expertise of the Carlysle brokerage firm, was likewise in no position to raise an effective stink. This was especially true, Anderson noted, where the trust would enjoy that profit.

There was always the issue of what *could* have been achieved, naturally, but getting into that would raise too many facts about the true control of the trust. That wasn't an area to be examined, and everyone involved would know it.

Laying that aside, though, there was the practical matter of what Judge Young could manage at a more subtle level. The judge's ability to control Anderson's fate was all too clear to a man who had nearly lost his job once before to a client's pressures. Anderson didn't doubt that the judge was more than willing to pull any strings he saw fit to pull.

Anderson wouldn't sell. There would be no phone call, and he supposed that he always knew it. No phone call, no sale, no problems. Just cruise along and do your thing and don't ask questions or get ideas. You just only stir things up when you do that, and Ian Anderson was no stirrer.

He stood and went searching for a cigarette.

36

THE BARBER glanced up only once, looking away as the afternoon sun first cut through the window and brightened his face. The yellow color, just shifting to orange, shone across the unlikely smoothness of his skin and caught in the muddy brown eyes. They closed momentarily as he felt the warmth of spring, then he turned back to the nightstand.

He gulped at a glass of cranberry juice, his weekend bout of acidic liquid that his mother once told him would stave off infections. He felt his jaw tighten.

His fingers worked deftly with the red strands laid out straight on the handkerchief. They steadily crossed and recrossed as before, the cord was tightened, and they were crossed again.

He was nearing the end, and he was already pleased with the result. The best one yet. When he first saw the hair, when he first noticed the woman across the small lake in the park, he knew it would be this way. It was soft and long and almost glassy, the color of the sunshine streaming in on it. It would require someone special.

He knotted it off and held it up in the sunlight. It glistened as he brought it down and rubbed it under his chin, feeling its slickness slide roughly against his unshaven neck as the cord caressed him.

He stood that way for almost five minutes, eyes closed as the blood coursed warmly through him. Five minutes before he pulled himself forcibly from the peaceful excitement that he felt. It was harder and harder to do, he knew. He knew it at some level, anyway. At some level that existed even now in what remained of the comparatively bright light of his full and constant coherence and capability and understanding.

As the sun edged toward the horizon, out of view through the thick-paned glass before him, the Barber considered going out, but he knew it wasn't quite time. How he knew that he wasn't sure. No one would ever understand precisely how he knew, how he *felt*, that it was time to go out. No one would be able to discern what motivated him at some point to take the thin hair rope into one of the parks sprinkled throughout the metro area. He wasn't able to do that himself. He simply knew when it was time.

And that would be tomorrow, he decided. Tomorrow he would go out and do what he needed to do to release the excitement built up in him. If he could wait that long.

He drank some juice and gazed out the window.

37

REBECCA WAS SNIFFLING her way through the boxes, which lay like empty graves in a sparse cardboard cemetery spreading around her. The thin streams of tears typically flowed steadily whenever she was alone, and they were doing so now, running from the corners of both eyes and down her cheeks.

It wasn't a gulping unable-to-catch-your-breath crying. She was past that, separated from that brief period by the unavoidable passing of immediate shock and the soothing and dulling progress of time. She cried that way for almost two solid days, even at work, where the tears were hidden under a stiff mask of concentration and frequent breaks.

That was over. This was just the next phase, with the growing sense of loss and the sheer aloneness that accompanies it. Everyone, she knew, goes through stages following the death of someone close. Everyone moves through predictable patterns of reaction. Those stages and the uncontrollable emotions that marked them had to be endured. Until they were over, she knew she could expect bouts of emotional overload, but that understanding didn't help her deal with them when they came.

This time, though, she at least knew exactly what it was that set her off. This time, it was the letters.

As she had promised Patchett, she'd found the letters and cards Tomlin had sent her while he was in Vegas. They were tucked at the bottom of the next-to-last box, blanketed by a wool stadium throw Tomlin had brought back with him from the trip. The blanket was now wrapped around her, and she occasionally without thought rubbed a cheek across its scratchy striped-orange and brown wool surface.

It was Navajo, bought from a roadside stand. There was more to the story, she recalled, dimly reflecting on the evening when Alex returned. They had lain on the floor in front of his fireplace. She could remember no more of the story and little else of the night.

One thing she could recall was the fact that Tomlin talked of his work that night. The common topic, the one that triggered the few true fights. And that night, as usual, she avoided listening.

The two letters discussed his work, too, as she told Patchett they might. She was reminded of that when she reread them. Scanning down a letter from December, she saw that most of the neat writing discussed Prohiva and some sort of problem they were having on the research in Arizona.

The rest was largely homage to her, a parade of "miss you" and "love you" sentiments that seemed out of place to her in the excruciating and exacting examination of grief-driven hindsight. She pondered whether the comments, the entire letter maybe, were obligatory, the kind that someone might write to stay in good graces with the person sharing his bed. She immediately doubted it, then knew it wasn't even possible.

Alexander Tomlin was many things, not the least of which was a distant and aloof man who was probably deathly afraid of most people and of most women in particular. He was also, though, a basically decent man who was, as she had told Patchett the day before, *nice*. His fundamental trait.

She was crying again as she studied the letter. It mentioned the men Patchett had asked her about. She wondered what it was that made him interested in them.

Nothing in the letters provided her with any clue that she could recognize. She folded them both and slipped them into their envelopes, jotted "Jon Patchett" on a slip, and stuck that together with the letters and three postcards. Two of those showed casinos, the other the Arizona desert in bloom. None of the postcards said anything that was really more substantial than hello. She banded them and laid them on the corner of a night table.

Rebecca sat, then lay on the bed and rolled to see the clock. It wasn't really evening yet, was barely even late afternoon at 4:50, but the March sun was already slipping and dimming toward the horizon, and she closed her eyes.

The tears dried as she drowsed. Some relaxation was what she needed. Something to calm her, divert her from thoughts of Tomlin and the job that haunted her with his image and his life.

Someplace peaceful.

She slept, dreaming of parks.

38

THE RAIN HAD STOPPED in early morning. The trademark Phoenix heat had risen since then, intensified by the out-of-place oppressive layer of humidity that lifted from damp streets to bathe the air of the Valley of the Sun.

The city sweated through the afternoon, then everyone stepped out of air-conditioned cocoons to enjoy the softly feathered grace of the early evening, then nighttime breeze. Parks filled with people eager to be comfortably outside in the "outdoor" season of the desert. Balls were tossed, picnics set out, Frisbees thrown. The sound of distant laughter rang across neighborhoods, just dying out as you neared the next park or playground or baseball stadium filled with teams in spring training. Then it would pick up again.

The sounds drifted that way, floating on the heavy air, until the light of the sky faded from a dusted desert blue to the reds and roses of another intense climactic sunset. The stars appeared, first above the far eastern reaches of ragged Superstition Mountain and the Four Peaks, which disappeared into blackness. The narrow columns of saguaros stood against the horizon, then seeped into it. Darkness settled into the valley, spreading a melancholy gloom street by street, turning on the corner lights as it went.

The one above Maggie flicked on as she approached the curb. It cast down the stark blue-white light of vapor lamps, cruelly pushing the shadows away from the top of every curve, line, edge, corner, or tuck of her body. The sharp undersides were thrown into dark relief as the shadows crept there in refuge.

Her cheeks were settled in below bags that ringed her eyes in even the most flattering light. Needle veins of red flushed her eyes, and her clothes hung on her shoulders and hips, held up by a tightly cinched belt.

The cough had vanished as abruptly as it had originally come, and her throat was beginning a struggle to patch up the raw rash that cascaded down it. She wondered for the briefest moment, all she could stand, just how long she would have before the coughing came back, perhaps to stay.

She was sick, and she knew it. She also knew that this wasn't just bronchitis. She was kidding herself to keep saying that. It wasn't the flu or a cold or an allergy or anything else like that. Maggie knew that this was something serious — pneumonia or TB or something she didn't even want to contemplate.

TB had come back in 1992 and again last year. She didn't know if that could be cured. She only remembered stories about people coming to Arizona because the air was somehow supposed to be better for you, but that was a load of shit. She sniffed and could smell the exhaust fumes even through the congestion that lingered in her head.

But *God* she hoped it was TB. Without even knowing if that could be cured, she hoped with everything in her that it would only be TB.

Not AIDS. Anything but that.

You didn't participate in this business without considering it. And you thought about it even more when you didn't always use a condom, when you didn't really pay attention to or care about who it was that was inside you on any given night.

God I hope it's only TB.

But whatever it was, the big man leaning against the car at the curb wouldn't know she was sick, she figured. She still looked okay, still managed to show a decent leg and a little cleavage. Occasional heads would turn as she walked a street, and this guy's was one.

He stood as a well-arranged bulk at the right rear of the car, which she immediately sized up as a typical rental. The car was a standard midsize, but the man's clothes suggested more than the typical renter of midsized automobiles.

The jacket was a bone-colored Italian silk and tailored number. It was an unusual weight for silk, a little heavy for the warm night. A winter jacket out of place on Phoenix streets.

The slacks were a vague brown underneath the jacket. Silk, too, by the sheen. They were bottomed by slips of leather shoes, make unclear. Thin gold circled his neck.

He looked, in short, like a dime-store gigolo, but she thought it more likely that he was a misplaced northeasterner. New York, maybe. He'd pay well.

"You're Maggie Washburn, aren't you?" he said, startling her. "You must be." He smiled, and she looked at him more closely, peering into the dimness that hung between them despite the street lamp. She tried to place the face.

"Tommy told me about you," he said, standing up on the curb. A car dashed by on the street. "Tommy Butler. Said you, uh . . ." The man paused before finding the words. "You were friendly with him a little while back when he was here. Man, he described you just perfect, and he was sure right. Said you'd be along here, too. Right again." The man laughed casually, easily.

Maggie smiled and took a step forward. She didn't know any Tommy Butler, at least not by that name, but she was friendly with a lot of guys recently who didn't use a name matching the ones tucked away in their wallets. Maybe this guy's friend was one of them.

"Sure," she said. "Tommy." Her smile got broader in response to his own as she moved up in front of him. "How's he doing?"

"Just fine," the man said. "Still talks about you, though. I had to promise him that I'd track you down."

Maggie liked him, felt comfortable with the sure and strong voice and face and the unplaceable accent. She traced a finger over his chest and looked into the shadows that filled his face. She looked for but couldn't see his eyes, which hid in those shadows, but she could make out the perfect row of teeth.

"And now you have," she said. "So are we gonna get to be friendly, too?"

"I hope so, after all I've heard."

Maggie raised her face into the shadows and kissed him. Her

tongue pushed his lips apart for a second and traced those teeth until he pulled away.

"How much?" he asked.

Maggie smiled slyly and rattled off the list, notching each item up ten bucks, despite the way she thought she looked. This one was clearly not going away. Besides, he'd never seen her before.

"Fine," he said, and she planted another brief kiss on his lips. "Where to?" He was fairly stamping from foot to foot with eagerness, too easily betraying his willingness to pay. She named a nice hotel not too far away. It could be a decent night for money, maybe even making up for what she had lost out on recently, and she didn't think that the nearest shack would bring out the big spender in this gentleman.

"Lead the way," he said. He opened the passenger door and she slipped in, feeling his hand on her ass as she did. He disappeared for a second around the back of the car, then was at the other door, opening it and getting in. He started the car, she pointed down the street, and they pulled away from the curb.

It was a Honda 70, an ancient trail bike patched together with mishmash repairs and a string of hopes, and it buzzed along the worn trail, jerking at each bump. Andy Littlefeather could smell the mixed scent of dirt and oil even under the oversized helmet sitting squat upon his head. The bike burned oil rapidly, throwing it from leaks, some of which Andy still needed to find.

He probably couldn't have repaired them even if he found them all, though. He was thirteen, and he relied on his father to pay for parts, although Andy was more and more capable of performing the work himself. But his father's store was having tougher times than usual, and money for motorbike repairs came at the end of a long list of other items crying for cash.

It was a wonder that he owned the bike at all in the first place, and that it ran in the second. It hadn't run when his father bought it almost a year ago, and the battered gold paint was even now barely visible under partial repainting and a spray of chips and spotted smatterings of putty and seals. But Andy continued to pour time into it, guiding himself with a dog-eared, oil-spotted maintenance manual that came with the bike.

So it fairly hummed in working order now, if you ignored the oil problem. Under the right conditions, it could even edge up to around forty miles an hour.

As he zipped around one of the large rocks that periodically jutted up in the trail, Andy considered with a typical child's level of incomplete understanding why his father actually got the bike. When Andy first asked for one, the response was abrupt and adamant. Both of his parents were opposed, his mother at one point on the verge of tears as she cried out various Navajo laments that Andy largely couldn't understand. But the bike showed up within a month anyway, with no further requests made. If he had known the full story with a more adult comprehension, he'd have been alternately pleased and a little disturbed at the well-meaning, manipulative, and patronizing gesture.

In truth, the bike was his parents' reluctant answer to their perception of a problem in raising Andy — his separation from the reservation. Although they lived and worked only twenty-five or so miles from Navajo Bridge and the canyon boundary for the reservation, the Littlefeathers and particularly Andy were always treated with the quiet demeanor given to outsiders. Only the members of their clan regularly dealt with them, and even they acted differently.

For the parents, that treatment constituted an understandable, if regrettable, annoyance. For Andy, who was bussed to a small brick schoolhouse on the reservation, it was a social trauma confronted almost constantly. And both parents knew that any stigma provided by adults was magnified by children.

The bike, then, was a diverting hobby for Andy and, admittedly, was also a potential way for the boy to attract friends who might not otherwise give him the time of day. True, essentially buying your son friends was no measure to be proud of, but the friends were there nonetheless, and that was better than before.

There were a lot of rules, of course. Always wear the helmet, so he did. No speeds over forty, but he couldn't anyway. No riding on the reservation, which was off limits because of its status and because he'd have to cross the bridge over Marble Canyon to get there.

And always be back at sunset.

Andy noticed with a start that he'd flicked on the weak and wobbling headlight at some point without thinking. It shone dimly down the ranch trail, a carrot that lit his path, one that the bike was eagerly chasing and seemed to be almost catching.

He spun the bike to a stop, something he had mastered really only in the past week, and he listened as the dirt and gravel kicked into the desert brush. He caught a whiff of dust under the helmet.

Andy wanted to follow the path out farther. It was one that he hadn't noticed before, one of a few on the flat that he hadn't traced to an end. But he knew he needed to get home to have any passable chance of avoiding trouble for this, and he turned toward 89A and the little town of House Rock, twisting the throttle open. More dirt plumed in a miniature rooster tail as the little engine gunned.

Andy raced down the trail, north toward home.

Something was wrong. Maggie looked at herself in the mirror and wondered what she had gotten herself into by agreeing to go with the man sitting just beyond the closed bathroom door. From almost that first instant, when he was so confident and comfortable and soothing — *when he knew who she was* — she should have realized that something was wrong.

It was in the way he carried himself. The way he acted and dressed. Maggie didn't attract elite clientele. Wealthy men who were looking for sex for hire didn't frequent Van Buren. That was the red light district, and any foray there at night triggered a risk of being seen or arrested. No mythical "Tommy" could encourage a guy like this to go there. She didn't care how great the reports this man heard were.

But here he was. He came off as a high roller. He looked like money, talked like money. That should have been the first sign that sent her running.

What confirmed it was how he handled her. Or rather how he

didn't handle her. He hadn't touched Maggie since she stepped into his car. No grabbing at breasts or stealing kisses or anything else that she frankly expected. He hadn't kissed her at all since they stood at the curb.

As she thought about it, in fact, he almost shied away at her touch and pulled away from even that first kiss. There were bucket seats in the car, so she couldn't sit close to him. But she'd leaned over for another kiss after getting in, and he literally had turned his cheek to her. When she reached over at a stoplight and pushed her hand gently into his crotch, he removed it with a seemingly short explanation that it'd have to wait. He was driving, after all.

What worried her most, though, was how the man acted on getting to the room. He didn't remove the jacket, despite both the heat and the fact that he was supposed to be here to have sex. And in a passing glimpse, as he reached over to flick on the TV, Maggie could have sworn that she saw a gun tucked under his left arm.

Which was *definitely* not right.

Maggie fretted her lower lip and brushed at her hair, pulling it away from her face. He could be a cop. Cops always carried guns.

But she knew even then — shifting nervously from foot to foot, her eyes flicking around the bathroom but always coming back to the door — she knew he wouldn't have known her name, and she wouldn't be here, if he was a cop. It would have been over after the exchange on the street, and she'd be sitting in a holding cell downtown.

But the alternative to cops was worse because the other possible explanation she could come up with was that he was some kind of crazy. She once knew a woman in Vegas who was killed while turning tricks. A psycho cut her to ribbons during a bad run-in with PCP. Maggie moved away from there shortly after that, thinking that the bad luck was because she was in Vegas. She didn't realize then that bad luck came with the trade.

Whoever he was, though, and whatever he was doing, the biggest problem was that she'd managed to box herself into the bathroom, a position that she most assuredly didn't like. The room door was maybe ten feet outside the bathroom door, and she could make a break for it, but she would have to deal with opening one door, covering the space, unbolting and opening the other door, and then getting out. Not a great feat, unless he was outside the bathroom door waiting for her. If that was the case, then she was in deep shit.

Maggie looked around for some type of weapon, anything that was heavy enough or sharp enough to use in short spaces. Despite the nicer-than-usual accommodations, however, the bathroom held nothing that looked like even a passable defense. In desperation, Maggie plucked the small complimentary hairspray bottle from the counter, aiming it into the sink and punching the button to make sure that it worked. The aerosol spray misted into the basin and ran down the starkly white porcelain.

Maggie palmed the bottle in her right hand, thumb on the button, and grabbed the doorknob.

The bike was parked in the shed, and Andy had squirmed under the covers in the narrow bed. He watched out the window above him, eyes fixed on the fat moon long enough to see it swing halfway across the pane.

He possessed an almost uncontrollable love for the desert, a trait perhaps passed to him by a father who gave up medical school at the university in Tucson to return to the land nearer where he was raised. Andy for hours would sit and watch and hear the elements come together in the world around him — the small animals, seen and unseen; the plants, sparse but beautiful in bloom; the huge sky with its unvarying summer blue, its passing fits in other seasons, and its palette of pinks, oranges, and reds at every sunup and sundown. He watched the stars out the window now and huddled deeper under the covers.

There were no problems coming in late. His parents were involved in some discussion and took little notice as Andy said a quietly respectful "good night" and slipped into his small bedroom.

He'd peered out the window then, too, and pressed a hand against the thin glass. Then he'd selected his warmest pajamas and wrapped himself in an extra wool blanket retrieved after being put away too soon. Even at thirteen, Andy understood the desert better than most experts. He shivered once, twice, bundled still tighter, and closed his eyes.

He knew it would be a cold night in Arizona.

The big man enjoyed the heaviness in his hand as he gripped tighter on the pistol and stepped within sight of the bathroom door. He could hear her in there, shuffling around. He clicked off the lights in the room and waited, gun pointed toward the door. This was a hunting blind like no other.

He would have enough light. The bathroom's would still be on when she came out, at least for the one fleeting moment he would need, and she would be outlined perfectly. *Like ducks in a row*, he thought.

He called to her.

"Maggie, baby?" he said. "What're you doing in there? I'm getting a little impatient." A duck call just for her. And it worked, he thought, as he heard the knob rattle. He took rough aim with the pistol.

He only just saw the light cut off at the crack below the door before he heard the door swing open with an unexpected bang. With no sight of her, he threw himself up and toward the surprising darkness. Sometimes it was best, he knew, to rush to finish the hunt.

Then he heard the steady hiss.

Maggie heard the shout of pain and felt the blow from an outstretched hand at the same time. It caught her on the right shoulder, jamming that arm up and knocking the can of hairspray from her grip. She heard it drop behind her, and she turned to find it. Her eyes, swimming with a lingering glow from the bathroom light, searched desperately for the can, her only weapon. She could see nothing.

And it hardly mattered. Immediately behind the blow to her shoulder came the weight of the man's body as he careened blindly into her by sheer momentum. They collapsed together against the bathroom door frame. Maggie felt it burn her cheek as her face slid down it.

"You fucking bitch," he was saying in a strange whispered shout. He straddled her. "You *fucking* bitch."

A blow cascaded across the bridge of her nose, and she saw a shooting spasm of nerve-charged light shoot through her head as she jerked in pain. The spray of liquid down her throat and over her lips told her the nose was crushed against her face. She barely had time to realize it before another blow sealed her left eye.

By the time the third blow glanced along her jaw, loosening a tooth, Maggie's arms were up. They struggled to reach the man on top of her, pulling at his shirt to bring his face within striking distance. When her hand caught the gold chain around his neck, she pulled as hard as she could manage.

She felt the thin slip of metal cut into her palm before the man finally tipped forward with a shout. Her free hand felt along his face, where her nails dug bleeding furrows of skin that triggered another scream. She'd reached his left eye by then, and she gouged her thumb into it. A howl of pain blew in her face.

A flashbulb popped. A brilliant burst of yellow in a small nova of light that illuminated his face like a picture while blinding her left eye. She noticed strangely, almost distantly, the red streaked mask over his eyes where the hairspray had flown in a cloud. It was accented by stripes of blood on his cheeks, another from the corner of his eye.

But her hand was no longer there, and she knew with alarming clarity that the entire right half of her body was numb.

Another pop of light, then a third. Each time there was a muffled slap that grew more distant and rang through her ears. Her head rocked, and it was all she knew, all she felt.

Her blood poured steadily onto the carpet.

39

HARRISON WAS CURLED UP on the floor grate of the heating vent, the tip of his tiger-striped tail flicking idly to an unknowable beat. Patchett watched him, splashing vodka into a glass of juice and sipping it for taste. Harrison looked up and meowed once before the doorbell rang, and Patchett shook his head in unspoken admiration of the cat's hearing.

"Don't get up," he said to the cat. "I'll get it." Harrison obliged.

Patchett opened the door to Anne, who was casual in a canvas jacket, blue jeans, and oversized chambray shirt. Her book bag was hitched over one shoulder, a thumb tucked under the strap. She was pulling her blond bangs off her forehead as the door opened.

"Come on in," Patchett said, and he stepped aside. She walked in and set the book bag on the nearby dinette table as he closed the door. She moved a clutter to find a clear space.

"Coffee? Something else?" he asked, and she nodded.

"Coffee's fine." Anne studied the apartment from a position fixed at the table. Without the furniture, which was unvaryingly blue, bland, and contemporary, the room would have been spartan. One print was hanging on the far wall, a nondescript, cheaply framed Monet—one of the lily paintings. There were no other accents to decorate the room or to hide a few pieces of electronic equipment that were sown about. It was a bare space just like Patchett's office, Anne thought—a bare space for what was an apparently bare and closed life.

Patchett handed her a steaming cup of black coffee poured from a brewing pot, and Anne thanked him, drinking from it and sitting. "I take it you got hold of Rebecca," she said immediately.

Patchett nodded.

"She have anything to say?"

"Nothing too different from what we knew or what we guessed.

She confirmed the trip to Vegas. Said she got a couple of letters from Tomlin while he was there. They talked about work."

"Lot 179?"

"She doesn't remember him mentioning it, but I think we know a little bit more than she might." He tapped at the table. All of Patchett's various notes sat there, the fax message rewritten in block letters on a single sheet of paper that rested on top. The words "Page, Arizona" and the date "December 12, 1995" were written below that.

Anne had left him a message about the call to Bateman, and he put that piece of the puzzle in as best he could, not surprised at the copy center's location but still unsure of its precise fit into the scarce information they had. Along with Las Vegas and Kanab, the various contact points for Tomlin's trip were scattered in and around northern Arizona, and Patchett wasn't sure why.

"How about Rayes and Bancroft?" Anne asked then.

"Same story, though she knew both names. She thought the letters might help some. Said she'd let me see them when she dug them out of her packing. I told you she moved?"

Anne looked up from the notes with mild interest. "No," she said.

Patchett nodded, sitting and crossing his legs. "Moved back in with her parents, which was pretty clearly a tough choice to make." The image of the Cartaways, glowing blue by the television as they watched him suspiciously, came back, and Patchett found himself instantly understanding Rebecca's difficulty in that decision.

"I met her father," he said, thinking of that. "Overprotective in a smothering way. She's had words with him before about Tomlin, and the old man feels vindicated and probably more than a little worried about this latest development." Patchett swirled a finger in his drink, lifting the vodka off the bottom, and he licked his finger.

"Sounds like it was a rough relationship," Anne said.

"Rebecca and Dad or Rebecca and Tomlin?"

"Her father."

"It was. Pop didn't approve and said so. Thought Tomlin was after sex and said so. She thought Dad was being a jackass and said so."

"So she moved out?"

"Spoken like someone who truly understands women," Patchett said, smiling.

"And fathers," Anne replied. She didn't return the smile.

Patchett noticed but went on. "Relationship with Tomlin seems to have been fairly solid. A few skirmishes, but all the obvious signs were okay, I think. She said they talked about marriage. It wasn't clear how seriously."

"Seriously enough to suggest that people maybe should be surprised at a suicide?"

Patchett considered that. "Yes," he said. "I think so." He fell silent as he recalled the conversation with Rebecca, the way she had looked and acted. "She's bright and attractive. And she loved him and said she thought he loved her. She was surprised by his death in any case."

"No idea why he did it, then?"

"Nope," Patchett replied. "In fact, she said she never thought he would. Loved his work too much."

They both sat quietly, the only sounds in the room coming from the occasional click of Anne's cup on its saucer and the soft purr of the furnace. Harrison slept on.

"We still don't have anything too concrete, Jon."

"I know," he said, and he began to flip through the stacks of notes and materials on the table. Anne saw the photograph, the notes about the fax, a few newspaper pages, and what looked like a Weber prospectus all folded intermittently into the papers. "That's why we're going to Vegas," Patchett said. He waited for a reaction.

It was slow in coming as she stared at him, trying to figure out how to respond. "Vegas?" she simply said in the end. "We're just gonna pull up stakes and fly off to Vegas?"

Patchett stopped thumbing through the papers, and he met her steady look. He pulled out the picture and set the notes and other materials aside.

"I don't know if we have any other way, Anne." He'd tried to think this explanation through all afternoon, but those practiced words failed him now. "You've told me several times," he struggled. "You've told me too many times, really, and I've told myself, that we need much more here before we can work out whatever the puzzles behind this are. And you're right. We're both right. But look around us. Look at this table." He lifted the stack of paper from the table, and it looked ominously, horribly insubstantial and empty.

"Notes," he said, his voice rising in a subdued and frustrated anger. "*Our* notes of conversations and of things people have told us about trips. Notes about documents that may or may not even exist anymore. We have lots of notes, one picture, and a rash of unanswered questions. That's all, and we're not gonna get anything better sitting around here or jawing with the people at Weber."

Patchett set his papers down and sat back. His face dropped back out of the light thrown weakly from the low-hanging dinette lamp.

"I'm out of people to talk to here," he said impatiently. "And that leaves Rayes and Bancroft."

"What about Rebecca's letters?"

"They'll help," Patchett said, nodding, "but I think they'll be a formality in the end. They'll just confirm what Rebecca said and what we already suspected — that Tomlin was working on Prohiva in Arizona. That's suspicious in light of everything else, but it's certainly not murder."

Anne propped her elbows on the table, which tipped unevenly toward her, and she rested her forehead on her hands. Thoughts of finals rushed through her mind. She was trying to reshuffle schedules.

It wasn't just a matter of the law firm's barking and her jumping. That was usually the case, but she felt that this was important. She *knew* it was. And she wanted a part in it.

"How long?" she asked finally, speaking down to the table, and Patchett felt a surge of relief.

"I need to talk to someone on Monday anyway," he answered, "and we'll want some help from a couple others. We'll leave afterward and shoot for a return on Wednesday."

"You know I have exams starting in a week?" Anne looked up at him, her chin now resting on her hands. "And class this Monday?"

"You can study on the plane," he suggested. "And you'll make the class. We'll leave later in the day. Tuesday if we have to." It was the way of all attorneys to somehow find a way out, no matter how improbable or impossible.

"If you're just going down there to talk to these guys, why do you want me along?"

"You know this stuff, and I want someone who *does* know it — someone besides me — to hear what they say. I want a second opinion on these guys, and you're the one who can give me that."

"A second opinion?" Anne asked doubtfully.

Patchett leaned forward into the light, eyes intent on her. "I'll level with you," he said with a calm that sounded artificial. He pressed his hands together in front of his face. "Ben thinks we're done," he said. "He would think it's a little foolish to be following up now. Unnecessary, what with the FDA's action."

"He doesn't know you're planning to go?" Anne asked uncertainly.

"No," Patchett replied. "He knows nothing about it." He scratched slowly, thoughtfully at his chin as his eyes found his lap.

"And if he did know," he went on, "he'd think I'm crazy." Patchett looked once more into Anne's eyes. "He probably already does for that matter." Thoughts of the outburst at Melissa Flare came to him, along with thoughts of the cool and sharp conversations with Clifton and everyone else Patchett came across now, thoughts of the pain in Rebecca's face, thoughts of the darkened balcony and the strange and frightening allure of understanding how someone might just consider taking that way out. He thought of all those things, and he questioned whether Ben might not be right.

"It gets to the point," Patchett answered himself, "that I think maybe he's not so far off." He watched for a reaction from Anne and this time found none. "I just want someone to confirm this for me. There are enough doubts in my own mind, so I want to make sure that there's really something there."

Anne studied his face, seeing the age valleys lining his forehead, just inches away and seeming almost cavernously deep in the stark overhead light. He had tired gray-brown eyes.

"We'll be back Wednesday," she said then.

"Wednesday," Patchett agreed. "And to make sure we are, I want you to get in touch with Gary and Linda. I want them to go, too. It'll save some time for us. You can talk to them tomorrow and we'll fill them in on Monday."

Gary and Linda Kane were young husband and wife law clerks. Both law students, they were hired by the firm three summers before, just in time to be thrown into work on the Prohiva indy application. They knew the facts and would require little startup time. Valuable extra feet, eyes, and ears.

"Bringing an army?" Anne asked.

"If I thought I could get away with it, I'd bring everyone on the damn team." Patchett was fixed on the photograph still in his hand. "We don't have much time," he said softly, "and they've got such a head start." He tapped at the picture, hitting Clifton in the chest.

"Someone out there already knows the answers, and we're just figuring out the questions. And I'm not sure how much time we have to catch up." Anne let him examine the photo a little longer before speaking.

"Do we even have any idea what it is we're trying to get the answers to?" she asked then. "Do we know what the bottom line here is yet?"

Patchett set the picture down, still looking at it, then answered simply, "Money, I guess."

"Money . . . for whom?" Anne replied, confused. "How?"

Patchett opened his mouth to speak before quickly shutting it again. He chewed at his lower lip, his expression betraying the thoughts, issues, and possibilities running through his mind. Those things, and all the doubts that came with them.

"You think he was killed," Anne said before Patchett could speak again.

"I can't say that," Patchett said instantly. "I don't know that at all."

"But you *suspect* it."

"I . . ." Patchett began before hesitating once more. "I don't know what I suspect," he said finally. "I only know that someone, probably more than one person, has a big enough stake in what-ever's going on that Alexander Tomlin's life didn't weigh much in the balance. Whatever the potentials were, they were more im-portant than the life of that man. Beyond that, I don't know. There's just not enough there yet."

"And that's the reason for the trip?" Anne asked. "To get more?" Patchett nodded. Anne picked up a pencil from the table and began rolling it nervously between her fingers.

"How far are we willing to take this, Jon?" she said. Patchett studied her face before he answered. Anne's brow was knotted, eyes absently examining the pencil. She was still young enough that the lines didn't remain, but Patchett at that moment saw clearly all of the creases that her concerns and a few years of life in this world would chisel across her smooth and clear skin.

Just like Rebecca that night, he thought suddenly, looking at Anne in the low light. *Just like Rebecca with her childlike innocence and outlook. And just like —*

The pencil twirled slowly in Anne's hand, and Patchett reached over just as slowly and wrapped his hand softly, deliberately around hers, stilling the movement. They both sat for a moment, Patchett feeling the cool softness of her hand, Anne feeling the warmth of his. She looked at him, her deep, navy eyes studying him, and in his face she saw the concerns of her question reflected back.

"We're willing," Patchett said over that thought. "*I'm* willing to take this as far as it goes." There was another lingering stretch of stillness before he squeezed Anne's hand gently, warmly, then let it go, sitting back again.

Just like Liz, the unspoken thought finally finished. *Innocence lost.*

"I have to," Patchett added then. "This time."

"This time?" Anne repeated.

Patchett looked down at the notes strewn across the butcher-block pieces of the dinette table. Alexander Tomlin's name graced most of the notes. A record of an airline ticket charged to American Express. A car rental in Las Vegas, the same card. A gas station in Kanab, Utah. American Express.

"For a long time," Patchett began, sorting almost nervously

through the materials, "for a *long* time I don't think I would have gone that far. Wouldn't have thought that anything I could do would matter. Not weighed against the world and everything that happened in it, anyway. And that may still be right."

"But?"

As Anne's question hung in the air, Patchett continued to shuffle through the papers until he again found and once more raised the picture of the four men. *It's always the pictures,* he thought. It was always the pictures that you remembered, that you came back to.

Alex Tomlin looked at something outside the photo, beyond that flat world. His eyes squinted under the high desert sun, an arm around the shoulder of the man beside him. Four men looking like friends, standing beside a rented car in a distant desert.

Patchett kept studying the picture — the faces in it — as he spoke.

"A few years ago," he began, his voice resonating hollowly, "five to be exact." He stared at the floor for a moment, confirming the time in his mind and finding himself surprised at it. "Five years ago," he repeated before going on, "I separated from my wife. My second wife, Liz."

"I'm sorry," Anne interjected automatically, but Patchett was already shaking his head.

"It was my decision," he said. "My doing entirely. But I realized — not soon enough, but still soon — that I was wrong."

"About what?"

"About everything really," Patchett replied. "Everything I did. Everything I said. *Everything.* And it cost me."

"Cost you how?" Anne asked, the confusion lingering on her face.

"I called her eventually," Patchett said as an answer. "It would've been a couple months later. Conversation didn't go well, not at first, but it got better, and she agreed to meet me for a drink the following week." Patchett grew deathly quiet, the room a tomb around him.

"I sat in that bar for hours that night," he said softly, almost inaudibly. "Waited for a long time. Far too long, probably." He tapped a finger against the cool glass of his drink. "Had too many of these," he said, "far too many, probably. For really the first but certainly not the last time." He closed his eyes at the admission, the lids draping down as though he were in pain. "Certainly not," he said softly. Anne heard his breathing, deep and long, almost labored. Patchett shook his head.

"I convinced myself at the end of all that time and all those drinks that Liz had changed her mind about coming. She had second thoughts, decided I was too big a fuck-up to take a chance on again. Something like that."

"But she hadn't," Anne said cautiously, expectantly. Patchett's sigh was heavy, resigned.

"She was killed," he said. There was a sudden uneasy quaver in his voice. "Raped and killed. On the way to meet me, I was told later." He paused a second, calming himself. "That cost me my chance to try again," he said then, his words leveling off. "For a long time, it cost me my only chance to do something that wasn't fucked up. Something that wasn't half-assed."

"I'm sorry," Anne said again. Patchett saw the pained look on her face and felt once more the long-dormant feeling of being viewed with uncomfortable pity.

Don't be, he started to say, but he managed only the first word. "Don't . . ." The rest was lost in a soft shake of his head. "I'm over that part of it," he went on. "I'm long past the guilt." He shook his head again, staring into his drink. There were colors glistening on the surface of the shining liquid.

"The only thing that's left anymore is the bitterness," he said. "The bitterness and frustration with the world. I suppose that's a too-sensitive reaction to the senselessness that seems to be behind anything these days."

"You don't blame yourself, do you?" Anne asked incredulously.

"Myself?" Patchett said. "No, I'm over that, too. I just blame everyone — *everything* — else."

"In what sense?"

In the sense that nothing seems to matter anymore. Nothing

seems to help. The world keeps moving on. And mostly it keeps moving downhill.

"Liz didn't have to die," he said. "Tomlin, either. Neither of them, nor a thousand others like them. But there are too many things spinning out of control, too many bad actions taking too many good people, and the way of the world has become blind acceptance to that. Nothing, *no one*, matters in the end, it seems. So no one does anything. No one tries to change anything anymore. Me included."

"Then why are you trying now?" Anne asked. "Why are we sitting here, planning to go across the country to try this without even knowing what it is we're really planning to do?"

Patchett silently set the picture aside. "Because I think now that we have to," he said finally. "*I* have to, anyway. I'm scared, terrified almost, that no one really tried for Liz when he should have, and I'm scared now that no one will stand up to look at this, to look at what might have happened to Alexander Tomlin. I don't want that to be the case. So I have to make sure that I try now. For as long as I can go and as far as I can go."

"You're being too hard on yourself, Jon," Anne said. "Too demanding." Patchett was shaking his head yet again.

"You should have seen Rebecca last night," he said. "Despite everything, she looked young and idealistic. Innocent. Untainted. Open to the world. But I couldn't help but think that everything still to come in her life would beat that out of her, would flatten those feelings and beliefs and dreams. I couldn't help but think she'd learn *not* to be those things."

Patchett leaned forward and looked at Anne's face as his own came fully into the light. Her smooth good looks were untouched by the photographs and memories that had made road maps of Patchett's forehead and the whites of his eyes.

"I see that in you, too, Anne," he said softly to her. "But I think that innocence and idealism should be the norm, not the exception. That people should always want to try." He looked absently at the papers spread across the tabletop.

"I forgot that over the years," he said. "A job where things like trying aren't really important, where *good enough* is the standard. A *life* where those things are true. A life where, in fact, I felt the need to keep most of the edges as far away as possible for fear I might have to do something about them." He tapped again at the glass in front of him, then wiped a line of dampness from it. "I'm just beginning to understand the problems in those things now."

They both fell silent, watching as Harrison glanced up sleepily from the radiator vent, then yawned and stretched, his paws splayed and his front legs shot out in front of him. The cat stood slowly and moved into the kitchen. They could hear him picking a small piece of food from the bowl on the floor, the only sound left in the room.

"Did they ever catch him?" Anne asked, breaking that heavy silence. In the light of the low-hanging lamp, Patchett's eyes were empty, colored with a dull pinkish cast that was the shade of a fading sunset.

"Yeah," he said softly, "they caught him. Turned out to be an eighteen-year-old kid. Drifter. Sentenced to life. Killed himself in his cell after two years. A little more loss. Death upon death."

"I'm sorry," Anne said for the third time when Patchett's words faded to stillness in the room. It was all she could think to say.

"The way of the world," Patchett murmured in reply. "The world gets worse and worse; the pains more and more painful. No innocence remains." He paused, frowning at the sound of his own words. "Things fall apart," he said quietly.

"And so you want to go to Las Vegas," Anne said.

"So I want to go to Vegas," he echoed. He began to gather the scattered materials. "I *have* to go," he added, and he couldn't tell if the look on Anne's face was one of mingled concern and interest or only the drinks trying to convince him that she could care about his rambling discourse. That she could care about him. He looked into the glass, and he watched the swirling lights twist.

The Sixth Day

40

"DID YOU FIND THEM?"

"Of course. It was simply a matter of time."

"And?"

"Margaret Washburn's dead."

"Blood?"

"Not checked. There was too much commotion at the scene. I guess she put up a bit of a fight. Probably something he doesn't get from too many of them. So he didn't want to take the time. Was afraid he'd be spotted."

The look that greeted this news was one of pure pleasure at another step made. The grin was about to get broader.

"Gordon Grant's dead, too" came the next report. "He was identified as a John Doe at Kingland Memorial in Seattle. Died last Thursday."

"So who's left, then?" the smiling man asked.

"Peter Steffens. Haven't been able to pin him down at all, but a man or two will free up now. Do you want them put on him?" The other man was already shaking his head.

"Leave it," he said. It must have been a good day, the smile was so broad. "And tell me," the man went on, "how is everything else?"

"Fine" was the answer. "Just fine." He thought to tell him about Patchett's meeting with Rebecca Cartaway but decided not to. That could be handled, he was certain. That *would* be handled. After all, Lew Franck was a very responsible man.

41

RAYES PULLED THE PHONE from his jacket pocket and set it on the counter in the trailer. He pushed aside the stack of plates crusted with the various remnants of the last three days of his life to find a spot.

He paid no attention to the dishes or anything else crammed into the small Airstream trailer. It sat at the northern tip of an odd collection of a few buildings that made up House Rock, Arizona, less than five miles west of the house where Andy Littlefeather lay sleeping on a Sunday morning. It was just a short two miles farther east to the Littlefeathers' general store. House Rock itself was only a bump in the stretch of road crossing the flat that carried the town's name, the store merely a speck on that road.

Rayes bought his food at that store, other supplies, too, during the times when he stranded himself out here. The few things that were still left from his latest trip to Littlefeather's would rot eventually, of course. In the meantime, he figured that there was just enough to get through a few more days in the trailer. He could grab something in Kanab tomorrow, too. His final trip in. After that, the trailer and its contents could all go to dust, a somewhat suitable end.

That wouldn't really happen, naturally. The trailer and the small plug of red land on which it was beached technically belonged to the Navajo Nation, although most of the handful of residents in House Rock didn't know that. If they had, some of them probably would have buried the thing themselves long ago.

As it was, though, Rayes would just slip out. Littlefeather

would notice sooner or later, the doctor supposed, and Littlefeather would tell someone on the res soon enough. Some of them would come out here then, sometime when little attention would be paid, and they would seal up the trailer until they could find someone else to live here from time to time. That person would do what Rayes did, trying to fill in for the lack of medical care that was pervasive on the near fringe of the vast chunk of Arizona that was the reservation. Rayes wished them good luck.

He dropped with a sigh onto the dirty blanket-draped love seat that sat opposite the door, its legs removed. It occurred to him suddenly and somewhat disconcertingly that in some odd and intangible way, he might actually miss the trailer and the solitude it provided. It was a sanctuary from the rest of the world, a refuge from the drift, and it came with a peculiar sense of purpose that Rayes wondered absently if he would ever again experience.

He doubted it. A few things were made perfectly clear at the beginning of all this. The chief of those was that, at the end, when all was said and done, there would be one final discussion by phone. Then each of them was left to his own, with an entire world in which to try to find new sanctuaries. But under no set of circumstances was anyone to stay in the States.

That was it, he guessed now, as he stared at a large stain on the brown carpet and wondered why he'd let Bancroft talk him into it. That was the real reason why he went along. No more drift. Just endless sanctuary. No bothers or concerns or people to account to. Choosing his own life, making his own decisions.

No more drift.

No more cellular phone, either. It was the one thing that could reach him anywhere — a long, annoying arm with the infuriating ability to break even the seclusion here. The phone belonged to Canyonlands Hospital, and Rayes would happily give it back tomorrow. He relished the idea.

A sudden sense of poetic justice came to him at that thought, and he stood and walked quickly to the counter and plucked the phone off it. He clicked it on and dialed the small hospital in Kanab. He would find the administrator, either there or at home, and he would resign over the phone. Just as they had reached into his life so many times in the past, he would reach into theirs.

With that done, he'd just shut the damn thing off once and for all. Maybe he could get some rest then. But as he listened to the wind rustle over the top of the trailer with an empty and echoing whistle, he doubted it. He doubted if he'd really ever get any rest again.

The phone began ringing as the call went through.

42

THE SMELL of the early morning air lifted her spirits for the first time in a week. It was the hinting scent of spring, hanging just above the stillness of the park as she moved down the path. She stared vacantly out at the lake, thawed now but with a heavy coat of fog shifting over it in a soft, twisting bank. That, too, was a hint of spring — a sign of the clash of temperatures as the seasons flipped from one to the other.

She last came here years ago, on the night before storming from her parents' home — only three blocks away — chased out by her father's words. There'd been no looking back at any of it. As she walked, though, she felt once more the calming effect that she knew routinely in high school. In better years, with better moments. It was, she imagined, her favorite place.

And even as she walked past the narrow tilled garden that sat brown at the divergence to another asphalt path, she saw the heads of what looked to be tulips. They rose just above the ground, decisively ignoring the day-long brush of snow a few days past. With the right dose of warm weather and sun, they would shoot up in an eventual burst of color.

She walked on. The coolness fought with the sun to warm her cheeks, but the slight skiff of a breeze over the water was turning the tide in favor of a lingering chill. Looking ahead, she saw a knot of trees. They would cut the wind and give her face and cheeks, blushed with light windburn, a break to warm up. She took the path that veered left toward the woods.

Her thoughts turned naturally, unavoidably, to Alex as she walked, and her conversation with Patchett hung with her momentarily. She'd told him that she had loved Alex, and wasn't that certainly true?

Wasn't it?

She thought it was, just as it was true that Alex loved her, more than he was ever able to convey. But there were her parents to deal with. They had always been of too important interest to Alex. He'd been a man of a different generation.

And there was the work. The whole truth was that it was his compulsive attention to his work, his obsession with Prohiva, that caused the strain that dominated their relationship over the past few months. *Not a strain that would cause his death*, she thought, *but one that was there nevertheless.* One that she first noticed, in fact, in the letter from last December that now sat bundled with the others at home, waiting to be handed to Patchett. Let him make of them what he could.

What mattered was that the problems had, she thought, been thawing slowly. Even as she heard of Alex's death just a week ago, she was beginning to once again believe that they would survive whatever it was that so consumed him for those months. There were the bad moments, of course, including a major step back toward his obsession despite an earnest promise to get away from it. But overall, he'd become warmer, more open, more like the gentle man whom she had come to know. And then he was dead, just as fast.

The tears came back. They no longer surprised her — not anymore — and she no longer made great efforts to control them, at least not when alone. A veritable flood of tears bothered her originally. But the weepy sob that largely replaced those extreme episodes since that time was now tolerated as an unavoidable but passing trait of her life over the past few days.

The world swam a little, lines doubling and wavering before

her as she walked. She tried to blink her eyes clear, and she felt a thin line of water trace down one cheek. She wiped it away with the back of a hand.

A mallard floated idly on the water, its green head catching the patchy sunlight in a sparkle of emerald. She watched it for a moment, clearing her eyes. She could just see the duck's feet, swinging back and forth beneath the water's surface as they paddled. There was a band of metal around one leg.

When the flash blurred before her, glinting in the tears that welled at the corners of her eyes, she jerked slightly, thinking for an instant that a bird had swooped down. But the sharp burn across her neck crushed her larynx with searing constriction, shocking all thoughts of birds out of her mind. It choked off her startled cry as she was pulled against someone who had not been there one second before.

She could feel the hot breath by her ear even above the terrifying force behind her and the flaring pain on and in her neck. She heard him whisper something, but it meant nothing to her, and she barely registered it.

Her heart pounded in her ears. Lungs began to ache shockingly in their realization that air was cut off. Her hands flailed up, and she felt the cord cutting tightly into her neck. She gouged at herself, trying and failing to pull it from the steadily growing crevice that circled her like a garotte. Her mouth opened. No sound came out.

The world swam again as she tipped back. This time, it moved not in the waved lines of teary eyes but in the black lines of growing unconsciousness. The mallard floated for one second more in her vision.

She felt her feet dragging across the path and onto the ground. They dug light furrows in the dead grass, but she felt nothing else.

The Seventh Day

43

THE NEWSPAPER splayed over the desk in front of him, the first page squared and flattened on top. Patchett was staring at it, carefully examining the words but not truly comprehending them. The pages were already smeared at the edges from repeated handling.

He wasn't really even reading it anymore. He had stopped long ago, and he sat now fixed only on a few of the words that continued to stand out.

Murdered. Victim. Barber. Strangled.

And the picture. Above all, the picture.

It was always the pictures.

Patchett thought maybe he'd even glanced at this one in her bedroom. It was probably taken from a high school's library of yearbooks within minutes of Rebecca's name floating over the AP wires in the city. Her parents might not even have known at that point. Their daughter wore braces in the picture.

The article, typical of articles on the Barber murders, was almost totally devoid of any real information. He saw the reference to the park. The street was noted as well, and Patchett knew that it was just blocks from her home.

Her parents' home, he corrected himself. He doubted that

Rebecca ever would have really claimed it as hers again. She'd gone back to her old neighborhood to find a little shelter. She found a murderer instead.

There were also the veiled allusions to a rape, and Patchett felt himself wince. *Just like Liz,* the inevitable thought came. As with every article on the Barber, this one brought the ready rawness of Patchett's past back into his life. With every article and every mention of the crimes, that pain became alive once again, washing over him with its cool drape of bitterness and frustration.

With it came another picture this time, an image of Rebecca with her hair pulled back in a ponytail, her stockinged feet curled against the cold. *Innocence lost,* the words rang in his head. Ideals, opportunities — hopes and wishes and dreams — all lost in the blinking seconds of a decision made by a madman. Lost and never to be found again.

"It's the way of the world," Patchett whispered to the empty walls of his office, his head tipped forward in otherwise silent anguish. *Liz,* he thought. *Liz. Tomlin. Rebecca.* His words to Anne were right — the world was consistently spinning out of control, and it was going nowhere but downhill.

"Things fall apart," Patchett said then.

Had someone been in the office, she might have noticed a slight tremble as Patchett reached for the briefcase. He found the flask inside without looking, his hands simply tracing leather seams until reaching and unsnapping the small pouch. He held the bottle up before him and twisted the cap, listening without thought to the crack of the seal — a new bottle to replace the one he finished yesterday.

But he froze at the sound, and his eyes fell searchingly on the clear bottle of clear liquid. He could see his own pained expression reflected in the glass.

No one tries anymore, echoed the voice in his mind. His own voice. More words spoken to Anne — what was it? — only two days back. *No one tries anymore,* the voice repeated, and Patchett caught the image in the flask once again.

Not even you, that image said to him. *Not even you.*

Every crisis in Patchett's life, every event good or bad, for that matter, was marked with the cruel touch of a bottle. He thought of Liz, the opportunities taken away there. He thought of Tomlin and the things he'd sacrificed. He thought of Rebecca, of her hopeless crushing love for a distant wish. Of things she never got and now never would.

And in those moments he wondered how many opportunities of his own he'd missed. How many loves, how many women loving him, how many wishes went unnoticed in the steady blur of alcohol.

There comes a time in every alcoholic's life when he holds a drink before him and assesses his existence through the liquid in the glass. And he drinks. Or he doesn't. The why sometimes escapes understanding.

Patchett tipped the flask slowly, and it first trickled and then flowed its contents onto a soon-to-be-dead plant. He didn't drink.

The taste hung in his memory, standing in place of other things that were missing, and he longed for it. But he didn't drink, and he tossed the empty bottle into the garbage can. He blinked once, twice, three times, suddenly trying to calm himself, trying to ease his mind enough to function. He breathed in heavily, then blew it out in a sigh that was just as heavy.

Turning uneasily to the paper, his eye caught references to the estimated time of the murder and the time that Rebecca's body was discovered. She was killed yesterday, in the early morning. A jogger —it was always a jogger, it seemed—came across the body a little past eight.

It was the times—the early morning hours—that first made Patchett trace his finger back through the article once more. A smudge followed his finger as he studied each paragraph briefly. There was something in his mind about the Barber murders, something that always turned him into the prosecutor he had once wanted to be. He was looking for the slim evidence that was ever present in articles on the murders, studying the words carefully, digesting the available facts, trying to read between the lines and trying to remember everything he ever saw or heard or knew during his short months in the prosecutor's office.

The rape. The strangulation. The cut hair. A cord still around the victim's neck. The park. The hallmark of the serial killer was the consistency between the murders, Patchett recalled, and that was here in spades.

Everything except for one thing.

The *times*.

Patchett checked the estimated time of the murder again and sat back unsteadily, realization dawning on him. If Rebecca was killed around 6:30 or 7:00 in the morning, as the article indicated, it was a marked deviation from the usual.

But the incongruity of that almost made him laugh. To expect that a deviant couldn't deviate was ludicrous. The "usual" murder for a serial killer?

Still, Patchett knew at the same time that it wasn't ridiculous at all. Serial killers were caught precisely because they were predictable. But this one just became unpredictable, because the deaths of the other women were all in the late afternoon or early evening, not the morning. And that difference was a shift that just didn't fit with what could be expected.

Patchett knew the typical profile well enough: a young white male, with average to above-average intelligence. Something of a loner, probably. Quiet. Usually never married. And according to that profile, the man would restructure his life before he would change the way he killed.

All of that suggested one thing to Patchett, and it was that one thing that made him sit back. It depended on an assumption, of course, and that assumption was marked out with neon lights for anyone who could stand far enough away to make out the clues and who looked hard enough at the pieces to make them fit together.

The Barber wouldn't change his schedule. Patchett felt that was true — he *knew* it was true with a sudden, loud clarity that seemed to ring in his ears with unsettling certainty. But there was no telling exactly whose schedule was at work here. All of the other signs — the location where a body might be found, the manner of death — were all a sufficiently controllable set of circumstances. With the single exception of the time of day. If you wanted to make it look like something else, some*one* else, you could manipulate

224 / PATRICK REINKEN

everything. Except for the time. That was up to fate. The opportune time would be dictated by chance alone.

That was only the case if the victim mattered, though, Patchett knew. If she didn't, then time was controllable as well, and this would look exactly like the Barber's work. Would, in fact, probably *be* the Barber's work.

But the victim *did* matter, Patchett suddenly thought. The victim did matter, and this wasn't the Barber's work at all. With a continuing sense of unease, Patchett was certain of that.

The times were too different, and that meant the victim mattered very much. That meant that Rebecca Cartaway was singled out. More and more, with each passing thought, Patchett knew that Rebecca wasn't claimed by some peculiar twist of chance. She was killed because of who she was. Just like her boyfriend. And that meant one thing.

Patchett lifted the front page from his desk and read its screaming headline. BARBER CLAIMS ANOTHER, it said boldly. The print stood out like an epitaph, high and black against the light-gray newsprint. TOLL CLIMBS TO SEVEN ran underneath in the subhead.

"Six," Patchett said quietly to himself. He tossed the paper onto the desk. "Still only six."

And he was scared as he said it. Even before he knew it. Rebecca was dead, and Patchett found himself scared as he suddenly realized that the list of reasons for that death was stunningly short, with his own name too uncomfortably close to the top.

It was the only thing that made sense really. Rebecca hadn't known anything relevant, although Patchett wondered in the same instant if her killer could have known that.

No, the attorney knew. Whoever killed her most likely couldn't have known that at all. What he *would* know was that, as Tomlin's secretary, Rebecca probably saw everything Tomlin ever did, which meant she probably knew, heard about, or at least looked at everything work related that Tomlin prepared.

And the killer might also know about the relationship, Patchett thought. That could have sealed her fate, and if it hadn't, Patchett's contact with her almost certainly did.

The numbing sense of loss returned, accompanied this time by a guilt that overwhelmed the growing fear, even if for only a moment.

Patchett lifted the phone and punched his secretary's number. "I need plane tickets for four to Las Vegas," he said when she answered. "Leaving tonight. Tomorrow morning at the latest."

"Returning?"

He thought of Anne again.

"Wednesday. Late though."

"Hotel?"

"No." Hotel rooms could always be found in Vegas, and he doubted that March was a big tourist season in Kanab, Utah. He doubted that there *was* a tourist season in Kanab.

"I'll get the tickets here as soon as possible."

Patchett called Anne's office next and got her voice mail before remembering she was in class for the morning. He called the college for a half hour after that, trying unsuccessfully to track her down. He left messages with five people, most of whom wouldn't have the slightest notion who she was.

He turned his attention back to the rest of what would be the first of a series of intensely busy days. The key would be Bancroft and Rayes. But one other thing was still out there, and he knew he needed to get that, too.

That one thing was the letters. Tomlin's letters to Rebecca unavoidably appreciated in value on her death. They were, in fact, probably the sole real evidence of Rebecca's relationship with Tomlin, Tomlin's work in Arizona, and the substance of the Vegas trips themselves. Patchett knew he needed to collect the letters from Rebecca's parents.

More than that, though, he would have to ask Dearson about Rebecca. Michael Dearson was a deputy district attorney and a longtime friend, and he'd know more than Patchett could guess at from reading between the lines of newspaper articles.

It was no accident they were having lunch today; Patchett had called him Saturday to arrange it. Dearson was the person he'd told Anne he wanted to talk to before heading to Vegas. That talk was supposed to be about Tomlin, of course, but the topics of conversation doubled with the morning's news.

Patchett collected the paper and took a long last look at Rebecca's photo. He wanted it to be an apology, but he knew painfully that his sorrow and any words or thoughts that came with it were worthless to her now. Those things were too late for Rebecca. He tossed the paper at the trash can. It covered the bottle.

44

RAYES COULDN'T BELIEVE his eyes. The track was clear. A soft rain had erased the flatness of the worn surface of the trail, replacing it with the slightly agitated look of raindrop-spotted dirt. And in that rough pattern stood the thin line of a motorbike tread. Even the wear bars in the tires were etched cleanly into the desert floor.

He noticed it first when he got out of the truck to open the gate, which was still barred against intruders. At least against the largest intruders, Rayes corrected. But the tracks were clear. Someone rode the bike up here, then got off to slip the bike through the fence. Behind Rayes, the snaking evidence led back toward 89A, crisscrossed occasionally by Rayes's own tire tracks.

Ahead, on the other side of the fence, footprints disappeared as the narrow tire print ran on again down the trail to the extent of his vision. A small bike, by the looks of it, and by the fact that it was lifted through. A small man, too. Maybe a kid.

Rayes snapped the key in the padlock and shot the bolt open with a twist. Jerking the key free, he scrambled back to the truck and jumped in. He was through the fence in an instant, the dust flying out behind in a red cloud that rose gracefully on the hot air rising in wavering rays off the ground.

As he drove, Rayes reached over to the glove box and opened it. The gun was there, of course, its slender nose needling up at him. He'd put it there not a half hour before. He pulled it out and set it on the seat, unsnapping the catch on the leather holster almost automatically.

He'd never really given this too much thought, to be honest about it. He expected the job of looking in on the site. He was the only one who was in the position to do it. And he also wasn't surprised at the 9mm that was provided to him as part of that job. But Rayes had never really thought it through until this point, as he hefted the black steel pistol.

Distantly, the echoes of a long-forgotten oath rang in his mind, but the unease growing in him pushed that away. This, Rayes realized as the desert flew and bumped by, this was working toward circumstances he didn't want to face.

He should have kept going toward Kanab in the first place. Shouldn't even have turned down the road. And he wasn't sure why he had. The site was checked only a couple of days ago. But the passing thought that he might not get another chance had come to him, echoed by the long-ago stated request to check frequently as they neared the end. So he'd hooked his finger into the cross-bar on the steering wheel at the last second, pulling the truck in a shuddering spin off the road and down the trail toward the fence.

Rayes passed his usual pull-off spot and headed for another point a half mile farther down the road. He slowed down to trim the dusty rooster tail that was following him.

A sufficient distance away, he slapped the truck into park, shutting it off. He stepped out and made his way up the slight hill, covering the distance in a trot, then dropped down the ragged edge of a wash before moving up the other side. From that edge, he could almost see the site, which sat down a gradual slope running away from him. He hunched and slipped over a few yards, keeping the gun out before him and an eye on the squared-off area.

When it came into view, he noticed two things in quick succession. First, he saw with growing anxiety that the outline of the site was still visible on the ground. A clear scar etched the desert despite the recent fading and his own fervent hopes that it would all soon be wiped away. Looking at it now, he knew he'd kidded himself in thinking that it was magically disappearing.

And then he saw the motorbike. Peering over the small jutting bluff that sat at the eastern end, above the site, Rayes looked out over the short distance of the flat that separated him from the bike, and he raised the pistol. He watched for movement.

Andy ran the trail all the way to its end, reaching the deserted and severely battered ranch house that sat there. It had obviously been uninhabited for years and had long been abandoned to the encroaching sand and grit of the flat. No window was left unbroken, whether by wind or by vandals. The sparse green weeds, which from a distance would make the valley look like a putting green, shot up through the cracks of the dried planks on the porch. A skeletal car sat preserved at one side.

Andy soon left the house behind to run the bike up some of the cattle paths that dipped into the ground in a helter-skelter web spreading out over the desert like crooked spokes. He wanted to try to locate the bike's oil leak, and he was running the Honda hard. He stopped frequently to wipe away the grime and reinspect.

He crossed miles of ground before stopping to survey where he was. It was impossible to get lost out here in the daytime. Some significant landmark from the Kaibab to the Vermilion Cliffs to Marble Canyon was visible at every point in the valley. Still, losing bearings was common at night. It was also expected of strangers who wandered into the area, with a few plucked out each month. But Andy, who knew the flat even in the darkness, soon figured precisely where he was. He turned slightly and set out again.

He was heading across the valley toward the main trail when he first came to the wound in the desert floor. There was no mistaking it. The squared-off lines were distinct to Andy, whose understanding of the desert exceeded that of most people. When he glanced down from the gentle slope, he caught sight of it, and he swung the bike to a dusty stop.

He rolled to the edge of the small bluff, then worked his way farther down. He lowered the bike's wobbling kickstand and pulled the helmet from his head. Getting off, he set the helmet down and moved to the nearest mark.

The marks were less visible close up; from the sky, they would have been like lines painted on a parking lot. But no one would have seen these from up there. The Grand Canyon pulled all the light plane traffic farther to the south, and the limits on jet travel over the canyon put the flat in the center of the Los Angeles, Denver, and Phoenix air corridors. Andy Littlefeather had only seen one plane flying in his entire life, and it wasn't above House Rock Valley.

He paced his way slowly around the lines. He figured that the whole thing was maybe fifteen feet by twenty-five feet total. A postage stamp in the vast reach of space on the flat.

Walking nearer the center, he studied more closely, sitting to examine the plants. Some were dead. And all had been planted by hand.

On that count, too, wetter locations would have eradicated any real evidence that otherwise remained to show that something wasn't right. Here, though, Andy could just make out some signs. Brush that looked like some radical form of sod. Cacti that didn't quite sit right. Whatever this was, someone had tried to turn it into desert again.

He stood and knocked at the dust on his black jeans. The red smudges remained anyway, and he ignored them. People couldn't get concerned about dirt in the desert, particularly on a thirteen-year-old boy.

He was actually scratching his head in puzzlement when he heard the small rock dislodge and tumble off the little bluff that outcropped over this place. He turned in time to see it roll in quick drops, zigzagging down to rest at the bottom of the bluff.

And it was only then that he saw the man. Dim recognition of what the man held was slow in coming. It wasn't that Andy had never seen a pistol before. He just had never had one pointed at him.

The man stood on the bluff, then moved down to stop a few yards away. Andy thought he knew him.

For the briefest second, Rayes's finger pressed on the trigger. He first saw the bike rider sitting and examining the brush near the

opposite fringe. He swung the 9mm over and concentrated carefully but briefly to steady a shaky aim. His finger tightened against
the trigger, not pulling on it but mashing it as a forgotten uncle
had taught him to do once upon a time.

And it didn't move. The trigger stopped dead, caught by the
safety. Nervously, Rayes fumbled the safety off. As he did so, his
elbow caught the bluff's edge where he lay, and a small tumble
cascaded a few feet down the hill.

Rayes thrust the pistol out again, but this time the bike rider
was standing. The doctor relaxed in a nervous release of fear and
quickly stood up.

The person before him was not some man furiously examining
the site. It was a teenage boy. Streaks of red dirt ran down one hip.
The boy was scratching at a mop of dirty black hair that shone in
the sun. A Navajo, Rayes saw.

When the boy looked up, he started at seeing Rayes, who
stepped carefully down to the level surface. The doctor lowered
his gun.

"What in the hell do you think you are doing here?"

The boy was frozen in place, as much an immobile part of the
desert as the cliffs rising in the heat to the north. They towered
behind Rayes in the distance.

The boy didn't speak. His arms hung stiff at his sides, his
shoulders hunched up slightly with a terrified look of apprehension.

When Rayes got closer, he saw he knew the child, that it was
Andy Littlefeather. He'd seen the boy running around his father's
store in House Rock. It was only then that Rayes put the safety back
on and slipped the 9mm into the back of his pants, pulling his shirt
over it. It felt cool and heavy against his skin.

Andy relaxed at the disappearance of the gun, but he still
didn't speak as Rayes came up beside him and squatted down.

"You are Andy, correct?"

The boy nodded and managed a quiet "yes."

"What are you doing out here, Andy?" Rayes's tone was softer.
The anxious shock was gone, replaced by the precisely delivered
moderate sound of a doctor.

"I was just riding my dirt bike," Andy said, his voice shaking. He lifted one arm at the elbow and pointed in the direction of the small Honda. It sat waiting in the sun, a tantalizing hint of escape.

Rayes glanced over more for Andy's benefit than his own. He'd already scared the shit out of the kid. Out of himself, too. And the only chance at calming the boy and what the boy might say was by acting as though the gun never existed. Thinking about his finger tightening against the trigger, he wondered if he could manage it.

"Nice bike," he said. He turned back to Andy. "But you know this is a private ranch. The people who own it might be a little upset if everyone came out here to ride around."

"Didn't mean to make trouble." Andy's voice was barely there in the massive, open space surrounding them.

"Of course you did not," Rayes said warmly. "And I am sure there is no damage done. But you did see the fence, did you not?"

Andy didn't reply. Of course he'd seen the fence. He'd struggled to get the bike through it. He could hardly claim something else.

He nodded.

"Well," said Rayes, "that fence is there for a reason, and that is to keep people out of here." He looked at Andy gravely, searching for a reaction and trying to judge how much of the story, worked out months ago, should be told. Still squatting down by Andy, he shifted his weight to his other leg, and he went on.

"You see, Andy, this ranch had a problem with its cattle. Something called brucellosis. It is a disease, and the cattle got it. So they were killed."

Rayes paused to make sure Andy was paying attention. The boy's face was intent, already tainted with the marks of fascinated fear.

"Some of them are buried right under our feet here." Rayes fell silent, watching as small eyes widened.

Although Andy wasn't raised in all the Navajo traditions and teachings, they nevertheless formed a part of him. He was exposed to them daily in his contacts with the foreign yet familiar social structure and religious life of the nearby reservation. His life was dominated by the Nation and by his contacts with it, from the schoolkids he saw each day to the soft and invisible tendrils of culture that seeped out from its borders.

And of all of the things that he knew of Navajo ways, the one that Andy understood best was the reverential respect for the dead. Any dead, including animals, which according to Navajo belief used to be people.

It was contact with evil, not bad deeds that made people bad, and contact with the dead was particularly dangerous. It could destroy the delicate balance of good and tip the level closer to the uncontrolled and disorganized world of evil. Even unintentional contact could lead to disturbance of harmony and cause illness. Even now, as he stood on ground that this man just pronounced to be a place of the dead, Andy trembled at the thought of ghost sickness and the Evilway ritual that he'd heard mentioned at school. Though he didn't know what it involved, the very thought of its name suggested the dangers of the infectious darkness to which he was so close.

The thought of the ghosts was the one lifelong lesson that came to Andy each night as he pulled covers up tightly under his chin. And it was staring him in the face now.

Rayes saw the fear in Andy's eyes so clearly that his own nervousness returned. He stood and moved toward the edge of the marked area.

"Come," he said, and Andy needed no more prompting as he ran to stand next to the bike. He picked the helmet up and held it against his chest like a shield.

"There is nothing to worry about," Rayes said, catching up to him. "There are no sick cattle left, but we still keep the ranch off limits, and we try not to alarm anyone unnecessarily. Do you understand that, son?"

Andy nodded but didn't look up at Rayes, who stood beside him. He concentrated on the trace of lines on the ground.

"All right. Head back to the highway. You can pick up the trail about a quarter mile over. I left the gate open. I shall go down to the ranch house to explain what has happened."

Andy didn't stop to consider the part about the ranch house as he jerked the helmet on his head. Rayes watched as the boy got on the bike, starting it without even pausing to fasten his chin strap. The Honda buzzed up the incline and disappeared from view.

Rayes listened until he could no longer hear the whine of the small engine, then he pulled the gun back out of his pants and sat on the ground. He stared at the pistol's black brushed-metal surface, resting it in his hand.

Rayes realized with unnerving shock that he had almost shot a boy who was barely a teenager. Without a moment's hesitation to even think about it, he had pulled the trigger to kill this person. Only the safety had kept him from *doing* it.

Looking up, he breathed a deep and ragged sigh.

He couldn't call anyone on this. The instructions were explicit. His instructions were, in fact, to "take care of" anyone out here. *Anyone.* The brucellosis story was only the last-ditch, whispered agreement among the others.

Rayes wasn't following those instructions.

He pondered whether he should have. Andy was just a boy, but boys talked, too. Still, it was just too close to be adding even more loose ends. If Andy disappeared, there'd be an investigation and search of the entire area within hours.

When his guilt began to rise at those thoughts, Rayes once more reminded himself of the bigger picture, sitting and working it out again under the rising sun and heat of the Arizona morning. He thought of the contribution to scientific advancement that was supposed to make it all even out.

But it didn't work this time, because when you came right down to it, he had just tried to kill a *child*. In the end, that was what mattered and what pushed him over the edge and back toward the course that would take him on the final drift. His life, Rayes knew, was not in his own hands. It never had been. Not since being blamed for the death of another child long ago.

Rayes set the pistol down in the red sandy dirt before him. He held his head in his hands to control his shaking. And he sobbed.

45

THE PRINTER DRONED as the carriage shot left and right, back and forth across the spindled paper that was tractor feeding into the machine. A twisted pile of connected pages was gathering on the floor like a crooked stream of soft-serve drawn onto a cone by a trainee at Dairy Queen.

The paper bridge stretching between the printer carriage and the neat stack of still-boxed perforated sheets churned out a steady stream of white pages filled with dot matrix rows and columns of names, addresses, dates, and numbers.

The first sheet sat on a table before Lew Franck, and he was running a pen down one edge of the page. He checked off names in a comparison to the notepad that also lay before him.

The computer list and the notepad both held the master list of hospital names. There were 125 entries on each, designating the hospitals that would, in turn, seek out 40 participants for the Phase III study of Prohiva. Most of the hospitals, notified weeks ago, were done collecting their names; they could start testing by Thursday.

The sheets coming off the printer contained the third draft of instructions and guidelines written by Weber BioTech and the FDA. When that finished spinning off, it would be reviewed a final time and printed again for inclusion in the Prohiva packages.

Those packages sat stacked one floor down. One hundred twenty-five boxes, blue-bannered with orange Federal Express lettering running across them. Each box held 100 vials of the Prohiva serum. Two vials per person for a total of 80 per hospital — one initial vaccine and one booster to be used as directed, should that decision be made. Plus twenty extras per hospital as a contingency.

Five thousand people would get the vaccine. Five thousand more would get injections of saline from more vials that were boxed one floor above Franck. But only the ones who got the Prohiva really mattered.

Franck doubted the contingency vaccines would be needed for those people, and he was certain that the boosters wouldn't be. Many of the 5,000 people who got the first shot of Prohiva would be noticeably sick within a few months, and all 5,000 would be dead in a couple years at the outside, give or take some time. There'd never be a need for a second shot for anyone.

He sat back from his hunched position over the paper. His pen lifted off the sheet and hovered there, a stalactite hanging over a community hospital in Wichita.

Did it bother him? That was a question that had long remained out of his mind, because the answer was no. Simply put, it did not bother him. And it never had.

Even as Alfre Rayes sat crying in House Rock Valley, the pistol with which he almost killed a child sitting as an accusation in the dirt before him, Franck bent once more over the sheet of names and checked Sedgwick Regional Hospital off the list.

Lew Franck was not Rayes. There never was the level of compassion in him, struggling up at inconvenient times, that there was in a doctor in whose arms a little girl died in El Cajon. Instead, Franck was always able to keep the ultimate goal firmly in mind: He'd be rich and living in the South Seas or wherever. Untouchable. What happened here happened, and no tears would be lost.

Franck checked off the last recipient of the vaccine, folded the paper, and tucked it into his notes. With only the slightest of smiles breaking his face at that thought, he stood and turned, stepping past the growing pile of instructions, then he stiff-armed the door and walked out.

46

WHEN SHE LOOKED over her book, he was still there. Not looking at her this time, but still there nonetheless.

Anne saw the man the first time outside her morning class.

She didn't really take much notice then. She barely registered that he was there at all, didn't actually remember it until later.

The next time, she was coming out of that class and was on her way to the second one. He was propped against the bike rack there, fighting a newspaper in the light breeze that was blowing steadily. It was the shirt that she noticed and recalled. A bright pink, long-sleeved T, neon-colored and vibrant even in the March midmorning sun. There were wraparound sunglasses, too, with pink reflective lenses like she hadn't seen in years. Those two things caught her eye and made her notice him.

She didn't know him, had never seen him before. It was a big campus with lots of faces she had never seen before, would never see again.

But most of the faces fit in better than this one. Fashions three or four years out of place. A face maybe a decade out of place, judging by the beard-shadowed, tough-skinned look. A *man* out of place. He would have blended into a crowd five years ago, but not now.

She saw him the third time at the union. The paper was gone, a jacket covered most of the shirt. But a fringe of the shirt's bright color was visible, and the sunglasses hung from the collar. A copy of *Newsweek* was open in front of him. He turned a page as she watched, but she saw him glance over at her, then look instantly away. He flipped another page without really looking at it.

Men had stared at Anne before. Every woman in the world has been stared at, and Anne was certainly attractive enough to come across that uncomfortably flattering but somewhat offensive indignity more than once. She had even been followed before — she hadn't liked it then, and she didn't like it now. But as she looked over her book once more and saw him, it wasn't just the instant, shivery crawl of being leered at. This was more, she realized, feeling a touch of fear edge up her back and settle at the base of her neck.

She watched for more than five minutes, one eye always on him as he paged briskly through the magazine. She watched the clock, too, waiting for the hands to swing up toward lunch. Anne read her own book and patiently bided her time.

•

The law school on the west bank of the campus, past the intervening Mississippi, sat square and low to the ground. Inside, the law library was a tomb, with its nondescript barrackslike interior and dim lighting. The concrete construction was bare, broken only by the endless racks of seemingly identical books. Students sat silently at long tables that were dominated by center rows of low fluorescent bulbs. An occasional pair or threesome was talking in hushed tones, fingers sometimes tracing arcane passages in a torts or contracts or property text.

Gary and Linda Kane pushed two thin volumes into a knapsack at the checkout desk beyond the divider doors and windows, and Gary slung the sack over one shoulder. "Maybe we shouldn't go," he was saying. They moved down the hall toward the door.

Linda looked at him with frustration and disbelief. They had talked about this almost every waking moment since Anne had called them Saturday night. Linda thought they already reached a decision, but her husband was backing away from it.

"I thought we went through this," she protested. They stepped out into the parking lot and headed to their small car. It sat on the far side of the lot, rusted holes perforating the metal like buckshot wounds circling the entire lower foot of the body.

"I know, but it doesn't seem right to just up and leave."

"Get used to it. If we expect to stay long at the firm, then we better be accustomed to 'upping and leaving' without much notice. You know that."

"It just seems so strange."

"It *is* strange. Being a lawyer is strange." That didn't seem to help. "Anne said that Jon would fill us in later today," she continued. "We at least have to hear him out."

"If we hear him out, then we'll have to go."

"I *want* to go, Gary. This is supposed to be exciting. We're supposed to be able to learn things and do things and see things. In a few years, it'll probably be a drudge to us. Or we'll never get the chance or have the energy to go at all.

"Besides," she concluded, "we never got a honeymoon. This

can be our honeymoon." She wrapped an arm around his waist, circling him under the shouldered knapsack. Gary looked at her.

"I don't think that this will be like a honeymoon," he said cautiously. "I don't think it'll be like that at all."

Gary hooked a finger into the rusted hole where the trunk lock once was and lifted the lid open. He tossed the knapsack into the back and closed the trunk, slipping a dangling coat hanger wire into the hole to connect the lid to what was left of the back bumper.

"You want to do this?" he said across the car roof to Linda as he climbed in.

"Yes," she said. "I want to do this." She got in the other door and sat on a squeaky spring buried in the battered bench seat. "If nothing else," she said, "it'll score some points with the right people."

That was true, and they both knew it. They also both knew the advantages in pleasing the "right people" at the firm. It could mean the difference between shuttling your résumé around for another year or having a $60,000 salary.

"All right," he said. There was reluctance in his words, perhaps resignation, but Linda also heard the unmistakable sound of Gary finally committing to his decision.

The car started in a roar of blue smoke.

Jason Burke was almost at the end of the *newsweek*, and he was very nearly asleep, too. He'd been back in town twelve hours or so. Barely enough time to think, really, but Franck already had him out after someone else. Burke glanced with shuttering eyes at his watch.

He got about four hours of sleep before getting to Anne Matheson's apartment this morning, and waiting for Matheson between her classes since that time was just about killing him. He would have taken little solace in the knowledge that it was an unusually busy day for her as well, with the hectic pace of preexam rushing. He wouldn't have cared had he known. He only cared about his exhaustion.

The schedule over the past several months was just too much.

Burke wanted to tell Franck that, was thinking of telling Franck that even as he was handed Matheson's picture and pointed out the door again with his latest instructions.

He went without complaining, of course. You couldn't really complain too much in the end — the rewards from acting without words were too great, the potential penalty for displeasing the wrong person or persons too severe.

And so Burke's complaints — about the frantic pace over the last months, about this new assignment tailing on the others even before he caught his breath — those complaints were dimly recalled frustrations right now. They were lost in the automatic responsive actions he was once again stepping through and in the slow and soft fog of his fatigue.

Burke closed the magazine and rubbed at his eyes, fighting to push the tiredness away and trying to mask it with the look of a weary student killing time between classes. He looked again at his watch and only then really noticed the passage of minutes and the growth of the crowd that filled the union wall to wall with a shifting lunchtime assembly of humanity. Hundreds of people milled through the room.

He shot up in his chair, heart-poundingly awake and aware and suddenly not mindful of either his covertness or the magazine, which flew unnoticed to the floor. A woman at the next table glanced over, then turned back to her own crowd, shaking her head slightly.

Burke searched through the swarming students, his head moving from side to side as he peered around people before seeing her table.

Anne Matheson was gone.

Anne tossed the book bag hurriedly into her car. It landed with a bounce on the seat. She got in, fumbling hurriedly in her jacket pocket for keys. She jammed one into the ignition when she found them.

She spun down the parking garage ramp and out onto the street, almost losing her toll card at the automatic gate. Anne was in a hurry. For the first time in her life, she went fast enough to make the car's tires squeal on the pavement.

She headed for downtown.

47

THE MINNEAPOLIS CLUB is an anachronism in the middle of downtown. It sits, squarish and small, with crenellated brown-brick towers that fall under the shadows of neighboring skyscrapers from earliest morning through the time that the sun falls slowly to the west behind the towering and black, glass-paneled face of the IDS Center and the lesser heights of the neighboring Baker Center. In the summer, the club's building is green with ivy, but it sat starkly this March, last year's growth clinging dead and dry in occasional corners.

It is one of the last bastions of power-brokered business lunches in the Twin Cities, a stiflingly cloistered world of overstarched linens and professionally designed and arranged food, a consistent choice of social-club driven powerful people and of people wanting to be among that group. Wanting to be seen and wanting to rub shoulders with those more well connected than they.

Patchett sat at a corner table with Michael Dearson, menus unfolded before them. Patchett drank from his water glass, surveying his friend over the list of lunches and wondering what would be the latest piece of information to try to cram into place.

Dearson was a big black man who didn't so much sit at a table as overwhelm it. His formidable frame, valuable and talented enough to put him through college on a football scholarship, controlled the space as effectively as it usually controlled a courtroom.

Dearson turned a page in the menu, and Patchett continued to study him. He first met the man while in the prosecutor's office. Dearson was new at that time, different from Patchett only in the law degree that he freshly held and the bar exam that he was in the process of studying for. One law clerk and one wet-behind-the-ears prosecutor who couldn't try a case without supervision until the bar results came back. They stumbled together through Patchett's few months at the Government Center.

Patchett remembered that he was afraid that his new friend wouldn't approve when it was ultimately announced that Allen, Sander had made an offer that Patchett couldn't refuse. Patchett had been right. At least to a point.

Dearson approved of the money. Everyone approved of the money. But there was the expected question from him and assorted others about "selling out" to that money. Selling out to big clients, nice suits, big bills, and comforts supported at some point by stepping on others.

Defending baby killers, Patchett now remembered someone calling it. He didn't remember who it was, and it didn't really matter anymore. But he still remembered the sound of it, ringing out as a joke with a too-heavy smack of seriousness pushing not too subtly behind it.

So, what's it like to be defending baby killers?

Patchett did his best to ignore the smirking question back then, but he knew that ignoring it never made the nagging accusation — right or wrong — go away. For there it was, once again, hanging in his mind, the slightly self-righteous and smug satisfaction that he once held in the face of that statement now replaced by a feeling that tasted more of uncertainty and mistrust — more of fear that the words were accurate — than of anything else.

Patchett considered the events he was here to discuss with his friend. He ran once more through the morsels of information that he knew, weighing them against the yawning appetite of questions backed up by even more questions, leading to . . .

Leading to what, he did not know.

Defending baby killers, echoed the old accusation in his mind as he reconsidered everything from the last week.

Defending —

"What're you so intent on?" Dearson asked, and Patchett's stare broke.

"Nothing," he said thoughtfully, looking at his friend. "I was just wondering if you were gonna answer some questions for me."

Dearson grinned. "I didn't really think you called me to catch up on old times." He closed his menu and set it aside before unfolding the napkin that sat pyramided on his plate. He draped it over his lap.

"What is it you want to know?" Dearson asked.

"A little bit of your business."

"I expected that. It has kind of a bad sound to hear it, though. Especially from you. You remember what happened last time?"

Patchett did remember. All too well. He'd once represented a client who was in a car accident, one that led to difficulties with the other driver. It reached the point where Patchett got a default judgment and started the process of attaching the man's wages.

That ended abruptly when the man disappeared.

Most would have written it off. Most would have let their own insurance cover the problem. But this client drove a Porsche and operated on a self-pronounced and defined set of "principles," at least when it came to getting his fifty thousand dollars or so back. Patchett had turned to Dearson to track the other driver down.

You would think that it wouldn't be that big a deal really. The criminal justice system has information ties that are tapped, properly and improperly, all the time. But Dearson was caught up in a transfer of authority to a by-the-book county attorney when word got out. He was clamped down on. Hard.

"That was different," Patchett said. "This is important. Very important."

Dearson didn't respond for a few seconds. "Let's hear it," he said finally.

"Rebecca Cartaway was murdered."

"That's not fresh news, Jon. I've seen the morning paper."

"Let me finish." Patchett's voice dropped to a whisper, the morning's thought of being followed suddenly haunting him once more. He gazed back and forth, studying the neighboring tables before speaking in a hushed tone, with a voice and look of boyhood treehouses and clubs, of imagined spies.

"Rebecca Cartaway was murdered. But she wasn't murdered by the Barber."

Dearson reached into a basket without looking and pulled out a thin slice of crusty French bread. He buttered it edge to edge and ate half of it before speaking. His tone showed the calm precision of carefully chosen words.

"What's your concern with this?"

"Something's not right with it, Mike. It doesn't fit together."

"Lots of things don't anymore. Why this? What's your interest in Rebecca Cartaway?"

"I knew her," Patchett said slowly. A measured cadence. It was his own turn to choose his words. "I'd met her in any case. And I spoke with her two days before she was killed."

Dearson stopped eating the bread, but it still sat between his fingers.

"I think that my meeting with her may have something to do with why she was killed," Patchett finished.

There, he thought instantly when the words were out. It was said. For the first time, he'd said it out loud.

Dearson put the bread down and sat back. He wiped his mouth with the napkin, knocking a crumb from the corner of his lips, and he dropped the napkin back into his lap. His eyes never left Patchett.

"I guess that makes you someone we'll want to talk to, Jon."

Patchett opened his arms, shoulders shrugging up. "So let's talk," he said. "That's what I'm here for."

"Let's start broad, then," Dearson said. "What do you know about this? And what makes you think it wasn't the Barber? Those sound like pretty good starting points."

"I don't know really," Patchett replied. "Just a feeling I got when I noticed some things."

"Like?"

"Like the timing mainly. You know the profiles better than I do, Mike, but I think I can understand this guy well enough. The time of death on this is too far off. And I think there are a lot more differences that maybe wouldn't be suggested in the paper."

244 / PATRICK REINKEN

"Differences like what?"

"Like her hair," Patchett said, the thought just occurring to him as Rebecca's picture floated uninvited into his mind. "Rebecca's hair was long, but it wasn't like the women in the other pictures, was it? It was medium length, to the shoulders. Had kind of a wave. The others — they all had longer hair, didn't they? And it was razor straight. Only one of them had anything resembling a curl."

Dearson was studying him, Patchett saw. Patchett expected as much, even from a friend. You didn't come in announcing murder theories without having people look at you funny. Maybe even consider for a moment that you might have just a little *too* much to say.

"And there's more than that," Patchett went on, despite that examining look. "At least I think there is. A lot more that I want to ask about, but first I gotta know if I'm right." He waited until he could wait no longer.

"I am, aren't I? Rebecca wasn't killed by the Barber."

The waiter appeared to take their order, but Dearson raised a hand to him. "Couple minutes," he said, without looking away from Patchett. The waiter disappeared.

It took almost a full one of those minutes for Dearson to think through the implications of what he was about to say. When he spoke, it was soft and deliberate.

"I have pictures," he said. "They're already stacking up around as evidence. They sit next to other stacks of similar pictures, none of which anyone really wants around. Pictures that are pretty typical of police fare. All the angles." He poked at the half piece of bread on his plate.

"You're right," he said finally. "They don't fit together, and everyone has some concerns."

Patchett's breath, held in silently and unknowingly, let out slowly. "Why?" he asked.

"The cord mainly," Dearson said. "The Barber always strangles and always leaves the cord knotted around the neck of the victim."

"So?" That much was implied in the papers.

"The cord was there," Dearson explained. "Shows up real well in those pictures. A bright and thin white stripe cutting across her neck." Dearson dragged a finger over his own throat.

Patchett didn't even want to try to imagine it, but the image came to him anyway. Rebecca's eyes, vacant and probably — *certainly* — bulging above a tongue that would protrude slightly between forever-clenched teeth. Dearson's white cord would knot at the back of her neck and cross improbably through a valley carved into the front, where it would be barely visible. Rebecca's face would be a death mask.

"What about the cord?" Patchett asked. His voice pulled them both back from the image.

"It wasn't the right type," Dearson said simply. "The police noticed it immediately, of course." He popped the rest of the bread slice into his mouth, chewed, and washed it down with ice water from a sweating crystal glass.

"Noticed what?"

"The Barber always uses a cord made from the hair of his last victim."

Patchett, who was raising his own glass to his mouth, stopped midway and replaced the glass on the wet ring that dented into the stark white tablecloth. He was frozen, mouth slightly open in surprise as another perfect picture inescapably came to him even as he tried to fight it back.

Dearson nodded a confirmation of the look on Patchett's face, then went on. "You heard it right. He kills one girl, cuts some hair off her, and braids it into a cord that he uses on the next one. A murder chain tied together by a serial killer's mementoes. Care to fit that into your profile, Jon?"

Patchett slumped back but continued to stare at the prosecutor. "And Rebecca?" he asked hoarsely.

"Electrician's wire. Less than a buck's worth at any one of a thousand or two stores throughout the area. Pretty much everyone has some of it in the house or in the car." Dearson gave a sad grin. "And you win a prize for that one — out of his profile, out of his chain. Not the Barber."

Patchett couldn't manage a smile at the confirmation of his fears, couldn't feel the slightest vindication. Just as absent, though, was the fear that should have come from knowing that a woman he had contacted turned up dead. And that her death was concealed to look like something else.

Instead of those things, he felt nothing but emptiness. He drank the water this time, and they both ordered without thinking when the waiter spotted the opportunity and returned.

"What else?" Patchett asked when the waiter left. "What other things did they find?"

"You sure you want to hear?" Dearson saw the blank look on Patchett's face, and he knew that it could be the look of professional detachment. But it could also be numbness and shock caused by whatever lay behind the questions and connected this man to a body in a park.

"I'm not sure anything could really faze me too much anymore, Mike," Patchett said, thinking of all his terrible expectations of the world, freshly renewed in the pictures that would be tucked into a folder in his friend's office.

"If you say so," Dearson replied. He leaned forward to lower his voice. The look of boyhood spies returned, two conspirators hunkering over the table, whispering coded messages.

"This is the whole thing," he said. "Rebecca Cartaway wasn't just killed in a way to look like the Barber's work. She was *assaulted* in a way to look like him, too. You read the papers?"

Patchett nodded.

"You read about the rapes?"

He nodded again, almost shaking at the word.

"Bureau of Criminal Apprehension found semen with each victim," Dearson said. BCA was the state forensics team. "All samples matched on DNA across the victims. No matches in the DNA library."

"What about Rebecca?"

"No semen at all," Dearson said simply. "No trace of anything.

"Assaulted?" he continued rhetorically. "Yes. Vaginal tearing and bruising show up, but nothing else."

"What kind of bruising?"

"She was alive at the time, if that's what you mean. Bruises were extensive across the inner thighs. Couple on the buttocks."

Patchett grimaced, and Dearson stopped.

"Not in the profile?" Patchett asked reluctantly.

"About as far outside as you can get. The others showed tearing but little if any bruising. Commensurate with rape after death and with comparatively minor force."

"But this was severe?"

"Severe enough to make some people think she was bludgeoned more than anything."

"Bludgeoned how? I don't follow."

"Bludgeoned like with a bottle, Jon. Flashlight maybe. Something that size. Hard. But definitely no guy. A guy'd break his dick off if he went at her that hard."

Dearson's voice was soft again, this time with the deadened demeanor that came with life in the prosecutor's office, but Patchett heard the underlying hatred in it. Mike Dearson was very good at his job because of his ability to stand back, but he was also very good at his job because he still always involved himself in it at some level.

"Not in the profile," Patchett said, to himself more than anything.

The two men quieted as their salads were set in front of them. They both ignored the plates in continued silence.

"Want a final confirmation?" Dearson asked finally.

Patchett looked up hesitantly, then nodded.

"Rebecca Cartaway was damn near bald," Dearson said. "Her hair was shorn off front to back, side to side. Bad job, too."

"And?" That, too, wasn't something vastly different from the newspaper articles, although Patchett knew what was coming even before Dearson said it.

"And no other victim lost anything more than a half square inch. Just enough to make a rope for the next one. You see?"

"The newspaper said—" Patchett began, but he stopped himself. The newspapers would report what the police let them believe or asked them to report. And the police wouldn't give them every-thing. It would make the inevitable cranks too difficult to weed out from the genuine suspects.

"A copycat?" Patchett finished.

Dearson nodded, picking up a fork. "Of some sort." He pushed a wad of dripping spinach into his mouth and talked past the chewy leaves.

"Which raises the question of who. And that, I suppose, brings us to you and to getting my own questions answered. Like why it was that you were talking to Rebecca Cartaway a couple of days before she was killed."

Patchett lifted a fork, too, and sat with it in his hand. He studied the warped reflection of the world on the shining steel surface.

"Rebecca had some potential information for me," he said, still staring into the fork. His words, as always in this conversation, were unnaturally careful.

"What kind of information?"

"Information that related to her boyfriend. Man by the name of Alexander Tomlin. I think you've probably heard that name sometime in the past few days, too." Patchett watched for Dearson's reaction and wasn't disappointed.

"I've heard it enough to be interested. Go on."

"Tomlin showed up dead last week." Out of the corner of his eye, Patchett saw Dearson nod and spear more salad, and he continued. "I wanted to see if Rebecca would have any knowledge relating to that."

"And did she?" Dearson chewed a new mouthful.

With that question, Patchett came to a cliff he had first glimpsed long ago. The answer to Dearson's simple question, Pat-chett knew, could be the entire story of the complicated, doubt-filled week.

Let me tell you what I think she might have known, that answer would begin.

Let me tell you what Rebecca Cartaway might have known without her even realizing it. Her boyfriend — her lover — was in-

volved in research on one of the biggest drugs in medical history. Research that no one was really talking about much, and so it was hard to exactly be sure what was going on. But one thing was clear. That research was important. Maybe important enough for murder, although that was tough to be sure about, too, really.

Patchett didn't give that answer. His look was intent, his eyes more focused and clearer that Dearson had known them to be in years.

Paths divide; choices are made. It was clear even to Dearson that Patchett had made a choice sometime recently. Maybe only in avoiding a drink this morning, a reprieve that might last a day at best. But he looked amazingly sane, Dearson thought. Amazingly sane and thoughtful. Neither of them even noticed the waiter clearing the salad plates and setting down meals.

"I don't really know what she knew about Tomlin's death," Patchett said finally to break that silence. "And it's far too late to find out now." He said it even as he thought of the unseen letters, which perhaps contained the elusive answer to Dearson's question. "I just know that something's wrong," Patchett continued then. "Something's out of place. Something about Dr. Tomlin is not quite right."

"I don't suppose you had any chance to ever talk to *him* two days before his passing?"

Patchett shook his head. "Tomlin was cold before I had any interest in him. But I've done my best to make amends for that."

"And what have you learned?"

Patchett smiled, a grin that was naturally more bitterness than humor. He pushed his hair back loosely with a hand, and he exhaled a soft sound of exasperation. "I have come to suspect something that you probably have already learned — that Alexander Tomlin also might have been killed. Not suicide, as might otherwise appear."

Dearson reacted more clearly this time, but it was only in the raising of an eyebrow. He took a drink of water to give himself something to do. To keep him from speaking too soon.

As subtle as it was, Patchett saw it. With perhaps the sole skill he'd mastered as an attorney, he caught Dearson's reaction.

"You knew that, didn't you?" he asked instantly. "Tomlin *was* murdered, and you knew that." Patchett's voice was rising, and Dearson casually raised a finger to quiet him.

"Easy, Jon," he said. "Just take it easy."

"*Level* with me, Mike." Patchett's voice dropped. "You level with me right now and I'll take it easy. I've got a lot of questions that need answers, questions that *beg* for answers, but too many of those answers are turning up dead. So you tell me. You let me know. Was Tomlin murdered?"

Of all the answers that flew through Dearson's mind, he chose the one he liked the least. It wasn't the best one for everyone, he thought, but looking at the man across the table from him, he knew it was the one Patchett needed to hear. For whatever reason.

"There's an investigation," Dearson said. Patchett sat back. "And what we know, what we *believe*," Dearson went on, "suggests that Tomlin was murdered."

They ate in silence, then finished half the meal, washed it down with water, and asked for more bread before either said anything more. A few tables emptied and refilled around them.

"The glass was too thick," Patchett said finally, almost nonchalantly as he set his fork down.

"Excuse me?"

"The glass. The window in Tomlin's office was too thick for him to break it out with anything that was in that office."

"True." Dearson pushed cooling fettuccine around his plate. "Sounds like you've been studying up on this one. What else you got?"

Patchett shrugged noncommittally.

"Lack of motive for suicide, pretty much. Plenty of reasons not to do it. Girlfriend, loved his work, so on and so on. Add the fact that there's no note."

"Suicides don't always leave them," Dearson said. It was part of a prosecutor's job to be the devil's advocate.

"No, but I think Tomlin would have. He was a scientist. He

liked resolutions of things. And he was a writer." Patchett thought again of the letters, which he hoped were still sitting in Rebecca's home. "There would've been a note."

Patchett continued. "There wouldn't have been blood on the window."

Dearson gave a look of reprimand that was more admiration than reproach. "That's a crime scene, Jon. You're not supposed to be in there noticing things."

"I noticed that and the clump of hair stuck there. Must be my fine training as a law clerk in the county attorney's office."

"So what did that training tell you?"

"That someone who'd go to the trouble of knocking out a window like that wouldn't gouge his head on the way out unless he wasn't too happy about the idea —"

"And someone's pushing him?" Dearson finished.

"And someone's pushing him." Patchett nodded and stared at the food on his own plate.

"Then there's the issue of the *way* he supposedly killed himself," he went on. "Tomlin's a doctor. He's got money and the smarts to find other ways to do this. Certainly less painful ways. But he jumps. He jumps from an office with an inch-thick pane of glass that he has to fight to get through."

He shook his head. "So this doctor who has access to every approved drug in the world and then some breaks the window without any tools and throws himself down eleven stories. But he accidentally scalps himself in the process? Doesn't fit."

"Well, let me tell you something else that doesn't fit," Dearson offered. "When Tomlin was pulled off that sidewalk, investigators found that he'd defecated in his pants." A look of disgust crossed Patchett's face, but Dearson went on.

"Pretty uncommon for jumpers. Not so rare, though, for people thrown from great heights. And he wouldn't have done that on the way down. He probably did it before getting tossed. But all we could find on the sill was —"

Dearson cut himself off. "Care to guess?"

Patchett shook his head.

"A trace of Top Job. Know what it is?"

"Commercial cleaner," Patchett said. He was thinking of the smell, the sweet scent in Tomlin's office. Flowery cleaner, he realized.

"Very good. The sill and part of the carpet and one spot of the window were scrubbed. A few other parts of the office, too. The phone. Desk edges and drawers."

"The file cabinets," Patchett said. It wasn't a question.

"Very good again. The file cabinets and a bookshelf. All with traces of the cleaner. The cabinets, in fact, were scrubbed enough to damage the finish in a couple of spots.

"All that wasn't done to remove this guy's shit, Jon. That was on him anyway. But there were no prints. Nothing except for Tomlin's, and his were fewer than expected. Only here and there."

"It seems strange that they missed the blood on the glass," Patchett said.

"Didn't notice it maybe," Dearson suggested. "Or didn't think it mattered. Someone was after fingerprints, not signs of Tomlin's exit through that window."

The plates were collected as the men digested the information together. The bill was slipped onto the table.

"So we know basically what probably happened," Dearson said when the waiter left. "We still need to know why."

"Which, I think, brings us to the end of this lunch." Patchett examined the bill with a cursory glance.

Dearson's face was marked by disbelief. "You can't just walk away from this, Jon. You've gotten answers. I still need some. We didn't even know about the connection to Cartaway, which leaves you as the only one with any real information on that." Patchett looked unconcerned.

"You'll have to give a statement, you know," Dearson told him.

"I'll give a statement in due time. But I don't have all my answers, Mike. I just have the ones you can give me. There are plenty more questions where those came from. Most of them involving who as well as why. And right now, I'm on my way to answer

JUDGMENT DAY / 253

some of those." He dropped the napkin into a small mound where his plate had been.

"When'll you be in for that statement?" Dearson asked, resigned to Patchett's decision. He wasn't prepared to haul his friend in to get him to change his mind.

"Thursday, if everything goes well. Maybe never if it doesn't, I suppose."

Dearson studied Patchett a final time.

"Jon," he said, "you're clearly intent on doing this yourself, and I know you well enough to respect that. But understand how much you've bitten off here. If you need someone to help you chew it, I'd be more than happy to lend a hand. A lot of other people would, too."

"You've done a lot already," Patchett replied. "Filled in some blanks. Helped assure me that the pieces can fall together the way I thought they might." He looked away to a distant window that let in narrow light. "Give me the opportunity to do some things first," he said. "Then I'll need that help. And you and I will have another long conversation. Maybe you'll tell me then that the Barber's been caught."

Dearson smiled sadly. "Maybe. But I'm not sure at times if it really matters." He, too, looked over to the window.

"It's a violent world, Jon. If it's not the Barber, then it's someone else. All the time. And everywhere. It's always someone. So be careful."

Patchett looked again at the bill in his hand. He was nodding at the truth in Dearson's warning.

Things fall apart, he was thinking. *The center does not hold.*

"I'll pay on the way out," he said.

He turned and walked away from the table.

Patchett finally emerged from the building, rousing the man's attention from the folded section of the sports page. He stepped out a few paces behind the lawyer, an eye on Patchett's back as they moved toward the corner and waited for the light to change.

He followed him that way until they reached the MET Building and Patchett was heading into an elevator. The man bought another paper and settled himself into the coffee shop at the base of the tower.

He read.

He waited.

48

IT SMELLED OF LEATHER. Leather imbued with the sweet and far-away smell of the pipe tobacco. Rowe ran a hand along the armrest in the back of the limo. He watched the river valley flit by between the trusses of the iron-girdered bridge. Each beam passed with a soft sound muffled by the tight seals of the car.

Whatever exterior sounds the car's engineering didn't conceal, the interior noises would. Two small color televisions glowed above a minibar. One was tuned to CNN, the other to CNBC. Both stations this day were attentive to only one thing — Weber BioTech and the FDA's announcement. CNN's *Moneywatch* was in the middle of an enthusiastic report on biotechnology in general. CNBC was focused on Weber's stock performance for the day.

It was, in a word, phenomenal. From the opening bell, Weber had spiraled up on the weekend news. Much of the gain was attributable to aftermarket trades since Saturday's close. But much of it also was new, the reaction of small traders who woke up Monday to live for five days in the world of business, only to find out that business hadn't waited for them at all. That it, in fact, had delivered a multibillion-dollar baby while they weren't even looking.

Rowe glanced at the screen filled with the talking heads of CNBC. He ignored the gibberish and the matching sound from CNN and concentrated on the small blue-boxed panel on the bottom. It was the box for the quote of the hour, and Weber's name was written in it: 67.125.

Rowe again looked out the window at the passing scenery. The skyline of Minneapolis was shrinking behind him. St. Paul's was invisible, hidden on the left by the hills of the southern suburbs. Those hills were just beginning to green, he noticed. The leaves would be out soon.

Weber smiled at the thought of spring. He was heading toward the broad expanse of acreage that surrounded his house. Once there, he planned to hole himself up for a couple of days to concentrate on planning. And counting.

He needed the next two days to lay some groundwork for the transactions that would begin in a few minutes and end on Wednesday or Thursday. The stock sales, the wire transfers and retransfers, a few select withdrawals and deposits in numbered and not-named accounts — he would direct it all over the next forty-eight hours or so.

He picked up a small handset and punched in the number of a broker on the East Coast. It would be operating most closely to the New York quote.

When the woman answered, he gave only one instruction: "Go with Group One," and he recited a twelve-digit two-lettered code.

Group One was the smallest of his holdings. Actually, it technically wasn't even his, although the ties to him could be tracked down by anyone with sufficient patience and resources. Anyone who did would find that Rowe controlled that small group of stock holdings through a limited partnership that was itself controlled by a corporate general partnership. The corporation reached ultimately to Rowe. There was a rank of other business entities that shielded the corporation a distance away from him, but Weber himself was at a loss to remember precisely how they fit together. The complexities of it all made his head swim.

But it wasn't his concern to figure it out. That was already done. *All* the work was done already, in fact. It was time to plan the next couple of days. And to count.

He smiled again.

The grass of the passing hills was bright green. He fell into the depth of the color, loving it.

The hills flew by.

49

THE GRAVEL in the gutter chattered like popcorn popping as Patchett pulled up the driveway of Rebecca Cartaway's home. Rebecca's *old* home, he reminded himself as he turned the car off.

Patchett walked to the door with no small measure of dread. He saw no lights through the thin, veiled curtains this time. No TV glowed, shining a cool, blue light across the room and casting dark shadows over watching faces. To all appearances, no one was home on what had become a dreary, cloud-covered, and dark afternoon slipping toward early evening.

There was no car in the driveway but his own. No lights on inside the house that he could see. No one here but the parents, who would be moving soundlessly around a house that once was full, emptied, filled again. Emptied again.

They would be here, he knew. They would be here, and the police would finally be gone. Patchett had called after lunch to be sure of those things. A necessary conversation to brace the parents. Showing up was presumptuous enough as it was. Too intrusive. But to appear without warning would have been unconscionable and undoubtedly would have meant being denied the letters, which he desperately wanted to see.

Patchett needed Rebecca's letters. They were the best evidence of the seemingly tight but nevertheless flawed and loosening fabric of lies that was built up around Prohiva, Tomlin, and Lot 179. It was critical proof, a small taste of what was out there for Mike Dearson and others like him. Without those letters, even the trip to Vegas would probably be useless in the end. With them, there might be enough to scare up further investigation even without the trip.

It was that thought that made him call in the first place, and it was that thought that made him reach out to press the lighted circle of the doorbell. He heard a muffled chime.

He waited for what seemed an eternity but which was ten seconds or so, no more. "Mr. Cartaway," Patchett said nervously. "Hello again. I apologize for bothering you at this time, but I called —"

"I know," the man interrupted, and his voice sounded, with no surprise, different from before. The strength and conviction it had shown just a few short days ago was scorched away by the past twenty-four hours. A layer of this man's life had been peeled cleanly away in minutes, leaving him only with memories that he probably now wanted to have captured better. Too late.

"The letters," Rebecca's father said. "She said she'd get them to you when you were here the other day. She collected them that night."

He disappeared without a word, leaving the door standing open as he sank into the dark house. He returned in a few seconds. He held a stringed collection of postcards bundled with a couple of tattered envelopes.

"Keep them," he said, holding them out to Patchett. "Everything went bad after she met him, you know. She changed. Everything changed. I don't want anything of his in this house ever again. So keep them."

Patchett took the small stack of papers from the outstretched hand. He searched for something to say. When he spoke, offering words so often repeated to him in the past, he knew it would sound empty. "I'm sorry, Mr. Cartaway. I'm sorry about Rebecca."

"Thank you," the man said.

"Now I wish you'd leave, Mr. Patchett."

The attorney turned and left. He heard the door click closed behind him. A deadbolt clacked.

A light rain began to fall, touching Patchett's face and dotting his shoulders with tiny cold spots of dampness. He tucked the letters into his coat pocket as he got in the car and drove away.

The man never turned his car off as he sat at the curbside almost a block down. He pulled out as Patchett left, keeping the distance between them respectable. Innocuous. He wasn't surprised to see where the lawyer was heading.

•

Patchett drove only as far as the park, stopping the car there and pulling the letters and postcards out. He didn't even realize at first that it was in this place that she had died. That her last moments occurred at a distance that could be measured in a few dozen yards from where his car sat. He would have been able to see the small woods and the edge of the lake where a mallard once floated, but the misty rain was already blanketing his windshield. He couldn't see the yellow tape or the men from the Bureau of Criminal Apprehension still combing the ground on hands and knees.

He skimmed the postcards, flipping each one over and studying the handwriting briefly.

I miss you.

I love you.

I'm thinking of you.

It was a litany of one-line endearments that looked and sounded cheap on the back of fifty-cent postcards with twenty-five-cent stamps. They scattered over the days that Tomlin had been in Vegas.

Or Arizona, Patchett saw. And Utah. One of the cards was postmarked in Kanab. Another was from Page. The cards spelled out the itinerary of Dr. Alexander Tomlin and his traveling road show.

After skimming the last one, Patchett gathered the cards together and tapped them on the steering wheel into a squared-off pile. He set them aside.

As he picked up the two letters, pulling the earlier one from its envelope, he watched the rain. He wiped a hand through the building fog that ran along the edges of the window.

He read.

50

May 5, 1994

Rebecca:

I apologize first for leaving without returning your call from the other night. I realize you were angry, and my not calling back only made it worse, I'm sure. I frankly didn't know what to say then. So I'll say that I'm sorry now, for what it's worth.

I hope you know that I had to make this trip. I know I said that before I left, but I also know how you feel about it. There's nothing else I can really say, though, that hasn't been said before. This just had to be done. At least for now, anyway, until we wrap this up.

The truth is that I'm still excited about the whole thing. I wish I could convey that feeling to you somehow.

You realize how important it is, of course. What we're trying to do, the reason we came down here, might be the most important medical advance in decades. It will change millions of lives. It's that important. Important enough that I'm even prepared to go along with the others' idea.

Simply put, time is of the essence. Each day when I pick up the paper I understand that more and more. So here I am. Here we are. We shouldn't be, I suppose, but we're here nevertheless to try to push this through as quickly as possible with whatever research we can accomplish.

The thought comes to me that this may save a month, a week, a day, and I don't think I'm being unrealistic when I say that saving that time will save lives. I'm sorry once again if it means more work, if it means being unable to be with you.

I care about you very much. Know that, and keep it in mind until we get the chance to see each other again.

My thoughts are with you.

Alex

•

Patchett folded the letter even as he remembered Rebecca's words. Before him was a firsthand glimpse of her frustration. Of Tomlin's obsession. That obsession drew Tomlin to Vegas to perform the research involving Lot 179.

And that research?

Patchett thought he knew what it was. He was certain of it, in fact, even as he plucked the letter from the second envelope and began to read. As he did, it struck him immediately — the letter sounded like a confession.

A final confession.

December 12, 1995

Dear Rebecca,

It's unfortunately been too long since you and I spoke. I don't mean in the common sense, of course. I mean since we truly spoke with each other about the things that I am more commonly finding are important in this world. It's a surprising development, I think. One that you have tried and tried to push me toward for as long as I've known you. One that I have failed until now to fully appreciate.

All that has changed. I, I hope, have changed. In the last few days, I've come face-to-face with everything I am and everything that this world is. I'm not sure I like either one anymore.

The research is going poorly. It's going worse than poorly. I came down here not expecting to find the things I've seen. The people I've seen. In some ways, I'm stunned that I even had a role in it, and I'm still trying to comprehend the magnitude of what it all means for our work and for the company. For me, for that matter.

It is too long a story to tell right now. And I don't think it can really be told at all until I have an understanding, until we all have an understanding, of just what it is that has gone wrong.

Some of the people we saw last year have been collected here, and they are all sick. Some have died. What's worse is that we really have no idea why. The vaccine should work fine.

The only possibility anyone can comprehend right now is that there was something wrong with 179.

Rowe has seized on the idea and has asked me to complete a full analysis. More work, I'm sorry to say.

I'm not sorry to say, however, that I imagine this will be the last work I do at Weber. Seeing this happen, seeing the reactions of the others — it has brought home to me the funda-mental differences among us. Rowe's greatest fear is that we'll never achieve human tolerance, because it will make Weber the small-town company it always was instead of the headline-grabbing entity he wants it to be. My own fear is for the people here and for the other ones who haven't been found.

My time here is almost done. I'll be home in a couple of days, maybe by the time you get this, and I couldn't be happier about that. Until then, I want you to think about what we're planning to do with our lives. I'm thinking of that now, I hope with a new outlook, a different viewpoint, and a better apprecia-tion for everything I do have. You, most especially.

Please take care. I love you.

Alex

Patchett slipped the second letter back into its envelope, think-ing he should be satisfied with what was written in it, but he found himself growing horrified instead. The words — written precisely in Tomlin's neat handwriting, like a careful, formal record — burned the realization into Patchett's mind.

Human testing. Lot 179 was given to people. It was given to people, with the worst imaginable results.

Some have died.

Patchett closed his eyes. It wasn't that human testing with unapproved drugs wasn't done, of course, nor that it couldn't be done. It wasn't illegal to test Prohiva on people. But to test it outside specified procedures and to have the results that Weber BioTech clearly got and then not disclose them? That was something else. It was something else entirely, and it was what was buried under the careful fabric of half-truths he'd stumbled into, Patchett was certain.

And he was just as certain that, to someone, it was well worth hiding, because it wasn't just Tomlin anymore. It wasn't just Tomlin and Rebecca and a clumsy effort to conceal something vague.

Some have died. It might be murder on a grand scale.

Patchett abruptly wondered how many. How many was Tomlin talking about in his letter? How many tested? When? Where?

Patchett rubbed his eyes, wanting a drink suddenly, *desperately*, to dull the persistent pound of all the new concerns, new thoughts, new doubts, new fears.

He looked up. Only then did he see the blurry figure peering at him through the rain and fog-blocked window, one hand lifted to shade its eyes.

What he saw first was the club, a black rod held out toward his face, prepared to tap against the tinted glass. But there was a police officer behind it, and the officer bent down to gaze in through the window as Patchett rolled it down.

"How are you, sir?" the officer asked. Patchett could hear the sound of suspicion in the man's voice.

The policeman towered ominously above him in a sea of the darkest navy. A bright shield of silver was tacked to the breast of the officer's thick jacket, which was zippered to the man's chin to shut out the soft, steady rain. Patchett's face was quickly dampened.

"I'm fine," he said, trying to sound calm. Trying to forget what he had just read, what he just was thinking, what he'd gone through and seen and felt and questioned over the past week. "I'm fine," he repeated, knowing it was a lie. "Is there a problem?"

"Well, I was just a little curious about what you're doing here, sir. We're trying to keep an eye on this place today."

It came to Patchett in a terrifying rush with those words, tripping his heart once more, and he felt stupid for not realizing it in the first place. Beyond that, he thought instantly of the letters beside him. He sat in a park where a woman was murdered the day before, and he was reading mail sent to her. He glanced at the stack of letters, despite telling himself not to, and felt his throat constrict tightly as he saw Rebecca's name written darkly on the envelope on top.

"I was just reading a letter from a, uh, friend." He struggled with the words, feeling them catch unnervingly. He felt his hand shake, and he fought to control that, too, as he picked up the stack of cards and the two letters and held them up briefly before slipping them into his inner jacket pocket. "Just got my mail. Hadn't heard from her for a while, and I got a little anxious to read it. She's expecting a baby soon."

The officer's gaze followed Patchett's hand as it moved. "I'd suggest you read your mail somewhere else, sir," the policeman said. "At least for a few days."

"Thank you, officer." Patchett rolled the window up, shutting out the rain. He started the car and backed slowly away, turning on the wipers, still keeping an eye on the cop for a reaction. He saw none, the man instead turning to the park and walking into it. Now Patchett saw the yellow tape in the distance, the men crawling over the grass, the BCA van parked beside them.

He drove away.

The man in the other car watched with some interest as the police officer spoke with Patchett, looking from those two to the crime team just visible from his position on the opposite side of the park. He wasn't particularly worried. Returning to the scene was never the right thing to do, but the risks were greatly reduced here. The original job was done early, without witnesses. The car was different. And he was hanging back, just a curious observer to anyone who noticed.

The man was content and unconcerned as he watched. He left when Patchett left.

51

BOXES STOOD STACKED along the far wall in the company's one unused research lab. They were arranged alphabetically for no apparent reason, packages running from Akron, Ohio, to the Sedgwick Regional Hospital in Wichita, Kansas. Select boxes among them were bundled in twos. Ten or twelve sets of shrink-wrapped, bound packages.

The woman wheeled the dolly in and slipped its lip under the first set. She rocked it back and pushed the stack out the door to the elevator. She flicked the switch to on, and the doors closed.

The Federal Express van was parked at the foot of the Weber Building. Not far, in fact, from the freshly patched cement square where Alexander Tomlin hit after falling from the sky.

The collection agent crossed the exact spot where Tomlin died. She rolled the dolly off the curb and up the ramp to deposit the boxes on the truck's floor.

The boxes would be at the airport within thirty or forty minutes. Memphis in a few hours. From there, they'd be shipped across the country. Overnight. A 10:30 delivery was guaranteed.

It was a marvelous world where things could spread so fast.

The agent went back for another load.

52

BEN FLARE was stewing in his juices. All four of them — Patchett and Anne, Gary and Linda — could see it clearly. Red streaks were agitating up his neck, shooting from his collar and clumping in blotches across his cheeks and forehead. One hand, which moments ago was proudly displaying a settlement check that was the work of the last two months and that had kept him here even into this heart of the evening, clutched arthritically at the armrest of the chair where he sat. Flare looked, in short, so if he might just pick this rather inopportune time to have a heart attack.

They were all in Patchett's office. Jon was seated in his own chair, Gary and Linda statued at either side behind him, unintentional minions as they leaned against the wall.

Both Linda and Anne, who sat opposite Flare at the small table in the office, were intent on the partner. They searched for any positive reaction, but they could see only the red skin and hear the rising inflection in the more frequent utterances Flare was making.

Patchett was in the process of spinning out what they knew, what they suspected, what they guessed. He was leaving out only the bit about his trip into Tomlin's office. Anything he learned there was instead attributed to the conversation with Dearson. Patchett thought it would carry more weight that way, and it avoided questions about illegalities. He could have saved the effort.

Flare snapped forward during Patchett's discussion of the letters. Just as Patchett pulled them out and extended them across the desk, Flare exploded.

"What in the *fuck* do you think you're doing?" he said in a rage. He leaned over and jerked the letters from Patchett's hand.

"And who in the hell do you think you are?"

Flare plunged a finger into one of the envelopes and hooked the letter with a pinch, pulling it out. He threw it down on the desk when he had finished reading it, and he dug out the other one, eyes fixed on Patchett. His face scowled as he read it.

"What do you think this really says, Jon?" He dropped it onto the desk beside the first one. "What in that letter says murder to you?"

"I think it's pretty clear," Patchett replied, knowing it really wasn't.

"You think it's pretty clear," Flare said, and then he repeated it. "*You* think it's pretty clear." Flare looked at the others, then at Patchett, who sat calmly.

"Then I'd really appreciate it if you'd fill me in a little more, because I think it's a pile of shit. I think it's a lovesick guy kissing ass to a woman who got pissed off at him and who let him know it.

"You don't have the slightest idea what he's really talking about, do you? Those people could have had the fucking Hong Kong flu for all we know. There's nothing in those letters linking whatever they had to Prohiva, if they had anything at all."

"The letter mentions 179. And the notes and the fax link 179 to Prohiva. I saw those notes and that fax, Ben."

"And where are they now?"

"I left them at Weber."

"You left these monumental notes and this key fax with your murderers and conspirators?" His tone dripped with angry sarcasm.

"Yes." Patchett's answer sounded foolish, and it revealed what was clearly now a foolish move. Everyone in the room noticed it, and Flare looked again from face to face. He was gauging the one jury that was available.

"Well how about this?" he said slowly. "Have you *asked* anyone to explain all this?" He waited. "Have you spoken to Rowe?"

Patchett shook his head. "No," he said slowly. "I didn't know anyone I could trust. I didn't know if Weber could be involved. I still don't." Behind Flare, Patchett saw Anne glance at him as she plucked a lock of hair away from her face. She turned to stare out the window. Lights winked against the black canvas of the city.

Across the table from her, Flare smiled bitterly and angrily. "Rowe's stupid, Jon," he said, the words tight and almost spitting. "*Plenty* stupid. But he's not *that* fucking stupid. The simple fact is that you didn't talk to anyone who probably could've explained this a week ago. Who could have done it easily. So you don't even really know *what* Tomlin was working on down there. Could have been a dozen things, but you don't know, because you . . . never . . . *asked.* Right?"

"No." It was Anne. Her attention was still fixed on the city lights. A steady stream of traffic was passing by below, red taillights merging alongside curving rays of white headlights. Flare turned to face her.

"He worked on Prohiva," she said to him. "It was all he ever did."

There was an uncomfortable silence as they watched Flare watching Anne. Gary turned to Linda. As they all waited for Flare to turn on Anne, Gary wanted out of this very badly.

"And how do you know that?" Flare snapped.

"I know Tomlin," Anne replied calmly. "I know what he did." She spun in the chair to look at him, meeting his angry look with her own, more measured gaze. Even from the distance across the room, Patchett could see that her eyes were a fiercely cold blue. "He worked only on Prohiva, and Jon's confirmed that."

Flare laughed. Anne's statement was all he needed to turn his attention to Patchett again.

"So you've '*confirmed it*,' huh?" He waggled his fingers in visual quotes. "And what kind of proof do you have for that, since you don't have any for anything else?"

"Rebecca Cartaway," Patchett answered quickly.

"Who's dead."

"Exactly."

Stillness filled the room again. Patchett and Flare faced each other off, Flare beginning to pace back and forth along the front edge of Patchett's desk. Patchett's head swung side to side, following him like a spectator at a tennis match.

Behind Flare, Anne turned back to the night. She was ready to go, Patchett knew. Ready to take off to Las Vegas with or without Flare's permission. Without his knowledge for that matter.

She was ready as soon as she set foot out of the student union earlier in the day, slipping into the swelling crowd and out the door. Patchett hadn't been surprised at her story. It worried him, more than he had previously thought possible, but it didn't surprise him.

But Flare? That was another matter. Anne's report of the strange man at the college was the only part of the whole tale that had brought an actual laugh from the partner during the telling.

But Anne knew what she saw at the school. She knew what she felt. And she was ready now to go to Vegas whether this sack of shit approved or not.

"Rebecca Cartaway," Flare was saying, "was killed by the Barber."

"Not according to the county attorney's office," Patchett countered.

"I'll tell you something, Jon. I don't really care what the prosecutor has to say. And I don't care what BCA or the cops have to say. Do they have any *proof?*" he asked. "No," he answered himself before going on to drown out any response.

"They don't have any definitive proof that it wasn't him, and don't give me any stories about *profiles* of psychotics. We're talking about a crazy man, and you're talking about trying to predict what he'll do." Flare shook his head in disbelief. "And you know what's more?" he said. "They certainly don't have any proof that this was in any way connected to Weber BioTech.

"Jesus *Christ*, Jon, this could have been done by a million people even if it wasn't the Barber. This could be a simple copycat killing committed by any one of the crazies out there. Lord knows there's enough of them. But you're sitting here pointing a finger at this company, at these people. Does that really make sense to you?"

Patchett leaned forward, raising a finger toward Flare. "You're looking at one piece at a time. You know you can't do that. You know you have to look at how everything fits when it's taken together. You've told me that yourself, Ben.

"Tomlin's death, Rebecca's death, the notes, the letters. Together, it's not a copycat killing. Together, I think maybe it's fraud that's topped off by murder, and that company might just be at the heart of it."

"Bullshit," Flare was saying even before Patchett finished. "That's bullshit."

"It's *not* bullshit, Ben. This vaccine doesn't work. The FDA is letting Weber BioTech ship it out in the next few days to start testing, when the company knows perfectly well it doesn't work." His voice fell to a hushed level as he plucked one of Tomlin's letters from the desk and held it up, not even looking at it.

"*Some have died*," he quoted. He dropped the letter to the desk. "And more people *will* die," he went on. "It's that simple. Anyone who gets injected with that stuff stands to die just as surely as if someone put a gun to each of their heads and pulled the fucking trigger."

Flare was silent. He looked in turn from Patchett to Gary to Linda and back to Patchett. He turned and looked at Anne, then away.

"I told you this was done, Jon," he said quietly, looking again at Patchett. Flare shoved his hands under his jacket and into his pants pockets, where they began to jitter with loose change. "I told you there was nothing out there and the assignment was over. You've clearly ignored that. You've brought these three into this. And you've concocted this convoluted and unbelievable scenario."

He pulled his hands back out of his pockets and leaned forward, bracing himself on the desk.

"You're out of your mind," he said. "You know that? I want you off this file. I want you off every file that I have." Flare straightened and moved to the door, where he stopped, standing next to Gary.

"This is done," Flare said to Patchett, who still sat. "We'll take it up again at associate review." He walked out.

When Patchett jumped up, the chair coasted back and slapped against the wall between Gary and Linda. They jerked with surprise as Patchett ran out, pulling the door closed behind him.

"I'm going to Las Vegas," he said loudly to Flare, who was retreating down the empty hall. "Eight o'clock tomorrow morning. I'm going to talk to Bancroft and Rayes."

Flare froze, then spun around to face him. He quickly paced the distance to stand almost nose to nose with Patchett.

"Like *hell* you are." The voice was a whispered fury.

"You want *proof*," Patchett said in his own whisper. "You want proof, the prosecutor wants proof, everyone wants proof. Real proof that you can sink your teeth into. That you can *taste*. Vegas is the only place I can think of to get it, and that's where I'm going."

"What the fuck's the matter with you, Jon?" Flare leaned against a secretary's station. He turned to face Patchett, shaking his head. "You're crazy. I gave you a simple project and you've made it out to be murder and medical fraud, securities fraud, conspiracy. What the hell is *that?*" He shook his head again. "You jumped down Missy's throat the other night, too, for no reason. Makes me think maybe you're seeing some ghosts. You maybe hitting it a little too heavy lately, Jon?"

There was a pleading tone in Flare's question that Patchett didn't like. The man was searching for some easy hook he could hang this problem on.

"Fuck you, Ben," Patchett said.

"Think about this, Jon." Flare moved beside him once more and took hold of Patchett's arm. The partner's voice was soft. "Think about this very hard and very long before you do something very stupid."

Patchett could feel the heat from Flare's breath and could smell a not-distant-enough odor of garlic and onion.

"This is your big career decision right here, Jon. One of our best clients. One of the biggest jobs we'll ever have. One of the most important." Each statement was emphasized with a tug at Patchett's elbow. "If you do something to fuck that up, then you're done here. You're done everywhere. I promise you that."

Patchett stared at Flare, just inches away. He could see for the first time the worn look on his friend's face, the tired look that comes from too many hours shaking too many hands, writing too many briefs and memos and letters, kissing too many asses and doing it with a smile and an overstated bill that you hope they'll pay without too many questions.

"If what I'm doing is fucking something up," Patchett said softly, "something that you believe it's our job to protect, then I don't want to be here." He tugged his arm free of Flare's grasp. "There's something here, Ben. Something bad that I don't want any part of, and I'll do whatever I can to stop it.

"And I would suggest that you think about any liability you and this firm might have," he continued. "Especially now. *You* think about that very hard. Very long."

Flare looked at him, eyes wide. "You *are* crazy," he said. "I want you out of here by tomorrow. You're fired." He turned and stormed swiftly down the hall.

"I'll do you one better," Patchett said after him. "I'll be out of here tonight." But Flare was gone, leaving Patchett alone with the sound of his own words. He entered his office again, cutting short a hushed discussion as the three people turned to look at him. He examined each one of them in turn.

"What'd he say?" Anne asked. Her voice was soft, and he realized she already knew the answer. They all already knew.

"He wished us luck." Patchett sat down and began to tell them his plans.

Flare sat brooding at his desk, running a finger along the edge of the blotter, pushing a line of dust, tiny dried clumps of correction fluid, and some assorted bits of paper off onto the floor. Now that various decisions made long ago were abruptly staring him in the face, he was looking alternately from the clock to the phone and contemplating, quite frankly, the rest of his life. Whatever he decided, he knew, it couldn't possibly be worse than the first part of it.

Nine-thirty at night.

There would be money in Geneva by now, if the preliminary estimates were still relatively accurate, and that money was his alone. It would soon be splintered off to Mexico, Argentina, and Bermuda before being filtered through other banks and repooled in the Grenadines. It could be collected at his whim then. But for now, Geneva.

He pulled out a pocket appointment calendar and flipped through it to "Important Numbers," finding the Suissebanc and the fifteen-digit account code. He had picked this bank out personally when in Geneva last year. Not for its security. Swiss banks were uniformly secure and secretive. He chose the bank instead for its stunning view of the *jet d'eau*, the water fountain that towered over Lake Geneva. It was a sight he didn't expect to see for some time anymore. Not until after all this faded a little from the immediate memory of the world. Then, maybe.

It was a computer-access receiver that answered when he dialed the bank, and Flare punched in the code plus another one that was also committed to memory. He waited for connections to be made. He waited for the file to be accessed. He waited for the slow, droning voice of the computer. It spoke, amazingly enough, in accented English.

"As of eighteen March 1996, account balance is two million two hundred eighty-two thousand three hundred sixteen dollars and twenty-seven cents American. British pound equivalent as of eighteen March . . ."

Flare hung up.

The money was about two thirds of the expected total, a little less. It would still be enough, though. Enough to support him. Alone. Away from Melissa and the mountain of debt she had forever attached to his name.

272 / PATRICK REINKEN

It *could* be enough, anyway.

It was the province of a good lawyer to be versed in decision making. In assessing the costs and benefits of going ahead as opposed to the results of getting out when the getting was good. Flare was a good lawyer.

He didn't think Patchett and the three cohorts he was going to drag along with him could succeed. Not against people who wouldn't think twice about simply making the four of them disappear altogether. Flare didn't even think Patchett would get very far outside of Vegas, and he planned to take steps to ensure that himself.

But there was always the other side, too. The side that weighed in as current benefits, available without the attendant risk of continuing down a more and more dangerous road.

$2.2 million. Almost $2.3. Without risk.

Flare picked up the phone again. He would make three calls. First, to Suissebanc. He could cut the transfer process now and filter the money himself through wire transfers later.

Second, an airline. Any airline that could get him away from here and on his way. His first home would be an island off the Mexican coast. It was rocky. Uncomfortable to some, probably. But it was warm and quiet. And it would be temporary.

Finally, to Franck, but that one would come later. Flare ideally needed a day to slip away unnoticed. For the first time, he had a card to play, and he planned to hold on to it just a little while longer. He would pass the word on about Patchett, but in his own good time.

After that? He was done making plans for now. First things first.

He dialed.

53

ANDY LITTLEFEATHER tossed in his sleep, his small body wrapping the sheets as he spun first one way, then the other. A narrow bead of sweat ran down his round face and made a damp spot on the pillow before evaporating.

He was dreaming. He would later remember nothing of what floated through his mind in the night, but the visions were now almost concrete.

He dreamed of strange men in the desert and strange markings in the earth. He dreamed of disease. He dreamed of ghosts.

In his dreams, Andy was riding the little Honda, and the desert was unfolding briskly in the thrown beam of the bike's wobbling headlight as he made his way west along 89A, then south along the ranch trail.

The turns and twists of the trail flew fast. Andy knew them well in the dream, although he had covered them only twice before. Each slight bend to the left, a dip in the road here, a passing cactus on his right. He saw it all, and he remembered it all.

Only the coyote was different.

He saw it ahead on the fringe of the road, freezing and turning in its tracks. Its eyes sparked red from the shine of the speeding headlight, growing larger as Andy approached. Its fur showed the patched wear and tear of dark and light brown tinged with flecks of peppery black. Andy saw it grin as he passed it, its tongue hanging out between rows of too-white teeth.

Despite the deep cold of the earliest morning, the animal looked hot. Exhausted. The coyote was traveling far, working hard in a spring that was marked even in a land of daily warmth and March rains by the remaining signs of seasonal death.

Its grin turned toward Andy, shining under red eyes. The picture of the coyote stayed with the boy, a Navajo sign of evil that haunted him for the remaining miles that unfolded until he reached the markings in the earth.

He stopped then, the bike parked on the overhanging bluff that looked down at the boxed-off area in the desert floor. He angled the headlight down, and it swung easily to add its feeble yellow hue to the dim moonlight.

And he watched.

In the dream, he watched until the dark of the night changed to the first purple of dawn, and he saw the ghosts circling the site below him.

They floated in lazy turns of bleary whiteness, the shadows alone revealing glimpses of faces. Black holes sat in those faces instead of eyes. The ghosts silently swirled in a wide circle, bounded by the perimeter of the desert grave.

Andy sat shaking on the bike, and he turned the light off in his fear, but the ghosts only became more visible. Arms, legs, the features of their bodies stood out. He wheeled the bike around but took a last glimpse over his shoulder.

It was then that he saw the coyote again. It sat behind him, its tongue still hanging between its teeth. The teeth were startlingly white even in the last remnants of night.

The coyote grinned.

Part Four

TUESDAY
WEDNESDAY

The Eighth Day

54

THE ARIZONA STRIP straddles the border between Arizona and Utah. Centered between artificial lakes, it begins low at the collected waters of Nevada's Lake Mead on the west and ends low in the submerged, red-cliffed buttes of the Rainbow Plateau and dammed-up Lake Powell to the east. In between, it rises over the mountains and cliffs of the high Arizona desert, from the Virgins in the west to Vermilion in the east.

To the north, its boundary is Utah's border and canyonlands; to the south, the deep breadth of the Grand Canyon separates it from the rest of Arizona. The Strip is crossed only by four major sections of paved roadway. Two of those form the lonely stretch of 89A that falls from Utah and weaves up and through the elevations of the Kaibab Plateau, sandwiched between the north and south boundaries of the Strip. That road then drops down into House Rock Valley, shooting due east to Marble Canyon.

Of the other two, one branches off 89A to dead-end against the Grand Canyon's north rim. The other barely loops down into the western reaches of the Strip before retreating back north through the Kaibab Reservation as though people started the road into the desert but then changed their minds. Wisely.

It is a place marked principally by its emptiness. By the ability of people to disappear there and never be disturbed again. It is the home of scattered remnants of a Native American culture that once roamed broader than the area of the Strip but that now is trapped there. It is also the home of a few remaining polygamous Mormons, who long ago left their native Utah when their church renounced that doctrine to pave the way to statehood. They settled here, cut off by political borders from Utah and by natural borders from Arizona, to be left alone.

The Strip is no-man's-land.

Just beyond the opposite end of the Arizona Strip, up the Colorado River, the generating station of the Western Area Power Administration sat, marked by lights still turned on against a night now gone. The station dispensed two things, as it had done for years. First, electricity, shipped to points far away from the Strip, the reservations, and the rare inhabitants of the region. It flowed to a six-state area draped like a blanket across the southwest from California to New Mexico and Colorado.

The other thing that emerged from the station, or more accurately from the station's control, was the river itself. Trapped behind the concrete and steel wall of Glen Canyon Dam, the waters of the Colorado collected in a reservoir that flowed through Glen Canyon hydroturbines with selectivity determined largely according to electrical demand.

WAPA's Glen Canyon station was a peak generator, a make-up service that filled the gap between community low and high demands. With those swings came variations in water release. Slow at night, surging as the morning arrived, peaking as the heat activated air conditioner thermostats in homes hundreds of miles away.

That pattern was supposed to stop in the early 1990s. The daily surges in water flow were melting the Grand Canyon beaches away, and the environmentalists and river runners were screaming.

But the reprieve that eventually followed the protests didn't last as Sun Belt demands and votes toted up. WAPA twisted the spigot on each day, off each night.

Right now, it was looking to be a hot one in Phoenix and Vegas. The surge was a few hours old.

Andy Littlefeather could almost hear the rush of the distant river as he slipped out the back and made his way from the house. He pushed the bike and slung a knapsack with a sack lunch on his back.

His mother thought it was a lunch for school, but Andy wasn't going to school today. When he was a little distance away, he started the small engine, and he got on.

55

LAS VEGAS WAS ELECTRIC. On every street, from those that stretched into the flat and open desert around the city to the Strip of Las Vegas Boulevard itself, the light shone even in the day. Coming in from McCarran, Gary Kane's attention was only half on Linda, who was reciting Patchett's instructions for the third or fourth time. The other half was permanently fixed on the passing signs that blinked the messages of the city radiantly and endlessly.

He pointed a finger as they passed the lion in front of the MGM Grand. A little kid in a candy store, he suddenly felt better about the trip. The image of Ben Flare swearing at them all was far away. As were all notions about their job offers, of course.

Still, there was always the possibility that they'd get those positions. It depended on Patchett and whether he turned out to be right or not. Gary had no opinion on the subject, despite his wife's fervent belief, but he was willing to give it a shot. He didn't have anything to lose anymore, and he knew it from the time that the first blush of red had colored Flare's neck last night.

"Look," he said, pointing again. Circus Circus stood on the left, shining its carnival façade. He glanced over at Linda and saw her smiling.

"What?" he said, and her smile broadened.

"I knew you'd like it," she said. Gary grinned.

"We haven't had to do anything yet," he pointed out. They drove in silence the short distance to Sahara Avenue.

"Which way?"

Linda glanced at the Hertz map in her hand and jerked a thumb right. They were looking for a motel.

Those were plentiful. Cheap, too, when you got a little farther away from the shiniest ones. They scanned the signs in front of the ones they passed, looking for posted prices.

"So what's the plan, commandant?" Gary asked. Linda would have that computed by now.

"Jon wanted us to find Bancroft early. The sooner we find him and maybe have a word with him, the sooner we can play."

"Which means?"

"I'd like to be out and about by noon."

Gary looked at the clock embedded in the plastic dash and groaned lightly. By the time they found a motel, got settled in, maybe got something to eat, it'd be edging past that time.

"Sure you're not pushing it a little?"

"We'll live." She patted his shoulder, then moved her hand to his knee and rested it there. "Could be worse," she said.

"We could be headed to Kanab?"

"You got it."

They kept driving.

56

THE MILES OF THE ROAD to Kanab sped away under the steady purr of the wheels of their car as they slipped into the land north and east of Vegas. It was flat at first, but it soon stretched toward a horizon of mountains that stood too close for Kanab to fall on this side of them.

Patchett listened to the wind whistle through his window. It was cracked a half inch, the cool air pouring in to keep him awake, if not fully alert. They had spent most of the night talking out some rough idea of how to approach this, a recitation of everything they needed to consider, everything that might happen. And they had paid the price in terms of sleep. He'd slept on the plane to try to make it up, but it was fitful. The uneasy rest of an uneasy man after an uneasy week.

Events of the past few days were catching up to him, the burden of Rebecca's murder especially so. It had hung in his mind almost constantly since he first unfolded the newspaper and saw the headline.

Rebecca Cartaway was dead because she talked to him for a few minutes one night. He couldn't talk himself out of that one. And he was tired of trying.

Anne was sleeping in the passenger seat, face turned to him, awash with the orange tints of the new sun. When she had told him about the man following her yesterday, she alluded to the something else that made him uneasy. "I've felt that before," she'd said about being followed.

Anne had said no more, but she hadn't needed to. Patchett didn't ask and doubted she would have told him if he had.

He watched her. His eyes flitted from the roadway to her face. Back again to the road.

Anne was dreaming, an uneasy look on her face. Patchett considered waking her but didn't. They had promised each other a division of the drive to Kanab, an hour and a half, maybe two hours each. Anne still had time left to sleep, and he would let her have it.

Bad dream or no bad dream, there looked to be little other time for picking up sleep before reaching town and trying to find Rayes. Using the Kanes as drivers while he and Anne hid in a car trunk, Patchett felt confident they had slipped past anyone who might have been watching them in Minneapolis. But if they *were* still being followed, someone would know where they were going, and Rayes would know soon thereafter. May know already, in fact. May be gone. But Patchett was out of other ideas.

A jacket, too thin for this time of year, was snugged up against

Anne's neck and draped off the shoulder nearest Patchett. He reached over and pulled it up across her shoulder.

She stirred at his touch, shifting slightly, and Patchett drew his hand away reluctantly.

The car flew down the road.

57

FROM THE BLUFF, Andy looked over the site, sitting astride his motorbike. The bike's engine rumbled a rocking, unsteady buzz. The oversized helmet was propped on the gas tank in front of him, Andy's hands resting loosely on it as he surveyed the scene. Had he remembered the dream better, he would have realized that this was almost the exact position, almost the exact pose of last night. He would have been even more afraid.

As it was, he was nervous but relieved. There was nothing different that he could see. Nothing appeared to have disturbed this place. And there was no sign of the ghosts.

They wouldn't have left signs, of course, and he knew it. He also knew that you wouldn't see them here now anyway, at a time when the sun was high enough in the sky to cast his shadow squarely and strongly over the markings below him. It was too bright, too warm, too much a part of this world. But he wouldn't have the courage, he thought, to come here at night to watch for what he knew must happen.

He hadn't been raised in Navajo traditions, but he did understand the balance between good and bad. He knew the dangers of being close to evil and how that could tip that precarious balance.

Even being here, he thought, just *being* in this place risked that. No matter what time of day, this was a place of evil. So he slipped the helmet on and turned the bike around.

As he did, his eyes fell on the narrow tire track of the front wheel, which was leaving a mark that really was too smooth. The tire should be replaced, but he lost than thought as it crossed other marks. Andy stopped and stood, leaning over the front of the bike and studying the dusty ground before him.

The tracks came in from the northeast and stopped beside where he was sitting. They stood out clearly — sharp images of a visitor that must have come in the night.

The tracks of the coyote.

58

EVERYTHING WAS DONE that needed to be done. Phone calls made, money handled, excuses out. A trip to Montreal, he told people. Discussions with a client there. Simple enough, and in exactly the wrong direction.

The engines of the jet were whining. He tugged at his seat belt for the third time. Said the silent prayer he always recited whenever he was foolish enough to fly.

The pressure he felt increased as the ground outside the window blurred by, and he could hear the seams of the runway slapping past under the tires.

The sound was gone with the roll of his stomach. The plane turned eerily still as it rose from the ground. The landing gear hummed up, and his ears popped. He yawned to open them again.

Ben Flare said good-bye his past, and disappeared into the early morning.

59

IT WAS CLOSED. After more than three hours of driving, Patchett and Anne stood before the Canyonlands Hospital in Kanab. The building was a classic statement of early 1960s boredom masquerading as functionalism. It had a plain façade outside in a color Patchett once heard someone call "baby shit brown."

And it was closed.

Peering in past the CLOSED sign that was suction-cupped to the window by the door, Patchett saw that the interior was similarly dated and plain. The most striking thing was the floor itself, which was covered by a wall-to-wall sheet of industrial green tiles. Each tile was dotted with flecks of black, white, and rust red, a smattering of spots that looked more like a galaxy of scuff marks than anything else. A row of neatly aligned, poorly padded, steel tube chairs ran along one wall, their split blue plastic covers looking battered.

Patchett turned to Anne, glancing again at the sign in the window. Hours were 3:00 to 9:00 until May 1, which was presumably when the tourist season would begin. Patchett never heard of a hospital that was closed, particularly better than halfway into the day. But it was a small town, so who knew?

He checked his watch. Between Minneapolis and Vegas and now Utah, they'd touched three time zones in only a few hours. And that wasn't counting the oddity of Arizona, which, he dimly recalled, didn't distinguish between standard and daylight savings time at all. He had no idea what time it was there, just a few miles away. But Patchett thought it was a little after 1:00 local time. That gave them almost two hours to kill before the hospital opened, and he searched the street for a restaurant.

"What now?" Anne asked.

"We eat." He looked at her. "We wait."

They glanced needlessly in both directions and walked across the empty street.

60

GARY WIPED A FINGER at the drop of water that ran between Linda's breasts, catching it just before it disappeared under her towel. He rubbed the dampness into her soft skin until it dried. She smiled, a coy grin that lit her face as she worked another towel through her hair.

"I think once was enough," she said, and she smiled again. "For now anyway."

"Never," he said. Gary tucked the finger into her cleavage and ran it under the towel. She twisted away when he crossed the nipple, which hardened at his touch.

"Once was *enough*," she chided, still smiling. She wrapped the second towel around her head and knotted it. "Just like one bite to eat was enough and one hand of cards was enough and one pull at the slots was enough." This last part was said with a menace that she didn't feel, and the lingering smile showed that. Gary wrapped his arms around her to pull her closer and broaden that smile.

On the way back from eating, they had stopped in a casino. "For a hand of cards," he said then. But that gave way to a roll of dice. A try on the slots. And so on.

They'd whiled away an hour or so before making their way out again, but Gary was so keyed up that they found another, more pleasing diversion from the immediate task at hand. But enough *was* enough. Linda leaned away from him, eyeing him suspiciously.

"C'mon, now," she said. "We are here for a reason. Remember?"

Gary looked to the ceiling as though searching in vain through his memory. "I recall something about a honeymoon," he said, looking at her lasciviously.

"Later," and now she did pull away. She held the towel to keep it up. No sense in baiting the bear.

"For now, let's just find Bancroft. We'll ask him a few questions like Jon wanted, then we'll leave it to Patchett to decide if he's worth a revisit when they get back."

She bent back toward Gary, who stood with a frown of semi-serious frustration half-mooned on his face, and she kissed him.

"After that," she said, "we can practice procreation all you want."

His eyes shone at the prospect.

61

ROWE WEBER opened his eyes at the first ring. He fumbled a hand over, grabbing the cord, then worked steadily up from there. The phone rang two more times before he could take the handset off the cradle.

Weber ignored the stirring form beside him. He wasn't sure he could remember her name anyway.

" 'Lo?" he said, a garbled slur more than anything. He tried to focus on the fuzzy numbers on the clock and closed his eyes instead. He had been up late to deal with foreign sales, foreign banks. Hadn't really gone to sleep during the night at all, in fact.

"Rowe? It's Lew." Franck waited a few seconds to allow this to register in Weber's groggy mind.

"What?"

"We have a small problem," Franck said. He waited on this, too. Weber would be fully awake in a few seconds, probably *too* awake. But it was best to go slow in any case.

"What?" Weber said again. He fought to clear his mind more, aware on some level that being contacted by Franck during these last few days probably meant something he didn't want to hear. But it also meant something he should probably pay attention to.

"Patchett's in Vegas."

Weber couldn't have snapped awake more quickly if someone had plugged his finger into a wall socket. He sat up like a shot, rubbing the sleep away from his face with his free hand before swatting the soft thigh bared and wrapped provocatively around a knot of covers beside him. The woman's head moved from beneath a pillow, peering out under a tousled mat of blond hair.

Brenda, he realized.

He slapped the thigh again, harder, impatient. A pinkish hue was already rising on pale, freckled skin.

"Out." Weber shook his hand in the direction of the door when her eyes opened. His voice was insistent, but she frowned once and tucked her head under a pillow, wrapping an arm over it to seal out the light.

Rowe ignited in a rage.

"*Out!*" he screamed at the woman beside him. He leaned with a hand pressed against her covered form, and he gave a fierce shove.

Brenda yelped once, the word lost in the muffle of the pillow. She landed with a hard *clump* on the floor. "You *fuck!*" she spat.

"Out," Weber hissed a third time. He pointed a finger at the door. Brenda clutched a loose sheet around her slender waist and breasts and stumbled from the room. She slammed the door behind her, the sound ringing like a slap in the room.

"When?" Weber asked after she was gone.

"This morning," Franck answered. He was nervous, Weber could tell, and he could also tell that Franck was trying to hide it. "He left with Anne Matheson and two others on the eight o'clock flight. Pierce hadn't seen Patchett come out of his apartment yet today. Same with Burke for Matheson. But Ben Flare called from his office around ten or ten thirty. Said he just found out that Patchett was on his way. Burke, Pierce, and Rettner should be there by now. They went out on the first available flight, maybe three or four hours after Patchett left."

Pierce and Rettner were faceless names to Weber. Wall's men, he knew. He dimly remembered that they were in on the search for Steffens.

"What about Clark?" Weber asked.

"He was still in Phoenix. Maggie Washburn got his eye pretty bad when he fought with her, and he was having it looked at, so I sent him direct from there. He's probably reached Vegas by now, too."

"How is he?"

"The eye's blind, at least for now. He wants me to tell you that it's not his shooting eye, though."

"Great." He meant it. Wall would obviously still have a role to play. "Anyone get word to Bancroft and Rayes?"

"Got hold of Bancroft about an hour ago. He's going crazy, of course. Jabbering a lot. But I think he'll be fine with a few people around to prop him up. No word that he's been contacted by anyone yet."

"Rayes?"

"Different story. We haven't been able to get in touch with him. He's apparently at the trailer out in House Rock, and the number for the cellular isn't in service. Not sure why. But we won't be able to call out there in any case."

"Wall's heading there first, I assume?"

"He'll check in with Bancroft first. See what's going on and if we can get a handle on whether or when anyone's contacting Rayes. But Burke's heading out to Rayes's place as soon as he touches down. Long trip, though."

"I remember. Listen, get all the others down there today, too."

"They're on their way."

"Good. I want to find these four little fucks as soon as possible." There was a pause as Weber considered something. "I want you to go down there to help, too, Lew," he said.

"I think—" Franck began.

"I don't care what you think. This is important. I can't leave this to a few hired thugs who couldn't scrape together enough intelligence to remember their names. Get down there. Take Clifton and Kenneth Miller with you, too. *And* Flare. I want everyone available on this. End it once and for all."

"I haven't been able to get in touch with Flare again."

There was another silence as Weber considered this news.

"Keep trying," he said. "Get everyone else in the meantime."

"What about managing things here?"

"Did the packages go out?"

"Last night."

"Then things here can take care of themselves. I'll arrange the press announcement today to speed things up. We should be able to finish tomorrow. You can help from Vegas."

"We're up on overnights," Franck said, offering one piece of good news. The only one that he had. "A run set off by the shipment," he added as unnecessary explanation.

Weber didn't respond to that, the anger at the rest of the news preventing it. "Get going" was all he said, and he hung up.

The sheets dropped from his naked body when Weber stood. He weighed the news that Franck had given and reassessed Patchett in the process. He reassessed Flare as well, his hands clenching and unclenching at the thought of those two men. Rowe had never really felt that Flare was a willing participant in this, and the news that he'd called in information like this and then suddenly disappeared made Rowe wonder exactly how far Flare could have gotten already.

No matter, though. He'd worry about Flare sometime in the future. Sometime when there was nothing better to amuse him. For now, he concentrated on Patchett, swearing at how far he'd let the attorney run. Swearing at the fact that he ever asked for someone to look into Tomlin's death in the first place. Swearing at the idea that a drunk like Jon Patchett was standing in Las Vegas already, uncharacteristically diligent and annoyingly persistent. Rowe Weber very suddenly wanted to tear Patchett's throat out for that.

"*Fuck,*" he said softly, but sharply.

He heard the shuffle outside the door then, and he turned to see the door crack open, Brenda's face peering through. When she saw he wasn't on the phone, she pushed it fully open and stepped into the room.

"So what the shit's the matter with you?" she said, annoyance in her own voice. The sheets were wrapped more securely around her, gathered in back with one hand, the other hand propped on her hip.

Weber turned to her, and Brenda regretted her question instantly. His eyes blazed as he crossed the room in three quick strides to stand before her. His own hand came up in a blur and caught her hair at the back of her head. He jerked it furiously, Brenda's head snapping back with it. She let out a cry of pain, and both of her hands went up to Weber's wrist.

Brenda grasped in vain at the steel strength in Rowe's grip as he pulled again, harder. The sheet slowly unwound from around her, and it dropped open to the floor. Weber's breath was hot when he whispered harshly into her face, an inch away.

"You disobeyed me," he said. "I told you to do something nicely, and you disobeyed me." There was a sound of near-murderous rage in the words. "I always get what I want," he went on. "I get what I want, and nobody — *nobody* — disobeys me." He hesitated, edging his face even closer. "Do you understand that?"

She was near tears, gasping at her instant fear and at the blinding pain at the back of her head. She tried to speak, tried to say *something*.

"*Do you?*" Rowe raged in her face.

Brenda clenched her eyes tight and screamed a terrified, garbled "*Yes!*" back at him. The tears began to flow as Weber tugged once more at her hair.

"I get what I want!" he said again, still shouting. "And you — and everyone else — better *fucking* understand that."

He turned at his last words, pulling and throwing Brenda forcefully to the floor. Her feet left the ground at the strength of it, and she landed prone, a few feet away. She was sobbing uncontrollably.

Rowe stood over her, staring down at her shaking, nude form. He bent, his own nakedness a terrifying, threatening presence over her, and he pulled one of her hands away from her face, holding it tight. Then his mouth was at her ear in final, whispered words.

"I always . . . get . . . what I want." He dropped her hand, and he stepped away.

62

ONCE PATCHETT and Anne were inside, the hospital was even more undesirable. Like every other hospital in every other city or town that dotted the countryside, it reeked of alcohol, an ever-present tinge of medicinal horror that brought the same touch of dread in anyone who caught it floating in the air. It was the smell of sickness, of shots, of thermometers, and of strangers doing things to you that you never wanted done to you by anyone. It wafted out even into the lobby, where Patchett and Anne stood waiting for the attention of the single receptionist, who sat ignoring them at the desk, a phone attached to one ear.

"Excuse me," Patchett said, just loudly enough to draw attention away from a phone call that seemed impossibly long for the middle of the afternoon in a drowsy Utah town. The receptionist didn't blink.

"Excuse me," he said again. This time, she looked up briefly in his direction, and he met her gaze evenly. "Could we get some help?" he asked. He spotted a name tag. "Barb."

She stared at Patchett as if debating it. "I'll call you back," she said, and hung up, killing the one glowing light of the seven on the black rotary dial telephone in front of her.

"What is it?" Barb asked. There was an open sound of exasperation in her voice, a tone that only the truly put out can muster at will. She reached up as Patchett spoke, patting a nonexistent stray hair back onto a head that looked shellacked with spray. The triangular wedge of hair seemed to sway as a unit under a nurse's cap that was impossibly out of date.

"We're looking for a Dr. Alfre Rayes," Patchett said, watching Barb's hair rock back and forth as she pushed it into place. "We believe he—"

She cut him off with a wave of her hand. "Not here," she said in a rush.

Patchett waited for an explanation that didn't come.

"When will he be in?"

"Won't. Dr. Rayes quit yesterday. Moving somewhere, I guess. Too bad. Nice fella." Barb began shuffling papers at her station. Her mission of providing information accomplished, she needed to look busy.

Patchett felt Anne look at him, and he knew the pounding concern running through him had hit her as well. If Rayes was gone, then maybe everything was already a couple of days ahead of what Patchett had previously thought. He wondered what else had happened, or was happening, then he thought of Gary and Linda and contemplated what they might find, if anything. Given the circumstances, he hoped it was good.

"Do you know where we can get in touch with him?" Anne asked hopefully. The question was uttered in a tone that Patchett hadn't heard before. She sounded like a lost child searching for her daddy.

Barb turned her gaze back and reexamined them both, eyes shifting over half-glasses from one person to the other. "Won't have a phone," she said, still looking from Anne to Patchett and back. She was sizing them up. "Had a cellular, but he turned that in." She paused. "Is he in trouble?"

"No," Anne said. "It's just that he treated my brother last year when we came through on vacation. We were in the area again. Thought we'd stop by. You know, say hello."

Barb was clearly comforted by the lie, and her pasty, aging face broke into a smile. "You can go out there, if you want," she said. "He sold his house in town. But he should still be around out there."

"Out . . . where?" Patchett asked, and Barb's brief smile faded. When she spoke, she spoke to Anne.

"He's got a little trailer down in House Rock, over the border. Other side of the forest, past Jacob Lake."

They both looked confused, and Barb sighed with resignation as she slipped a sheet of memo paper from a tray on the desk.

"Follow 89A south out of town," she began, and she didn't stop until she intimately described what was probably all of both streets in House Rock. The piece of paper said exactly three things: 89A, Kaibab, and silver trailer. She handed it to Anne, who took it and glanced at it as if to reaffirm everything it said.

"Bit of a distance," Barb said as they turned to go.

"How far?" Anne said.

"Fifty miles about, but the hills will slow you down some." Barb studied the ceiling from the corner of one painted eye, running the course of the road over the Kaibab Plateau through her mind. "An hour at least. If you hurry."

"An hour," Anne said, nodding. "Thanks." She and Patchett stepped out squealing doors and into the bright daylight.

"An hour," Anne repeated one more time, squinting. "Any idea how you're gonna do this? What you're gonna say?"

Patchett looked at her honestly and started to the car, parked alone in a packed-dirt lot. "Not the slightest," he said.

Anne followed him.

63

WHEN THEY REACHED and then crested the top of the Kaibab Plateau, Patchett and Anne could see virtually the entire breadth of House Rock Valley stretching out before them. It swayed off to the left and then the right as they followed the switchbacks of 89A. The view of the valley flicked at them between the pines, which jutted up incongruously.

House Rock itself was down there somewhere. Patchett hoped that the silver trailer would be there as well, with Rayes inside.

Anne watched the approaching valley, too, and Patchett's attention flitted between the road and her face, which was focused intently out the window.

"What's on your mind?" he asked. It was a terrible question, he supposed, but he could no longer tolerate the silence between them. Coupled with his growing unease as House Rock came nearer, the tires steadily and unnervingly thumping against the road, the lack of conversation was too much.

Anne answered without looking at him. Her eyes only closed more narrowly into tight squints behind nondescript sunglasses. He heard her sigh lightly before she spoke.

"Have you ever stopped your car and gotten out on the side of a road like this one?" she asked. "A road that seems out of place in its surroundings? No one around?"

Patchett considered it, shook his head, and Anne turned her gaze back out the window. She held a map backfolded and rolled in her hand. He could just make out a section of the Utah border on it as she tightened and loosened her grip, crushing it.

"I remember once," she said, "driving up to my mother's house one evening. It was in the middle of winter. January. Maybe February. I can't remember why I needed to stop, just that I did, and I remember getting out of the car beside the roadway." She was picturing it in her mind—the road stretching forward and back through a desert of snow. Much like the scene before her now, but done in a thousand shades of whiteness. No one but her at that place and at that time.

"After you get out of the car," she continued, "it's like stepping out of a little box you've been crammed in for hours. You get out, and it seems as though the world has exploded almost past your sight. Past all your senses. No one's around. It's just you standing under a sky and in a place that seems impossibly large."

She sounded like she was talking to herself, her voice had faded so much.

"And it's perfectly quiet."

Anne noticed for the first time that she was crushing the map, and she stopped. She set it carefully on the dashboard. It fell off quickly onto the floor. Out of sight.

"It'll be like that down there," she said. She tipped her head toward the valley below them. "Big. Empty. Silent." She stared at the flat as it flitted between trees, then she turned to Patchett.

"You think the answers to your questions will be down there," she said to him. Her voice was stronger, a touch of fearful conviction in it. "All the answers to everything we don't know. But I'm afraid that it'll only be silent. Nothing at all, and everything still unknown."

Patchett's attention was fixed on the road, but he stole glances at Anne and the approaching flat. It looked, as Anne had said, horribly silent. And vastly empty.

"The answers are there," he said confidently and calmly. "We just have to find them."

"How?"

He really couldn't answer that. Despite the fact that he'd come here, bringing the others with him with an announced "plan," and despite the growing nearness to Rayes and the answers that Patchett wanted and now even needed, he simply had no idea what he would say or do when he knocked on that door and Rayes opened it. *If* he opened it. Patchett didn't know how to handle that at all.

He shook his head, and they continued without saying anything more until the road first began to level below them. The pines changed over to rough and scrappy shrubs interspersed among scattered rocks and a few taller trees. Then it was brush and clumps of sage that twitched gently in a light breeze.

"So where were you heading on that trip?" Patchett asked then.

Anne turned to him. "Pardon?" She'd missed the question, engrossed in thoughts that she wouldn't have been able to identify if he had asked.

"The trip," he said. "Where were you going? Where are your parents?"

"Hibbing," she said, almost noncommittally, and she pulled absently at a lock of hair, tucking it once more behind an ear. Her eyes turned to the passing scenery once more.

"They still there?"

"Mother," Anne said to the window. "Father's long gone. Stepfather, too, for the past few years."

Patchett felt the discomfort of a question that shouldn't have been asked. "Sorry," he said.

"Don't be," she replied in a toneless, flat voice. "I understand your bitterness at the world, Jon. Despite what your perceptions of my innocence or idealism might be. I probably understand too well, unfortunately." She turned from the window to face him.

"So I also understand why we're doing this," she went on, tipping her head toward the road ahead. "I understand it perfectly well."

Anne's words lingered between them, hanging like a passing reflection on lessons learned and youth lost, until hints of House Rock appeared before them. A battered pickup truck with a mongrel dog in the debris-laden bed was the first sign of life. Then a green highway sign marking the town, bullet holes through it, and they were there.

Patchett turned into the small town and headed for the silver trailer that he could see even now on the slight incline above it. They were a couple of miles away, no more.

64

THE DESERT MOUNTAINS rose thousands of feet to the left, and they were a breathtaking orange hue as the high sun struck them fully, but Jason Burke paid no mind to either that or to Marc Clifton, who appeared to be trembling in the shotgun seat.

Burke watched every pull-off spot as he passed it, scrutinized each car that he roared by. He had no description of the car he was looking for. Just two pictures — black-and-white law firm directory photos of Jon Patchett and Anne Matheson, two faces he already knew.

He didn't have any pictures of Gary and Linda Kane, who were also supposed to be down here with Patchett. He had only brief descriptions. There wasn't time for anything better.

But it shouldn't matter. They'd be along here somewhere. One, two, or all of them maybe. He would find them.

Burke figured he and Clifton were about three hours behind them because of Patchett's head start. Maybe a little less. But Burke checked the pullouts and passed cars anyway. The people ahead were probably unfamiliar with the area, and they wouldn't feel as pushed as they should have on top of it. Add to that the fact that there could be as many as four of them together ahead of him, and you got all sorts of possibilities for delay. He pressed harder on the pedal and heard the engine shift up, saw Clifton tip slightly toward the middle of the seat to glance at the speedometer.

Burke didn't know that Patchett and Anne — just those two — had spent almost two hours waiting in the Old Paria Coffee Shop across the street from the hospital with a flecked green floor and a receptionist named Barb. He didn't know the margin was now down to an hour and a half and narrowing still.

It wouldn't have mattered if he had. They were speeding along.

Donald Pierce and Terry Rettner exchanged the briefest of amused glances as they occupied Bancroft's couch, watching the doctor pace. He was shuffling his overweight bulk like a penguin across the worn carpet as Clark Wall lectured him on what was going to happen over the next few hours. Pierce and Rettner were old friends of Clark's. Friends who'd been around long enough to see what Clark could do, what he sometimes *had* done. Friends who'd been around long enough and were trusted enough to have helped him do some of those things, and who were helping him once again.

Bancroft wasn't that kind of a friend. To him, Clark Wall was only a huge, foreboding presence in the center of the room, methodically laying out the probable hows, whys, and wheres of what they were going to do. Eric Bancroft was terrified at every word Clark uttered.

Someone would show up here, Wall said, and it would be sometime today. Ben Flare had told them that return tickets for the four were purchased for the next day, and there simply was no other way to cover the territory between Rayes and Bancroft in that amount of time. So someone was coming here today.

After explaining the plan to deal with that, Wall moved over to Bancroft's desk and sat down calmly. He was wearing a light-weight leather jacket despite the redness that was still inching its way up the Pepsi Cola thermometer at the AM/PM store across the street. It was a March scorcher, possibly touching an incredible 95 degrees, but Wall wore the jacket anyway, snapped cuffs and neck strap left open as the sole concessions to the heat. He occupied Bancroft's desk chair, tipping his large squared-off frame back in the recliner.

His feet were planted on the edge of the desk, chipping away at the simulated-wood Formica. He, too, watched Bancroft, but with just one eye. The other, his left, was hidden behind a black cloth patch with a wide elastic band that wrapped around his head.

A series of scabbed gashes ran in parallel rows under that eye. The marks from his enraging battle with that slut Maggie Washburn.

"Would you please sit the *fuck* down?" Clark said finally, as Bancroft's pacing and the pain in his eye caught up with him. "You're driving me apeshit."

"I can't help it."

"Try."

Bancroft retreated to an old coil radiator that was camouflaged by a layer of paint to match the walls. He propped himself against it.

"Where's everyone else?" he asked.

"Burke and Clifton are going out to see Rayes. Franck and Miller are at the hotel, coordinating the final steps. Just like I told you. You forget any of the rest of what I said?"

"No." And he hadn't. In fact, Wall's speech laying out the day's events so thoroughly scared the piss out of Bancroft that he thought he'd never forget it.

An unnerving void filled the room, broken only by Wall's rocking his foot against the desk edge. A chunk of the Formica freed itself and jumped to the floor, where it lay on the clear plastic carpet protector.

The silence got to Bancroft first.

"I'm not an assassin or anything, you know," he said weakly. The three men turned their attention to him as though he were a dull child they'd rather ignore.

"I mean, I don't know if I can really do anything when it comes time to do it."

"Well, Eric," Wall said, "I think there are probably some people who've got that pretty well figured out already. But don't worry too much about it. I think you'll find your motivation when the time comes. Couple a million motivations, probably. What do you think?"

Bancroft didn't answer, turning instead to stare out the window. He could see the heat shimmering off the pavement in vertical waves.

Rettner and Pierce were laughing at a private joke that was

whispered between them, no doubt at Bancroft's expense. Wall watched Bancroft for ten, then fifteen minutes more, the other two men on the couch continuing to trade occasional comments and chuckles to pass the time.

When it happened, it came sooner than anyone but Wall had expected. A buzz that stopped Pierce in mid-punch line. Bancroft turned to the desk. Wall sat perfectly still, the one eye covered, the other closed in concentration and not in sleep. He was just imagining how the day would go, and this was fitting in just fine.

"Dr. Bancroft?" said a speaker on the desk. It was Bancroft's secretary from the outer room.

"There are two people here to see you. A man and a woman. They don't have an appointment, but they insist it's important."

Bancroft was immediately frozen in terror and shocking indecisiveness. He looked at Wall, who didn't return the look but who nevertheless nodded serenely.

"Send them in," Bancroft heard himself say, and the line clicked closed. They waited a few seconds.

They had thought they wouldn't get through at all at first, and Linda was already trying to figure out how to contact Bancroft in some other way. The phone was always out of the question. It was too easy for the other person to control the conversation that way. Getting away from phones was the primary motivating factor for the entire trip. The only option left was to wait for Bancroft to leave his office before getting the chance to talk to him, and Linda didn't like the odds on what might happen if they waited that long. Too many things could go wrong. Too many problems could arise to prevent their ever getting the chance to corner him.

Which left the secretary. She was firm enough, convincing enough, discouraging enough. Dr. Bancroft wasn't seeing patients or anyone else today, they were told. He'd canceled all appointments and was to be left alone. Family death or illness or something else vaguely defined. He was tied up in arrangements. Could they come back?

Gary and Linda pressed, then pressed again. It was, they said, terribly important that they see Dr. Bancroft immediately. A matter of life or death. Linda wondered if that was so terribly far from the truth.

After the prodding, the secretary had shown the one crack that would allow them in. She said she would check with Bancroft, and both Linda and Gary felt silent shouts go through them. The task was already proving a little tougher to accomplish than either had really expected, though Patchett clearly set out the potential difficulties before leaving Minneapolis.

They watched in nervous and total silence as the secretary rang through on the intercom, and they listened on edge as she reported their presence. The patch of quiet that followed frayed nerves once more, but Bancroft's delayed response washed the nervousness away.

This was going to be relatively simple, Gary thought as he half listened to the secretary mumble about going right in. She gestured to the door, and they headed toward it.

Go in, he thought. *Ask a few questions, get the answers, and get out. Talk to Patchett later. Spend whatever time was left tonight and tomorrow enjoying Vegas. Enjoying Linda.*

This would be all right.

The first thing they noticed was the huge man sitting at the desk. Then they saw that he was barely a man at all. Was probably only twenty-two or twenty-three years old. And he appeared incredibly young and old at the same time, a doubtful mix of youthful features next to the scars of age.

It was the eye patch, of course. The patch that you noticed immediately and that made you think of pirates on coloring-book pages, and you asked yourself why this person was wearing that thing. People wore patches in the nineteenth century and in fairy tales. Not now and not here. Then the scratches leaped out. Four slashes across the cheek.

He wasn't Dr. Bancroft, and it wasn't even surprising to see him lift a pistol off the desk and point it in their direction. Gary and Linda heard the door swing closed behind them, and they knew there were more of them, but they didn't turn to look.

"Gary and Linda Kane," the big man said. There was no questioning in it, and there was obviously no denying it. Gary felt his stomach tighten uncontrollably, and he found now that he *was* surprised. Not at the man sitting before them. Not at the gun. Instead, he was surprised that this day, which had started with such low prospects but had grown to great heights, was crashing to this incomprehensible depth once more.

"Welcome to Nevada," the man behind the desk went on. The gun still didn't drop. It appeared cast in cement. "My name is Clark Wall. Donald Pierce and Terry Rettner are behind you, and they'd appreciate it if you didn't cause any problems for any of us. Over there"—and Wall gestured into the darkest corner, where Bancroft stood attached to the shadows—"is Dr. Bancroft. We're all really pleased to see you. Won't you sit down?"

Wall swung the gun from Gary and Linda over to the couch, and they moved stiffly to it, not taking their eyes off Clark except to sneak a confirming glance at Pierce and Rettner. Then they sat nervously and tightly together. Gary could feel Linda tremble against him.

"I imagine you're here," Wall said, "to speak with Dr. Bancroft. Is that correct?"

The Kanes looked at each other, at Bancroft, at Wall. Gary nodded without a sound.

"Right," Wall said. He rested an elbow on the desk, the pistol rocking alternately from Gary to Linda. "I'm afraid that Dr. Bancroft can't talk to you today. Maybe the secretary mentioned that on the way in. But I'd be more than happy to talk to you both.

"What do you say we start with Jon Patchett?" he said, and he grinned.

The pirate came to life.

65

THE COKE CAN in Rayes's right hand was full but warm. He'd gotten it almost an hour ago, popping its top and taking just one sip before once again being overcome by the visions that were haunting him ever since he had scared Andy from the site. The images were more frequent now, and they were lasting longer. Whole stretches of pictures ran together in bright streams in his brain.

The duration of his treatment of Marguerite Ruval so many years ago was there, etched in his mind in precise strokes of color. Rayes could see the people who had stood around her as the last seconds of life seeped from her small body. The death of a child, coming at his fingertips.

But that was a death he could understand and tolerate, even if he could not forgive those who were involved alongside him. Marguerite's death came through negligent misguidance. Something overseen. Something forgotten. Something done too late.

But the other pictures? The images of Andy Littlefeather that passed through Rayes's thoughts presented a different situation altogether. They were not some long-ago event created at the hands of others but left on Rayes's doorstep. What happened with Andy was a very real, very recent development drawn wholly from the pages of Rayes's more modern existence. Created wholly by his own hands.

He had almost killed a boy.

Tears and a shaking doubt flowed freely over the two days since finding Andy at the site. Rayes was racked during that time in an almost uncontrollable purging of the emotions that built up inside of him for all the years of his life. All of the events that were dammed up had tumbled through the small gap made by Andy Littlefeather's small and round face, which that day looked up at him with such innocence and trust before turning to fear of Rayes's making.

That face was unmindful of the violence that Rayes had been planning, and that was perhaps the worst thing of all. A small boy, accepting without question the word of an adult stranger who stood above him, not realizing the danger.

Rayes wiped at his eyes with the back of a hand just as he heard the sound of a car crunching over the gravel spread thinly in a parking area at one end of the trailer. He rubbed his eyes again and stood, moving to the dirt-encrusted window and peering through it.

He didn't recognize the car that parked between the pickup truck and the small Bobcat sitting beside the trailer. He didn't recognize the passengers, either, as he saw them get out. The driver was a tallish man, weight average to his height. He was dressed casually, in jeans and a purple long-sleeved shirt. His hair was poorly cut, on the long side. He was stretching one shoulder as he talked to a woman getting out on the other side. She was a bobbed-hair blonde who looked impossibly young, even with the sunglasses hiding half her face. They were making their way to the door.

Rayes glanced once at the cracked mirror tacked to one wall and grimaced at his appearance. It wasn't that he disapproved of people seeing him this way; it was just disconcerting to see how far he'd fallen in the span of a couple days. More disturbing, he found that he didn't really care.

The knock came at the door.

Patchett noticed that the breeze was stiffer, more urgent when he stepped from the car, and he examined the horizon as he worked the knot from his shoulder. The sky was marked by the puffed tops of clouds that floated high above the valley, but the coolness in the light wind suggested something ominous behind the seeming peacefulness of the weather.

He glanced at his watch and wondered if there was a motel in House Rock, someplace to wait out a storm that might greet them on a trip back, but he knew immediately that he would find no such place in this small town. It was really nothing more than a collection of ramshackle clapboard houses and trailers that looked out of place in a desert more suited to the one or two hogans that dotted the town. The closest thing to commerce was a gas station that marked the end of House Rock like a period under an exclamation point of a town, laid out here under the watchful eye of the cliffs. A sign had indicated a general store farther east. But no motel.

"Ready?" Patchett asked across the car to Anne, who was stepping out the other side.

"Looks like he's here, so that means I'm as ready as I'll ever be."

They walked up a path marked by stones that were largely kicked out of place. Outside those markings, the red, packed dirt looked exactly the same as the path itself. Looked, in fact, exactly the same as every other square inch of land they could see.

They mounted the creaking steel steps, noting the worn black paint, and Patchett rapped at the door. There was a shuffling inside, and a curtain twitched to the right of the door. Then the door jerked open with an obviously difficult tug.

The man who stood before them looked both haggard, fitting in remarkably with this place, and distant, as though indeed dropped here in a place he didn't belong. His face was lined deeply, wrinkles cutting through his brown skin, his hair black. His eyes were shot through with a red that was familiar to Patchett, and he needed a shave.

"Dr. Rayes?" Patchett asked, almost doubtfully.

The man looked at him as though trying to place him, then did the same for Anne. He nodded wordlessly.

"My name is Jon Patchett. I spoke with you once before. This is Anne Matheson. We'd like to talk to you about Prohiva and Lot 179. May we come in?"

Rayes looked from face to face without surprise. In an instant, he ran through everything pushing him along for the last two years, but he ended again with Andy Littlefeather's standing out in the middle of the site, a pistol extended toward him. A pistol in Rayes's own hand. There was that picture, and the picture of Marguerite.

"I suppose that I should have expected you sooner," he said resignedly. "Come in."

Rayes stepped aside to allow them in, extending an arm into the dark trailer. "Pay no attention to the mess, please," he said. Patchett noticed the familiar, slight accent and the precise formality in the man's words this time. "I was packing. But you probably expected that."

Patchett and Anne entered the trailer.

•

Burke and Clifton didn't stop in Kanab, and they couldn't have even if they had wanted to. A call from Franck already confirmed that Rayes wasn't there and wouldn't be anymore, and the stop would have been a waste of precious time. So they took the more direct route to Jacob Lake, avoiding Kanab altogether, and they picked up 89A to follow it into the valley beyond the Kaibab Plateau. That would shave nearly fifteen minutes off the distance separating them from Patchett and Anne.

Clifton said nothing. He was maintaining his silence in bowing deference to the intensity of the driver. Burke's manic concentration destroyed any opportunity for discussion of what they were supposed to do.

Whatever that was, its time was nearing. They were closing the gap.

If anything could be called a living room in the trailer, this was it. Patchett surveyed the room once briefly when he stepped in, but he examined it more thoroughly while Rayes was pulling two more cans of Coke from a refrigerator that groaned when it was opened. The room was dominated by traditional trailer decor — cracked plywood paneling and bad carpet. But the level of filth, both in terms of junk and dirt, was alarming.

No flat surface appeared free of some object. Dishes rambled across the kitchen counter and into a tiny dining area, where another assortment was stacked on the table. The garbage can was capped by six inches of piled-on refuse of various kinds. Soft drink cans appeared to be the dominant species.

An unidentifiable smell exuded from somewhere that was strangely enough *not* the garbage can, and a large heart-shaped stain marked the center of the room. Patchett and Anne sat on opposite sides of it, with a folding chair for Rayes pulled up at the edge of the cracking linoleum that signified the kitchen.

"I apologize again for the mess," Rayes said as he handed the drinks to them. "My attention has been on some other things these past few days."

"Would Prohiva and Lot 179 be among those things?" Patchett

asked, and he was surprised to see the mask that was Rayes's face crack with a smile.

"Mr. Patchett, those two things have dominated my recent life so thoroughly that not a day passes when I do not think about them. But you cannot possibly comprehend and probably do not believe how I now wish for the day when I had never heard of either of them."

He looked at Patchett with a face that the lawyer usually saw only in the mirror on mornings when he awoke with a powerful hangover. It was a look of painful, rampant lack of self-control. A look that told the viewer that it was damn well time to start changing a few things. What the person did on seeing that face, however, was ultimately up to his own determination, as Patchett well knew. He wondered what decisions Rayes had made.

"You are here," the doctor said, "because you have become convinced that Lot 179 is associated with Prohiva, despite what I told you previously?" Patchett nodded without a word and sipped at the can of soda pop.

"Well, you are right, Mr. Patchett. They are linked. But before I spill all of it out to you two here, why don't we make this much simpler. Why don't you tell me what you already know about Lot 179?"

Patchett felt more than saw Anne look at him, and he questioned for a moment if Rayes was merely fishing for something to shape a story around. He looked again at Rayes's tired face, and he answered honestly.

"We think that Lot 179 was the testing of Prohiva on humans. We believe it failed for some reason, and the results were not provided to the FDA."

"And you base this on . . . ?"

"On Weber documents. On assorted notes and papers as well as some notes that should be there but are not. And on two letters sent to a woman by the name of Rebecca Cartaway. They were sent by Alexander Tomlin, and they suggest the situation I just described."

Rayes was leaning forward in his chair, eyes focused on the

stain in the carpet. "Alex," he said, thinking back to him. "Perhaps too romantic for his own good. For the good of *both* of them, for that matter." He looked up at Patchett. "I understand that Ms. Cartaway is dead."

"Tomlin, too, by strange coincidence."

Rayes shook his head. "No coincidence, Mr. Patchett, but I am sure that you two have already reached that conclusion as well. I am impressed with your other conclusions after all. I find that, despite all I have seen in the relatively few years that I have been around, some things still do surprise me. You have done so. But I am guessing that you are here to fill in the 'for some reason' in your statement?"

"If you're asking me if I want to know everything about Lot 179, then I'll say it. Yes, I want to know *everything* about Lot 179."

"Very well." Rayes tipped his warm Coke can against his lips, taking a slow drink while he thought.

"There is a street in Las Vegas," he began after a moment, leaning forward. "A street that stretches off the Strip. It runs a few blocks. Perhaps a half dozen. No more than ten." Rayes's tone drifted to softness, his gaze turning in, seeing the scene he was describing and only that.

"I was there two and a half years ago," he went on, his voice a faint, entranced monotone. "There with Eric Bancroft and Marc Clifton. We had a small stack of flyers and an equally small stack of money. Not that we needed more."

"What about Tomlin?" Patchett interrupted. "Was he there?" Rayes's steady gaze broke and turned to the attorney, then Rayes seemed to run the question again through his mind, as though he had heard it only distantly the first time. He began shaking his head.

"No," he said. "Alex was not there at that time. He remained up at Weber BioTech." Then the doctor spoke to answer Patchett's next, unasked question.

"But he did know," Rayes said. "He did know what was happening down here. He did not approve necessarily, but he did know what was happening, at the beginning."

"What *was* happening?" Anne asked. Rayes turned to her, but when he spoke, his eyes cast downward and found a neutral refuge in the carpet, as though he were ashamed.

"Fifty people," Rayes said. "We found fifty people and paid them each one hundred dollars."

"Fifty people from where?" Patchett asked.

"From the street" came the answer. "They were the homeless, the prostitutes, those down on their lives and luck enough to take one hundred dollars for a quick needle prick and the chance to help out what they thought, I am sure, was the government. If you walked down that Vegas street at that one time, you had the chance. And fifty of them took that chance in less time than any of us originally guessed."

"You gave Prohiva to fifty people off the street?" Patchett repeated in disbelief.

"Yes, Mr. Patchett," Rayes confirmed, nodding his head. "We gave Prohiva to fifty people."

"What . . . happened to them?" Anne asked hesitantly, and Rayes's response was hesitant as well. He took a final drink from the Coke can, emptying it, and he set it on the sole clean spot on the table beside him. It tapped the table with a soft, metallic, and hollow *tink*.

"About thirty of them were dead within a year" was all he finally said in answer to her. He looked at neither of them.

"How?" Patchett asked.

"When the initial deaths came," Rayes said, "we tested each carefully. There were seven of them almost immediately. Within months. And the results were . . ." But he trailed off. Patchett and Anne waited for him to finish, watching the doctor's changing expression as Rayes searched for words that were lost to him.

"Were *what?*" Patchett prompted. Rayes didn't move, didn't blink.

"Extraordinary," he said finally, and both of the people listening to him knew instantly that the word wasn't used in its positive sense. "Those first seven died of AIDS," Rayes continued, explaining. "And it was unusual in the rapidity with which it developed. But what is more — what is *worse* — was the virus itself."

"How do you mean?" Anne asked, her tone cautious.

"To a person," Rayes replied, "each one of the first seven deaths resulted from a previously unidentified different strain of HIV." He waited for his words to sink in, looking to each of the two people in turn. "Everyone got the same shot from the same lot," he said matter-of-factly. "But inexplicably they all ended up with different viruses."

"And all those viruses were fatal?" Patchett said.

"Yes, Mr. Patchett." Rayes nodded again. "The viruses were all fatal."

"So after those first seven, what happened to the rest of the recipients?" Anne asked. "What happened next?" Rayes looked nervously at her, mopping at a light coating of sweat shining across his face.

"We collected all the others we could find," he answered.

"Collected?" Patchett said. The word was sharp and examining. Rayes's eyes closed tight as he waited for more from the attorney.

"Collected," the doctor repeated when only silence followed. "Collected them in one place in Vegas, where we could observe them. A place where we could see what would happen."

"Like guinea pigs," Patchett said bitterly. Rayes winced at the comment, then went on.

"We collected them so we could take care of them," he said.

"And what did happen?" Patchett asked then. "In the end, I mean."

Rayes shifted uncomfortably in his chair. Its metal frame squeaked once under his weight before it, too, fell silent, waiting.

"In the end," Rayes said, "it did not matter." His voice tapered off in a melancholy whisper accented by another squeal from the chair as he shifted again. Then the stillness swelled into the room, battled only by the sifting sound of the wind against the trailer's roof and walls.

"Why didn't it work?" Patchett asked finally.

Rayes sat up slightly, regaining some of the composure that had leaked away during the story. "That is unfortunately a question best asked of the late Dr. Tomlin. He was studying what happened in Lot 179 during the months immediately preceding his death. In truth, though, I do not think it would ever really have mattered what he found."

"Why's that?" Anne asked.

Rayes looked at her and shrugged as if the answer were obvious. "The project had moved beyond Prohiva by then. Weber had bet his future on the vaccine, and 179 was the signal that it would not work well enough to pay him back. At least not in time. So he went on with the approval process and kept Tomlin at bay by letting him run with the studies."

Patchett had looked up abruptly at Rowe Weber's name, and he spoke now with the conviction of another puzzle piece dropping in. "So he *knew*," he said. Rayes looked to him in bewilderment. "Weber knew," Patchett said, and Rayes smiled weakly at that, despite the circumstances.

"Of course he knew," the doctor said simply. "How could he not?" And at that seemingly uncontestable statement, Patchett found himself wondering the same thing.

"Who else at Weber was involved?" he asked.

"Me, of course," Rayes said, the absoluteness of the confession halting his words. "Rowe. Marc Clifton and Eric Bancroft. Kenneth Miller, too, to a lesser extent. And Alex. Reluctantly, but perhaps unavoidably."

Patchett slipped the photo out of a pocket and passed it to Rayes, who took it and sat back.

"Is the big guy Bancroft?" Patchett asked him.

Rayes was looking at the picture almost wistfully, the memory of it crossing his face visibly. "Yes," he said. "That is Eric." He examined the picture more closely. "This was taken when 179 was just beginning. Things seemed very bright indeed."

He handed the picture back to Patchett.

"It is strange," Rayes said more to himself than to either of the other two. "The usual approach during the FDA approval process, of course, is to seek an exemption from new drug restrictions for the express purpose of doing investigational studies on humans. But Rowe never sought such an exemption. In fact, through connections at FDA, he specifically sought additional animal testing for Prohiva. He *asked for* a unique approval process heavily weighted toward animal studies, with human studies only at the end. He characterized it as a concern for people, and the FDA, hearing that, obliged and delayed that testing."

"Rowe Weber threw a highly public fit about that delay," Patchett said.

"Ah, but the key there is *public*, is it not?" Rayes's statement echoed alone in the small room until Patchett spoke once more.

"It was the stock, wasn't it?" he said expectantly. There was uncertain anticipation in his words and surprise in Anne's face. She looked to Patchett, wondering exactly what he meant and, whatever it was, how long he'd been considering it.

"With every step through the approval process," Rayes answered, "the stock climbed higher. If human testing was ordered earlier, Prohiva never would have gotten off the ground with the momentum that it has built. Instead, however, we have seen a frenzy."

"Wait, wait," Anne interjected. "Just *wait*. What is all this?" she asked, not knowing whether to look to Patchett or Rayes for the answer. But it was the attorney who spoke first.

"Rowe Weber owns around forty percent of the stock in his company," he said. "He's got ties to another ten percent or so, mainly through complicated holdings. He's probably got other ties, even more indirect, to holdings beyond that." Patchett was talking to Anne, but he was looking at Rayes, who was returning the steady stare.

"What's the price of a share?" Anne asked, comprehension already dawning on her.

"Around seventy dollars," Patchett replied.

"And how many shares outstanding in the company?"

"Weber BioTech was overissued," Patchett answered. "Too many shares. Too fast. It was one of the reasons that the price plunged so low at the initial offering."

"How many?" Anne repeated insistently.

"Around twenty million."

Just like that. Those few statements, and the cash register in Anne's mind began to ring out of control.

Twenty million shares, ten million or so of them controlled by Rowe Weber himself.

Seventy dollars per share.

That meant $700 million for Rowe's holdings alone. More than that with each additional dollar in stock price.

"He could never pull it off," Anne said, but her voice was an uncertain whisper. "Trade imbalances would shut it down. And even if they didn't, the sales would destroy the market for the shares as they were sold." Even as she said it, though, she knew she was wrong, and Patchett knew it, too.

"It'd be fairly easy, I think," he said. "Heavy-volume trading, with mutual funds buying and selling in a stock rapidly spiraling upward. Over the course of a couple of days, sales could be worked out. Some sales early, I'd expect, with other sales late. Most of them probably through nondescript neutral-faced holding companies. Maybe some sales aren't reported at all. And best of all, there's always program trading." Patchett shook his head at the thought, at the realization of the myriad possibilities.

"It's always been possible to take advantage of deficiencies in information in the market," he went on. "Problems like time differences, insufficient phone lines, things like that. They can make possible any transaction that was previously thought impossible. Arbitragers can still make some money in this world simply by understanding the interplay between operating hours in different markets and the time zones that separate them.

"With things like those, it's easy. The speed of modern communication would allow the last sales, which would probably be the biggest. You could get a transfer of the funds out of the country before the market itself could fully react. It'd still be thinking up for Weber BioTech, after all." Patchett shrugged, shaking his head.

"The market would flush it out by then," Anne said, but Patchett continued shaking his head.

"I doubt it," he replied. "Sure, the market *may* notice. The ticker alone would reveal much of the information needed to give it away. But I think it'd be tough to link them to Rowe Weber until it was too late. And other large purchases and sales by institutional investors, along with any resulting investor confusion, would mask it for a few more hours. Maybe even a day."

"Someone would notice eventually," Anne protested.

"No doubt," Patchett conceded, nodding at that next hurdle from the series of questions and problems he knew were running through Anne's mind, questions and problems Patchett himself remembered from his night staring at the Weber prospectus.

"No doubt," he said again. "But it wouldn't matter by then. It'd only mean that he's able to get half of it unloaded, or three fourths. So he ends up with only half a billion or so, not the whole thing. But either way, all or part, all that's left is the counting and the laundering."

Anne looked at Patchett with lingering uncertainty and, the attorney thought, a measure of fear. "It couldn't possibly be pulled off," she said. "It *couldn't.*" But the response to that came from an unexpected source.

"Look around," Rayes replied. "Look at this," and he pulled a copy of *Time* magazine from a stack beside him, tossing it to her. She caught it and looked at it.

GENETIC BLANKS the cover declared. THE MIRACLE CURE MOVES FORWARD. The magazine's red border wrapped around those white block letters, which were imposed over a skull and crossbones labeled AIDS. A hypodermic stretched across the cover, two twisting strands of genes floating in the green serum in the syringe.

"It *has* been pulled off, Ms. Matheson," Rayes said. "And no one has found out but you two." He looked from Anne to Patchett and back. They both were staring wordlessly at the magazine in her hands.

"Do you not see how simple it is?" the doctor went on. "Mr. Patchett is correct — it is simply a matter of timing. Keep everyone blind long enough to get the stock high, and then, good-bye. Whatever happens after that simply happens."

"Did Tomlin ever even get close to figuring out the problem?" Patchett asked pointedly, but Rayes answered him with a question.

314 / PATRICK REINKEN

"Do you know how Prohiva works, Mr. Patchett?" the doctor said. "The antisense?"

"Blocking of portions of genes, right? Cancel out the dangerous portions to create a genetic blank that triggers antibody response without starting disease."

"Precisely. In 179, however, Alex found out that the antisense did not work. Sometimes it failed entirely to blank out the targeted genetic coding, sometimes it affected just a few portions, sometimes it affected the wrong portions. What effectively happened was that all the recipients were injected with HIV that contained an inherent variable."

"A little more English, please."

Rayes rubbed a hand through his hair in mild frustration. "You understand, don't you?" he said to Anne, and Patchett could see by the look on her face that she did. The fear and comprehension there were growing.

"They weren't blanks," she said. "You injected those people with live viruses that were unsuccessfully treated in a way that made them even more dangerous. Even more unpredictable."

Rayes was nodding, head in hands. "In many ways," he said, "the viruses were stronger and faster, with latency almost written out of the picture. People became sick in months, not years. But other than that common thing, the individual viruses were totally unique."

"What caused it?" Patchett said. "What made the antisense not work?"

"Alex was working on two theories. The first was that Lot 179 had degraded due to age. There was a significant lag between manufacture and use. If that theory was correct, then it was correctable."

"And the second theory?"

"The second theory was based on physiological differences between the studied subjects and humans. Prohiva was initially tested on monkeys. And it was tested against simian immunodeficiency virus, not HIV. It is conceivable that enough variables, possibly including the age of the lot, entered into the mix to bring this result about."

"Which would mean what?" Patchett asked suspiciously. Rayes stared at him.

"Which would mean that it might never work," he answered.

"But you don't *know*, do you?" Patchett whispered heatedly. "It could have been old vaccine. It could have been the monkeys. It could have been overheated or too cold. It could have been given on a Tuesday or during the rainy season, for Christ's sake." Suddenly, Patchett was on his feet, trying to pace off cool rage building inside him. "You just don't *know*, isn't that right?"

The color flared in Rayes's own face, and he appeared momentarily young again, revitalized by the anger flowing at him.

"That vaccine can work, Mr. Patchett," he snapped. "Yes, there are problems. Yes, it needed more study. And yes, FDA should have known. I'm as guilty as anyone else for not speaking out earlier. But that vaccine — that *technology* — should get a chance. It needs that chance, and it must be studied."

Patchett stood before him, raising his hand and pointing at the doctor with a trembling finger. "You can't tell me it'll work, though, can you?" he said. "Right now, when it matters, you cannot tell me that this vaccine will do anything other than kill people. Do we need to study *that* a little more?"

Rayes started to speak, but Patchett cut him off.

"And tell me something else, doctor," he said tightly. "Has anyone ever given any consideration to what would happen if one, just *one*, of these souped-up viruses got out in public and started spreading? Has anyone actually sat down to think about what might happen if a virus like that could spread similarly unpredictable viruses? Do you even know? Isn't that the ultimate question — do you, or does anyone else even know what truly could happen? Or do you want a study on that one, too?"

Rayes looked at Patchett till he could look no more, then his eyes found those of Anne, who looked less menacing, if nothing else. The images of Andy and Marguerite were reshaping in his mind.

Patchett walked to the small window of the trailer and looked through its rotated panes out onto the foreign landscape of the Arizona Strip. He'd forgotten it was day, Rayes's trailer was so cut off, so separated from all other existence. But he could see now that the sun still slanted down on red dirt undisturbed save by the puffing and gusting breeze that was running ahead of thunder-clouds in the distance.

Patchett sighed deeply, then turned back into the room. "Do you know, doctor?" he said again, his voice quieter and almost reserved. "Do you know what would happen?"

Rayes simply shook his head.

Patchett looked down at the doctor, who sat with slumped shoulders in the folding chair. "Tomlin," Patchett said. "Rebecca Cartaway. Everyone in Lot 179. That's quite a legacy you partici-pated in there, doctor." He rubbed at his forehead lightly as Rayes slipped farther down on the chair. It was Anne who broke the silence.

"How many people are planned in the Phase Three tests again, Dr. Rayes?"

"Ten thousand in the first group, with half of those getting the actual vaccine."

"And they might pass it on?"

"They will be closely monitored and probably will never have the chance. The fifty in Lot 179 were the problem. They could have passed it on. One or two might still be out there doing just that, for all I know."

Patchett looked up at that. "I thought you said you found them all."

"No, Mr. Patchett, I said that Weber collected most of the recipients. At last report, he was still hunting down a handful of them."

Patchett caught the tone in Rayes's voice, and he leaned over, one hand braced against the back of the doctor's chair. "Hunting them down in what sense?" he asked. "For what?"

Rayes looked slowly up at him, only inches away. "To kill them," he said softly. "Just as he has already done with several of those whom he could not originally find."

Patchett's head tipped back in disbelief. His eyes shut tight as Rayes's words sank in.

"A few more for the books" was all he said. But Rayes was instantly before him, standing and whispering furiously in Patchett's face.

"Your self-righteousness is not lost on me, Mr. Patchett, but it is also not helpful. The simple fact is that I am here, talking to you now, because of the way I feel about everything in which I have become involved."

The lawyer leaned toward Rayes with a practiced courtroom intensity. He spoke softly as well. "The fact is, Dr. Rayes, that your help now might just be too late. We're talking about turning loose a virus the likes of which this country — this *world* — has never before seen. The likes of which it may never recover from. Your virus makes regular AIDS sound like the fucking sniffles, doctor. *That's* what we're talking about people being exposed to here. *That's* what everyone seems to have forgotten."

"I know that," Rayes said, his voice calm and smooth. "You know that. She knows that. Many people know that. But Rowe Weber?" Rayes shook his head.

"Rowe Weber is many things, Mr. Patchett. A moderate genius, perhaps. An eccentric, certainly. Quite possibly a madman. But he is not an understanding man. He is not a compassionate man. Those are things that do not matter to him. Those are *people* who do not matter to him.

"For Rowe Weber, we are ultimately talking about perhaps a billion dollars. Life can be good with a billion dollars, and that is the *only* thing that matters to him. Balanced against it are the people you speak of, but those people are faggots to Rowe Weber. Drug users. Prostitutes. Immigrants." Rayes spat the words out. "They are not really considered people by Mr. Weber."

"That's a nice speech," Patchett said bitterly. "Nice sentiments. But how much did you get?"

"How much I would have gotten is irrelevant now. All that matters is that I am talking to you. And I am prepared to repeat it wherever necessary."

"You never said anything before," Anne said.

Rayes shook his head, turning to her.

"You never did anything."

He shook his head again.

"Why now?"

Rayes's gaze grew distant, and he was silent for a few moments. "I have recently become reacquainted with things that I used to think were more important than money. Things that I forgot for a time."

"Things like what?" Patchett said. He'd stepped away from Rayes and positioned himself once more before the window, watching the approaching storm.

"Things that are my business and not yours."

Patchett looked at him briefly but let it slide.

"Be that as it may," he said, "your recent change of heart helps us, but we could still be a lot better. I'm willing to go to the proper parties tonight, but I'd rather do it with some proof other than the stories of a man who's never been linked to Prohiva before. We came here for proof, and we've found some, but I'd like more if you have it."

Rayes didn't hesitate, his eyes leveling at the attorney. "I have all the proof you need," he said. "More than you would ever want to see. And I would be happy to have you help me get it." Rayes tugged a jacket off a nail driven into the wall by the door. "Shall we go?" he asked.

Patchett looked at Anne, who got up, startled at the suddenness of it. Rayes stepped out the door, and they followed.

66

GARY AND LINDA could barely breathe in the cramped space. Their noses pressed near the crack through which a hint of light came, and they sucked in as much fresh air as they could. Their heads throbbed from the smell of exhaust and the effects of carbon monoxide poisoning.

If suffocation or asphyxiation didn't kill them, the heat would. They had been folded into the car trunk for at least an hour of the hot afternoon, and the movement of the car failed to deaden the building heat. Even now, as Gary struggled once more against the rope knotted around his wrists, he could feel the sting of sweat seeping into the burning cut that he was making in his skin. Another drop ran across his temple.

He stopped pulling at the rope when another muscle knot rippled through his shoulder. He straightened the arm as much as he could to force the pain out.

Linda had stopped struggling against her own ropes some time before, directing all her effort to finding some measure of space and the best available air. He could feel her knees spooned up behind him, and he figured that her head would be cornered near the taillight.

That was confirmed at the next bump, when he heard the dull *thunk* of her head striking the trunk lid. There was a sound muffled by the strip of packaging tape that ran across her mouth. A similar piece covered his.

The bumps and jolts were becoming more frequent, and Gary decided that, wherever they were heading, they were already off the main roads. Beyond that, neither of them really understood what was happening or what they should do.

Gary had tried to track the car's movements after he and Linda were bound and gagged and tumbled unceremoniously into the trunk, but the duration of the ride and his unfamiliarity with the area prevented it. He was working on the ropes instead, also without luck.

He lay quietly for what seemed like hours, knowing it was really minutes as he listened alternately to Linda's forced breathing, the strained and unintelligible conversation from the front of the car, and, eventually, the slowing sound of the engine. They both received a final jolt and a collision with the trunk lid as the back tires sprang over one last bump before coming to a halt.

The doors opened, and now they could clearly hear Bancroft

and Wall. Two others as well. Gary caught a reference to Pierce. Then the trunk lid opened, and they looked up at the silhouettes of the four men—Wall, Bancroft, Pierce, and Rettner.

The bright sunlight radiated out from around those shapes in a burst of brightness. Gary and Linda closed their eyes against the light.

Burke and Clifton stopped in Fredonia just long enough to get gas, then they set off again toward the plateau that rose before them. From Fredonia, you could make out a dark crown on the mountains—trees that, to someone on the desert floor, seemed to have an impossible existence.

The road went out of town toward those trees, soon passing a sign declaring that the area was a national forest. There was no forest at that point, but the two-lane highway began to rise sharply, thousands of feet being marked off by improbably short distances. The car strained at the climb, and Burke pushed it harder. The rough shrubs appeared, then individual trees, and finally the dark foliage of the Kaibab Plateau's approaching heights.

Burke and Clifton kept climbing.

The rock was large and square, just big enough for Clark Wall to sit on. Still, it wasn't so large that his knees didn't jut up at skewed angles. He was resting his elbows on them, one hand holding the pistol, which dangled down between his legs. He was staring at the ground, watching a beetle tote a compacted sand pebble on legs lifted over its back. He poked at it with a long leaf.

Wall made no sound at first as he prodded the insect, waited, then prodded it again. A grin spread across his face, a mischievous smile that warned of danger. Wall pushed at the beetle once more, almost furiously, then looked up at the Kanes. They stood before him, still bound, still gagged.

"Mr. and Mrs. Kane," he said brightly, as though greeting business associates he hadn't seen for some time. He smiled broadly, warmly at them. "You didn't really have anything to say back in town. Would you like to rethink that now?"

Gary and Linda looked at each other, squinting against the desert glare, eyes searching, confused.

"*Oh,*" Wall said suddenly, "I apologize." He gestured at Terry Rettner, swinging the leaf blade from Rettner to the Kanes. Rettner moved to them and tugged the packaging tape from Linda's mouth with a sharp pull before doing the same with Gary. Then he moved behind them and, pulling out a short-bladed knife, he cut the ropes at their wrists.

"Better?" Wall asked when that was done. He could see a thin line of blood running from a tear on Linda's lip. He waited for an answer, the smile still bright, his face expectant. Gary rubbed at his wrists, Linda at her mouth.

"Well?" Wall prompted.

"I know you," Gary said in response. Linda turned to him at his words, but Gary's eyes were only on the big man sitting in front of them. "I know you," he said again. "I couldn't place you at first, but now . . . Clark Wall." Gary hesitated, as if confirming it in his own mind, running the name through once more. "You're Eugene Wall's son," he said then.

Wall was positively beaming. "Very *good,* Mr. Kane," he said. "Keen eye you've got there. Very observant. You'll make a fine lawyer."

"Like your father?" Gary asked smartly. "I worked with him on the Prohiva application for the FDA, coordinating various parts of the submission." Gary shook his head in dawning realization. "So what's his role?" he asked then.

Wall actually laughed out loud at the question, a sharp, barking noise dulled only by the reach of space around them. But the laugh faded, the grin slumping away with it.

"Ah," Wall said, "Dad." His words were burnished with a light touch of seeming melancholy, seriousness setting in about him. "Father," he went on, almost to himself. "I have him to thank for this job, you know," he said. "My father had contacts with Rowe Weber, and Rowe Weber needed a hunter. I fit that bill."

"A hunter?" Linda said uncertainly, and Wall's gaze turned to her. His grin returned, sharper and cooler, more dangerous in its taut control.

"Never mind," he said. He looked down again, eyes searching for and finding the beetle. It had progressed almost a yard since they began talking. Wall started to prod it once more.

"We have a problem, Mr. and Mrs. Kane," he said, watching the beetle. It was still making steady progress toward his toe, despite the leaf poking at it. "You are reluctant to help me, and your visit in any event is . . . how should I say this? *Untimely*, I suppose. As happy as we are to have you here, it would have been better if you'd shown up later in the week. Can you appreciate that?"

"You'd have been gone," Gary said.

"Exactly," Wall replied. "That's just it exactly." He looked up, the smile fully back, looking fresh and new. "Again, the well-trained mind of a lawyer-to-be who understands precisely my point. So I'm sure that you'll also sympathize with the problem that this presents us. That problem, of course, is that you're here *now*, and we frankly have a lot of other things that require our attention over the next few days. Which means that you're going to have to find other ways to amuse yourselves. And that's why we've brought you here."

Wall swung his arms open, throwing the leaf a short distance. The gesture pointed at nothing, instead sweeping across the vast emptiness that surrounded them. Gary and Linda could see no distinguishing features other than rolling, brush-covered hills and a few assorted mountains they didn't know. There was no visible road, paved or otherwise. The car, a nondescript sedan, sat squarely in the middle of the desert. A fine layer of dust decorated its sides.

"You're going to leave us out here?" Linda said doubtfully. One of the other men — Pierce, Gary thought — laughed lightly.

Wall shrugged. "Think of it as an opportunity to embrace nature," he said. "In fact, we'd so much like for you to experience fully this beautiful countryside that we'd appreciate it if we could have — and ma'am, I'm particularly embarrassed to ask you this — if we could please have your clothes."

Linda made an unrecognizable noise and Gary jerked toward Wall only an instant later. He made it precisely one yard before

Rettner stepped into his path. There was a blur of black as Rettner's own pistol swung out at the end of his reach. It contacted Gary's nose and a wide spray of red speckled into the air.

Gary dropped backward like a felled tree, feet knocked from under him. He gasped and raised his hand to his nose, finding it wet and flat against his face. Linda fell to her knees beside him and rolled him partly over. The blood drained in a stream down his cheek and onto the ground.

Wall never flinched. He looked at Gary, then at Linda, and finally at Rettner, who stood over them both, and he shook his head.

"That's not too cooperative an attitude, Mr. Kane," Wall said. He stood up from the rock, dusted the seat of his pants with one hand, and strode over to the couple as Rettner stepped aside. "But now that you've gotten it out of your system," he said, leaning over them, "I'd like to have your clothes, please."

Linda's head whipped toward him. "What do you need with our clothes?" she spat. Her voice was low and intense, a whispered fury. Gary wiped a bloody hand at his more bloody face.

Wall looked at her with impatience. "I told you we need time," he said. "And right now, our best way to get that time is to make sure you two don't just come strolling out of here. Not having your clothes will be a big step in that direction, don't you think?"

Linda felt Gary struggling to sit, and she lifted him with one arm. "It doesn't sound like we have too much choice," he said, spitting blood between his words. "Doesn't feel like it, either."

"Once again, sir, very astute. I'm impressed with your perception." Wall straightened up and moved away, waving the pistol at the Kanes as if to confirm Gary's words. "So let's make it today."

Gary tugged his shirt off where he sat, leaving a smear of blood inside it that soaked through to the outside like a red shadow. A streak ran up his face by the time he finished pulling the shirt off. His forehead looked stained with juice.

Gary was pulling his shoes off when Wall looked at Linda, who stood fixed to the ground, unmoving.

"You, too, Mrs. Kane," he said.

She didn't reply, instead looking with undisguised anger at the four men, three of them armed, who stood arrayed before her. She caught hold of the bottom of her shirt and pulled it up and out of her jeans.

She dropped the shirt on Gary's, ignoring stares from Pierce, Rettner, and Bancroft. She watched Wall alone, and he returned her glare with his own poker-faced gaze.

No one stirred as the Kanes removed their pants, piling them together. When they finished that, Linda was standing, Gary still sitting. His head was pounding, but the blood was slowing.

Wall looked expectantly at them and waved the gun once more in their direction. "Everything," he said, and Gary started to speak before cutting himself off.

He stood carefully and stepped out of his underwear. Linda unfastened her bra and slipped it off onto the pile before hooking thumbs in her panties and dragging them down.

Someone behind Wall made a single-word comment, but Wall didn't look away from Linda's eyes. She tossed the panties to him, and they hit him in the chest, falling to the ground at his feet.

"Happy?" she said in a mocking voice. She stood with her arms defiantly at her sides. Her skin was pale under the dying brightness of the Nevada sun. Even with the clouds that now hung heavy in the sky, edging out the most intense light, she would be red in minutes.

"Yes, thank you," Wall said. "I am." He kicked at the panties, and they landed with a scattering of dirt near the other clothes.

"Don?" he said, and he pointed the gun at the clothes. Pierce tucked his pistol in the back of his pants and moved over to collect the clothes. He kept a wary eye on Gary and a lecherous one on Linda, who stood tantalizingly near. The clothes and shoes gathered, he retreated to his position, and he waited.

Wall was stepping up in front of the Kanes. "Your cooperation was really quite helpful and very much appreciated," he said. "And now that you've done the difficult part for us, I'm afraid that it's time to go."

He lifted the pistol in a short arc and aimed quickly, choosing a target according to the hunter's maxim that you always took the strongest first.

He fired once. The second shot was accompanied by Linda's scream as she saw the spouts of fresh blood running from Gary's head in twin streams. He collapsed once more, and Linda stood over him for one fleeting second before seeing the gun swing in her direction. She turned and sprinted.

She was so close to Wall that it seemed to him that he had the luxury of slow motion to choose his precise actions. He leveled the gun at her, bracing his aim with his other hand, and he squinted his swollen and bloody eye behind the patch.

"Pity," he said, as he watched Linda's running figure above the notched point at the tip of the pistol. He squeezed the trigger.

A pea-sized spot of red appeared in the center of Linda's back, and she tumbled to the ground as though pushed by an unseen hand. She screamed again as her bare skin swept the ground in a slide across the sand, gravel, and spiked plants of the desert floor. Then she was up on her hands and knees, struggling to her feet, and staggering forward once more.

Wall turned to the men watching from behind him. "Wait here," he said calmly, and he paced deliberately across the desert, stepping carefully over cacti, the pistol in one hand at his side.

When he reached Linda, he stepped in front of her, blocking her desperate walking crawl, and he crouched just beyond any possible reach. Linda struggled to raise her head to see him. A thick line of spit fell from her mouth as she did so, and she froze that way, staring at his knees. A single hiccup was the only sound she made as she waited.

"I'm an excellent hunter, Mrs. Kane," Wall said to her, but he was looking out across the desert, studying the mountains in the distance. "I hunted them down," he said then. "I hunted the rest of them down when everyone else fucked up and didn't collect them all." He looked at her, bending his head forward, his eyes searching hers coldly. "I mopped Mr. Weber's problem up for him, because I'm an excellent hunter. And an excellent hunter knows how to follow everything, and how to cover up tracks."

Wall stood abruptly as Linda's eyes shut tight. "Running wasn't going to change that," he said softly, and he swung the pistol toward her head. "In fact, nothing you do can matter now." He pulled at the trigger three times. Linda Kane was flattened against the hot desert floor. She twitched once across her right arm, then lay still.

None of the men in the near distance stirred until Bancroft sat back heavily against the fender of the dusty car. He was mumbling what sounded like a prayer, no doubt the first he'd uttered in years and probably the only one he could remember. No one paid attention.

"You want ID removal?" Rettner asked Wall from a few yards away.

Wall considered that, his gaze remaining on Linda's pale white body. It lay perfectly still at his feet.

"ID removal" would mean removal of fingertips or hands, the same for toes and feet, and destruction of dental work. A shotgun blast to the mouth, maybe. It would take additional time and would make more noise and mess.

"No," Wall said, pulling his attention away from Linda's body and turning toward the car. "We've got the clothes, and we'll take them back and burn them. There'll be no instant identification if someone finds the bodies. But I don't think even that will happen. We'll just roll them into a hole somewhere. We only need a couple of days."

"What about Patchett and the girl with him?" Rettner asked then.

"They're on their way to see our friend Alfre, I'm sure," Wall replied. "Burke will have to see to them." At that, Pierce and Rettner moved to the car trunk and opened it, searching for a collapsible shovel tucked into the spare tire compartment. Wall walked slowly over to Bancroft, who was wiping a hand over his face.

"You don't look too good, doctor," he said, the hard smile returning. "Maybe you need a chance to get back to nature yourself?" Bancroft's head shot up, and Wall laughed loudly at the fear that he saw in the man's face.

"Just kidding," he said. "Just kidding." Moving away, he caught sight of the beetle once again. Still with a smile on his face, he stamped down with his boot heel and crushed the bug into the ground until he heard a light crack.

He moved over to help the other two men carve out a shallow hole.

67

ANNE COULD SEE the trailer swinging from side to side behind the truck as they sped their way back up a short stretch of 89A and down onto a ranch trail that extended south into the flat. The wind whipped, pushing the trailer and the truck itself in unpredictable directions. She could see by Rayes's hands on the wheel that he was fighting the stiffening wind and the drag that it was having on their load. His knuckles were white.

Patchett wasn't saying a word. None of them was. No one had spoken since Rayes led them out of the trailer with a bang of the door, walking over to the small Bobcat minidozer parked next to Patchett's rental car.

The dozer looked as though it had been there for years. A thick red fog of dust was caked on it, turning its chipped white paint to a pinkish tinge. Assorted tumbleweeds were piled against its trailer, having somehow worked their way into the crevices beneath it. They'd been poking out like spidery legs until Rayes pulled them away and hitched the shaky and battered trailer to his pickup. Then he took a few minutes more to clear a path to the Bobcat, started it up after two sputtering attempts, and maneuvered it up the tipped-back trailer.

The last thing that had been said by anyone was said then, as Patchett questioned what Rayes was doing. Rayes had merely brushed it off with a brusque stare.

That was fifteen minutes before heading down the dirt path,

and the steady jarring the road was delivering was only heightening the tension. Patchett clutched a battered door handle with each jolt, pushing or pulling himself more fully into the seat as necessary. He twisted his neck to peer out the window when he dared, watching clouds that were forming a heavy line in the sky. The clouds hung gray and thick a few miles off, and evening was coming.

"Where the hell are we going?" he asked finally.

"You want your proof, Mr. Patchett," Rayes said. His voice was loud against the sound of the truck's engine and the disconcerting wrench of metal parts in unidentified parts of the vehicle. "And you will get it," Rayes continued.

Patchett glanced out the dirty windshield, past a crack that glistened in it, and he looked at what was still visible of the countryside. It was barren, totally devoid of anything meaningful, totally empty of any life.

"Out here?" he said, waving a hand toward the reach of space outside the window. Anne, too, was staring out with a look that clearly betrayed her doubts.

"This is not just any *out here*," Rayes said, turning to Patchett. He had the sudden appearance of a man in control of his life once more. Alfre Rayes knew that he commanded the one piece of this puzzle that Patchett needed, and he would deliver it. But for now, he relished the upper hand that he could enjoy.

"Just beyond this rise, there's a fence and a gate," the doctor offered, and Patchett and Anne saw that it was true just as he was finishing his sentence. The gate was visible in the distance even in the dim color under the clouds. Rayes flicked on his headlights.

"That fence marks property owned by Claymore Ranches. Now, even *you* probably do not know this, Mr. Patchett, but Claymore for the past year or more was a subsidiary of . . . Do you care to guess?"

"Weber BioTech," Anne said softly, but both men could still hear it even above the competing noises.

"One and the same," Rayes confirmed, nodding.

"Are you going to tell me that the Lot 179 studies were conducted out here?" Patchett asked.

"No. There is nothing big enough out here for that. Too far out of the way. The closest — the only — paved road is the one we left near House Rock, and this flat is bounded on the east and south by canyons and on the west and north by mountains and cliffs. The only thing out here is an abandoned ranch house and some remnants of a barn. No cattle, no people, nothing. No, the studies were done in Las Vegas, in facilities arranged by Bancroft."

"So what's Weber have the land for?"

Rayes didn't look at either of them as he spoke. "The studies were not done out here," he said again, and he hesitated before going on. "But the results are here."

"What does that mean?" Patchett asked.

Rayes didn't answer. He stopped the truck and got out to unlatch the gate.

They drove through.

68

CLIFTON JUMPED when the trailer's door banged closed, bounced open once more, and closed again under the driving force of the wind. He was standing beside their car, his back to the trailer, waiting for Burke, but Burke stood now on the swaying steps. One hand was on the fragile rail, and he was looking left and right down the slope and past House Rock, which spread below them toward the flat. Burke's other hand shielded his eyes from the stinging dust rasping into their faces.

"What's wrong?" Clifton asked, raising his voice against the wind.

"Not here." Burke pulled his sunglasses from his pocket and slipped them on. It was actually getting too dark to use them, but the wind demanded it. He pointed to Patchett's rental car, which, save for Burke's own car, sat alone in the graveled parking area. "Truck's gone, this car's here, and no one's inside. Hard to tell 'cause it's such a fucking mess in there, but it looks like a couple of them were here with him."

"So where are they now?"

"How the shit do I know?" Burke said, and he hurried down the steps. "Don't know why Rayes's truck'd be gone and this'd be here, unless they're with him. Maybe he's taken them somewhere."

"Out here?"

"Don't know. But the Bobcat's gone, too, and I'm not sure if that's good or bad."

"What's your concern?"

"That he took them out to the site," Burke said, glancing up. "Alive or dead, that he took them out there. And I think that's where we should be headed, too."

At that, Clifton cast a look up at the ominously darkening sky and listened for a moment to the shrill, driving wind. The sky couldn't have been changing to a more definitive black if someone had been pulling a tarp across it, and the air carried the thick, musty smell of heavy dampness. It would be raining on the plateau to the west. A hard, driving downpour.

"Can we make it before the storm?"

"No," Burke said without hesitation. "Do we have a choice?" He gestured for Clifton to move around and get in the car, then he opened his own door.

He stopped for a moment before plucking an army knife from his pocket and unfolding it. He jogged over to the rental car and bent over the two nearest tires. With quick movements, Burke slashed the valve stems on those tires. They hissed flat as he got back in his own car and pulled out, heading down the hill to House Rock.

"What do you plan on doing when we catch up to them?" Clifton asked after they traveled a few miles.

Burke glared at him. "Second thoughts, Marc? A day away from a few million is a little late for that, isn't it?"

Clifton knew he was right. Too many things had gone before. Too few things were still to be finished. This close to the end, this near the reward, it was too late to stop. True, he was no assassin.

No more than Bancroft, who had previously voiced the same concern more definitively to Wall. But he probably wouldn't have to be, he thought, looking at Burke. The other man was once again intent on the road, Clifton's question already forgotten.

They both fell into silence as Burke turned off 89A and onto the ranch trail. They headed south, deeper into the valley.

69

THE BOBCAT'S ENGINE was rattling the headlights atop the minidozer's cage. Their white glare wavered down to cut the darkness in front of Rayes, who had driven the Bobcat down off the nearby trailer to begin moving the blade forward and back at the etched border in the soil, working the dirt loose and starting a small trench. The sandy soil broke easily. The plants, still unsettled even after the intervening months since they were laid down, were pulling up in clumps.

The wind was dropping off to an eerie, still pulse, and Patchett and Anne no longer needed to squint against the blowing dust as they watched from the small overhanging bluff. The truck sat beside them, its own headlights aimed down a few feet to the area where Rayes was working.

Flashes of lightning were beginning to illuminate the scene, with thunderous crashes following each burst of light. Looking west, Anne could just make out the drizzling fog that signified a drenching on the Kaibab.

"We don't have much time," she said to Patchett, and he nodded nervously, following her gaze. They watched Rayes wordlessly as he edged first forward and then back, carving out a broad and sloping hole that gaped darkly into the earth.

The smell of diesel exhaust was hanging in the air, only barely being pushed out by the advancing rain, when Rayes idled the engine and waved them down from the bluff. They stepped carefully, choosing their footholds gingerly in the shadows and glow created by the truck headlights behind them. Anne took Patchett's hand once as she moved lower, and he felt its cool and damp softness. Then they were down and crossing the short distance to where Rayes sat in the Bobcat. When they stood close enough, they saw that the darkness of the hole was lightened by a layer of something that shone bluish-white in the storm-muted last light of the evening.

"What is it?" Patchett shouted to Rayes over the Bobcat's engines, and the doctor throttled the dozer forward until its high headlamps shone into the pit more clearly. In the light, the color was a pristine white, contaminated only by its mixture with the last of the layer of dirt that Rayes had dug away.

"Lime," he shouted back.

"Stone?"

Rayes shook his head. "Powdered," he said, and he reached down to his feet to pull out some objects Patchett couldn't quite make out.

He and Anne caught them when Rayes tossed them down, and they saw that they were half-face respirators. Twin-filter canisters projected from either side of a slotted speaking outlet, and elastic straps sprang from the rubber nose-mouth cup. When Patchett looked up at Rayes, he saw that the doctor was pulling a similar mask on. Rayes began edging the dozer forward once more. Patchett waved him to a stop.

"If we're talking about HIV here, and I assume we are, we won't need these," he said, speaking as clearly and loudly as he could over the rumblings of engine and thunder. Patchett held his mask up. He could just see Rayes shake his head and could barely understand Rayes's garbled words through the doctor's own mask.

"Not virus," Rayes was saying. "The smell."

Even as Rayes finished speaking, the dozer roared to full life and bit deeply into the powdery lime, scooping it away. The doctor once again began advancing and backing, gradually moving farther into the hole each time before retreating with another load of lime and dirt.

The white layer began to disappear from the deepening trench and reappear piled beside it as the thunder clapped more loudly and the first light sprinkles of rain dotted their faces. Patchett studied the sky, feeling the water begin to soak into his skin and clothes.

A few minutes later, Rayes stopped with a jerk as soon as Anne cried out.

"There!" she shouted, and Patchett jumped a little at the sound before stepping up to the edge of the hole. His eyes searched frantically through the soggy gloom of the pit, flicking back and forth as he tried to pick apart the shadows. Then, in the cast of the dozer's headlamps as the Bobcat swung around, Patchett could just see it—an arm, thin and frail, bones traceable along its length and a tattering of skin running across the back of its hand where the blade of the dozer had cut through. It thrust out from the hole's edge into the dim light and the wetness of the stormy night.

"In the glove box!" Rayes shouted down as he idled the Bobcat and leaped down. "A camera in the glove box of the truck!"

Anne scrambled up the bluff as Rayes came up beside Patchett, a shovel in hand. The doctor didn't look into the hole. He only studied Patchett's face, which was fixed on the darkness of the pit.

Patchett couldn't pull his sight away from it. With each tiny shift of his head, another horror leaped out from a previously unnoticed niche. As he looked now, he could barely see an emaciated, white-powdered face, a thin thigh, a foot jutting out at an awkward angle. Some were marked or mangled by the digging, but all were recognizable. All of Patchett's doubts, all of the concerns for whether he was right or wrong, any unanswered questions that remained—all fled at the sight laid bare before him. He didn't hear Rayes next to him until the man spoke.

"You wanted proof," Rayes said in a strong and harsh whisper that forced through the respirator and into the night. His voice hissed. "There is your fucking proof, counselor."

Two sets of headlights floated like ghostly sticks west of the road as Burke and Clifton drove stealthily past. The two men drove slowly and without their own lights. Burke hunched over the steering wheel and occasionally stuck his head out of the open window, searching in the shadowy and dank world ahead of them for the slickening road. The car slipped sideways with occasional lurches, and Clifton's grip tightened on the seat with each one.

Burke was talking about a second pullout up ahead, but Clifton wasn't listening to particulars. He was remembering his last trip out here. It wasn't raining that time, but it was just as dreary nonetheless. And just as dark.

They were all there except Tomlin back then. The doctors had come first. Rayes brought the minidozer, just like tonight. He did the digging. That was probably the same, too, Clifton thought.

Wall and Burke and a couple of the others showed up later, pulling a nondescript trailer behind them. The trailer was loaded with bodies. The last twenty or so of the Prohiva recipients who had been collected by Weber.

Clifton never asked what exactly had happened to them. They hadn't all died naturally. That much was obvious. And they hadn't been stored until all were dead. Quite simply, all of them were killed that day. But Clifton never knew how or by whom. He never wanted to know.

It had taken just a few minutes to unload the trailer, and Clifton recalled now seeing one or two bullet holes in the process. The strongest ones, presumably. Awake and aware still, it wouldn't have been a simple matter of slipping something unseen into an IV line.

The bodies had been lined up roughly in the pit and covered with a shallow layer of dirt. Then a thicker layer of lime, as a barrier to odors that might otherwise make the coyotes restless. The pit was filled in. Clifton had once heard that the scars in the earth were mended the next day, tamped down and covered with fresh desert topsoil and an assortment of plants.

"A few months," he remembered Rowe saying that night. "A few months, and it'll be like Lot 179 never existed."

It was a few months now. Rowe had been wrong.

Burke was nudging him, and Clifton looked over, realizing

that they were stopped. "Out," Burke said. He jerked a thumb at the car door, and Clifton glanced out at the rain before opening the door and stepping into the night.

"We'll walk back a little from here," Burke said as he moved to the trunk. He opened it and pulled out a long, slipcased rifle. An oversized scope looked like a tumor growing from its back.

Burke closed the trunk lid, and they walked into the rainy night, bearing on the dim rods of light still visible in the distance.

The flashbulb flared in miniature accompaniment to the more infrequent but grander flashes of lightning that bolted across the sky. Patchett and Rayes were in the pit, stepping carefully over and around bodies as they picked their way through the sandy mud. "Here," Patchett said, and he pointed. The flashbulb caught a clawed, reaching hand.

"And here." The bulb flashed.

They were making a grim tableau. Patchett's proof was winding onto a spool of Kodacolor 400 with each push of the button. But he didn't feel any better for it, the morbid scene crushing any sense of achievement for what he'd found and for what he could now do to Rowe Weber and the others.

Patchett crouched at one point, catching sight of the hole punctured beneath the eyesocket of one man's body. "Here," he said, barely hearing his own voice through the slots in the mouth of the respirator. But Rayes heard him, and there was a bright flash over his shoulder. The bullet hole stood out in blue-brightened horrible detail, then Patchett's eyes swam with the unearthly green and orange picture of the same scene. He blinked against it, trying to force it away.

"He murdered them, didn't he?" Patchett said. He didn't wait for an answer from Rayes. "Weber collected those people all right. The first ones did die of AIDS from the vaccine. Just like you said. But he didn't wait after those first few, did he?" Patchett turned to Rayes, studying the doctor through the fog of rainfall that was lit by the truck and dozer headlights.

The attorney could smell a faraway mingling of chemicals,

dirt, and the unmistakable taint of spoiled meat. The mask, not fitted properly first, was leaking somewhere, bringing the stench of death to him. Patchett pushed it tighter against his face.

"He murdered them," he repeated. He spoke in clipped sentences so he could be understood through the mask and over the rain. "Then he stuck them here like it never happened. He hunted down the ones he hadn't managed to find earlier. To make sure that no one else would know it happened. Isn't that right, doctor?" But Rayes only stared back until he could look at Patchett no more, then he turned and trudged up out of the trench in slipping footsteps, the attorney following behind him.

Patchett spotted Anne as they reached the top. She stood, drenched, over toward the small bluff and the truck. Just far enough away from the pit's lip, a good location. Far enough away that she couldn't see what she'd already seen enough of.

"Your proof, Mr. Patchett," Rayes said then, and he slapped the roll of film into Patchett's wet hand. The attorney pocketed it without a look as Rayes was digging a wallet out of a back pocket. He plucked a folded and worn sheet of paper out of it.

"You will want this, too," Rayes said, handing the paper to him. "It is a little worn. I have read it too many times. But you should have it."

The paper was glistening with water instantly, and Patchett didn't want to unfold it and risk more damage. He shoved it into a pocket as well.

"What is it?" he shouted to Rayes. The lightning flared, lighting their faces.

"A list of the original Prohiva recipients," Rayes answered in his own shout, but the crack of thunder drowned his voice. Patchett leaned closer.

"What?" They were screaming at each other.

The thunder cracked again at that moment, but it came distantly this time. A sharp and short sound, without a rumble that shook them where they stood. Only that cracking noise, and the steady rain.

Without lightning.

Rayes didn't answer, and Patchett looked directly into his face, seeing already vacant eyes.

A spurt of blood channeled through the mouthpiece slits in Rayes's mask, then it became a gush. The doctor collapsed against Patchett. The attorney dropped him and ran.

The world was all green light through the scope. The beams from the headlights of the Bobcat and the truck were blinding glares in it, and Burke had to avoid tracking them through the sight. But the people showed up perfectly. Their images were as clear as the picture of a black-and-white TV, despite the surrounding night. Faces shone brightly in the glow-in-the-dark color of children's toys.

The first shot took Rayes in the back, just inside the left shoulder blade. Burke considered a head shot initially but passed because of the small size of the target. But the chest was easy and could be just as lethal. With the scope, he could have done it with a slingshot.

The next shot wasn't so easy. The flare from the burst at the end of the rifle hung in his eye and the sight, casting a dull green fog over his view. And Patchett was moving. He had bolted almost immediately, unexpectedly, toward the truck's headlights.

Burke fired once more, then again as Patchett ran for the truck. The scope went blind as it followed him.

At the second shot, Patchett was at the incline to the bluff, and he could hear the bullet smack beside his head. Mud sprayed, flecking his cheek.

Patchett could see Anne running above him, and he heard the sound of the truck door screeching open even over the sound of the third shot.

The blow was like a razor slashed high into his left arm. He fell forward into the mud, tasting its grit, feeling it grind between his teeth. Then he was up again, staggering higher.

The wounded arm went numb, and it hung beside him like deadweight, a sandbag swinging at his side. Dislocated maybe. More likely broken. Patchett could feel only the warmth of blood streaming down it. He cradled the arm until he reached the top of the bluff, ignoring the first shocking pain that radiated into his neck and back.

He jerked the passenger door open and climbed in, his shoulder screaming in pain as he landed inside and tugged the door closed behind him.

"*Go!*" he shouted at Anne. She was already in the driver's seat, cranking the key, and the engine caught mercifully as a star of cracks shot through the windshield, dwarfing the one that was there from before. They both saw the hole centered in the radiating lines.

The back wheels spun for one hanging, interminable moment before catching and pulling the truck backward. Anne swung the steering wheel around, and the truck jackknifed back, pointing toward the trail. Toward House Rock and 89A. Toward who knew what else beyond that. The empty reaches of the Arizona Strip, which may or may not be full of the same people who were shooting at them now.

The truck's engine roared as she stomped the gas pedal, and they shot forward with a spray of mud. The desert bobbed in front of them with each bump that jolted the truck, but the scene soon disappeared under the mat of rain. Anne yanked and poked at steering stalk levers and dashboard knobs until the wipers flipped to life.

When they hit the muddy road, Anne angled the truck in the direction of Patchett's pointing finger, hoping it was the way out as the pickup fishtailed in that direction. The truck's wheels churned at the road for a mile before either of them spoke.

"There's a gun in the glove box!" Anne screamed.

"What?"

"*A gun! The glove box!*"

Patchett popped the compartment open and grabbed Rayes's pistol from inside. "You don't think this is really gonna help things, do you?" he shouted. Anne never had the chance to answer as the sight opening before them pushed her words away.

The ranch trail dipped through Claymore Wash just ahead, and they could pick out the brown flood of water building across the road. A foamy white froth reflected in the shine of the head-lights, looking too deep, too near.

Then she glanced in the mirror and caught the bright spots of headlights behind them. But not far enough behind.

Burke and Clifton also saw the wash, and they saw the truck's one working brake light flash red. Clifton smiled with ill-disguised glee, but the grin evaporated when the taillight went dim once more.

The truck caught a little air at the near lip of the wash, and it went a few feet over the stream without touching water. When it hit, there was a spraying cascade.

The pickup hydroplaned a few more feet before sinking a little deeper. Then it sideslipped, wheels churning the truck forward as it moved sideways downstream. It caught once, lurching toward the opposite shore. Sideslipped more. Caught again.

Then it was out.

Burke and Clifton watched the truck's wheels chew the earth into a flapping, muddy shrapnel even as their own car reached the wash. Its clearance vastly lower than the truck's, it mimicked the pickup's performance only in skimming above the first few feet.

The car landed with a dull smack and sank almost immedi-ately. By the time the tires found any purchase, they were pointed back toward the ranch house and the grave.

Burke pressed the gas, hearing the wheels whine the sandy mud into a slick surface. The car vaulted back onto the shore and buried itself to the axles.

Anne turned east on 89A, heading for the only lights she could see. The dim beacon, barely visible through the falling rain, sat far down on the highway, maybe four, five miles away. That would be past House Rock, but it was a sign of civilization that she hadn't otherwise seen in the small town.

Patchett sat spewing a stream of profanities next to her as he rewadded her jacket once more and pressed it hard on his shattered shoulder. The jacket was seeped with red.

To his credit, he was conscious. He knew that gunshot victims frequently didn't die so much from loss of blood as they did from shock. He also knew he was avoiding the latter, but flirting with the former.

"We need to stop," Anne said to herself more than to Patchett. It was the one thing she was certain of in a terrible and uncertain place where people were being killed while digging up mass graves before her eyes.

She didn't really know what lay before them to the east. She knew only that it was more barren desert. And it was no better to the west, where a mountain ride separated them from distant towns. With Patchett sitting shot and bleeding beside her, his eyes shut even as he swore on, they needed to stop. Soon. She pressed harder on the pedal.

She saw that the light was coming from a general store when they reached it. The paint was cracking and dusty, the door propped open to let in the cool air of the rain. A generator growled somewhere.

The sign in the window said CLOSED in fluorescent orange letters. But the lights were on, and a tall man sat rocked against the outside wall. A battered straw cowboy hat was perched on one knee. He was holding a torn paperback so that the light from inside fell on it through the windows. It was a tattered novel by Larry McMurtry.

When the man glanced up at the truck as it pulled in, Anne could see a small glint from glasses propped high on his nose. He plucked the hat from his knee and stood as she jumped out and came toward him.

"Sorry, ma'am, but we're not open," he said. He pointed at the small sign. She was close enough now to read the name — LITTLEFEATHER'S — but she ignored both that and the hours posted below it.

"This man's been shot," she said hurriedly, moving around to Patchett's door. She opened it, and he almost tumbled out. He woke from an uneasy sleep.

The man was beside her instantly, and together they eased Patchett out of the pickup and into the store. Anne pulled the chair from out front inside, and they sat him in it carefully.

"I need to use a phone," she said, noticing in the light the darker tint of the man's skin, the blue sheen of his black hair. A Navajo.

She also saw a scar that jagged in a shining gleam along one arm. A knife cut maybe, but she was too preoccupied with Patchett to have a concern for just what type of shopkeeper she'd run into.

"Phone's out," he said simply. He was pulling Patchett's shirt back, looking underneath it at the wound.

"How can I get an ambulance?"

"The phone," he said. He saw the blood drying into the shirt, and he pulled the cloth down again. "If it worked," he finished.

The Navajo stood and moved to one shelf, skimming over it and picking out a package of gauze, some antiseptic, some tape, a pair of scissors. He came back to Patchett's side.

"Ambulance wouldn't come anyway," he said, glancing at Anne. He set the materials on the floor and tore open the gauze. "It's out of Kanab. It'd take hours, and they'd never cross the mountains in this weather. Probably got six inches of wet snow up there. Helicopter'd never risk the trip, either. Too dark, too windy, no lights for landing. Power's out."

He studied Patchett's shoulder again, assessing how much shirt to leave and how best to clean the area. "Give me a minute to patch your friend up," he said, beginning to cut the shirt. "Dr. Rayes is in town, so I'll go get him after that. Only a couple of miles away. No time at all."

Anne leaned heavily against the checkout counter, a wave of oppressive heaviness running over her. She rubbed at her eyes, not noticing the blood she was smearing over her face, then she looked at William Littlefeather.

"Don't bother," she said softly. "He's not there."

Littlefeather gave her a questioning look. He worked on.

"Every man," Burke said. A cellular phone was pressed tight against his cheek, the short rubberized antenna rising from it as though springing from his ear. He was shaking his head. "Everyone. I want everyone. This is one wounded attorney and one fucking girl. They can't get very far, and they can't do very much if we hurry. We can end this now." There was a pause, and Burke started to speak, stopped, started again.

"We only need till Thursday, damn it! Thirty-six fucking hours to find two people who can't be more than a few miles away. If we don't find them within that time, and if they get out of here with the information they have now, then we'll all be sitting on our fucking thumbs in prison."

There was another pause, and Burke calmed noticeably.

"Meet me at the bridge," he said. He shut the phone off.

The Ninth Day

70

PATCHETT THOUGHT HE WAS DEAD. When his eyes opened against the better wishes of his throbbing head and searing shoulder, treating him to a vision fuzzed at the edges, he thought that he'd died during the ride. He moved his head carefully from side to side. Even the contact with the pillow hurt. He looked across the ceiling of the room, then down each wall, trying to figure out where he was.

It was a simple room, decorated simply. The couch he was on sat in a small office, a bedroom conversion, probably. A bright, zigzag-striped blanket hugged the back of the sofa, and there was a lifetime of photos attached to one wall. A father and mother, a son. A grandfather in one, lines creased in a face deeply, mapping years that looked to have run out long ago. His hair was snowy white and down his shoulders.

Under the pictures was a worn sewing machine table. Papers were spread over the top of it. It doubled as a desk, by the look of it.

Beside the desk stood Anne, her back to him. She was talking in hushed tones to the father in the pictures. A tall Indian.

"Yours is an interesting tale," the man said when he noticed

Patchett looking at him. Anne spun around, a lock of hair falling onto her forehead.

"Where are we?" Patchett asked when she came over to him.

"Back in House Rock," she said, and she pointed to the man. "This is William Littlefeather. He helped us last night."

Littlefeather said hello, and Patchett nodded to him. "Thank you," the attorney said, not knowing but wondering exactly what had been done. He turned to Anne, and he asked her what time it was.

"Four o'clock," she said, and Patchett thought briefly that he didn't hear her right. He looked to the window and saw the light of day.

"Four?" he asked. Anne nodded.

"The next afternoon," she said.

Patchett looked at Littlefeather as though the man could magically fill in the lost time, could explain where it went, but William only stood perfectly still and expressionless, staring at him.

"Where are the police?" Patchett said finally.

Anne's gaze fell on Littlefeather for a second, then went back to Patchett's pasty face. He looked almost deathly lacking in color.

"There are no police," she said.

Patchett's grogginess faded, and his face knotted.

"What?" he said doubtfully.

"No police," Littlefeather said. His voice was a strong bass, and it filled the room. "No phones, either. No power. The whole valley's out, just like always after big storms. And it'll take two or three days before we get it back. Just like always."

"Two or three *days*?" Patchett said.

Littlefeather nodded. "Days," he confirmed. "No one cares about the Strip, so it may not even happen that soon."

"The storm's just broken in the past few hours," Anne explained. "We couldn't realistically get out; the police couldn't realistically have gotten in."

"So what about now?" Patchett said. "How about a radio?"

"We tried to reach the highway patrol on the citizens band," Littlefeather answered.

"And?"

"No response. There's only one highway patrolman in the area, and we haven't been able to locate him. He may be on the far side of the plateau. There was a lot of snow there late last night and this morning. That would slow him down. He may also be on the reservation side of Marble Canyon to our east."

"Or he may be dead," Patchett said quietly, almost to himself. He was thinking of Rayes. Of Tomlin and Rebecca. Of the bodies stacked like cordwood.

"The young lady has suggested that," William said. Anne was staring at the floor, looking almost guilty for having said it. Patchett ignored her look.

"What about the Navajo police?" he said.

"Too far away," Littlefeather replied simply. He pulled a chair over from in front of the desk, turned it backward, and sat down. "The reservation is vast, and we are miles from the closest fringe even here."

"And they're in the heart of the storm right now," Anne added, William nodding in confirmation. They had already discussed all of this before.

Patchett shifted his weight on the couch, wincing at a pain that shot through his arm. It was splinted somewhat crudely, but it was stiff enough to be unmoving.

"I apologize for the rough first aid," Littlefeather said, noticing the expression. "Ordinarily I would have deferred to Dr. Rayes, but I'm sure you understand the difficulty there."

Patchett closed his eyes at the thought. The shoulder was flaring, and Littlefeather and Anne could see it in his reaction.

"There is aspirin and Tylenol," William said. "I suggest you take liberal doses of both. And there is water or juice."

Patchett looked up with an almost frightening but still-tired gleam. "Any vodka for it?" he said, but he rested his head back before Littlefeather answered.

The Navajo didn't blink. "Not in this house," he said. "Not in my store."

The attorney closed his eyes once more. He didn't need it

anyway. Didn't even want it, strangely enough. He just wanted this to be over, one way or another. "We need to get out of here today," he said. "The film and Rayes's list need to be seen as soon as possible."

Anne stepped forward, closer to Patchett, and spoke. "That's a bit of a problem, too," she said, and Patchett's eyes opened once more to her.

"What now?"

It was Littlefeather who answered.

"You have some determined people out there. Friends of mine have told me that there are men at either end of the valley, where the highway goes out from the flat. They're stopping cars passing through." Patchett's attention was now very clearly focused.

"And do you hear that sound?" William continued, looking toward the ceiling. They all listened quietly until they could pick out the flipping drumbeat in the distance.

"A helicopter," Patchett said.

"Exactly. Helicopters almost never pass over House Rock. But this one has been sweeping back and forth ever since the storm moved on."

"What the hell is going on?" Patchett whispered.

"They're looking for us," Anne said. "Looking for us to either kill us or to make sure we don't get out of here until it's too late."

"Where in God's name *are* we that something like this could happen?"

"I'll show you exactly where we are," Littlefeather said. He stood and stepped to the desk, searching through it until he located an old weathered map. He unfolded it to reveal Arizona.

"We're here," he said, pointing to the top center. "This is the Grand Canyon, and this is Marble Canyon." He traced imaginary lines along the south and east. "This is the Kaibab Plateau, and these are the Vermilion Cliffs." Lines went along the west and north.

He had drawn a perfect rectangle, tracing the barriers that Rayes had mentioned and that Anne had run through her own mind during the chase the night before. House Rock sat at the center of the box, a point on a bisecting line that was 89A.

"With a storm like that," Littlefeather explained, "people could sit for days at the ends of this road, and no one would really pay any mind. We get maybe a dozen cars a day through here at this time of year. The storm will cut that down to almost none. Without phones, without traffic, no one will notice." He dropped the map on Patchett's chest.

"We might as well be on the moon," Patchett said.

"No," William replied. "Someone might be watching if you were on the moon."

Patchett raised the map and looked halfheartedly at it, holding it up with his good arm. "None of this changes the fact that we have to leave here today," he said. "We have to get that film developed and to someone who can get word out. Any ideas?"

Littlefeather considered it. "If you want out of here today," he said, "then you must go out on that road."

"There's no other way?"

William shook his head. "No phone," he said. "No plane. No one responding to radio. Miles of difficult desert terrain surrounding us. There is no other way."

"Then tell me how we can do it."

Patchett handed the map back to Littlefeather. He glanced at it for a moment before setting a finger on Navajo Bridge.

"Here," he said. "Without knowing what the roads are like over the Kaibab, this is the only way." He folded the map and set it on the desk.

"It will be dark again in a few hours. It'd be best to wait till well past sundown. It'll be better then, even though the moon will be full." He came back and sat down again on the chair, looking steadily at Patchett with calm, serious eyes.

"And there is one other problem, of course," he said.

"What's that?"

"Unless you are able to recall, we don't really know where your grave site is. During the rush to get away, there was some confusion."

Patchett looked at Anne, who nodded, her face set firmly. He started to speak then, but he realized that he couldn't pin down where it was, either. The desert looked the same everywhere. Each turnout was like the next. And how far had Rayes gone before turning off 89A?

"I know, father." The voice was impossibly small, and it came from the doorway. They saw a young boy, the boy from the pictures, when they looked. He appeared ashamed at having been caught listening, but he walked into the room.

"I know where it is," he said.

And Andy Littlefeather began to tell the tale of the coyote.

71

THE JUDGE WAS RIGHT. Anderson had to admit now that the judge had been right. The broker pushed himself away from the desk and stood, plucking the cigarette from between his lips and letting the smoke drift out. He was perfectly at ease with himself and with the developments of the day.

The trading in Weber stock was almost uncontrollable all day. The company's announcement about the shipment of vaccines had come earlier than expected, exciting the Street. And the *Time* article had galvanized it with the scoop of Monday's cover story.

Traders hadn't looked back. The price hit a slight drop-off Tuesday morning but recovered to finish up. And it went farther up all day, despite occasional blurbs from inevitable profit takers.

It sat fat at $84.50 a share. The judge's stock was worth more than $11 million, on an initial $400,000 investment. A stunning return, almost incomprehensible in its magnitude.

Anderson dragged on the cigarette once more as he glanced at his watch, then at the computer ticker. Trading time was done in New York, but he wasn't worried. Weber looked to be high for the week, if not forever.

He exhaled.

Life was sweet.

•

The clerk was checking yet another airline as Weber waited impatiently on the line. Rowe was nervously looking at the time, thinking of the remaining calls to make.

He'd heard from Franck, who assured him that Patchett was still in Arizona somewhere, effectively boxed in and stranded. So there was time enough so far as that threat was concerned. But the vaccines were out now, adding a heightened sense of risk. More important, the stock was on a crest that would peak this week, probably tomorrow, before settling down to await further developments. Weber didn't think that those developments would be appreciated by the market.

Which gave him tonight. Tonight, to arrange the remaining smaller sales. Tonight, to arrange a trip out of here. The last sales, the big ones that would set off alarm bells, would be triggered tomorrow, from safer places.

"I have a five ten flight tomorrow morning," the clerk reported. "American's first flight out, arriving in Dallas for connections to Antigua."

"Anything nonstop?"

"No, sir. I'm sorry."

Weber nodded absently to the unseeing phone, knowing this was his earliest realistic shot for tomorrow.

"I'll take that," he said, and he gave her the information she needed before hanging up.

That done, he dialed a Seattle broker. It was his fourth call there in two days.

When the phone was answered, he said one thing: "Go with Group Twelve." He gave the coded number.

Weber hung up, a smile on his face.

72

THE DESERT SMELLED DAMP in the last trace of the warmth of the
sun. The Navajo men moved steadily along, guiding a small flock
of sheep toward a makeshift fence. Two dogs nipped the sheep into
a tighter formation. One of the men barked commands in Navajo.
The dogs swerved at his order.

On the western horizon, the sky was erupting in pinkish-
orange hues under deep blue darkening steadily to black. The land
was indiscernible and dark beneath the sky, the full moon pale
white above it.

The world was vastly different from the night before, when the
desert sands were swimming with rainfall and the night sky was lit
with lightning and broken with thunder.

Tonight, in the places outside House Rock Valley, the world
was peaceful.

The connection between the peaceful world and the valley was the
Navajo Bridge. It sat high above the Colorado, a steel, arch-
supported span attached to canyon walls like a spider on glass. A
glance over its sides would look down hundreds of feet to the
green-tinted, calm river that meandered at night through sheer,
red-rocked walls. A few hours later, rising from yesterday's storm,
the river would roar frothing white.

Officially, the narrow stretch of Marble Canyon was part of
Grand Canyon National Park, but it was almost wholly inaccessible
at this point. The parking lot at the western end of the bridge was
for gawkers, not for anyone who wanted to walk the canyons. The
drops were too steep for anything more than peering carefully over
the edge.

Patchett, Anne, and William were headed for the bridge at
roughly 50 miles an hour. Patchett couldn't tell for sure because

they were running without lights, despite the darkness that enveloped them.

Patchett had tried to talk Littlefeather out of coming. He had also tried to convince David Talkingbird not to ride with them, but Talkingbird sat staring into the truck's cab from the bed. Rayes's truck followed them as well, the same speech having been given to its two passengers, the same rejection having been received. They were Littlefeather's friends. They had all volunteered without hesitation.

"Why?" Patchett asked suddenly, breaking a silence otherwise tainted only by truck engines. His arm was taped to his side, and it throbbed and burned dully against massive doses of over-the-counter painkillers. The wound was infected already, and the broken bone occasionally ground into muscle. But the pain cut back the tired weakness of blood loss.

"Why what?" William's eyes didn't leave the road. He knew the surface intimately, but you used whatever senses you could.

"Why are you here? Why are *they* here?" Patchett gestured back with his head. He didn't expect any answer at all and had, in fact, largely forgotten the questions when Littlefeather finally spoke.

"Andy," he said, and he said nothing else for several more seconds. Patchett and Anne could just see the man's profile outlined darkly beside them. That and his form pressing against Anne, who sat in the middle, were the sole reminders that someone was really driving the pickup.

"I was a student in Tucson for a time," William said, breaking the silence once more. "Nice city. Not too small. Not too big. But a city nonetheless." Patchett now actually did see Littlefeather glance over at his passengers, his shadow shifting ever so slightly.

"There were the usual things that come with a city," Littlefeather continued. His shadow shifted back. "The things I couldn't tolerate and that pushed me back here when my father died.

"Bad people. *Bad spirits*, people here would say. Too much out of balance. Too much money. Too much drugs. Crime. Greed. You name it, there was too much of it. Too much death, certainly.

"And now the cities have reached up here, up into this secluded desert valley where I hoped I could remain undisturbed for the rest of my life, to bring death and incredible danger to this place and to my son. When that touched Andy, when he crossed its path, I had to get involved and do whatever it takes. *Whatever* it takes. Not do so would be to deny the reasons that had brought me here in the first place. Perhaps you do not understand," he added in a hush, and Patchett heard in his voice a touch of sadness, of resignation to taking actions you didn't agree with.

"I understand," Patchett replied softly, thinking about this man's concerns and remembering his own conversation, his own thoughts, expressed to Anne a few nights ago. "Perhaps better than you would expect," he added, and he was surprised to hear the same things in his own words.

"But what about *them?*" he asked Littlefeather, referring to the other three men with them. "Why are they here?"

"The same reasons, for different people," William replied. "Nothing really is safe from this type of influence, Jonathan. On the reservation, there've been cases of AIDS. Too many. Probably in higher rates than in many of the cities. It's a problem that would be amplified by the conditions there. And for all they know — for all any of us know — some of those people might have been connected to Weber." Littlefeather turned once more to Patchett and Anne, looking at them for a dangerously long amount of time while he spoke.

"My father once told me that when the devil knocks at your door, you must answer it and send him away for good. Or he will come in and live with you the rest of your life." William turned back to the road. "We have only answered the knock on the door. Now we must send him away, and to do that, we will do whatever it takes."

Patchett thought of his own life and how accustomed to it he was. He thought of Liz.

Innocence lost.

And Patchett knew then, as the truck ate the miles toward Navajo Bridge, that the devil had long ago come to live in all the places and things that he knew. And he wondered now if he had already lost the opportunity to send him away.

"The devil," he said. "That doesn't fit with peaceful people, with the idealistic and innocent people here. It doesn't fit with this *place*."

"It fits everywhere," Littlefeather replied. "Whatever name you call evil, whatever face you put on it, it fits in all places and can find its way into everything. Into every aspect of your life, so you must always be diligent against it."

Anne and Patchett listened intently. The few other sounds melted away, and the danger of dark roads passed from their minds.

"The *Diné*, the People," Littlefeather went on, "the Navajo to you — they would see it in other things. The spirits or ghosts of the dead would be evil. And they could be found in anything — a whirlwind can be a ghost. The lightning of last night has great evil in it. Some animals, too. The coyote from Andy's dream, for example.

"Contact with all of these things can upset the harmony and balance in life, and they are found everywhere, in smaller or larger doses. We don't need this new evil here. The world has enough evils already. So we will do what we must."

They drove for another mile without words, cutting through the dark until Patchett could just see the first distant line of lights that marked the canyon's span. It was the first sign of power, the first sign of life outside the flat.

"In many ways," Littlefeather said only then, "that is the other motivation." Patchett felt the truck slow almost imperceptibly as William tapped the brake to signal the men behind them.

"This land and these people," William said. "What has happened here will affect us regardless of what happens tonight. But it also would touch us even if the danger was uncountable miles away. Everything is tied together in this world; it will all hold together or it will all crumble together."

He nodded as they drifted to a stop, and he tapped the brakes again. "That is why I am here. Why we are all here. Explanation enough?"

"Yes," Patchett said. "More than enough." He heard the second pickup stop on the shoulder behind them.

Clifton ignored the useless binoculars at his side and waited for the cellular phone to ring. He sat with Kenneth Miller at the valley's western end of 89A. A small one-car post at the foot of the Kaibab.

They were there as a formality more than anything. Wall and Burke were working on the assumption that, based on the snowfall on the western plateau and the desire to move fast, Patchett would run east if he ran at all. If he was alive, for that matter. So Clifton volunteered to hold down this position.

They had stopped exactly two cars that day, giving their lame and quickly worked-up speech about agricultural diseases and a "Could we check your car, please?" to the drivers.

They didn't expect Patchett to just slip whatever he may have to some stranger who could smuggle it to the other side. No, Patchett's best information was in what he knew and his ability to put it all together. If the news of Lot 179 was going to come out of House Rock Valley in time to make a difference, it would come with Jon Patchett or Anne Matheson. And they would be coming past Wall and Burke and the others at the Navajo Bridge.

Clifton relaxed at the thought and at other thoughts of options still open to him in any case. He'd picked this spot because it was out of the direct line of fire, true. But being out of the way brought another benefit as well.

Up and over the plateau behind them was Jacob Lake or Fredonia or Kanab or whatever podunk town had the first available airstrip. Come dawn, no later, and he would be there. By then, it would be done, whichever way it went. Clifton suspected that Weber would be out by then, and if Weber was out, then *he* was out.

Miller could go with him, Clifton supposed. Or he could kill Miller, if he really had to. Whichever way, he would be gone at dawn.

•

It was edgier at the bridge, under the watchful eyes of Clark Wall and Jason Burke. Their two cars were parked at the bridge's western end, angled nose to nose toward the valley so that they would fork back into a tight, locking mass if anyone tried to ram through.

Bancroft and Franck stood at the doors of the two cars. Designated drivers, since they were largely worthless for anything else. Pierce and Rettner were on the valley side of the roadblock. They chatted in yet another meaningless conversation and waited for another car, any car, to arrive to break the daylong monotony that had stretched into a dark night that would itself become another morning in a few hours.

Wall and Burke occupied the bridge on the other side of the cars. They hadn't spoken since Wall chewed Burke's ass for missing Patchett in the first place. Wall scratched absently at the eye patch, wiping a bead of sweat from under it.

They watched the road.

Patchett and Anne waited four minutes before starting Rayes's pickup and slipping back out onto 89A. Littlefeather and the others had edged out ahead of them after delivering explicit instructions — wait four minutes, then follow. Be prepared for anything.

Patchett wondered what that meant as he watched Anne pull Rayes's 9mm pistol from the glove box once again. But he pushed the concern from his mind, pushing aside the concerns for the delicate shoulder and his own weakness as well.

They moved along the highway, jarring on the potholed road. Lights out. Patchett's heart pounded in his chest.

Roy Hendrickson watched the needle swing one more mark through the notched arc. The small glass box covering it was centered above a label designating the Central New Mexico Energy Conservation District. The people would be waking up soon in Truth or Consequences and Raton. The eastern fringes of New Mexico first. Then Santa Fe and Albuquerque.

Hendrickson checked the digital clock on the console and flipped a toggle to light the temperature map. It'd be cool enough in Santa Fe and Albuquerque, but hotter everywhere outside the mountains. Phoenix and Las Vegas would bake today under the combined force of record temperatures and humidity from the drenching they took yesterday.

Despite that rain, the gauge showed that the reservoir was 23 percent down, but Hendrickson knew the demand would be high today, and high demand didn't care one way or the other about water level. All the dials and lighted boards and screens in the world couldn't predict it or limit it, but seventeen years in a windowless room buried beside Glen Canyon Dam gave you a pretty good idea about what you needed to do and when you needed to do it.

He pulled at the card key attached to his breast pocket and it clicked off. It fit the door panels and all the other slotted controls installed in the dam control room two years ago. He inserted it into the slit on the console and waited for the beep of recognition.

When it came, Hendrickson punched at the keypad. Lighted numbers flashed up in sequence, the coding command for the floodgate. It clicked to vibrant, steady green as he completed the set of numbers, and he reached for the palm-sized dial.

The building seemed to rumble as he moved the dial gently, a one-eighth turn. Beyond and below the wall of rock that separated the room from the staggering height of the dam, the gates swung wider. They turned on great cogged wheels, their grinding sound washed out by the increased rush of water that spilled through them and by the blaring alarm that sounded through the predawn air. The water cascaded through the rock wall and the turbines within it, moving down to the Colorado River at the dam's foot.

The river bubbled up like a spring at the spillway's output pipes. Anyone who had dared to be nearby would have been able to watch it rise steadily and smoothly even as it rushed free from the confines of the reservoir.

It built, and it headed south and west. Toward the narrower reaches of the nearest canyons, then it would go farther, through to the Grand Canyon and ultimately the gulf beyond.

Another day of destruction was coming in northern Arizona.

73

"BULLSHIT," RETTNER SAID. He pushed at Don Pierce disbe-
lievingly. "You've never even seen her." They were talking about
women, and they were talking about them in the bragging, sexual
style known to all men who have been awake long past commonsen-
sical hours.

Pierce was claiming to have met an actress once, a face known
to fans of bad TV sitcoms. Claimed to have met her and claimed
to have slept with her. Rettner stared at him with eyes that were
bleary red even in the pale light from the moon and the bridge.
"Bull. Shit," he said again. Two words, drawn out for effect. He
shook his head.

"Look sharp," Clark Wall called out. Rettner followed Wall's
gaze and caught the gleam of approaching headlights. It was still a
mile or so away, but Rettner strolled back to take a position closer
to the gap between the angled cars.

"This one's yours, Superman," he called to Pierce with a
chuckle.

"Like hell it is. I got the last one."

"Like hell you did. You probably don't remember anyway,
you dumb fuck. Thinking about women too much. Too much
testosterone." Rettner smiled and thumbed the safety catch on the
gun holstered under his arm. He pulled the state agricultural jacket,
a leftover from their last trip, back over the pistol to hide it from
view. "Do you good to do a little work. Get rid of some energy."

Pierce clicked the safety on his own weapon off and also
tugged at his state-issue jacket. "Fuck off," he said, also smiling.

"Pierce," Wall said, and the smiles disappeared. "This is yours."
No one said anything else as the pickup approached, then slowed
to a stop as it pulled near the car barrier.

Pierce waited until the man's head appeared through a rolled-down window before moving. A Navajo, he saw, and he stepped up next to the truck. Another Navajo sat on the other side.

"What's the trouble?" the driver asked. He tipped his cowboy hat away from his face and looked at Pierce with casual interest. His eyes were deep brown behind his glasses. The irises were almost black in the poor light.

"Nothing. Just running a checkpoint for out-of-state ag products. Anything to declare?"

Littlefeather could see the bulge and caught brief glimpses of the pistol as Pierce came up beside the car. He didn't know of any agricultural officers who carried guns. Particularly in shoulder holsters hidden under their jackets. And he didn't know of any ag officers who traveled in packs of six in unmarked cars and stopped people at barrier points in the middle of the state and the middle of the night. Everything he'd heard was right. He settled himself into the seat and took a single, deep breath. It sounded like a sigh.

"How about this?" he asked quietly as Pierce peered in at him.

The shotgun across his lap swung up.

Littlefeather caught the startled expression on Pierce's face for a second and saw the man scrabbling a hand under his jacket. Pierce was reaching for the concealed pistol as his mouth dropped open in angered surprise. Then William pulled the trigger.

There was a sparking burst of orange smoke at Littlefeather's chest and a deafening roar that filled the cab and shook the sliding back window in its frame. The center tray between the bucket seats cracked with a *pop* as the recoil sped into its braced position.

And then the still of the night was lost in an explosion of noise that opened up to swallow it.

The first small burst of light in the distance was like the glow of a Fourth of July firework fountain spurting up in a tiny spray of sparkling flame. Patchett knew instantly that it was a shotgun blast, and he knew just as quickly that the smaller licks of yellow light that followed it were return fire from handguns.

He crushed the truck's accelerator to the floor, wincing as the pickup jerked faster forward and reignited the pain in his shoulder.

He did his best to ignore it, concentrating on the bridge and the sparks erupting there.

Anne was quiet beside him, her eyes also locked on the lighted bridge. She was cursing Patchett silently for insisting that she, with her comparative clear-headedness, handle the pistol. She weighed the gun's heft. Her hand trembled around it.

Together, she and Patchett were wordlessly counting the seconds it would take to be there, measuring them against the amount of gunfire, wondering who would — maybe who *could* — survive that race. They could see Littlefeather's pickup obliterated in front of them. One of the Navajos was barely visible, crouched behind a concrete support for the bridge railing at the right side. Patchett saw that it wasn't Littlefeather when the man jumped up and fired a shot toward the car barriers and the men positioned behind them.

Not an inch of glass was intact in the truck — the remnants of the windows were scattered on the ground like ice chips — and Patchett and Anne could see the holes that dotted the pickup's sides. The passenger door hung like a wounded wing off the right.

Three bodies lay perfectly motionless off to the left. One was another of the Navajos, Patchett saw. Who, it was impossible to tell. The two other bodies lay beyond it.

Counting Littlefeather, four men had started this attempt to cross the bridge. One was clearly dead; another was still firing from the bridge's right side. Neither of the other two could be seen as Patchett and Anne came roaring down the last hundred yards. But others were visible on the other side of the roadblock — three, Patchett saw — and the car on the left was just working its way out of a tight space and turning toward them.

Patchett cut the distance in half before painfully reaching over to turn on the headlights.

They made it almost to Littlefeather's truck before drawing any fire. By then, it was too late. The first shot barked harmlessly off a side mirror with a whizzing whine; the second cut higher and missed entirely.

"Duck down and brace yourself," Patchett said. He saw Anne turn to him, a questioning look on her face, and he reached over with his right arm to bend her down in the seat. His left arm screamed once more as it fought to control the speeding truck in the last few yards along the rutted road.

Bancroft thought he was home free when he finally found the relative safety of the car, got in, and began to manipulate it out of its tight spot. He glanced over at Wall and Burke, who were firing from the other car, then looked to the shattered pickup, which stood destroyed in front of them. Only after he stepped hard on the gas did he glance up.

Patchett's headlights filled his windshield.

For one fleeting moment, as the lights chased all shadows from his face, Eric Bancroft had two distinct thoughts. First, that he recognized the oncoming pickup and its barely discernible rust-orange paint. He was certain he'd seen it before, even if he couldn't remember where.

Second, that he would quite possibly die here. And he found at that second thought that he was terrified of that idea almost beyond comprehension.

He had just enough time to think those things, then to wonder why he'd begun this so long ago. Then he wet his pants in a steady stream of warmth.

There was an unidentifiable noise when the oncoming truck hit his car. It was the airbag, and it opened with such force that it shattered Bancroft's nose, flattening it in a break that, for now, was painless but bloody. He shook his head once to try to push away the startling confusion from the blow, but failed. He struggled with the car door then, opening it with a groan, and he stepped out, stunned.

Bancroft's head swam, and the world tipped once each direction. He could just make out the two people in the truck, staring back at him, but their faces vanished in his blackening vision.

He collapsed to the ground in a faint.

There was a pause in the gunfire at the sound of the crash. Wall and Burke just watched for a moment, eyes fixed in amazement at the two joined vehicles that stood where only one car was before.

Wall, knocked to the ground, recovered first, and he began scurrying back on his hands, moving away from the wreckage toward his weapon, which he had dropped on the pavement.

At the ebb in shooting, Littlefeather jumped and rolled out the pickup's passenger door, the shotgun tight in his hand. Brian Echohawk, the man at the right side of the bridge, bolted forward onto the road at the same time.

They darted toward Franck. He turned at the sight and squeezed off a shot before starting to run.

Echohawk got to him first, cutting Franck's legs out from under him within ten feet of the car. The gravel scraped away portions of Franck's shirt and pieces of skin as they slid together, the Navajo on top of the smaller man.

Franck rose against the weight and reached for his gun before collapsing under Echohawk. His arm slipped through the gap under the bridge's guardrail as he fell back, and he felt the terrifying emptiness just inches away from his face.

Echohawk straddled him and stood with a jerk, one hand on Franck's collar, the other sweeping up the gun. He pulled the man to a kneeling position.

Littlefeather had slowed at Echohawk's tackle and turned to Burke. The other man didn't hesitate. He leveled his pistol and fired a single unaimed shot, then turned for the far end of the bridge.

"Stop!" William yelled at him, pulling the shotgun up under his arm.

"Stop!" Littlefeather shouted a second time, knowing that the running man wouldn't. The shotgun swung up.

In the five-second span from Burke's turning to run and Littlefeather's raising of the gun, the Navajo considered giving chase. But he knew he was too old and would probably be killed in any close quarters fight with the man. He also considered letting him run.

But then William thought of Andy. Of Patchett's tale of the bodies and the grave. Of everything that had happened around them without their even knowing it.

He thought of how close this had come.

Whatever it takes, he thought.

He pulled the trigger.

Patchett jumped from the truck as soon as he worked his seat belt free and kicked the door open. Anne was raging at his side, unfastening her own belt and screaming about what he'd done without any warning to her.

He ignored her. He was looking for the man with the eye patch, who had been at the junction of Bancroft's moving car and the other, parked one. Patchett knew the man from somewhere, he was certain, and he also recognized the cool determination in the man's face. He saw how the man had held his ground despite the oncoming pickup.

Patchett was out of the truck and past Bancroft's unconscious form and the smashed car in a second, closing in on Wall, who was crawling toward a lost weapon. There was a commotion at the other side of the bridge — gunshots, yelling — but Patchett's attention was fixed directly ahead. He leaped as the man started to stand.

Patchett caught Clark Wall's jacket with his good hand, almost blacking out from the wash of pain that swelled through the broken shoulder. Littlefeather's crude splint, hastily applied at the house, cracked neatly in half with a splitting noise. Silver-gray strands of duct tape remained as the only things holding it together. Patchett bit a scream back as he dragged Wall to the ground once more.

He collected a handful of short hair at the back of Wall's head and repeatedly tugged and pushed. The face bounced against the asphalt with each blow until gravel began to stick against reddening skin.

A sweep of Wall's arm caught Patchett at the left elbow. The pain ratcheted through that arm as Wall rolled and threw him off.

They went for the gun at the same time, both moving in a scramble, and Wall would have reached it first but for the ringing sound of a shot and a splintering of asphalt in front of him.

Anne had watched the struggle over a brief span of seconds as she fought in growing desperation with her door. It groaned at one point, the sound of metal bent against its will, and opened an inch or two before jamming firm. She'd shouldered and kicked at the mangled door one more time before moving across the seat and out the driver's side door, the 9mm in her hand.

Her second shot hit the sprawling Wall high on the right thigh, burying itself into his femur and stopping cold his grab for the gun. Instead, he fell forward before rolling over to Patchett, who had pulled even in the race for the pistol.

Wall encircled him with a massive arm, and they struggled together to the edge of the bridge until hitting the railing. Then Wall stood, his frame towering over Patchett's, and he dragged the attorney to his feet. A cut above one of Patchett's eyes seeped red fluid into his vision. Wall's hands clasped warm against his throat, and the attorney felt himself tipping back against the railing. The water rushed far below, its level swollen deadly with the dawn release.

This is how it feels, he thought suddenly.

This is how it feels to die.

But Wall's hands were gone just as quickly, and the man's weight lifted off Patchett.

"Back off him," Patchett heard Anne say in a shaking voice, and he coughed once as he straightened up to see her just behind Wall. The tip of the 9mm was buried in Wall's ear.

"You wouldn't dare," the big man sneered. He was back-tracking from Patchett just the same, Anne moving with him.

"I would," Littlefeather said then, stepping up beside Anne. Wall stopped at the words, and he turned to see the shotgun riding on William's hip.

Wall said nothing at that sight, his lips thin and tight. He stepped toward the rail as Patchett moved aside, and he leaned heavily against it.

Wall's gaze never left the shotgun, not even when Brian Echo-hawk dragged Lew Franck across the road and dumped him next to Wall. Not even as the third surviving Navajo — David Talkingbird, Patchett saw — limped up on a wounded leg, driving a crawling

Eric Bancroft ahead of him like a cowboy running bloodied cattle. The doctor collapsed when he got nearer Wall. Only then did Wall look down, giving Bancroft an expression of disgust.

"Clark Wall," Patchett said, drawing Wall's attention away from the doctor at his feet. Patchett studied a man he had once met casually, almost accidentally, in Eugene Wall's office two or three years before. He hadn't enjoyed the experience.

"Clark Wall," he said again, and he shook his head. "I can't say I'm surprised to see it's you." The pain was flaring in his arm, an ache in his throat matching it, but those feelings were far away as he spoke.

"I found out what you did, Clark," Patchett said hoarsely. "I've learned what you—what all of you—did. I've found out all the secrets. And I'll be there in court to tell everyone who wants to hear it. I'll tell them, just to make sure you each get what's coming to you for this. For *all* of this."

But Wall was smiling as Patchett finished. A thin smile, firmly closed at the corners. Patchett couldn't know it, but it was the same dangerous smile last seen by Gary and Linda Kane. It was a smile of madness.

Wall looked at Bancroft first. The doctor was sobbing tears down through the blood that spread from his nose, across his face. He was steadily repeating the soft, whispered word "why?" as he rocked with a smooth, rhythmic pulse.

Wall looked to Lew Franck next, still smiling. Franck actually glanced up at him once before turning away. Franck buried his head in his hands as he sat quietly on the curb near the bridge rail.

Only then did Wall look once more at Patchett, who stood now before him, Anne on one side, Littlefeather and his friends on the other. Wall kept smiling.

"You think you know all the secrets now, Patchett?" Wall said menacingly, mysteriously. "You think you can possibly know everything about what has happened?" He smiled even more broadly, his teeth shining white in the night. "You think what you do can matter now?" Wall's hands reached to the rail behind him, where they rested easily.

"I spoke with Linda Kane about that," he said then. Patchett and Anne went rigid at the name. "Nothing she could have done mattered, either, and I told her that. I'm sure she wanted to send me away, too, you know." Wall paused, appearing thoughtful for a moment, almost wistful.

"I'm sure she wanted me to get what was coming to me, just like you do. But I told her that nothing she could do mattered anymore. I told her I was an *excellent* hunter, Mr. Patchett." Clark Wall's uncovered eye closed at that statement, the smile beaming. "And I know how to cover up tracks." Wall opened the eye slowly, and the smile leveled off finally, as Wall's face died to emotionless flatness.

"I told her all those things," he said simply and plainly, without inflection. "*Nothing you do can matter now*, I said to her. And then I shot her, Mr. Patchett." Anne let loose a gasp.

"Just like her sniveling husband before her, I shot her dead."

Patchett started forward at that instant, the one hand upraised, but Wall was already gone, up and over. His hands gave a light squeal as they wrung on the rail, then they, too, disappeared.

They didn't hear a scream. They heard only the roar of the swollen river.

Clark Wall was gone.

Patchett stood still in place. He blinked once, twice, not believing his eyes, then stepped up to the rail to peer toward the raging river that was lost in the fathomless black below them. He heard Anne behind him, her breath coming in ragged rushes. She stood beside him and raised one hand to wipe the blood carefully off his face, the heavy oppression still hanging on her, made newer and fresher by Wall's final announcement.

William made his way toward the cars.

74

PAGE, ARIZONA, appeared first as a few lights under the dark sky. The road simply meandered between eroded mesas and buttes, aiming toward the water-filled canyon beyond Page until the small community rose in its path.

Patchett didn't see it. He was unconscious — sleeping, apparently — in the backseat. Anne and Littlefeather, who was urging Franck's battered car along with gentle coaxing words, didn't really notice it, either.

Anne was hoping that all the effort wasn't for nothing, that it wasn't too late, but she was thinking at the same time that it wasn't worth Gary and Linda, whatever the result. Littlefeather was thinking the same thing, weighing in the life of one of his own friends.

The dead lay back at the bridge, collected and lined up in the beds of one of the trucks. Brian Echohawk was also there, watching over Bancroft and Franck and waiting for help to be sent by Littlefeather.

"Where?" Littlefeather asked, snapping Anne out of the staring look of a tired daydream.

"I don't know," she said, but even as she said it, she did know.

"Corner of fifteenth and North Navajo," she said. "Next to the Burger King." The Bateman 24-Hour Copy Center. Full circle.

William headed that way.

When they got there, Anne and Littlefeather checked on Patchett, then went in. She plucked the film and Rayes's list of names from a pocket, where she'd put them after retrieving the items from Patchett, and she set them at the counter.

"I need . . ." she started before stopping. *What do I need?*

She stared at the woman across the counter, who stared even harder back at them, caution and a slight bewildered fear on her face as she looked over the bright and ugly cuts and scuffs covering the two people in front of her. The marks looked starkly black under the piercing fluorescent lights.

"I need a copy of this." Anne slid the list to the woman. "Then I want you to take the copy and start faxing it to every newspaper you can think of. Start with the big ones — *New York Times*, *Wall Street Journal*, whatever — then go to the small ones. After that, magazines. *Newsweek*, *Time*, *U.S. News*. You name it."

"Uh, okay," the woman said uncertainly. "What about this?" She held up the film canister.

"Can you develop it?"

"Um," the woman faltered, "sure. The, uh, the machine's in back."

"Do it. Then can you get them out?"

"I can scan them and send them electronically."

"Send them to the same places. You got a newspaper in town?"

"A weekly."

Anne thought for a moment. "Radio station?"

That brought a nod. "Back down the main road here. Left at Cameron." The woman took the list from the counter as she spoke, skimming it briefly. She looked up at them when she finished, and they could almost see the wariness turn to concern at the sight of the two battered and tired people.

"Do you need some help?" the woman asked. She was studying the marks on Anne's face again, her own face wincing in sympathy. Rayes's list seemed to tremble in her hand, but her words were steady.

Anne smiled at the question, as warmly and reassuringly as she could. "You're already helping," she said. "And I'm on my way to get some more. All I need is that copy back."

"Can you stay?" Anne said to Littlefeather while the copy was being made.

"If you'll be okay."

"I'll be fine. But it's more important that someone stay with the film."

"I'll be here."

"Thanks," Anne said. She kissed him lightly on the cheek before retrieving the list and heading out the door.

75

THE TOWERING red-and-white antenna marked the tiny radio station well before they saw the building itself. The station building sat like a toy cake at the antenna's base, the antenna an immense candle with a blinking red tip.

Patchett was awake and relatively coherent, although pale and gray. The arm, Anne was certain, would be badly infected, possibly the bone as well. He needed to see a doctor. Needed to sleep and eat and heal and kill the furnace burning under his skin. Needed to do something unrelated to Weber BioTech or Prohiva, or anything else associated with them.

But that would come later. For now, he slowly moved into the station with Anne at his side, her arm thrown around him, her body supporting his.

The night receptionist nearly screamed when she saw them, but she was content to merely shoot her chair away from the desk. Out of reach. Away from the beaten and bleeding people. Her heart was jumping.

"Yes?" she said, one hand pressed to her chest.

"Do you have an AP wire?" Anne asked.

The woman looked from face to face, her mouth open, and nodded.

Anne and Patchett looked at each other. For one moment, wear and tear, permanent and temporary, floated away, and they both smiled.

"We need to use it," Patchett said weakly. "We need to get some information out as soon as possible." He took a pad and pen from the desk and began to write, patiently shaping the words on the paper.

"I . . ." the woman began. "I'm . . ." she trailed off. "You can't just come in here and ask to use the wire," she managed finally, trying to sound authoritative.

Patchett's weary gaze turned to her, and he stopped writing. "Ma'am," he said patiently, "we've just had a hell of a night, as you can see. And I expect a hell of a day to follow it, because this town's about to get more attention than it's ever had. So we don't really have the time to dance around with you on this just this second. We need to use your wire to get a story out, and we need to do it now."

Patchett blinked once. The secretary could see blood pooled in the whites of his eyes as she stared at him.

"So what'll it be?" Patchett asked softly. Anne stood wordlessly beside him, her hands clenching and unclenching nervously.

"I'll . . ." the secretary sputtered. "I'll call the police," she said, unsure. But Patchett and Anne smiled at that. Just barely.

"That's fine," Patchett said in a whisper. He reached over the counter and lifted the phone handset, holding it out to her. "That'll be just fine."

The secretary took the phone and began to dial.

EPILOGUE

The Day After

76

THE PLANE CIRCLED for an hour before landing in Dallas. Then it sat on the ground for the same amount of time, waiting to take off again. People up and down the narrow aisles muttered among themselves, grousing at the delay. At the heat and humidity. At the fact that if they had to wait, they could at least damn well let them wait in the terminal, where you could get something to drink and something bigger than a bucket to pee in.

When the plane jolted once and started to move, a cheer went up. The smattering of applause lasted right up to the moment that the extension arm connected to the plane's door. The cheers turned to grumbles intermingled with curses when the captain announced there would be an additional delay before disembarking.

Another thirty-five minutes' worth of sweat seeped from the passengers' pores despite the air vents, now hooked up to the terminal once again. Shifts were run to the bathrooms, with flight attendants monitoring the crowd.

Another cheer went up when the seal popped on the doorway, but it was weaker. The passengers in front stood to retrieve luggage before being politely told to return to their seats. One of the flight attendants grabbed a hand mike.

"Ladies and gentlemen," she said, "we are once again sorry for the delay, but we need approximately ten minutes before we can leave the plane. Please bear with us. Thank you."

A man in a gray suit came onto the plane at the same time, four others trailing behind him. One of the men was uniformed airport security. The others wore suits and sunglasses. Wires snaked from behind their ears, disappearing under their suit coats. A flight attendant spoke to the man in the gray suit and pointed once.

The men walked directly to seat 4C and arrayed themselves around it.

"Rowe Weber?" the man asked. The passenger looked up from a newspaper, noticing for the first time that the people who had been seated immediately around him were nowhere to be seen. He looked at the five men standing in the aisle.

"Mr. Weber?" the man said again.

"Yes?" Weber folded the paper carefully and lay it across his lap.

"I'm Special Agent Steven Thurin. Federal Bureau of Investigation. These are agents Hoper and Brooks. Thomas Salkind, Department of Justice. Officer McCallum, airport security." He gestured at each in turn while keeping his eyes fixed firmly on Weber.

"Gentlemen," Weber said, tipping his head.

"Sir, you are under arrest for suspected violations and conspiracy to commit violations of the Securities Exchange Act. You are also under arrest for suspicion of federal murder and conspiracy to commit murder. You are also under arrest for suspected violations of the Racketeer Influenced and Corrupt Organizations Act. You are under arrest for suspicion of unlawful interstate flight from authority. You are under arrest for suspicion of federal kidnapping and conspiracy to commit kidnapping.

"Sir, I am also authorized to take you into custody, pending federal grand jury proceedings and any necessary extradition proceedings, for suspicion of murder and attempted murder in the states of Arizona, Nevada, and Minnesota. The same states have requested that I also take you into custody for suspicion of administration of illegal substances. Nevada and Arizona are considering charges of improper disposal of a corpse.

"You may rest assured that this is only the beginning of the list.

"You have the right to remain silent. Anything that you say can and will be used against you in a court of law. You have a right to an attorney. Should you not be able to afford an attorney, one will be appointed for you. Do you understand these rights as I have read them to you?"

Weber sat perfectly, flawlessly still, hands clenched at the arms of his seat, the newspaper crushed in one of them.

"Sir," Thurin repeated, "do you —"

"Yes!" Weber snapped.

"Do you wish to make any statement at this time?"

Weber's face was gaunt. He couldn't have made a statement if he had wanted to.

"I would like to speak with my lawyer," he managed.

"Very well. I would ask you to place your hands on the seat before you and stand slowly, with your feet apart."

Rowe Weber stood up and stepped into the custody of the FBI.

77

DAYLIGHT SAVINGS TIME was beginning soon. That and the following summer's early morning light would erase all hope of seeing anything interesting in the hotel, so Ian Anderson was arriving early all this week and dedicating his mornings to peeping. Strangely addictive, he'd decided. Like playing the stocks. Exciting. Always an underlying touch of illegality, of getting away with something that no one knows about. Reward without cost.

He felt the fluttery twitch of nerves in his stomach, and he glued himself to his position at the small window. A Merit dangled from his lips. He was looking toward the hotel windows rather than at the computer ticker when the first Weber BioTech quote crawled across the screen: $63^{3}/_{8}$.

He spotted someone almost immediately, and he thought luck was going his way when he saw that she was tall, with fabulous quarter-horse legs that Anderson could just glimpse as she stepped into thin panties and pulled them snugly up.

58 ⅞.

Her breasts were full and they bulged against the fabric of the lace bra she was fastening. Anderson's breath caught at the sight, then began to race.

53 ⅛.

There was alarming news on the Street, Weber BioTech effectively dropping off the map even before the TRADING SUSPENDED label could flash on. But Ian Anderson stared his merry way through it. He dragged on the cigarette, a smile on his face.

Ian Anderson's job had disappeared in the night.

78

MELISSA FLARE was shaking as she dialed the phone, the fingers of one hand punching furiously at the number pad. The handset was wedged in the crook of her neck, and her free hand held a small card. Through bleary, tear-filled eyes, Melissa was trying to make out the number on the card, which was for her bank's twenty-four-hour computer phone service. This was the third attempt to dial, and she was determined to get it right.

That was made difficult by her agitation, which had been building steadily through the afternoon. Ever since, in fact, she'd tried to do a little shopping earlier.

The shopping was cut short by a trip to a teller machine to get some cash. When the request was rejected, Melissa really hadn't thought much about it. When a similar request to her savings account was also rejected, she'd been upset, but still far from her current state. But that all changed when she tried to contact Ben at his hotel in Montreal.

The hotel showed no registration in his name, and the law firm couldn't confirm the need for any trip to Montreal in the first place. Melissa chewed on that information all afternoon, then started her calls.

She started with airlines and rental car companies and got nothing. Then Ben's possible contacts in Montreal, with nothing there, either. And then she called the banks.

She'd contacted two so far, and the results in each were the same — accounts closed. Eyeing the card in her hand, the number of their last bank blackened on it, Melissa punched in the final digit and listened to the purring ring.

The computer picked up on the third ring, and Melissa dialed her way through the options, weaving her way through the instructions to reach an automated service on account balance. Then she pushed the final numbers, identifying the account, and she listened.

Two people walking past the Flare house actually heard the cry when it came. A long, drawn-out, wailing *No!* that was deadened but not entirely muted inside the suddenly empty brick walls. The people paused at the sound, looking toward the house's elaborate façade, then turned back to their walk, moving along, heads shaking. They heard no more screams, and they most assuredly couldn't have heard the much-quieter sobs that were following the first one.

Melissa Flare was crying softly, and she was crying alone.

79

No GODDAMNED MESSES!

The Barber ran it through his head again and again, the words singing soundlessly, tauntingly in his mind even as he continued shredding the newspaper. He was tearing it up in narrow strips. A seemingly endless pile of newsprint rested in his lap, and it was building steadily as he destroyed everything in the newspaper. *Everything.*

Everything except the picture.

No goddamned messes!

But he ignored that, at least as it applied to the paper. He shifted restlessly once, and a few of the pieces fell from his lap and cascaded twirling to the ground. He concentrated only on what was left of the newspaper, tearing it carefully as he reached the black-and-white yearbook photograph of Rebecca Cartaway. He edged around it as though neatly trimming a lawn.

"No . . . goddamned . . . messes," he whispered in the stark and quiet room. The picture tore neatly free at the last word, and perfect silence fell across the air. No words in his mind. No ragged rending of paper. Only the silence, then the softest rustle as he shifted once again, sending more of the piled-up newspaper strips to the floor. He ignored those as well, his eyes intent on the picture.

He hadn't done this one, of course. Looking at her and knowing the picture was old, the girl having grown to a woman, he knew she would have been perfect for him. *But he hadn't done this one.*

He never got the chance, unfortunately, and he trembled with anger at that thought. Someone else got her, took her, had her, and the Barber never got the chance on this one.

"No goddamned messes," he said again quietly. The picture, held close to his face, fluttered at the exhalation of breath.

His mother always said *No messes, no messes, no goddamned messes,* but oh my God, was this a mess.

He'd have to clean it up. He knew that. This was his fault, his doing, and he needed to clean it up. It would take work, of course. It would take a little more looking, a little more learning. But he would do that, and he would find out who did this, and he would deal with him. He would clean this up.

That could mean big trouble for someone. But that wouldn't be surprising in this world, he thought. That wouldn't be too shocking. Because after all, it was a violent world.

He looked out the window, and he began to plan.

80

ANNE SAT ON THE EDGE of the bed, and Patchett felt it sag, a comfortable sign of her nearness. She reached gently to his face, her hand hanging before it for one second before touching it, lightly tracing one eyebrow, a cheekbone, his chin. She felt a rough touch of beard stubble.

She pushed a lock of his hair back as she had her own so many times. She looked at the cast, at the hard whiteness that ran across his chest and over his left shoulder. The arm was free only at the wrist and fingers.

"I wanted to tell you," she said finally, "that I think what you did was . . ." — she searched for her words — ". . . *incredible.*" Her eyes arched at saying it. "I mean, I don't really think most people, certainly not most attorneys," she said with a laugh, "would have tried so hard or followed up so far."

Patchett was shaking his head as best he could. "Any real credit goes to you. And to William and his friends."

"And Rayes?" Anne said, thinking of the doctor and seeing, as she always did and always would now, the slight jolt of his body and the rush of blood that followed — only the start of a terrifying thirty-six hours.

"And Rayes," Patchett said.

Anne bent over him suddenly then and kissed him lightly on the forehead. "I still think that what you did was great," she said, her face just inches away.

His good hand found the back of her head, and he pulled her down, touching her lips with his own and smelling her wonderful smell. "I couldn't have done it without you."

He ran a finger over her face, tracing her light features. When he came to her hair, he hesitated, then touched it with a caress. It was smooth against his fingertips. Silky. A glint from the light fell over it, and his eyes caught in the color.

He touched it again.

He thought about Tomlin, Rebecca, Liz. Thoughts and images of all three, mixed together. Pictures of the grave site, indelibly stamped in his memory, Rayes dying at its lip. Death upon death. They were the kinds of images he had tried to hide from for years in drinking.

He pushed them back.

He pushed them all back.

Anne's eyes were deep blue, focused once more in front of him, and he plunged into them, forgetting all the concerns of before in favor of her face. His hand graced her hair, running through it.

"I knew I had to try," he said then. "It was all I could do, so I knew I had to try." His words were a whisper.

"It was enough," Anne replied. "*More* than enough, really." But she caught the concern, the touch of anguish that hung still in Patchett's gaze.

"What is it?" she asked. "What's wrong?"

"Will it always be enough?" he asked doubtfully. "The next time, whenever that is and whatever that is, will it be enough then?"

Anne was shaking her head, and she reached a hand out to Patchett and brushed his cheek. He turned his face into her open palm. He could feel its softness even against his rough, unshaven skin.

"You know, you don't have to fix everything, Jon," she said. "You don't have to fix it all. It's enough — it'll always be enough — if you just try to fix the things that affect you, the things that *matter* to you."

There was a sigh from Patchett as he listened carefully to Anne's words, weighing them against everything that had come before. Weighing them against everything he'd done or believed prior to the past week.

"I think I've done that," he said then, his hand finding and tightening on Anne's. "I think I've finally done that."

He pulled her to him again, their lips meeting with the barest brush, the fearful images locked away. They retreated into the farthest recesses of his mind.

And at last they were silent there.

Author's Note

When you get to create the world, you have the right to change it a little bit, and I've done that here. For starters, the science depicted here is intentionally somewhat stretched. Antisense exists, it works to some experimental degree, and it seems to work better than is suggested here. It is not, however, the basis for a preventive vaccine for AIDS. At least not yet.

I've also played to some degree with this country's securities markets and laws, though not remarkably so. And I've altered the FDA approval process in minor ways. Changing those procedures is a power fully within the FDA's capabilities — one that it has exercised for review of AIDS-related drugs.

I haven't changed the settings. Minneapolis, Phoenix, and the Arizona Strip are precisely as they appear in these pages, the sole exceptions being changes to House Rock and Kanab and the addition of the Minneapolis Exchange Tower Building and the Weber Building to the Twin Cities' skyline. A keen eye could, however, pick out where those buildings are said to be located.

Finally, I have not changed the disease that underlies this story, other than to speed its destructive process. With that in mind:

Centers for Disease Control and Prevention
National AIDS Clearing House
1-800-458-5231

Centers for Disease Control and Prevention
National AIDS Hotline
1-800-342-AIDS

Enough said.